TEN BEFORE THIRTY

YANA KAZAN

MANHATTAN
BOOK GROUP

Ten Before Thirty
Copyright © 2023 by Yana Kazan. All rights reserved.

This is a work of fiction. Names, characters, places and incidents are products of the author's imagination or are used fictitiously and should not be construed as real. Any resemblance to actual events, locales, organizations or persons, living or dead, is entirely coincidental.

No part of this book may be used or reproduced in any manner whatsoever without written permission, except in the case of brief quotations embodied in critical articles and reviews. For more information, e-mail all inquiries to info@manhattanbookgroup.com.

Published by Manhattan Book Group
447 Broadway | 2nd Floor #354 | New York, NY 10013 | USA
1.800.767.0531 | www.manhattanbookgroup.com

Printed in the United States of America
ISBN-13: 978-1-958729-45-8 (Paperback)

"I am out to sing songs that will prove to you that this is your world [even if] it has hit you pretty hard and knocked you for a dozen loops."

—Woody Guthrie

CONTENTS

YOUNG ANNIE. 1

LEAVING HOME 34

MADISON 94

EXCOMMUNICATION .237

THE FINAL COUNT 251

YOUNG ANNIE

Dead Flora Zechman is in Annie's bedroom. Her great-grandmother is wearing a white wedding dress that widens at her hips like a river broadening from a narrow bay of a waist. Annie recognizes her from the portrait on the living room bookshelf.

"I can't stay long, dear, so pay attention. Ten really bad things are coming—you can get them early in your life or later. Your choice."

"What do you mean by really bad?"

"Really bad."

"Will I live through them?"

"It will be up to you."

"Ten seems like too many."

"We all get a different number, dear."

"What should I do?"

"Pick one."

Flora is shaking in small tremors.

"If I have to choose, then early, I guess." Immediately, Annie wonders if she should take it back. "And what is early?"

"Thirty." Flora expels a long breath like a deflating balloon and disappears.

Annie's heart is snare-drumming, her short legs driving lanes down the center of the bed. Hannah is asleep a few feet away. The mantle clock hands point to four. Last week Annie read that the hours before dawn are when most people die and nightmares seem real.

1

She tiptoes to the living room to see if Flora is still in her silver frame. She is.

Only three Zechmans fit at the small kitchen table. When they eat as a family, Annie moves to the wooden cutting board that slides out of the counter on the other side of the kitchen. Daniel moves to the typewriter table next to the oven. Hannah doesn't like to move, so she never does. Dad sits by the steps heading to the back door. Mom sits by the entrance to the hall.

Today the three siblings are at the table waiting for breakfast. Dad stirs oatmeal in a small pot. He's singing their favorite poem, "Three Little Mousies." His tall legs dance around the kitchen in brown wool slacks belting a white undershirt that doesn't fully cover his dark chest hair. He ladles oatmeal, lumpy the way they like it, into their bowls. In a few minutes, the dishes clink into the sink. This is the signal for Mom to get up. Dad's fifty-two-year-old legs dance down the hall to finish dressing for work. The three little mousies pull on their coats and mittens for the walk to school.

Seven hours later, Annie opens the heavy storm door, jumps the stairs two at a time to the kitchen, and heads down the hall to change out of her school clothes. The door to the living room is closed. Turning the knob just enough to peek inside, she sees Hannah and Mother on the sofa. Hannah is crying into a clump of tissues, head bowed. Mother's head is bowed too.

No one seems to notice Annie walk through the dining room to take a seat on the piano bench in the living room. The oil painting Annie loves is centered above the piano. Sailboats moored by a copper-colored house with a single high window facing rough winds. The sails are worn yellow, the white-capped sea so dark it could be dusk or early morning in the Italian town where Annie dreams of living.

"What's wrong?" Something must be wrong—the living room door is never closed.

Mother never looks up when she whispers, "Daddy. Died."

"What?"

"Heart attack. Hospital." Mother sounds like she's talking from under the water.

Annie leans forward to try to hear her mother better. "When? Were you with him? Who was with him? Where is he?"

Mother seemed talked out. Annie focused on the rising tissue hill between her mother and sister. The limp, wet tissues were saying it was bad. No one could do anything.

But they just had breakfast together—he was dancing and singing. Annie didn't know if she should join them on the sofa—they still were not looking at her. It seemed better to go. She walked to the door and closed it quietly behind her. That seemed respectful—to be quiet and stop asking questions.

She passed Daniel's room down the hall. He was hunkered over his homemade baseball game on the floor—scoring papers spread around him.

"Did Mom tell you?"

He looked up. Usually Annie wanted to play after school. But she was sitting now on the floor cross-legged in front of him. She picked up his scoring papers and shuffled them, her black braids making crescent moons around her face and neck.

"Something happened. To Dad. At the hospital. He's not coming back. It happened fast," she adds though the tissue hill didn't say that. She made that up because Dad was singing just hours ago.

"Is it ok to play?"

"Yes, but stay here. Mom will probably come in soon." She drops the scoring papers to the floor. Daniel starts shuffling them into their right order.

She thinks it's best not to change out of school clothes. So she lies down in her bed to try to understand what has happened. Just two weeks ago, Mom made a chocolate cake for Dad's birthday. Annie licked the frosting bowl and asked if she could have frosting for her next birthday—no cake. They celebrated Mom's fortieth a month ago. How long are people supposed to live? More than fifty-two, she's sure. Her great-grandmother Flora lived to one hundred and six.

The doorbell rings in rounds like it's Halloween. But Halloween was two weeks ago. Annie dressed like a Spanish Flamenco dancer in Mom's red crinoline slip that ballooned around her thighs like a bell. Her long dark hair swung loose. It was so cold outside she had to wear a wool hat, and no one could see the sparkly earrings she'd found in her mother's jewelry box. She and her friends ran through three neighborhood blocks collecting candy in white pillowcases. Mom and Dad offered Three Musketeers and Hershey's Kisses from their front door.

The doorbell-ringers drop off casseroles and fruit baskets. Someone pulls Dad's scotch out of the mahogany hutch in the dining room and sets up shot glasses on the silver tray they use for company. Before long, aunts, uncles, cousins, and strangers are huddled on the grey sofa, on every chair in the living and dining room. Someone has brought up dusty chairs from the basement to fill in the empty spaces. Women in dark dresses with polka dot scarves and crying kerchiefs drink whiskey and sob. Heavy floral perfumes waft to the back of the house from the new way station.

Annie has never seen adults cry. A woman is wailing in high-pitched discordant bird cries. Someone says they're sitting Shiva and will sit in their house for days. Annie wishes they would go away—who invited them?

Two of her aunts argue about mirrors. "Let's count how many need to be covered. We can drape sheets and towels over them." They ignore Annie standing behind them.

"They're reform. *He* was conservative. We don't need to cover them." Annie didn't know her dad was a different kind of Jew than she was.

The two sisters pour more scotch into their glasses and head back to the couch to sit more Shiva. The hours pass in a fog. In the middle of the night, Annie wakes to a stranger sobbing over her, "You poor child."

Annie didn't know if it was bad manners to tell Shiva people to leave, so she pretends to be asleep. Hannah is a few feet away. Maybe she is pretending too.

Grandma and Grandpa arrive the next morning. Someone tells Annie to move to her parents' bed so Gram can sleep in Annie's bed. Grandpa will share Daniel's bed. Annie asks what side of the bed she should sleep on. Gram says to take Dad's side.

Two rabbis arrive early in the afternoon. The young rabbi sits on Hannah's bed, with Hannah and Daniel next to him. Annie sits across from them on her bed.

"You're going to have to help your mother," he says, looking at them intently. "And Daniel, you're the man of the house now." He says he will see Daniel in Hebrew School and look out for him. He does not tell Annie he will see her in Hebrew School though she will be there too. Doesn't he know that? He does not explain why people die or ask if the mousies have questions.

After he leaves, Hannah asks, "What did you think?"

They agree he was no help. Annie asks if he uses Vaseline to slick his hair down. Hannah doesn't think so.

The old rabbi never speaks to them. He is busy ministering to the Shiva people. He advises Mother it will be too scary for the children to attend the funeral. There will be hundreds of people because everyone knows—the newspaper published a half-page obituary with Dad's picture. The obituary listed Annie, Hannah, and Daniel's names and all their aunts and uncles. The article said Dad ran for city council last year. The article did not say he lost because he was Jewish—her uncle told Annie that. It will be better to take the children to the cemetery when life settles down, which it will, the rabbi assures Mother. Dad's doctor friend came to the house to give Mom a sedative—Annie saw the needle and asked Aunt Hazel if Mother was sick.

"No, she isn't sick," she answered, dabbing her eyes with a fancy handkerchief. Everyone said Aunt Hazel looked like Betty Grable, the Hollywood actress. But not today—her blue eyes were red and swollen from crying.

On Dad's second night dead, Mother's animal howl races up the hallway to the bedroom where Annie is still awake on his side of the bed. "Why didn't God take me? He was the better person! Why didn't God take me?"

Annie can't hear what Aunt Hazel is saying but wishes she could. Mother is asking a good question. Dad would say, if he wasn't dead, that was a good question, and he liked good questions.

During the hours everyone is at the funeral, the neighbor from the upstairs duplex ushers the children to the playroom in the basement, with the black-and-white checkerboard floor tiles and clown-face tile in the center of the floor. Annie never liked the clown face with garish red lips.

They don't know what to do in the playroom. Read Archie and Veronica comic books? Make clothes for the dolls with no heads? Hook up

Dad's train set in the room across from the washing machine and furnace and run the puffing black locomotives and boxcars around the town he built? Nothing feels right. Annie has a vague understanding that someone is putting her dad into the ground while they're standing awkwardly on the black and white squares in the playroom, and the three little mousies are not there to help him. The quiet in the basement is deafening.

That night Annie gets out the yellow legal pad Dad brought her from his office. She writes in pencil on the first page: "Thursday, November 15, 1956—having my first real thoughts. I can't count on anyone. I'm an adult now. Dad left, and I'm not going to cry. I'm going to act like a man—and I will not sit Shiva."

Annie's first decision as an adult is to drop out of school. She's embarrassed to have a dead father. No one else has one. And there's no hiding it. Her fifth-grade class sent a fruit basket with a sympathy note. Her creepy teacher with her thin black hair brought it by, her thick eyeglasses peering around the front door. The basket is still wrapped in plastic paper on the kitchen counter. Annie can see the bananas she doesn't like. Mother says Annie has to go to school. Annie thinks it's best not to fight with Mother, who is looking pale, red-eyed, and defeated.

Walking slowly to stall her arrival at school despite the biting wind, Annabelle runs up to walk with Annie. "Did you hear about Maryann? She had to go into an iron lung. She couldn't breathe."

Just a month ago, all the classes in their school lined up in the gym to get the new polio vaccine developed by Dr. Salk. The nurse gave them a sugar cube with the vaccine on it. Dad told the family at dinner how lucky they were to have the vaccine—the number of cases was up to 30,000 this year, and so many were children like Maryann. Mother made them promise they would never drink from someone else's glass—ever—and not to touch the drinking fountain at school with their mouth.

Annie was still shaking her head about Maryann when Annabelle starts chattering about a scene in a movie—men were lowering a casket into the ground using metal pulley chains, and people were throwing dirt on top of the casket. She never mentioned Annie's father, but Annie was feeling queasy, trying not to listen. She would have to smash Annabelle into the ground if she kept talking. But they were at school. Annie hurried to the coatroom at the back of the classroom. Benny was hanging up his coat, mumbling, "I'm sorry about your father."

Annie ignored him, heading to her seat in the last row. Class started, and everyone pretended there was no dead father in the room.

Waiting to fall asleep in her bed that night, Annie wondered how heavy caskets are with a body inside if there have to be pulley chains to lower them, how long before maggots get inside, and could her father just singing in the kitchen a few days ago really be inside one of those and under the earth now? Are these the kind of good questions Dad would want her to ask?

Annie's second decision is to never again say his name aloud. The plan is to go on with her life during the day as if nothing has happened and think of him at night when it's safe. And maybe he will help her understand why Mother is coughing so much and whether Mother is leaving next, and if their house will blow up again from a furnace fire. The last time they had to move to a downtown hotel while the acrid smoke smell dissipated.

Annie plans the escape route through the window over her bed. Luckily, the hospital is close. All she has to do is bust out the screen, jump through the window, and even if she breaks her legs falling to the ground, she can crawl to the street in front of the house and attract a passing car or crawl up the hospital driveway. She does not think about saving the rest of the family.

But she does think about saving animals—and some people. Mother tells her to let things be. "You can't save the world. Leave the bird alone. The mother bird will help her baby."

Annie doesn't think the mother bird is going to help, so she carefully puts the baby bird in a shoebox to take to the old veterinarian next door. She rings the doorbell, peppering him with questions when he opens it half-way: "Dr. Frieze, look at the baby I found. Are the air holes big enough? Can she eat Cheerios? What should I do? How old do you think she is? Will she die?"

He pretends not to hear her and closes the door. Mother says he's retired, hard of hearing, and doesn't like to be bothered. He doesn't like Annie because she ate the petals off the tulips he planted between their houses five years ago.

There was the stray grey cat too, who hung around the yard, bony and miserable.

"Mom, can Gracey live in our house?

"We can't have a cat. I'm allergic."

"Even in the basement?"

"I have to do the laundry in the basement."

"What about a dog or a rabbit?"

"I'm allergic to fur."

Annie didn't know if Mother really was allergic because they never had an animal in the house. Annie knew Mother never had an animal at Gram and Grandpa's house either because they were scared of animals. Annie had to cross the street on walks with Gram when they saw a dog ahead. Gram told her Grandpa's father died tied to a tree in the Carpathian Mountains in Europe after a rabid dog bit him. But Aunt Hazel had a poodle named Napoleon—Mother didn't get allergic when she visited there. So, Annie was not sure about allergies.

And there was Hans. When the class lined up at school after recess to get water from the drinking fountain, Miss Dark made Hans wait against the corner wall because he was German and talked with a thick accent. Miss Dark said he was a Nazi. Hans cried, facing the corner wall, and Annie whispered to him it was unfair that Miss Dark pulled him out of line. Annie didn't like Miss Dark, and she didn't like her any better when she dropped the fruit basket by her house. It was creepy the way Miss Dark was looking around their living room.

Annie talked to her classmates behind Miss Dark's back, "Don't you think it's wrong how Miss Dark is treating Hans?" Heads were nodding.

"What can we do?"

No one had ideas.

"What if I write a petition for Hans to be able to drink at the fountain, and we all sign it and give it to the principal?" Heads nod. Normally she would ask Dad about things like this. Mom would tell her not to make waves. And if she tells Hannah, Hannah will tell Mom.

Annie writes the petition that night. She draws nineteen lines with a ruler where classmates will sign their names. The next day, they fill up the lines with signatures. After school, Annie drops the petition by the principal's office, wondering if she is going to get in trouble.

Christmas break starts the end of the week. She's hoping for snow for this first holiday without her father though she knows this will not be a holiday. They barely got through Thanksgiving. And the very next week, it was Hanukah, but it didn't feel like a holiday. The gold menorah was weathered from dried candle wax after the first three nights of lighting. Annie didn't think they should even be lighting candles, given the pall in the house. She did not say this out loud.

When school started back in January, a substitute teacher introduced herself, telling the class she would be with them for the rest of the year. There was whispering that Miss Dark had health problems. At mid-morning break, Hans was lining up behind Annie at the drinking fountain, and a teacher was reminding them not to touch the faucet with their mouths because of polio. No one said anything about the petition, but she knew the petition was connected to Miss Dark's leaving. It had to be. Annie thought she saved somebody and Dad would be glad.

A month after the funeral, the partners of Elias, Kolinsky and Zechman notified Mother they were renting Dad's office to another lawyer. She should pick up his personal effects.

Mother, Hannah, Annie, and Daniel made the trip downtown. School was out for winter break. They brought empty boxes to bring items back. Annie expected to see his large wooden desk and office chair on wheels. Bookcases lining two walls, filled with law and history books in leather and thick cloth bindings, with gold titles on their spines. Two wooden chairs for clients to sit across from his desk. Three black-and-white lithographs on the walls. Standing lamps with beige silk shades on either side of the desk. An expanse of windows along one wall, ten floors up, overlooking the busy downtown street. A large spitting radiator under the window. A thick office door with the transom open to let air in from the white-and-black marble hall. The door had the name of the law firm painted in fancy black letters, and under it, her father's name: Neil R. Zechman, attorney-at-law.

When the Zechmans opened the locked door with the key Mother had, half expecting to see him sitting at his chair, the office wasn't looking right.

"Where are all the books?" Annie asked first, running to the wall of bookcases.

"The partners must have taken them."

"But aren't they his?"

"Yes. I don't think they should have taken them without asking." Mother looked dismayed.

"Me too," Annie agreed, "I want the books. I want them back."

"Let's see if there are things in the desk drawer. You can pick out things for yourself."

Hannah wanted the thick book on Abraham Lincoln the partners left on the shelf and a silver pen from the desktop.

Daniel wanted the pile of stamps and silver dollars from one of the desk drawers.

Annie wanted the glass prism on the desktop. She played with it every time she came to the office. When she looked through the glass as she stepped forward, each step took her down a sloping hill she could fall from, and rainbows rimmed every surface on the floor. She liked the feeling of danger at the rainbow's edge. She was surprised no one was fighting for the prism. She quickly put it in her box, ready to fight if she had to.

The longer they were there, the more disconsolate they became.

Mother sighed, "I could have sold his books—they're valuable."

The Zechmans took their boxes filled with pens, paper, coffee cups, leather desk blotter, typewriter, the few history books that were left, and artwork from the walls, and left the office for the last time. Annie vowed to keep the prism always. He told her just weeks ago that it was good to go down steep hills even if it was scary—and to see rainbows.

The afternoon they cleaned out Dad's office, they wrapped up two photographs from his bookcase: Mom and Dad with the three little mousies on vacation in Florida and Flora's wedding picture. There was an identical picture of Flora on the bookshelf in their living room. Flora must have been important to have a photo at both Dad's office and their home. Annie heard how Flora ate chocolate cake and danced at Aunt Ava's wedding when Flora was one hundred and six years old. That night Flora died in her sleep. Everyone said that was the best way to go—to die in your sleep after chocolate cake and a last dance. Annie wondered what Flora would think of her grandson dying at fifty-two, leaving the mousies with no father.

So it wasn't a surprise Flora visited Annie the night they cleaned out his office—four months after Annie turned ten. She did not want to believe bad things were coming. Was Dad's death one of them? Wasn't death just nature's way? The doctors said a blood clot traveled up his leg and lodged in his heart—blood couldn't get to his brain. Annie pictured a narrow garter snake making its way from his foot to his heart, rolling into a pinwheel to warm in the chambers there.

"It's not your fault," the doctors assured Mother. "There was nothing you could have done." Was the clot moving up his leg while he was dancing and singing in the kitchen that morning?

Even if Flora was right, that bad things were coming, should Annie prepare? And what were bad things anyway? She wrote "10B430" at the top of her legal pad like it was a code to her bicycle lock. Then she wrote down the worst things that already happened.

When that boy she didn't know pushed her off the diving board, and her foot hit the cement on her way to the water. She pretended she *wanted* to hop on her left foot because she didn't want to tell everybody she couldn't walk—she didn't want to ruin their Florida vacation.

When she thought her eyeball turned inside out after her eyelashes got stuck in her eye.

Spinning in the ocean undertow—she couldn't tell where the surface was in the blinding sand and water mix, out of air.

Reaching for the checkered tire by the Virginia creek when the triangular head raised to look at her. Mother screamed from the top of the hill, "Run! Run, Annie." She ran up the hill as the motel owner ran down with his rifle. It wasn't right to shoot the snake taking a sunbath by the moss-heavy trees bowing to the black water.

And Dr. Erikson's shots. Arms stiff from polio, he plunged the needles in like railroad spikes. Hannah and Daniel made Annie go first, telling the doctor she was the bravest.

Were these what Flora meant? Were they bad enough? Annie decided to rate them between one and ten. Really bad would be anything eight or higher. A parent dying, at least a parent you love, would be a ten. Cracking a bone in her foot, five; going almost blind, four; nearly dying in the ocean, five; a snake dying for her, seven; and getting spike shots, five. So far, only one scored high enough. Were nine more as bad as Dad's death coming? That seemed like too much.

She wondered if her father and Flora would help her from the other side—she was pretty sure they would not. And she was not about to tell anyone about Flora's visit. Mother would worry and restrict her even more. That's what they fought about. Annie wanted to go somewhere, and Mother said no, but she wouldn't say why. It was always 'because' or 'because I said so' as if she ruled Annie's world. Annie knew she did not. Just like she did not rule Dad's world. Because if she did, he would not have left them.

There wasn't much Mother could control. Annie could see that now. Annie concluded her Mother was powerless, like so many women. This was not the life Annie wanted. Flora must have come to warn her so Annie would be prepared—because she was going to be a woman. That might be one of the really bad things. That Annie was going to be a woman.

<hr />

Though Mother never really said, 'someday you'll get a penis,' what she said led Annie to believe she was in the offing for a major change of life, and this would have something to do with a penis. Just when this change would come, Mother didn't say.

The week after her eleventh birthday in August, one thick splotch of blood made a perfectly round red pool on her white underpants. She left the bloody pants on her bed, changed to a clean pair, and headed outside to play. The wound—she was sure it was a wound—healed quickly.

Mother found the bloody panties and walked Annie to the bathroom where she showed her the shelf with two boxes of Kotex napkins. Mother handed her a small unopened box with an elastic contraption that held two garter attachments. She was to slip this elastic sling over her hips, attach a bulky pad that looked like a giant bandage to each of the garters, hoist it into place like a harness, and walk with this bandage between her legs hoping no one noticed. And worse, put up with this wedge in her butt all day, even at night. She was to carefully roll each bloodied napkin inside toilet paper and place the package in the trash can by the sink. Annie didn't ask if this meant she would never get a penis. Standing next to the Kotex shelf, she realized her fate.

"Now you're a woman," Mother said with pride, adding a last unflattering thought, "I hope you and your sister don't inherit the family breasts."

Why would she say this? Auntie Sarah and Ava's pendulous breasts made a convenient shelf for their formidable, crossed arms. Annie shuddered at the thought of shelves growing from her flat chest. No one talked about the size of the uncles' penises like they talked about their aunts' breasts. Maybe breasts were more important than penises.

Annie's favorite place was the red-brick library a mile from her house. Two golden lions guarded the books between sturdy white pillars. Annie and Hannah walked to the library most Saturday afternoons to check out books for the week.

Today Annie walked alone. She was thinking about the biographies she liked—people's lives lined up on two bookshelves near the comfortable leather chair she hoped no one would be sitting in. The biographies were bound in plain orange jackets as though orange was the best color for people's lives. Who decided to wrap people's lives in orange?

She passed the corner house where the student nurses lived when they were training at Oak Hospital. She was halfway down the next block where the neighborhood was less familiar. Though it was a cold afternoon, her coat was unbuttoned, and her thick braids trailed down her back. A noisy car stopped at the curb. A man in a dark jacket got out and moved toward her. "Let me give you a ride. It's so cold," he said, reaching for her shoulder.

Without thinking, she pulled away and slipped out of her coat, her short legs pumping like a windmill to carry her up the hilly lawn toward the row of old Victorian houses. She stopped between two houses to catch her breath and look back. He watched from the sidewalk, then hurled her blue coat hard to the sidewalk and got back into his car and sped away, tires squealing. She was too scared to go pick up her coat. She ran through two blocks of backyards until she was home.

The next day Mother noticed Annie's coat was missing.

"I lost it but don't know where."

"You're always losing things; you have to pay more attention!" Mother snapped angrily. She bought the blue coat for winter just weeks ago.

Annie nodded. She did not tell her mother what a good runner she was.

Annie kept her word. She never spoke her father's name out loud. Gram was visiting from Buffalo, and they were setting the table for dinner. Annie put out the tablecloth Gram had embroidered with purple and blue flowers and the place settings—fork on the left, knife and spoon on the right. Gram was watching quietly. Then for no reason, Gram blurted like an accusation, "You're going to have to say his name!"

There was a quick glance between them, then silence. And not a silence because Gram wasn't wearing her false teeth because she was. All Annie could think was, if Gram guessed her secret, why didn't she try to help? Annie knew Gram was smarter than she let on. She had secrets but she wasn't talking. When Annie asked how her son Andrew died, looking at his picture in his fine military uniform, Gram said he died in the war. Annie knew that wasn't true. She had heard things.

Annalise Kaylah Zechman was the name on Annie's birth certificate. Too weighty, Annie thought. And it sounded like "Analyze" Zechman. And what was Kaylah—some Hebrew name her parents came up with?

"Where did you come up with Annalise?" she kept asking her mother.

"We thought it was so pretty."

"Who thought it was pretty?"

More vagueness. One day Annie overheard Mother say, "We were looking for an *A* name." She's sure she heard that, though Mother later denied it. Jewish families usually name children for someone who died. The only *A* dead person was Mother's brother, Andrew, who committed suicide at twenty-three, though Gram said he was killed in the war. Then Gram would purse her lips like a pocketbook closing coins inside and leave the room.

What Annie knew about Andrew she mostly gleaned from his picture on the brick mantle above the fireplace in Gram's house. The mantle hosted Gram's collection of elephants—one carved out of wood, another ivory, several jade. One of the jade elephants was a mother with a baby elephant attached behind her. Mother said elephants bring good luck, and that's why Gram liked elephants. Andrew's eight-by-ten-inch black-and-white photograph sat in a brass frame in the middle of the elephant herd. He was Hollywood-handsome: wavy black hair, dark eyes, even features, distinctive in his uniform. He enlisted in 1941 to serve in World War II after a couple of years of college. He married Esther when he enlisted.

Andrew found out Esther cheated on him when he was overseas, but they stayed together when he left the Army. They had a child. The baby contracted polio and was so crippled by six months old that Esther and Andrew had to put the baby in a hospital. When Esther decided to divorce Andrew, he dissolved into dark moods, unable to cope. He had never dealt well with emotional problems, Mother said. She told Annie in a hushed voice one day about the fight when he was thirteen over who should pay the fine for an unreturned library book. Andrew grabbed his fifteen-year-old sister around the throat and slowly cut off her airflow. She thought she would die. Their younger brother separated them.

When the family thought Andrew should get help for his moods, Grandpa told Andrew to be a man. No son of his needed a doctor. Andrew was in a dark mood that July night when Grandpa told him to act like a man and locked Andrew out of the house. Aunt Hazel's husband agreed it was best to lock the door—they didn't know what Andrew would do, and Hazel was ready to have a baby any time. Mother didn't know what to do, but her vote didn't count anyway—Grandpa made the rules.

They found Andrew the next morning in the garage, head curved to his knees pressed against his stomach, dried blood around his nose and

16 • YANA KAZAN

mouth. He had swallowed a container of rat poison. Grandpa drove him to the hospital where Andrew died—the same hospital where Aunt Hazel went into labor, delivering her baby daughter by dinner time. In the space of a day, a death and a birth. The family never celebrated Annie's cousin's birthday on the right day after that for fear it would upset Gram. A month later, Gram had a heart attack. She teetered on the edge of death for weeks in a hospital bed. The doctor said she lost her will to live. She did live but went mostly mute—presumably, there was not much worth saying anymore. She started a walking regimen: miles most days, her white hair leaning into the wind no matter the weather, no matter the pain in her gnarled arthritic joints. She moved out of Grandpa's bedroom with the mahogany wooden frame twin beds, to the double bed at the head of the stairs, the bed with the creaky metal frame that Annie's mom shared with Hazel when the sisters were growing up.

Annie was born two years later, the *A* for Annalise forever linking her to Andrew, though Mother denied this.

A few months before Dad died, he took the mousies to a music store to pick out an instrument they wanted to play. Daniel chose drums; Hannah, violin; and Annie, flute. This was their second instrument. They all took piano lessons, practicing at the piano in the living room under the painting of the Italian fishing village. Annie practiced scales imagining they were waves flowing up and down the keys. At the end of the scales, she crashed a few intense ten-note chords—all strong fingers on deck.

"Stop banging on the piano!" Mother yelled.

"I'm not—those are waves crashing on the beach," Annie yelled back. The flute would be different—it would echo in the air like delicate bird calls.

Annie met Fran Vogel when they learned how to play the flute in the middle school orchestra. When they went to high school, they signed up for band. Annie's house was farther from the high school than Fran's so Annie picked up Fran to walk together to morning practice. Fran was always waiting outside her house.

Annie was first flute, Fran, second flute though they were even in their skills—Annie blew harder, and Mr. Perry, the band director, liked louder playing. Annie almost lost first flute when the band sold candy to raise money for new uniforms. She was eating candy bars in practice, and chocolate was dribbling out of her mouth when she was blowing.

"It's bad for your instrument, Annie, to have chocolate in your mouth! I'm going to switch you to second flute if you don't take care of your instrument!" Mr. Perry's normally red face turned redder when he yelled. The trumpet and drum boys laughed. Annie kept the candy bars hidden in the folds of her skirt.

"The candies are gone now," she lied. When Mr. Perry turned his back to work with the tubas, Annie quickly stuck another piece in her mouth. Rich chocolate with almonds.

Fran lived in a beaten-down cabin on an alley near the grocery. Plain looking with thick glasses and thin blonde hair, she had a nice voice but talked fast as if she was running out of time in her conversations. Her boyfriend played the trumpet in the band. She told Annie she couldn't meet him at her house because her parents would beat her if they found out he was Black. So she sneaked out to meet him.

It was early November when Fran told Annie she wanted to tell her something, but she had to promise not to tell anyone. Annie agreed.

"Pa-John makes me have sex with him. I try to say no, but he's threatening to do it with my younger sister if I say no." Fran's voice was breathy and shaking. "I don't know what to do."

Annie was shocked. "Your father?"

"Stepfather."

"Can you tell your mother?"

Fran's head was shaking like a puppet with loose guide wires. "I told the girl who lived across from my house in third grade—her mother called the police. They came to our house and took my stepfather to jail for one night. They wrote a report about everything." Tears were falling down Fran's face though her eyes faced straight ahead while they walked. "When he came back from jail, they said they were going to get him help—put him in a special program. The police told my mother to decide if she wanted him to stay at the house or else they had to take me and my sisters to child services. She wanted him to stay. She said he is a good husband."

18 • YANA KAZAN

Annie's snare drum rattled ominously in her chest. "What—your mother knew—five years ago?"

Fran nodded. "They took me and my two sisters to child services. We spent a lot of nights there. They locked us up separately at night in sleeping rooms. It was like jail. I just wanted to be home—for him to stop."

Annie remembered the day she saw Pa-John getting out of his car after work. Big. Sausage-shaped. Red-faced. Tan boots. He tipped an imaginary hat at Annie and smiled when he opened the whining screen door to the house. She was scared for Fran.

"My sisters and I went back home, but he still made me have sex. Now he's going to start with my sister. He's always yelling how I'm Black-boy crazy. He says if anyone comes around, he'll beat him up. He says I'm causing all the problems, to stop acting up."

How could this be? Fran seemed so quiet and timid at school. "Is there someone at child services you can call?"

"I called the lady there yesterday—said there's more trouble. She says she can't do anything unless my mother asks her to. She asked if I was messing around with my boyfriend. I told her I wasn't doing anything that I didn't do with Pa-John. You have to promise you won't tell anyone, Annie."

"I promise." But all that week Annie wondered what Pa-John made Fran do and why no one could make him stop—and whether Annie should break her promise.

Weeks later, Annie and Fran were standing side by side to perform a flute duet in the center of the wood-planked high school stage wearing identical white blouses and black skirts, instruments raised perpendicular to the floor, hands cupping the silver keys in readiness. Mr. Perry played the opening notes of the piano accompaniment, signaling with his index finger for Annie and Fran to start. No sound came out of Annie's flute though she was blowing hard. Fran's notes were coming out strong. Fran took the lead for those terrifying moments, and no one knew the truth but Fran, Annie, and Mr. Perry. Annie's notes finally came in halfway into the piece. Annie was mortified by how she let Fran down, how she was first flute and could not make even one note come out.

Annie's mother came to hear the performance and wanted to sit close to the stage. Annie begged her to stand at the back of the auditorium. Fran's family did not attend.

TEN BEFORE THIRTY • 19

That night was the last time Annie saw Fran. She heard Fran dropped out of school. Annie didn't know if she should knock on the door at her house to ask where Fran was. Annie was too scared to go to the house. She wondered if a really bad thing happening to someone else could go on Flora's list. She thought it could and didn't think it would be breaking a promise not to tell to put it on her list.

⁘

The band was learning the halftime show for the last football game of the season. "You're going to be car pistons," Mr. Perry explained.

"What's a piston?" Annie asked.

Mr. Perry gave a brief explanation and drew the marching pattern on butcher block paper taped to the wall. "Percussion, your pistons will march north, like this." He alternated waving his arms up and down. "Woodwinds and brass, your pistons will march south."

Annie was dubious people in the stands were going to know they were pistons, even though they were playing the car song, "Beep-Beep." Thankfully, the black and red helmet with the wide chin strap would hide Annie's face so no one would know who she was.

"Annie, please stop by my office," Mr. Perry called out after practice.

She wondered if she was in trouble for not knowing what a piston was. She put her flute in its case, picked up her coat, and walked to Mr. Perry's office next to the practice room.

"Annie, I want you to play the piccolo. You'll be the exclamation mark to the 'Beep-Beep' piece," he said, smiling at her from his reddening face. He showed her a small instrument case, opening it carefully. "We have this piccolo for you to play."

"I don't know how to play a piccolo."

"It's the same fingering as your flute—it's just a small-size flute, but higher pitched, more staccato." He handed it to her. "Try it. Do a scale."

She started to blow into the mouthpiece tentatively, pressing her fingers to the keys. The sound was shrill.

"Louder, louder, you're going to be the exclamation mark!"

She forced more air between her lips into the narrow mouth hole.

"Yes, yes, that's going to sound great! This is the first time we're going to use the piccolo in the band. I just got the instrument. Take it home and practice."

The band practiced every day that week on a corner of the field. The football team and cheerleaders practiced nearby.

On game day, the team was losing at halftime when they headed for the locker room. The band marched onto the field behind the front row of big bass drums booming loudly, snare drums rattle-tattling a fast pace, and cymbals clashing for extra verve. It was exhilarating to march in unison tucked among the soft woodwinds, buoyed by the loud blasts of trumpets, trombones, and tubas, punctuated by the cries of her high-pitched piccolo.

First, the band played the school march, then "Beep-Beep" began. The pistons were alternating their marching patterns north and south. The marchers were swaying their instruments to the beats. Annie was trying to remember where south was while she focused on blowing forcefully into the little piccolo so its shrill exclamation marks would ride the high waves of the band. The song was ending, and she was delivering her best marching steps, twelve inches long with legs alternating to a height that matched the other marchers. She was marching off the field relieved the halftime show and her debut piccolo-playing were over when she realized the drumbeats that set the cadence to march off the field were dimming. There was no one to her left and right. She heard people yelling, "Go the other way, the other way!" She turned to see that the band had marched itself nearly off the field by the goal post, and the football team was running back to the field. Annie had marched alone halfway down the field toward the opponent's goalpost where the visiting team was waiting. Mortified, she turned to run toward her goal line, dispensing with the required twelve-inch marching steps, to the crowd's loud clapping and laughing. Mr. Perry was waiting by the sidelines directing the band to take their places quickly on the bleacher's first-row benches as the game resumed. Annie shrank gratefully among the soft clarinets and oboes, burying her exclamation mark against her chest.

She rated this episode as a four because she figured hardly anyone recognized it was her in the helmet she was wearing.

Annie didn't like marching without Fran. And she didn't want to play the piccolo though Mr. Perry complimented her in front of the band for the unique sound she was bringing to the group. Lilly was trying out for cheerleading, and she was Annie's new best friend. Annie decided she would rather be a cheerleader than be in the band. Annie and Lilly lived in the same neighborhood so they could practice together. They were both good jumpers though they had different looks. Lilly smiled a lot and had a contagious warmth. Annie's look was darker—she didn't smile widely because her teeth were crooked. She had been perfecting a sultry, mysterious smile in keeping with her dental situation. She knew this didn't align well with cheerleading but thought she could compensate with athletic prowess— when she jumped high to form jackknifes and leg splits and signaled with strong arms her true fighting spirit, yelling each letter and imploring the imaginary crowd to respond to the B- and the U- and the double LL- and the D- and the O- and the G-, asking what that stood for, and everyone screamed BULLDOGS, she put on a convincing show.

Annie and Lilly never talked about what would happen if they both lost or if one of them lost. Annie was hopeful they would both be selected. She wondered if Lilly felt the same—they hadn't been best friends that long. They dreamed about what they would look like in their short pleated white skirt, white sweater with red B for Bulldogs, red and white striped socks, and white sneakers. Annie would look mysterious and sultry, with a faint smile like a French woman she imagined, mimicking pictures she cut out of magazines and taped to the back of the door in her bedroom.

They were standing side by side at tryouts, stomachs grinding from acid nerves, when the roll call started. One by one, the hopeful twenty-five teenage girls stood in the center of the gym alone, launching a cheer and yelling BULLDOGS with no one to answer back, facing three judges: the perky brown-haired director of the cheerleaders, the muscular squat male coach from the football team, and the blond overweight physical education teacher who was always barking at the girls to change into their gym clothes faster and line up on the field.

Lilly's last name started with "J" so she went up before Annie. Lilly's blonde shiny hair was pulled into a high-swinging ponytail, and she had tied a large red and white bow in it to match the school colors. Her straight white teeth glistened under the lights, conveying exceptional school spirit.

When it was Annie's turn, last as the only Z, she delivered a rousing cheer, hopeful in her athletic prowess but mindful she did not look like Lilly. Annie had smoothed her long dark hair into a low ponytail held by a brown rubber band. She aimed her most alluring French look at the judges as she lifted her arms and legs into high kicks and yelled the Bulldog code.

Annie and Lilly walked home from school, debriefing their performances.

"You did so good, Lilly! Your bow really stood out!" Lilly never told Annie she was going to put a bow in her hair. Annie wished she'd tied her hair with something nicer than a rubber band. Lilly told Annie how scared she felt waiting in line. She thought she was going to vomit.

When the results were posted the next afternoon outside the cheerleading office, the loud-chattering group pushed forward to see the winning names, shouting them out one by one: "Adam, Connors, Janes, Hoover, Lincoln, Smith, Walters, Washington."

"Congratulations, Lilly Janes!" Annie turned to tell Lilly who was pressed behind her. No names after W made the list.

The winners were clumping together, congratulating each other. Lilly was in the center of the new group, her fine ponytail and bow swinging above them. Annie backed away. Should she wait for Lilly? Should they walk home together? In an instant Annie knew something changed.

The week after the results were posted, blaming herself for not being blonde, not having straight teeth, and not being perky, Annie was called to the principal's office. The principal and cheerleading director were standing side by side.

"You need to stop telling people you were not selected to be a cheerleader because you're Jewish, Annie! This is not true!"

This was the first Annie was hearing this. Her heart was banging like a bass drum. Who could be saying this?

"I never said that!" Annie protested, her face reddening with anger.

They didn't believe her. "You're fueling rumors throughout the school, Annie. You're not demonstrating good sportsmanship. It must stop!"

Annie held her tears in, trying to be strong in the face of so many injustices. She's never going to be a cheerleader. There's a rift with Lilly and she doesn't understand why. They haven't walked to school any day that week, and they can't walk home from school anymore because Lilly has practice. Fran disappeared and Annie thinks she knows why. And being Jewish means something important to so many people—but why? And what no one knows, Annie isn't sure she's Jewish anymore. Because of what happened at confirmation.

Annie thought confirmation after nine years of Saturday school at the synagogue would be like eighth-grade graduation—getting dressed up, gifts and thank you notes, a dance, and cake with frosting flowers.

In the weeks leading up to confirmation, each student received a paragraph to memorize in English, not Hebrew. They would present their passage to the congregation after they walked up the steps to the pulpit under the ark that held the Torah. They would wear white graduation robes and Mother would buy Annie a new dress to wear under her robe. She would have her picture taken in her robe at a real photographer's studio. Their class picture would hang in the hallway of the synagogue with pictures of the other confirmation classes.

The class sat like blossoming tulips in the front pews of the synagogue on confirmation day in May. The old rabbi blessed the tulips, inviting them one by one to come to the altar. Annie didn't understand the meaning of the passage she memorized but delivered her words with confidence. Then the rabbi kissed her forehead—a warm kiss, she thought with surprise, thinking he was too old to have soft lips. She returned to her seat in the wooden garden.

Now the rabbi was leading the fourteen-year-olds in what ominously sounded like a marriage oath. He stated the lines they should repeat after him—'they're entering a sacred community committed to Judaism and Jewish living.'

Annie didn't know this is what confirmation was. She cannot stand before God and lie—commit to something she hasn't even thought about. When were they going to teach her how to be a Jew? So far, she learned how to speak and read some Hebrew, but she was not allowed to have a bar mitzvah like Daniel, no matter how proficient her Hebrew, because she's a girl. And the women spend every holiday in the kitchen while the men have the speaking parts in the ceremonies and command the women to be quiet and listen—to them. The weekly classes she's been sitting in for years are about wars—why are we always fighting, why are people trying to kill us? Should she grow up to be a warrior to protect her views when she doesn't even have views?

In an instant, Annie decides her only course of action is to abstain. So when everyone pledges their commitment in unison, she is mute. After the pledge, the rabbi instructs the tulips to walk back to find their families in the pews, kiss them, and thank them for all they have done for them. Annie heads to the last row where Mother, Hannah, and Daniel are sitting. She half-heartedly thanks her family because everyone is watching. Mother doesn't seem to notice how angry and confused Annie is. Luckily, there are no family photos of the un-confirmation. The family did not own a camera. And there were not going to be photos of Daniel's bar mitzvah in two years either when he pledges to be a Jew at thirteen—and become a man. Maybe it didn't matter—the rabbi already told Daniel he was the head of the household when he was eight. He had powers. Annie's only power was to say no or go mute. But she knew those were not powers, really.

Two months after the un-confirmation, Jack, who was confirmed, called Annie on the phone to invite her to a dance. Annie later found out it was his mother who asked Annie's mother, and the two mothers decided Jack and Annie would go to the dance together.

The dance was at the Jewish country club located in the middle of a field on the outskirts of town. You turn right onto a wavy concrete road and go until you get to the parking lot. There's a short winding walkway to the main building with meeting rooms on the top floor and dressing rooms and showers on the first floor. There's a small hut-style building where you can order ice cream bars, burgers, candy, and chips. You don't need money—you can put orders on the family bill. Picnic tables line a rectangular cement apron that gets slippery when it's wet from swimmers who race over for food when the lifeguard blows a whistle to close the pool for fifteen minutes each hour for adult swim. On the other side of the picnic tables are barbecue grills where you can cook your own food. Mother stocks their blue cooler at home with thick steaks and corn on the cob wrapped in aluminum foil that they will grill after they swim. It's Annie and Daniel's job to grab the handles on each side of the cooler that they nest in the trunk of the car and carry it to the grill.

Mother said Annie was too young at fourteen to have a date, but she was making an exception so Annie can go to the dance with Jack because he called like a gentleman and comes from a nice family. Annie has to wear a dress which she is not happy about. The material of the caramel-colored dress is light cotton. Mother says to wear a slip under it so no one will see her legs through the dress, and the dress will not stick to her body because it will be hot and muggy that night. Annie's mother will drive Jack and Annie to and from the club. She'll stay and talk to other parents who will be there as chaperones.

Annie sits in the passenger seat next to her mother on the ride to Jack's house, the windows open to the welcome wind. "Go let Jack know we're here," Mother says when they arrive.

Annie runs up the steps to ring the doorbell. Jack's mother comes out on the porch to wave at Annie's mother. When Jack and Annie get to the car, Mother has opened the car's back door and ushers them into the back seat. Jack slides across the seat and scrunches his body as close to his door as he can. Annie takes her seat, leaving as much space between them as possible. They peer out their windows as if something truly gripping is going on outside. There is silence in the back seat for the thirty-minute drive to the club. Mother makes small talk over the hot wind pushing at them through the car. Is this what a date is? Why didn't someone warn her she would have to talk to Jack?

The clubhouse is decorated with banners, lights changing colors from red to blue to green, and music from a chattery disc jockey. Annie and Jack know most of the teenagers. The girls immediately group together—as do the boys. They're talking in groups and eating food while a few brave couples are dancing. Mother sits at a table in the corner with some chaperones, smiling and talking. The lights lower and turn an ominous blue. The DJ calls for a slow dance to "Mister Blue" by the Fleetwoods. Jack walks over from the boy's group to ask Annie to dance. She doesn't know how to dance but thinks she can copy whatever the other couples are doing.

Jack puts his left arm around her back and pulls her right hand into his hand which feels sweaty, and they are in a dance position Annie has seen in movies. To Annie's surprise, he knows how to dance and is tracing a box pattern as he moves. She tries to trace the pattern too, without stepping on his feet. There is no talking. Annie is desperately looking at other couples trying to learn how to dance. She knows the lyrics. Halfway through the song, when Mr. Blue is crooning sadly that he's sitting by the phone but knows his love isn't going to call, Annie feels her slip pulling away from her waist and heading south. Maybe it's the frayed elastic on the old slip Mother lent her or Annie's narrow hips. Annie uses her left hand that she's been holding against Jack's back to try to pull the slip back into place. But her slip keeps edging down. Annie is afraid to breathe—the slip is at her hips, and she knows it is poking out below the hem of her dress now. She's trying to think what to say or do while Mr. Blue's heart is breaking.

Now the white slip is resting fully on the dance floor, circling her feet in the final chords of Mr. Blue. Annie is unable to make the slow box pattern with the ring of silk bunched around her feet, and what if Jack's feet step into the ring of silk? She decides the only thing she can do is break away from the dance hold Jack has on her and pad with tiny steps to the nearest wall, and from there, step out of the slip entirely and carry it to the women's restroom where she will be able to pull the slip back into place. If Jack notices that Annie's slip is around her feet as she shuffles away in the dim lights to Mr. Blue, Annie will never know. Her face is crimson, and she is barely breathing.

The rest of the dance is a blur except for the ride home. In the dark, Jack and Annie thankfully cannot see each other. They press against their separate doors in the back seat. Mother chatters: 'Did they have a good time? Did they like the music? Did they like the food?' Mother thinks the finger sandwiches were delicious and the brownies too.

Back at his house, Jack politely thanks Mother for the ride and races to his porch. Annie climbs out of the back seat to get in the passenger seat.

"Did you have a good time, Annie? You looked so beautiful."

Annie sucks in the humid wind through the passenger side window. "No." She does not want to talk about coming undone. And why there is so much concern about anyone seeing her legs or her underwear through her dress. And why anyone would want to go on a date. She's sure Jack would agree if they were talking. Which they never do again.

The last straw comes to the fragile hut the unconfirmed Annie lives in, months after Daniel's non-photographed bar mitzvah. Mother asks Hannah, Annie, and Daniel to come to the living room. They stand side by side like a police lineup.

"I have something important to tell you," Mother is saying.

Annie exchanges a quick glance with Daniel.

"I met a very nice man in Dallas—his name is Benjamin Cohen. He's a widower—he lost his wife to cancer five years ago. We're getting married. We're moving to Texas when school is out. We'll have a better life there—we need a new start." Mother smiles hesitantly, waiting for their response.

Hannah doesn't care because she's leaving for college in the fall.

Daniel is ok—he wants to get away. Whenever he left the synagogue late afternoons while he was preparing for his bar mitzvah, three boys who lived by the high school across from the synagogue chased him to beat him up. He never told Mother how he had to run home so many days, but he told Annie. Annie's advice was to run fast.

Annie doesn't want to move. Things settled down after the cheer-leading debacle, and she's working on the school newspaper. But her vote doesn't count. Mother has made up her mind—they are moving twelve hundred miles away.

It was just a few months ago Mother visited her girlfriend who moved to Dallas to marry a man she met after her first husband died. "There are lots of single older men I can introduce you to," she told Mother.

Mother was in Dallas two days when she met Benjamin. He asked her to marry him before she returned to Pittsburgh twelve days later.

Benjamin flew to Pittsburgh in a few weeks and stayed at a hotel when they were packing up. Mom lined them up again in the living room. He had a speech prepared. He said he loved their mother, and he loved them. He was not going to try to replace their father. He had two adult children in their thirties. He owned a dress factory in Dallas—he moved there from New York after he got his start in the dress business in the garment district. He said they could ask him any questions.

Annie raised her hand like she was in school and her mother looked dismayed. "I have two questions—what do you want us to call you and what is the garment district?"

Benjamin smiled. "How about you call me Ben?" Mother nodded with approval, and they all agreed that would be good.

"I grew up in New York where my whole family worked in the garment industry making hats and women's clothes. My parents and uncles were immigrants from Europe—they used their sewing and tailoring skills from the old country to earn a living. My uncle told me I could make a good living if I got into women's ready-to-wear clothing because women were wanting to wear more dresses than skirts and blouses. So I learned everything I could, like designing, making patterns, buying and cutting fabric, and where to sell the goods. After the war, a lot of the people I was working with were moving to the South and West, so my cousins and I decided to head to Texas to build our own dress factory."

Hannah asked if they could see his factory when they got to town. Ben said he would give them a tour and some dresses from his sample line. At dinner he told them about the new neighborhoods springing up in North Dallas where he had an apartment. He promised to find a big house for them—they could have their own rooms, including Hannah when she came home from college. Mom was hanging on every word.

"I don't know if we should trust Ben," Annie confided to Hannah later that night. "What if this is a lot of bullshit—Mom only dated him for two weeks."

"Don't start a fight. It's Mom's decision. She trusts him. She wants the best for us."

"It's fine for her to have a new husband—I want her to be happy—but I don't need a stepfather, and I don't want to move. You don't have to worry; you're leaving for college."

"It'll be ok, Annie. Give it a chance."

"I'll go for a year, but I'm going to come back and live with Sarah's family and finish high school with my friends if I don't like it."

Hannah nodded. They were packing clothes in boxes Mom stacked between the beds in their room. They were moving in a few days.

The ragged herd headed that early June morning through Ohio to connect with Route 66 in Illinois in Mom's grey Chevrolet sedan. Annie read in a historical guide that Route 66 would take them to Texas, "land of oil wells, cowboys, and the conservative Bible Belt." The three little mousies, mostly grown, were crowded into the narrow back seat, Annie in the middle. She offered to let Daniel and Hannah have the windows because they were taller.

Ben drove the entire two and a half days, unwilling to stop at spots featured in Annie's guide where they could have had chocolate ice cream sodas, visit live snake displays, and shop for key chains, mugs, and jewelry. He said they had to make good time. The farther south they descended, the hotter it got. The car windows were open and steamy air blew in their faces. They arrived ruddy-faced in Dallas—one hundred and three degrees. Ben said it was a dry heat, so it was not so bad. This made no sense. He was pretending again, like he pretended to love them, when he didn't even know them.

"It's a cement and glass city, with no trees and sidewalks," Annie wrote in a postcard to her friend Sarah. The picture featured a Texas longhorn cow smiling and wearing a red scarf and gold earring. More pretending.

Annie's favorite place those first few weeks in Dallas was submerged in the swimming pool at their apartment building. The pool was bath warm because every day exceeded one hundred degrees. The water was covered with a thin scum of oil from tanning lotions. Women with high-teased hair and gold bangles sprawled in shiny bathing suits on lounge chairs around the pool. Annie found the fashion show at the pool fascinating. Was she supposed to turn into one of these women? Was that the plan?

Hannah left two months later for college. Hannah and Annie had shared a bedroom for sixteen years—Annie was glad to have a bedroom to herself. Now it would be just Annie and Daniel in the new concrete and glass city, friendless.

The high school that served the new apartment complexes and single-family homes in their neighborhood was large, moneyed, and white. The high school advisor assured Annie when she and her mother went to the office to register that this school was going to give her a better education than she could get in Pittsburgh. They were telling her she could work on the school newspaper, but in Pittsburgh, Annie was already the feature editor of the paper. She could take third- and fourth-year Latin but was that more valuable than starting a new language like Spanish in Pittsburgh? And there would be no driver's education at the new school. So Mother would have to teach her to drive—no telling how long that would take.

The student parking lot was larger than the staff lot. Everyone seemed to have their own car and more freedom than Annie was going to have. In the new neighborhood, there were no sidewalks—no one walked, no one rode a bicycle, and there was no city bus. Mother would drive Annie and Daniel the two miles to and from the school every day. It was embarrassing to lose her freedom at sixteen, and there would be so many occasions for unwelcome parental lectures. Like the lecture Annie and Daniel got one day about dating, preceded by the question, "Are you both gay?"

Annie didn't know anyone to date, male or female, and Daniel was fourteen. They whispered to each other in the back seat that Mom must be having a nervous breakdown.

Annie's new classmates looked like movie stars—coiffed hair, gold arm and neck jewelry, expensive outfits. Girls in their junior year gabbed about the sorority they would join at the University of Texas or the University of Oklahoma. Monday chatter was about weekend dates and vacation plans.

Annie read about the Junior Achievement program in the city newspaper, how it helped high school students set up businesses, make money, and develop business thinking skills. She needed that type of thinking, so she convinced her mother to let her take the city bus downtown to an orientation session. In Pittsburgh, she always took a seat at the back of the bus, so she headed down the aisle on the bus in Dallas. A white woman turned to watch her, then got out of her seat to walk to where Annie was settling in. "Dear, you shouldn't be sitting here. This is where the colored people sit."

Annie didn't know what to say. The lady was waiting for an answer. Annie stammered. "I like sitting in the back." The lady shrugged and went to her seat at the front of the bus.

Annie's high school in Pittsburgh was half-white/half Black students. She had never heard rules about where people sit on the bus. But she knew the rules for Jewish people. The hotel in Florida where they weren't allowed to stay. Why Dad lost the election for city council. Why people thought she didn't make cheerleader.

A week after the bus ride downtown, Ben took the new family to a basketball game at the university. The band opened with a rousing rendition of Dixie and waving of the Confederate flag. There were more cheers for that than the "Star-Spangled Banner." Her English teacher called Annie a Yankee because of her accent. She didn't know how she was going to adjust. And why should she adjust to something that felt wrong?

A month before school was out for the summer, Annie told her mother, "I don't have any friends. I don't like it here. I don't fit in." She reminded her mother of the plan they made before they moved—to try life in Texas for one school year, and if it wasn't working, she could go back to finish high school in Pittsburgh. She could live with her best friend Sarah's family.

"I don't know what you're talking about, Annie."

Was Mother denying their plan? Mother was using the because-I-said-so voice that meant there would be no discussion.

"But we talked about it. Sarah's family said I could live with them senior year." Annie reminded her, trying to stay calm while she felt herself unraveling.

Mother was shaking her head no.

"Then I could apply to college now. I have good grades. I'm sure I can get in someplace. Other people skip a year of high school and go right to college."

"You're not done with high school. There will be no more talk of this."

Her mother had a way of pulling her lips inward from all directions when she wanted to convey disapproval. Annie recognized this was the way her mother signaled she was not going to say what she really felt like saying. If Annie kept pushing, the yelling would begin. Then the choking cough from thick spit that formed in Mother's throat at tense times.

A sigh that started in the pit of Annie's stomach moved through her, expelling sadness, just plain sadness. This betrayal set off weeks of bitterness and a numbness greater than any she experienced since Dad died. She recognized Mother was trapped in a rocky new marriage. For nearly a year, Annie listened to Mother rant about how weak Ben was. His daughter was trying to take money which was supposed to be his new family's money too. His ex-mistress, the designer in his dress factory, retaliated when Ben married by reporting him to the IRS for tax issues—which turned out to be unsubstantiated, but he closed the factory anyway during the investigation because of the turmoil, the house he promised to buy never materializing. That's not what Mother uprooted her family for— mistruths, wishful thinking, pretending. She told Annie she would never leave the marriage, that vows were sacred—they had no place to go now.

Betrayed and trapped, Annie retaliated by announcing she would not be speaking during her last year in high school. She spoke to Daniel in his room at night but stopped talking with the rest of the family. Annie was never going to forgive her mother for not even trying to understand how she felt. And the betrayal, for sure, was going on Flora's list. Betrayal was worse than an eyeball turning inside out or rag-dolling in a blinding ocean undertow. Betrayal was an eight.

On her darkest mute days, Annie thought about the grandfather who escaped from Russia when he was a teenager conscripted in the Cossack army because he was a proficient horseman—she imagined him encouraging her to get on her horse and ride out of Texas like he did fleeing the Cossacks. The other grandfather who escaped Germany as a teenager after a fistfight with a German soldier—she imagined she could find a new geography like he did.

When she planned her escape during her seventeenth year, she couldn't imagine what was coming. The high school public address system would crackle in November that President Kennedy was gunned down just miles away. Jack Ruby would shoot Kennedy's killer days later, and she would see it live on television. On Sunday nights, Ed Sullivan would introduce Elvis Presley and the Beatles to screaming teens waking up in tumultuous times—the Vietnam War; civil rights workers like her cousin Saul marching in the South to help Blacks register to vote; and Bob Dylan delivering the gravelly benediction that "The Times They Are a-Changin'."

Then high school was over. She was leaving for college two weeks after she turned eighteen. On her birthday, she dug out the African proverb Saul gave her the day before they left for Texas:

Every morning in Africa, a gazelle wakes up.
It knows it must run faster than the fastest lion
Or it will be killed.
Every morning a lion wakes up.
It knows it must outrun the slowest gazelle
Or it will starve to death.
It doesn't matter whether you are a lion or a gazelle.
When the sun comes up, you better start running.

She took stock. She was hopeful but something inside felt dead. She didn't know if that's how everyone felt. She hoped Flora's dream—if it was a dream—would fade into her childhood. She wanted to be done with bad things. She was sure of four—Dad dying; Pa-John forcing Fran to have sex; Mother's betrayal; and President Kennedy's assassination. She wasn't sure if almost being kidnapped from the street should be five. Seeing Flora's list grow these last several years was eye-opening. It was dangerous to be a woman. No more mute years. No more hiding in the sand. Her gazelle and lion would have to run faster.

LEAVING HOME

"Come in. Sit down, dear. What are your college plans?" The high school counselor had summoned Annie for the obligatory session in March. "You're a good student—good grades, you've taken hard classes." She was looking at Annie's file on her desk. An orange shine smeared the counselor's lips like a new highway line—bleeding paint above her upper lip.

"I'm going to attend Titus College for Women in Missouri where my sister goes." Annie didn't explain that going to college was a transportation decision: get on a train or plane or in a car and travel a long distance. Annie would be applying because it was six hundred miles away.

"Well, good for you," Miss Conklin said, launching a tired smile in Annie's direction without looking at her. She jotted down notes in the file. She was relieved to get through the alphabet of seniors. Zechman was last.

It was August now, and Annie was talking to the family because she was leaving. She packed her belongings in three dress factory cases Ben brought home: clothes, bedding, towels, shoes, toiletries, books, typewriter, knick-knacks. Two cases would travel ahead via Greyhound Bus for Annie—and two for Hannah who had come home for the summer and was returning for her third year. One case each would go with them on the train.

Mother, Ben, and Daniel said quick goodbyes at the station on a melting afternoon. They left the house late, and Ben had to drive fast to get them to the station. There was no hugging—Mother explained the

34

rules when they were young: Dad's side of the family hugged, her side of the family did not. Annie didn't know if her mother was tearful because Annie did not look back. She focused on her luggage as if it would melt in the heat and watching would prevent that.

Alone now, the sisters tugged their heavy cases along the hot cement apron next to the tracks, listening to the faint, high-pitched whistle of the impending train. As they positioned their cases next to the loading edge, the whistle cried loudly, low-pitched train vibrations earthquaked through their feet, then the sounds of squealing metal and brakes slowing. The train doors opened quickly, and a conductor stood between two railcars calling, "All aboard. All aboard!"

Annie and Hannah helped each other hoist their cases up the metal stairs and into a baggage bin inside the car. They found seats mid-car, relieved to be out of the heat. In minutes, the doors closed, and the train blew its whistle like a mantra to focus them on their journey. The engine picked up strength to head north, and the sisters settled in for the fifteen-hour ride. Hannah would later stretch across two seats to sleep. Annie tucked her legs up and looked out the window all night at passing lights and towns, though much of the time she only saw her reflection in the dark window. She had a good talk with Daniel last night. She worried about leaving him behind, but he was sixteen and had made friends at school. He would be okay with Mother and Ben, he said. Annie promised to write.

The farther the train pushed north, the calmer Annie felt. Distance was calming. She had been praying for distance for months.

A bus the college sent met several students at the train station the next morning. Miles later, the bus pulled into the long campus driveway, passing through an elaborate archway. Annie had been waiting to see the archway featured on the cover of the college brochure. She had written a report on archways for Latin class—"The Magic of the Keystone." She learned archways were a mainstay of architecture in the Roman Empire. They held up aqueducts, buildings, and monuments. She had a hard time understanding how the form could be strong—looking at an arch, you'd think it would cave in under duress. But there was the keystone, the wedge-shaped piece at the top—the last piece placed during construction locked the stones into position—allowing the arch to bear weight. That's what Annie wanted, a keystone to hold her parts together.

The bus headed down the driveway ending at a Y, dividing two east-west roads edged by green grassways and sturdy trees. And there they were—stately Victorian brick buildings that Annie knew from the brochure were built in the 1920s.

The girls called out to the driver which building to stop at. Hannah was living in the new dormitory for upper-class women. That was the first building on the Y's far-left edge. Hannah got off the bus, and the driver pulled her heavy case out of the luggage compartment under the bus. Hannah was going to have to pull her case to the dorm by herself, Annie thought, watching from the window. The driver was already back in his seat, and they were moving again.

Annie would be living in the oldest building, at the far-right end of the Y. Annie was last off the bus. The driver pulled Annie's case out to the front walkway, and Annie looked up to propped-open, arched wooden doors and an expansive, white-painted porch. She grabbed the thick leather handle of the case with both hands and eased it up six worn stairs to the porch. Then another push to get the case over the door lip. Finally, she was standing in the entry. On top of a mahogany desk was a check-in book with a sign: *All Students Must Sign In.*

As Annie was signing in, a middle-aged woman with short blonde hair came to greet her. "Welcome, welcome. I'm Mrs. Lichtenberg, house mother." She looked at the sign-in book and sounded out the new girl's name: "Ann-EE Zech-MAHN."

"ZECH-man, Annie corrected her, breathing heavily from pulling her case up the stairs.

"Welcome, Annie. I'm so glad you're joining us! You're in room 204. Your roommate is Laurie Fishman. She isn't here yet. Do you need help getting your bag up the stairs? This is an old building—no elevators or air conditioning, I'm afraid."

"No problem, Mrs. Lichtenberg. I can manage." Annie double-gripped the leather handles and eased her case up the wide oak stairs to the second floor. She was tired from the all-nighter but invigorated by the distance she had put between herself and home.

TEN BEFORE THIRTY • 37

The next morning Annie met the balding, heavy-set economics professor who would be her academic advisor. Annie was going to major in economics because that was the class she liked best in high school. Professor Thomas motioned her to sit in the brown leather chair next to his desk. Pictures of his family smiled down from the shelf above—dark-haired wife, two dark-haired teenagers, and a grey Weimaraner dog. Three ornate frames showcasing university degrees took up another shelf.

"Hello, I'm Dr. Thomas," he said, reaching forward to shake her hand. "I see you're Annie Zechman from Dallas, Texas—the town that kills presidents." He's reading from a manila file folder.

Annie catches her breath. Did he say what she thought he said? The squealing announcement of the president's shooting on the school public address system less than a year ago was seared into her mind. And the fight with Mother. Mother wouldn't let her go to Dealey Plaza to report on the motorcade. Annie was the photography editor—they were planning a photo spread for the school paper. Annie was still raw from that day and the shocking days that followed.

The journalism team was going to stand on Houston Street. Annie would have missed the shooting because the four-car motorcade turned from Houston to Elm Street next, where Oswald was waiting at the sixth-floor window of the Texas School Book Depository to fire his rifle as Kennedy's limousine drove past at twelve-thirty. The first shot missed the president but the second struck him—rupturing his trachea and a lung. The third shot seared through the top of his skull. The president was declared dead at one p.m. at Parkland Hospital. News reports hit the public airstream a half hour later. Annie would never forget the scratchy PA system at her school, trying to relay the news. She strained to hear through the high-pitched screeching. It was like the PA system did not want to relay the horrific news. And then everything went quiet.

That Thanksgiving, Annie added Kennedy's name to Flora's list on the worn yellow legal pad Dad gave her eight years earlier. Dad left them on the fifteenth day of November, the President on the twenty-second day. That Thanksgiving, the twenty-eighth day of what always seemed like a dismal month, was sad. Kennedy had pressed his presidential seal on a proclamation just two weeks before his death that Thanksgiving would be celebrated on the twenty-eighth in 1963. He proclaimed they 'give thanks for the ideals of honor and faith inherited from our forefathers—for the decency of purpose, steadfastness of resolve and strength of will, for the courage and the humility which they possessed and which we must seek every day to emulate. As we express our gratitude, we must never forget that the highest appreciation is not to utter words but to live by them.' She shuddered at the thought he had only two weeks to live after he proclaimed they should be grateful.

Annie did not feel grateful that Thanksgiving, and now she's wondering if she will have to take all her economics classes from Dr. Thomas. She did not think she could bear it.

"How many economics professors are in the department?"

"There are two of us. I teach all the core classes in economics."

She makes up her mind in those fifteen life-changing minutes that even though a Weimaraner lives with his family, a point in the professor's favor, she has no recourse but to change her major. She has read about small colleges: each major is a small community—an academic herd. If you don't fit in, best to find a different herd.

That afternoon Annie resets her goals. The advising office assures her she does not have to explain her change of mind to Dr. Thomas. So on day two of college, she declares two majors: English and biology. If she doesn't like one of them, she can drop it later.

Laurie Fishman's Cincinnati family drops her off quickly late afternoon on day two. They waste little time stacking boxes in the corner of the bedroom and hugging their sobbing, convulsing daughter goodbye. They were handing their red-faced, puffy-eyed daughter over to Annie now.

After Laurie washes her face and resumes normal breathing, Annie faces Laurie, who resembles a fish with red-rimmed bubble eyes, for their first decision. Who should take the top bunk? They each climb the ladder to try out the top. Laurie hesitates at each rung to look down, anxious. Annie offers to take the top.

They discover this was the right decision when Laurie explains her going-to-bed regimen. She'll be winding several thick metal rollers into her hair, and then wrapping a cloth cap around her head to keep the rollers in place. She's sure her head would be too close to the ceiling with her rollers in when she sits up in bed, so she would never be able to sleep on the top bunk. She will also be using a bronchodilator, inhaling medication from a white plastic pump to keep her airways open. It's anxiety, not asthma, that causes her airways to close, she explains. It will be easier to access her breathing gear if she keeps it on a table next to the lower bunk. And she will be going to sleep every night at ten.

Though she never explains her music-listening process to Annie, when music comes on the radio or the record player, Laurie conducts, accompanying the instruments with an imaginary baton, pointing to the woodwind section when they should come in, the string instruments, and the drummers. Laurie is not a music major—she's majoring in education.

Annie concludes they have little in common. She keeps a night-owl schedule, leaving the library at nine most evenings to return to the dorm to visit with new friends down the hall until one or two in the morning, tiptoeing to her room to climb the ladder to her bunk for five hours of sleep. Sometimes Laurie is crying quietly into the blanket pulled up around her face, her roller-helmeted head propped starkly on top of the pillow. Annie apologizes for waking her up and often asks, "What's wrong, Laurie? Are you ok?"

There is typically a quick muting of the crying, and Laurie sniffles she's ok. Then sleep comes to them both. Annie leaves the room most mornings before Laurie for chemistry and biology classes. Laurie does a lot of letter-writing and calling home.

It's months into the school year when Laurie's crying is not muffled when Annie asks late one night if she's ok. The crying grows louder as Annie tries to guess what could be wrong.

"Are you sick? Are you hurt? Did you get a bad grade on a test? Is something wrong with your family? Are you out of money? Did someone say something bad to you?"

Each question is met with more crying. Annie is about out of questions when she thinks to ask, "Did you miss your period?"

Laurie lets out a shriek-cry, which means that's the right category. So Annie pursues this line of questions.

"How long have you gone? You don't think you're pregnant, do you? Have you had sex with anyone?"

The little fish mumbles in her tearful, trembling voice that she has not had sex with anyone. She hasn't even had a date with anyone.

"You know you can't be pregnant if you haven't had sex." Annie tries to reassure her with this declarative sentence—maybe Laurie doesn't know this. Maybe her anxiety is so severe she can't be rational. Maybe there's something wrong medically.

Laurie's crying levels off. There's breath-catching to do with the bronchodilator while Annie advises her to go to the student health clinic in a few hours. It is probably the irregularity many girls have.

During the bronchodilator deep breathing, Annie makes up her mind to request a new roommate next term—or better yet, a single room. She spent sixteen years living with Hannah, and now Laurie. Annie wants to swim through the night alone.

She writes a letter explaining the incompatibility of their schedules to the Dean of Students and is approved for a single room next term. Laurie cries when she hears the news. Annie points out their schedules are too different—Annie's majors require her to study late at night to keep up, and she's a night owl who needs less sleep than Laurie. Laurie reaches for her bronchodilator, and Annie knows she has betrayed the little fish by abandoning her for the girls down the hall.

At Thanksgiving break, Annie and Hannah cannot travel to see family because they don't have enough money. A small number of classmates, including the international students who cannot travel long distances for such a short week, stay at the college. The dining hall cooks a big turkey dinner, and the small tribe of students eat together at round, white-clothed tables. Annie tells herself to be grateful like President Kennedy proclaimed for them to be last Thanksgiving. But she does not feel grateful though she does give thanks for the extra days of quiet without classes or Laurie, who left for Cincinnati to see her family.

At Christmas break, the college closes, so Annie and Hannah have to leave. Hannah travels to Texas. Annie is still angry with her mother, so she travels to her grandparents in Buffalo.

Gram is ailing—there are more angry-looking bony growths on her toes and fingers. Her false teeth float most days and nights in the glass jar by the kitchen sink, and Gram is quiet. She tries to walk daily, cook meals, and embroider tablecloths though Annie does not know how she can thread the eyes of the small needles with her deformed fingers.

Her grandparents do not ask if Annie is fighting with Mother, and Annie doesn't tell them anything is wrong. The family is used to sweeping disputes under the rug, and Annie correctly counts on no one asking questions.

Annie spends the break reading books, playing the tinny-sounding piano in the back room overlooking the garden, and cleaning. Gram doesn't ask her to clean, but Annie goes through each room, scrubbing away the dust and grime of the old house. And she studies her namesake on the fireplace mantle, who sits in his frame among the miniature herd of elephants.

Annie sleeps in the small corner bedroom on the second floor. This is Andrew's teenage room, across from Grandpa's room. The house is noisy. Radiators clank and spout steam like trains heading in and out of the station. The cherry-wood grandfather clock gongs every hour and once on the half-hour. Grandpa winds the clock every day, turning the brass key in the clock's keyhole and checking the weights on the chain at the top of the cabinet. At night there is Grandpa's loud snoring, reassuring because Annie knows where he is by his hard rumbling. Gram sleeps at the other end of the hall, in the room Mother shared with her sister growing up.

On the third day, Annie discovers Gram standing before a row of glass wine bottles lining the long hallway across from the small bathroom on the first floor.

"What are you doing?" Annie asks.

Gram lifts her deformed second finger to her lips to signal her to be quiet. Then she pours water from a carafe into each wine bottle. Annie watches Gram struggle to pull the corks out of each bottle with her nearly useless fingers. A narrow stream of sunlight from the small window at the end of the hall flickers on the bottles, lighting the process. Annie steps forward to help her pull out corks. Annie knows she's diluting Grandpa's bottles—when he drinks, though Annie doesn't know how often that is, he fills the house with crazy singing and taunts, trying to stir movement in the nearly empty train station.

The two weeks pass quickly. The rooms are clean, though Annie knows they may never be cleaned again like she has done for the rest of their lives.

Back at college, Annie sets up her single room, deciding where to put the bed, what color spread to have, and where to hang the bulletin board and pictures. Her room is just down the hall from her old room, but two new roommates are living in the old room because Laurie did not return after break. She decided to stay with her family and go to school in Cincinnati. Annie blames herself. Had she embraced a friendship with Laurie, Laurie might have stayed. But Annie's gazelle and lion were too busy running—that is all she can focus on.

That and book-divining. Annie believes that books containing answers she needs to improve her life come to her by divine intervention. She has a process to help the divine deliver them: she walks slowly past the stacks in the library and in bookstores like she is searching for water with a divining rod. When the feeling is right, she stops to select a book and flip through the pages for answers, for inspiration.

That is how she finds *Beautiful Losers* by Leonard Cohen, before she discovers his music and he sings to her in his low hypnotic voice. That's how she finds the dream analysis book, guiding her to curate themes in her dreams and set alarm clocks to wake herself to remember dreams. And how she finds ee cummings, who tells her to use lowercase letters and stay flexible, oh so flexible, when she's laying out words on a page, to free her voice. And the book of Salvador Dali paintings that show her new ways to think about time. Does she want to spend her time like a parched clock drying in the desert? Because she is. Parched. Her gazelle and lion are pawing at the dust of a dried oasis.

Annie learned from her encounter with Dr. Thomas that if you don't like the professors in the department of your major, it's best to change majors because you'll be having those professors for most of your classes. Dr. Rickson was one of the few professors Annie was happy to take all her classes from. He worked on the Manhattan Project before he came to teach at the college.

"How did you get involved in the Manhattan Project?" Annie asked when she went to his office for approval to be a biology major. His white lab coat covered most of his short, stocky body. His round face and thick glasses emanated kindness and no affectation. His limbs were constantly shaking from Parkinson's disease, mostly his left arm. One leg dragged as he walked, tipping him slightly off balance.

"I was a new PhD out of graduate school when I was recruited in the 1940s. President Roosevelt had authorized research to develop atomic weapons because of the research going on in Nazi Germany. We were doing our research at the University of Chicago and a nearby site which became the Argonne National Lab. Our teams developed the first atomic reactor in an old squash court at the university," he said chuckling.

Annie remembered the horrific pictures of the bombings of Hiroshima and Nagasaki, and her father talking with his brother about the dangers of an atomic arms race. Annie wanted to ask if her professor's Parkinson's came from working with radiation, but she thought that was too personal.

Another time he told her he was developing an experimental course, Radiation Biology, that she could take after she completed enough biology courses. Annie liked the idea but shared her biggest concern about being a biology major, "I don't like live animal work, Dr. Rickson." They already had to do so much dissection, though the animals so far were dead. But she knew they would be working with live eggs in embryology, and she heard they would be working with the eggs until the very day the chicks hatched, and then the chicks would die. She didn't want to think about what was ahead—all the killing.

"That's part of the scientific method, Annie. You have to do lab work in the major," he explained matter-of-factly. He would let her do lab work any time during the day because she would be trying to fit labs in between other courses.

"Dr. Hill says I can't major in English and biology. He thinks they're too different. But to me, science seems a lot like English—words and stories seem so organic. Hill won't be my advisor if I major in both."

"I don't agree with Hill. Biology and English are compatible. It's best to make up your own mind, Annie."

She was satisfied she was making the right decision. Rickson agreed to help with biology, and she would work with a less opinionated advisor for her English major.

"Everyone is going to be working with three frogs in lab experiments over the semester," Rickson explained to the class. "These are experiments on the heart."

"Can our lab partners team up and set some frogs free?"

"No, you have to do your own work."

Annie felt the pit in her stomach whenever they did animal work, whether they were already dead or alive. The frogs were torpid and soft in the refrigerator's vegetable bin, resting in a few inches of chilly water. By the end of the term, Rickson explained they would all be used in experiments.

Rickson gave the class directions: "Before any experiments, we render the frog insensitive to pain. Pithing is how we do this. Pithing destroys the brain, in the frog located between the eyes—in some cases, pithing also severs the spinal cord."

Annie tried to listen dispassionately, thinking that words like *sever* and *destroy* are so harsh.

He continued in a monotone, "Pithing is relatively painless. We use this little tool—it has a wood handle headed by a thick needle—to drive the needle quickly into the central spot at the base of the skull to kill the frog instantly, or else the frog will suffer. When you hit the right spot, their legs stiffen—this means you have severed the spinal cord."

He demonstrated: "Hold the frog away from your body with the lower extremities extended. It's best to hold the frog with one finger on the nose and the second finger under the jaw," his fingers shaking from Parkinson's. "Flex the frog's head away from your body and move the needle down the midline until you come to the soft spot. No need to put pressure on the frog's skin—the skull is hard cartilage. You'll feel a soft spot at the end of the skull. This is where you insert the needle quickly. Move the needle from side to side inside the cranial vault to destroy the brain. Don't worry.

The frog won't feel anything. Without the brain, perception of sensory phenomena is impossible."

Several classmates squirmed uncomfortably on their metal lab chairs. Most grimaced, but a few looked on dispassionately as Dr. Rickson wiggled his needle inside his victim's cranial vault. When the demonstration was over, he handed his severed-brain frog to one of the girls so she could work with that frog.

"It's your turn, class. The experiments are described in the lab workbook."

One by one, Annie's classmates moved to the refrigerator to pick out a cold frog. Some girls were scared and clumsy. They were used to anesthetizing frogs with ether. Some pithed their frogs, missing the spot. Annie had the knack. They begged her, 'Do this one. Do mine.'

Annie took their frogs one by one, believing the frogs would suffer if they didn't do it right, sure Rickson was wrong about the frogs' lack of feeling. She lost count of how many frogs she pithed that afternoon and had no recollection of conducting any experiments. What was she supposed to be learning about the heart? She was just trying to aim for the right spot so the frogs would not suffer. She was learning to kill.

She left the lab at the end of class—she would need to return to finish the assignment. It was nearly five when she returned—she had an hour before dinner. She dropped her books on the counter and walked the few steps to the refrigerator. There were still a dozen frogs in the vegetable bin. Cold and quiet. When she held the bin open, the frogs began to stir, crying for warmth and freedom, she thought. She couldn't hold the drawer open too long, or they might jump out. She pulled out the one she had named Otto.

"Well, Otto, today's the day, my friend. I'm sorry." He'd been submerged in the shallow water for days, a fine sleek frog with yellow dots across his back.

She reached for a needle, drew Nembutal into the syringe, held Otto by his legs and neck, and stuck the needle into his belly. At least no more pithing, she thought. He blinked and actually croaked. The needle drew out, slippery. "I'm sorry, baby." She felt a kinship with this frog. Otto blinked his fine high eyes, a thin protoplasm lid slipping. He clung to her hand like skin. She pulled on his leg to see if he was asleep. He slept laxly on her palm, without her holding him there. She moved him to the wood plaque where she would tie the frog to a metal turnstile with a graphite needle that would etch his cardiac waves on blue and white graph paper.

The workbook said to write down the readings and keep the heart wet throughout the experiment, or it would dry out. She looked about the room to stall. Broad glass shelves, beakers, gas jets, metal needles, chemical bottles in alphabetical order behind glass doors. She picked up Otto in her hand. The wall clock moved its angular hands like needles. She felt drugged herself, like Otto, who was sleeping soundly now, on his way to death. The centrifuge whirled in the room next door. Water was running in a tap behind her. Someone came in and slammed the refrigerator. She heard frogs cry out before the door slammed closed. She thought about putting Otto back, about using another frog. But he would be used eventually.

She spread him out on the board, so his front side was fully exposed, picked up pins from a small metal box, and began sticking them through his webbed legs and arms. He didn't move. She placed three pins in each hand, three in each foot, to keep him taut. It's so strange that the skin didn't rip. It just punctured, she mused.

She took tools she would need out of a nearby box, picked up the scalpel, looked at Otto again dozing quietly and vulnerably, pinned on his back on the wooden board. His leg stirred; she placed her finger on him. The cut she made turned red quickly. She cut across, under his chin, down by the bottom of his belly, and down the center, between the two crosscuts. He opened like pages in a book. He was shining, clear, and transparent underneath his skin. She remembered the lines in a novel, where Christ comes to earth without a skin but within a transparent envelope, barely concealing inside heavy organs, blood rushing underneath, bubbling lightly like tears. She moved fast to lift the organs, feeling cool and slippery. She noticed he had something in his stomach. She attached electrodes to his heart, worked the machines about his body. So much machinery for such a tiny muscle. Otto stirred again, coming to life. She was startled: it's impossible. It must be a natural reaction that he should stir.

The readings were coming clearly. She lined up the chemicals before her, ready to drop them on his heart to register the different rates. The clock ticked slowly. She began to record in her notebook which chemical she was using, watching the rates come, mechanically. The workbook asked her to observe things like atrial and ventricular systole and diastole in Otto's heart; the effects of epinephrine, acetylcholine, atropine, and pilocarpine on the frequency and amplitude of cardiac muscle contraction. Would she ever use any of this information in her life?

She wondered if it was still snowing outside. It was starting when she walked to the lab. Otto continued to send steady beats. She was done with the readings and would let him dry out. She cut the tubes holding the heart in place and took it out, shining, still beating, and put it on the counter. She unpinned his legs and arms. His appendages slipped into comfort. He looked little different when she closed the flaps and pieced him back together, Otto without his heart, with a red cut down the front. A little juice dried on the wood plaque. His heart continued to beat. She could have stitched him up then, but he wouldn't have lived without a heart. Now what are you, she thinks, Otto without a heart—dead. His heart kept beating.

She walked across the room to look out the window. It was snowing. The frogs that had been used that day were wrapped in tissue, disposed in a garbage pail at the corner of the lab. Annie looked at her hands. She was a killer. Her Otto was a puzzle, with body parts that fit together. She turned back to the desk and looked at the clock. Her friends would be waiting in the dorm for her to go to dinner. She pulled a candy bar from her pocket and bit the paper away with her teeth because her hands had saltwater and Otto's juices on them.

Otto's heart kept beating. She couldn't leave until he was dead. He'll be dead when his heart stops, she thought. "Come on, Otto, die." She picked up his other body parts and wrapped them in paper. Some fluids seeped into the paper. He felt heavy wrapped like this. She walked to the basket by the refrigerator. Several brown corpses lay there, soaked with juice. She threw Otto into the pail. The candy bar tasted stale and a peanut was caught in her tooth. She walked back to the table. Otto's heart was still beating. "I didn't want to kill you, Otto," she muttered out loud. She wrapped his pulsing heart in a Kleenex, walked to the metal pail, looked one last time at the shrouds soaking the paper, and decided she could not let him go until he was dead. So she held his wrapped up heart inside her hand and left the lab.

Outside the science building, the wind blew into her tired face. She tucked her face into her woolen hood and pushed her hand into her right coat pocket. His heart beat in her pocket for some time. She kept asking herself, is this what scientists have to do? Is this what I have to do? And why am I so good at killing?

Annie knew about radiation experiments and the nuclear detonations in the western states before she enrolled in Rickson's radiation biology course. Every time there was a blast, the news reported the speed of the winds carrying radioactive fallout across farmlands and mountains, cities and towns. People worried about the people and animals that lived downwind. How could it be true that low doses of radiation were not harmful? Annie read that radiation could lead to cancer, heart disease, birth defects, genetic mutations, and other diseases. Her physiology class took Geiger counters outside for days following a detonation in the west to measure the ionizing radiation in the air. The numbers went up several days after a detonation, so they knew the winds were blowing fallout across large distances.

Annie learned in Rickson's course how sensitive biological systems are to radiation—cells and tissue. She imagined these effects were like the detonations that go off in people's lives too—relationship blasts that damage people's bodies and spirits, sometimes beyond repair, and maybe cause their very cells to mutate. There were days she imagined the winds were blowing the fallout from her fights with her family to damage her body and spirit. How bad does a blast have to be, how many traumas, before her own cells would mutate from assaults? Her experience with Flora sat inside her head, raising the questions: how bad is bad, and what really counts as bad? If only there was a Geiger counter of toxic relationships to warn her when the damage was getting too great.

For the final exam, Rickson injected a large box turtle with an unknown radioactive substance for each student. The assignment was to run tests—dissect the turtle and measure the radioactivity in different organs—to discover what the unknown was. Because of Annie's schedule, she would be working in the lab late afternoons by herself, though Rickson would be in his office nearby.

Annie carefully removed her turtle's organs—the stomach, heart, thyroid, other organs. She measured each with the Geiger counter and entered the amount of radioactivity into her lab notes. The highest counts were in the thyroid, so she realized her unknown substance was radioactive iodine which had moved through the turtle and settled in the thyroid.

Annie was cleaning up after her lab work was done. The turtle shell was so unique—she would wash it carefully and put it on the night table next to her bed in the dorm.

"I'm leaving, Dr. Rickson," she called out. "I'm done."

He poked his head around the corner. As always, his lab coat was so long it skimmed his shoes. She was picking up her books and holding the turtle shell.

"What are you doing with the shell?"

"I washed it really good so I can keep it."

Rickson shuffled over, back leg dragging, and took the shell from her. He moved to the Geiger counter, placing the shell on the counter's attached metal tray. He turned on the machine, and it started emitting loud, regular beeps.

"Annie, this is hot. Do you know what would have happened? You would have gotten sick, and no doctor would think to check you for radiation sickness."

She watched Rickson put the shell in the receptacle for radioactive materials. That's where Annie already disposed of the organs she removed from the turtle and the papers used to wipe up the workspace.

Annie was dismayed at her carelessness. "I'm sorry, Dr. Rickson. I should have realized."

He gave her a tired smile and waved her away with a tremoring arm. Annie thought about the dangers you can't see—the dangers you don't think about. She wondered if her professor was sick because no one looked out for him when he was young, as he looked out for her.

Annie was uncomfortable dating. She was sure there would be a penis coming along on the date, trying to talk to her. She was sure something was wrong with her. She decided to design a course of therapy to find answers, writing four steps in a notebook she kept hidden under her mattress: 1) read up on dating, intercourse, frigidity, sex therapy, penises, vaginas; 2) observe the dating practices of her friends; 3) keep a journal of dreams to search for psychological clues; and 4) find an appropriate man to have sex with—a sex therapy man.

She told her friends she was thinking of becoming a sex therapist like Masters and Johnson. No one questioned this because she was a biology major, and they all knew about William Masters and Virginia Johnson's research studying human sexual response and treating sexual disorders. Masters and Johnson had visited their college—Annie heard they were recruiting women to have sex in their lab, to collect data on the anatomy and physiology of the human sexual response.

Everyone knew who was having sex in the dorm because they talked openly at night when they gathered in one of their bedrooms, and someone pulled out a bottle of liquor they weren't allowed to have. They talked for hours about their periods, birth control, gynecologist visits, socially transmitted diseases, underwear they thought men liked, the kind of underwear they thought their professors wore, and penises. They especially liked to make fun of Nancy's underwear—the plain granny panties and pointy bras she got at Sears. Nancy was the only one still wearing Kotex pads, not tampons. They chided her to switch over.

"I've tried—I can't get it in!"

Lucy gave her the box with the drawing showing how to insert it. "Try again. We'll stand outside the door and talk you through it."

Nancy reluctantly went to one of the stalls in the shared bathroom down the hall, and Lucy, Annie, and Ruthie gathered around the door.

"I might be trying to put it in the wrong hole," Nancy called out with a high-pitched groan. She was ready to give up.

"Keep trying. Look at the picture. You know where your butt hole is—don't put it in there. And relax. It's easier if you're relaxed," Lucy said.

Nancy called out, "It's in." She unlocked the stall door and emerged, face flushed with embarrassment. She was tucking her shirt into her jeans.

They congratulated her, and Ruthie said wryly, "Your boyfriend is going to be happy you know what hole to put it in." Nancy was talking with her boyfriend about having sex for the first time.

Annie wondered if men in their college dorms helped each other practice putting on condoms and talked about what types of condoms they liked the best.

For the next few months, the girls moved their attention to a new project, outfitting Nancy's white china dog with sexual regalia when she was out with her boyfriend. The dog was two feet high, and his stately, noble expression made him a good subject for dress-up. They hung a pair of tennis balls between his legs or put a pointy red and black bra around his chest or hung a garter belt from his hips. Sometimes he had a Kotex pad between his legs instead of a tampon. Or they borrowed a stuffed animal from someone else's room, and the errant elephant or teddy bear would be humping Nancy's china dog on her bed, on her pillow, or on the rug on the floor when she returned from her date. The girls would hide in the room across from Nancy's to hear what she said when she opened the door, laughing so much their stomachs hurt. They piled into her room to hear what happened on the date, while she removed the accouterments from the dog, begging them to leave her dog alone, reminding them how upset her mother would be if she saw what they did to the dog, a prized family heirloom.

Since Lucy was the most sexually experienced in the group, Annie especially liked to hear her stories. She asked Annie for advice about Sidney, the married medical student she was seeing. He always jumped up immediately after sex to take a shower.

"Do you think that's normal? Do you think he thinks I'm dirty? I've been douching. He won't go down on me either."

"Maybe he has a phobia about sex. Just ask him why he showers every time."

Lucy didn't want to ask—he might feel insulted, and she wanted to keep seeing him.

Annie wondered if he was feeling guilty for having sex with someone other than his wife and wanted to erase the evidence. She kept that thought to herself.

To ensure she would wake at different points throughout the night to track her dreams, following the advice of one of the dream analysis books, Annie placed alarm clocks in three drawers of the dresser. One alarm rang sixty-five minutes after she went to bed. The second, an hour later. The third, two hours later. After a time with this protocol, Annie learned to wake herself on this schedule without alarms.

The books advised finding recurring themes in dreams and noting any change in the scenarios. It took months of writing down dreams to have enough to identify key themes. Once Annie paid close attention to them, she recognized that many themes had recurred for years.

Like the water themes: rivers, oceans, and swimming pools where she saw parts of her life being enacted in waterways. And bridges and ships: bridges falling in, ships running into bridges, people dwarfed and intimidated by ships hundreds of times bigger than they were. In one dream, she and Daniel were floating down a brown river in a rectangular willow basket, trying to make their way in the steep waves created by looming, darkly painted freighters around them. Annie was sitting in front of Daniel, looking back at him often, the two sitting carefully, so they didn't flip over, comforted by being together.

In some water dreams, there were bizarre and fanciful creatures Annie had never seen in any aquatic book—part fish, part bird, and body parts that made new assemblages of fantastical creatures. Some were dark and deformed. Sometimes the creatures started out small and morphed into larger species right before her eyes, crowding the bodies that were trying to swim in the pond or lake.

And there were the train dreams. Phallic trains coming down the tracks, sometimes through water in rivers, barreling at her, from behind, loud steam hissing, whistles deafening, dark and imposing, drowning out any cries she might have made.

She wrote the dreams in her notebook, noting where she was in each. Run over? Knocked off the tracks? Standing in groups with friends? The train dreams—the scariest—continued until the last dream signaled a solution: move away from the oncoming train. All she had to do was step off the tracks, get out of the way of the trains.

There were also war dreams. She was embattled and attacked, and many of the attackers were in Hitler's armies speaking German.

Then came the vacuum sweeper dreams. Big hoses spewing out of her mouth, endlessly. Her jaws were so tired of trying to excise hoses. And chewing gum. She was trying to pull the gum out of her mouth, but it was endless wads of gum she was pulling out of an exhausted mouth.

There were good dreams too. She would be flying low, a few feet above the ground, moving quickly and deftly through the woods, above lakes, weaving in and out of trees—effortless, fast, swooshing, her body comfortable and capable of flight.

The dreams messaged what she already knew—except when she was low-flying and free, she felt run over. If she tried to speak, no one saw or heard her. And often she was being run over by powerful phallic shapes. She was a woman without power.

Annie sought help from the student health center because she was falling into half-sleep trances. She could hear conversations outside her room and have them verified later by her friends, but she was paralyzed on the bed, unable to move any part of her body. She would begin to sweat and try with all her strength to move the little finger on her right hand. When she could do that, she could emerge from the paralysis.

At the health center, the doctor asked her questions: "Do you think anyone is trying to hurt you? Do you think anyone is trying to kill you? How many hours of sleep do you get at night?" There was no physical exam.

She recognized he was searching for delusional, paranoid feelings.

"I don't think I'm paranoid," she said, wondering if he would believe her. "I'm not a good sleeper—sleep a few hours most nights. What can I do to stop going into these trance-like states?"

"I don't think there is anything wrong except you don't sleep enough. Try to develop better sleep habits."

She thanked him and walked back to the dorm. Why didn't he do a physical exam? What if she had a brain tumor or a neuromuscular disorder starting up, and this was a sign of another bad thing for Flora's list? Was he right—she just needed more sleep? She didn't tell the doctor she was waking herself up with alarm clocks three times a night to write down dreams.

The disturbing phone calls with Mother came in weekly. Annie took the calls on the phone at the end of the hall because no phones were allowed in dorm rooms. One of her classmates would yell out: "Annie, you have a call!"

"So, how are you?" Her mother started with innocuous questions. Annie reminded herself to answer questions with well-tested answers and keep it simple.

"Ok," worked for some of the questions.

"Are you going to class and studying?"

"Yes."

"Are you smiling enough? You're such a pretty girl."

Silence.

"You're not wearing black all the time, are you?"

"Yes, I wear black a lot. There's not a lot of emphasis on fashion here."

"Are you eating? I'm worried you're too thin."

"I'm eating, but I'd like to be thinner."

"How's your money situation?"

"Ok."

"Are you having sex for money?" Invariably there was a trick question about moral values and sexuality.

Silence for anything in this category.

"So, how many boyfriends have you actually had?"

Silence for this one too. Boyfriends means sex partners.

In between questions, Annie was expected to listen to the latest about Ben. He wasn't giving Mother enough money to help with the household. His daughter from his first marriage was trying to take everything he owned. Mother has to work hard in the dress shop Ben bought when he closed his factory. He won't pay Mother's Social Security though she works full-time managing the shop. She can't do anything to break out of the marriage. She won't do anything to break out.

There is usually the "I'm worried about your brother" part of the call. Annie tells her not to worry. Daniel has common sense. Mother is not sure—what if he turns out like Andrew—they have to be careful.

Then discussion about how costly the long-distance calls are.

The wind-down: "Don't forget to smile. You're such a pretty girl."

"Ok."

"I miss you so much. I love you."

"Ok."

"And don't wallow in the past."

Silence for this one.

"Take care of yourself. I need you in my life."

Hang up.

By the summer Annie was turning twenty-one, she'd completed all the steps in her therapy except the deflowering. She didn't count as deflowering the night with the pilot-in-training she met last summer when she was a camp counselor in the Ozarks. They kept their clothes on all night through their dry humping.

Annie found her sex therapy target in an Irish bar downtown. Duncan spent a good part of the evening leaning over bar tables introducing himself to women, his breath smelling of Guinness. He was English which was funny because his last name was English too, and it was "hello luv, hello, luv" to all the ladies. He was blond, handsome, twenty-six, confident, worldly, and he smoked a pipe. Annie thought he might be the man for the job.

She accepted his offer to play a game of darts. Before the game ended, he asked for her telephone number. He called two nights later. She was living with three college classmates in a two-bedroom apartment in St. Louis for the summer. She worked as an EKG technician at the university teaching hospital clinic for low-income people. She was filling in for a technician taking the summer off to have surgery. Annie got the job because she learned how to do EKGs in Dr. Rickson's physiology class.

Duncan was in the Army, stationed at Fort Leonard Wood. He was divorced and interested in her. Annie selected him as a sex partner because he was experienced and would be persistent. She didn't want a man who would listen to protestations and back away.

He knew someone throwing a party the next weekend and invited her to go with him. By the time they arrived, it was a mash of strangers making out in different rooms of the house. Annie thought it was too public to move her plan forward, so she put Duncan off. She was wearing a new green and grey striped dress with a long zipper down the back. She liked the dress better than the evening. Duncan kept pulling the zipper up and down, testing boundaries. He had her dress down around her waist on a stranger's bed in one of the rooms he found for them, despite her decision that nothing would proceed that evening. She managed to pull her dress up, pretending she had morals, telling him she did not feel comfortable in a stranger's house. She told him she wasn't on the pill either and was worried about getting pregnant.

"Don't worry, luv. You're safe with me. I had mumps when I was young and can't have children."

Annie knew mumps was a viral infection that could affect the testicles but had he been tested? "How do you know?" she asked him.

"I was married for three years, luv, and we never got pregnant. I went to a doctor—he said I was infertile because I had mumps at fifteen."

"In England?"

"Yes, luv."

Annie wasn't sure she should believe him.

Her friends talked about birth control a lot—how unfair it was that men could do whatever they wanted and women could not. The college health center would not give out birth control when girls asked for it. The health center told them to go to a gynecologist off campus. Her Catholic friends couldn't decide if contraceptives were sinful like their priests were saying. Two years ago, the Supreme Court ruled that state laws prohibiting the sale of contraceptives were unconstitutional, but their professors didn't say anything in their classes about this, even the science professors, and her friends didn't know if things really were changing.

But Annie thought they were—she'd been seeing the words "sexual revolution" in her reading. And Masters and Johnson were talking about how women liked sex as much as men, though this seemed like news to many people.

Lucy's boyfriend said a birth control pill for women was coming out—he was hopeful he wouldn't have to use a condom. Lucy asked Annie about it, but Annie hadn't heard about it. Annie had never had a gynecological exam and was hoping she would never have to.

They worried about getting pregnant. In high school, everyone knew which girls had abortions. Some girls ended up in the hospital when they got infections from back-room procedures. So many states outlawed abortion—there was hope for a national law that would let women decide what was best for their bodies.

All of this felt overwhelming. Annie wanted desperately to be normal and stick to her therapy plan. She would have to trust Duncan, that he was telling her the truth. She decided the deflowering would occur on their second date when things could be more private. It wouldn't be romantic—it would be business, like going to the dentist or the gynecologist.

That early evening, heading up the stairs to the third-floor apartment Duncan borrowed from someone he knew for their second date, there must have been small talk, but Annie would never remember any. Duncan was on top of her quickly on this stranger's bed. He worked vigilantly, as she knew he would, to take off her clothes. She congratulated herself for her careful planning. She noticed how winded he was, trying to get inside of her now that she was naked. She was surprised that sex was so much work. She willed herself into a silent fog while Duncan proceeded. Never had a man worked so hard to get laid, she figured. Her muscles were iron clamps, resisting his efforts for what seemed like hours. She was sandpaper, raw and dry. He spit on his fingers several times for lubrication. She hoped it would be over soon. She could not imagine what he must be thinking. She was looking at deep cracks in the dull plaster ceiling. Lucy called watching cracks in the ceiling during sex "ceiling fucks." It was a shabby apartment. Annie wondered who lived there. There were no picture frames in the room. It was the end of the day, and she watched the sky through the window by the bed turn a soft navy blue.

Duncan was inside of her now, huffing and puffing like a tugboat pushing a dead freighter to port. She was thinking of laughing at the seriousness of his efforts when she became aware of someone else on top of her. An old man was huffing and puffing in that same way, a thin white cotton sheet moving between them. He was balancing on his strong left arm while his right hand tried to press his cock into the apex of her short legs. She played dead, wondering if Grandpa noticed she was dead while he was humping. He didn't notice. He was talking in his raspy voice, in his German accent, about the summer weather like they were neighbors kibitzing over a backyard fence. He did the talking. She saw him heading for her bedroom through the one-inch crack in the seam of her open door just moments before. No one else was home. He was visiting from Buffalo and slept last night in Daniel's room. Annie was just waking up. She weighed her choices in an instant. Run past him to the bathroom and lock the door or pretend to be asleep. She closed her eyes to feign sleep. When he climbed on top, she pretended she was dead and tried not to breathe. Maybe he wouldn't touch her if she was dead.

"What's wrong, luv? What's wrong?" Duncan was asking. Her mouth was open, eyes fixed on the ceiling, making no effort to move. She tried to form words but nothing came out. He thought she was lost in the ecstasy of the moment. He liked to have a virgin, he told her later.

She took a quick assessment: she was in pain, raw, and dry. But strangely exhilarated—her therapy worked!

Now other scenes were flooding in. She was three years old, needing help getting dressed for bed. Her grandparents were babysitting the mousies, but she was alone in Grandpa's room. She was naked, trying to pull her pajamas on. He was rubbing her toddler body up and down. She was struggling to pull away, to cover herself.

She never liked his scratchy long underwear and the loud snoring that filled the quiet of the house from his bedroom with the dark furniture twin beds—Gram always slept in the bedroom down the hall. Annie didn't like how he called the mousies pigs when they ordered double-dip ice cream cones at the shop down the road. He thought one scoop was enough. And he thought they should get vanilla but no one wanted vanilla. Gram didn't seem scared of him but she didn't talk back. She sat silent, sipping her coffee in the kitchen, dipping breads and buns in her chipped white china cup. Most of the time her false teeth were soaking in a glass by the sink as if they were waiting for another mouth to service if she wouldn't be needing them. She didn't like to wear her teeth because they didn't fit. It wasn't that she couldn't talk without her teeth. She could. Annie had conversations with her without her teeth in. But when Grandpa started yelling, Gram stopped talking. Whoever was in the house ignored him. Then he would quiet down and watch television or read or ask if someone wanted to play checkers. That's when he looked at Annie and Daniel when they were visiting.

The black-and-white checkerboard was waiting on a small rectangular table in the center of the garden room, off the living room. There were big windows on two sides of the room and the dark wood upright piano against one wall. Grandpa sat on the large, cushioned chair on one side of the checkerboard. He held Annie on his lap during games with Daniel just feet away, sitting in the smaller wooden chair on the other side of the board. Grandpa made moves with his black checkers while he jerked off against her little bottom held tight against him like a pillow as she huffed and puffed to pull free from the open flap of his long underwear. All the while he was saying to her brother, "I'm going to beat the pants off you."

Daniel would be leaning over the board to decide where to move his red checkers. He never noticed Annie struggling to pull free. Grandpa was so strong she could not get away. She could not use her voice to tell him to stop, to let her go. Why didn't she cry out and tell Daniel? Would Daniel even know what Grandpa was doing if she asked for help?

Annie learned to run when she saw him. She pretended to fly like an airplane from room to room in the house in Buffalo, her arms outstretched, balancing her lithe body from side to side, adding sound effects so they would think she was trying to fly. She especially ran away from the garden room. Her family laughed, exchanging glances. Surely she was old enough to know she couldn't fly.

That morning in Annie's house when she was twelve, the last time Grandpa touched her, she figured she could not outrun him. So she played dead. If only she had run, she would not be spread-eagled in front of Duncan like a desert parched for rain, like Dali's melted clock.

The first naked night with Duncan marked a new course of therapy. How to feel something other than deadness or pain. Duncan was the penis she used to prod her memory, to see if there was anything alive inside. He conveniently kept after her for months before the Army shipped him to Vietnam. He'd been drafted just two weeks before he turned twenty-six, when he would have been too old to draft. With his master's degree in education, he was assigned to intelligence work which meant a safe desk job. But it would be dangerous wherever he was going and Annie worried for him. The year he went through basic training, the casualties for Americans were nearly twelve thousand. The predictions were seventeen thousand for this year.

Amid the chaos around them, Annie felt she had gained some control over her life. At twenty-one, she finally had some answers.

◆

Now that Annie's memory was coming back, she marveled at the phenomenon of repressed memory. Should she tell anyone? Was nine years too long to tell someone, anyone, that Grandpa turned her into a statue? Should an aging grandfather claim the title of respected elder without so much as a mention? No one would believe the silly girl who tried to fly through the house. And she would be mortified to tell anyone the details if they asked. What if they brushed her off without asking? That might be worse.

Annie knew some scientists did not believe there was such a thing as repressed memory. Others believed memories could be blocked when they were associated with a high level of stress or trauma, and these memories could emerge later. Doctors identified a list of behaviors people had who had repressed memory from trauma. Annie had most of these—feeling detached; difficulty maintaining eye contact; blank staring she couldn't control; hoping other people didn't notice when she felt herself separate from reality for troubling, painful moments; suicide seeming like a logical solution; ambivalence toward family and friends, withdrawing into her own world.

She thought about her memories. What happened to close her mind down, keep her from facing what was so horrifying it caused her to repress the memories? She felt powerless around physically stronger people, and that meant most men. And this was incest—a family member she trusted invaded her body and mind. How could she forget everything for nine years? Somehow, the forgetting made it worse. Was her mind saying it didn't matter what he did to her? But it did matter. It mattered so much. And whether Annie should blame Mother and Gram was a question. Did Grandpa come looking for Annie because she was named for Andrew, because Gram moved out of his bedroom, because Annie was a girl and had no power, and he had all the power?

There was the driving lesson when she was eighteen. Grandpa agreed to let her practice driving in his car. He had wood blocks attached to the gas and brake pedals to make them closer to his feet because he was so short—so driving felt like using a pair of stilts. His car was big and heavy. They were on a busy street in Buffalo. Annie kept scraping the car against the curb while she drove, unable to gauge where the car was in the lane. She ran into the curb several times, rebounding from the scraping each time. Her mouth was half open and horrified. She didn't know if she was breathing, fixed on trying to stop ramming the curb. He did not give her directions, did not say anything. The car went faster than she expected, and she did not understand how to slow it down while traffic moved around her. Her mind was racing in slow motion. Should she brake? And if she braked, how much? Should she brake when she's scraping the curb? It was frightening that the car was mostly out of control, and Grandpa was not stepping up to help.

Eighteen-year-old Annie in that practice drive had no memory of what he had done when she was younger. Why didn't one single synapse of hers link up when he was sitting so close on the passenger side of the seat, while she tried to manage the too-fast car, her feet jacked up on his stilts? And if that one synapse had linked up and she saw him on top of her trying to drive his cock into her dead curb, what would she have done? Confront him in the car? Demand to know why he touched her like that? And did he remember, or did he have repressed memory too? Does a toddler's memory, a few checkerboard memories, and a dry hump between the sheets at twelve make him a pedophile? For decades he had dutifully taken care of his family. The family said he was a wise man, but she knew he was a sly man. She figured he knew what he was doing. How do you assess a man if he's done bad things but good things too? Does bad trump good on the scales of justice?

Annie chided herself for overanalyzing and rationalizing. She was turning into Ann-a-lyze, her legal name. Was she supposed to forgive him? He probably didn't know she knew, or more likely, assumed she was never going to talk about what happened because other people didn't talk in the family. Gram didn't talk about things she didn't like. Mother didn't talk. Annie knew Grandpa would not ask her to forgive him, ever.

While she struggled over whether to tell anyone, Duncan kept her busy. His incessant grinding at her crotch and the pain of dryness inside did exorcise a bit of the old man's visage from her legs. There was even a surprise orgasm in a green field the afternoon she laid on her back on a scratchy woolen blanket watching dense clouds roll by—clouds with cauliflower towers, flat tops, and dark bottoms. These were her favorite. They noticed the clouds earlier and agreed thunderstorms would likely move in later. Duncan pulled the old blanket out of his car and spread it out in the field. He pulled her jeans down around her ankles and pushed himself inside her, and she came while she was enjoying the clouds, disassociating from her body. Watching clouds was so much better than watching cracks in the plaster ceiling. The orgasm was simple and she felt free. It never happened again with Duncan but she knew it could.

Years later, during one of Mother's insulting calls about morality, Annie blurted out in anger, "What did you expect when I was molested by your father?"

Mother paused for a moment to process this information, then came back with the strangest response: "I thought it might have been the other side of the family."

Annie was dumbfounded. Did Mother have an inkling Annie was in danger by *any* family member?

"It was *your* father," Annie said matter-of-factly.

"Well, was there penetration?"

There was a long silence while Annie tried to process her mother's question. Annie finally answered, "No." Was Mother implying if there was no penetration, it was not so bad? Is dry humping on a petrified corpse's genitalia a lesser crime than penetration followed by humping? There was no apology from Mother. No recognition of how hard it was to live with memories that assault you. Annie was never going to trust her mother— and her mother did not ask more questions—she was moving to a maxim.

"Try not to wallow in the past, dear. Learn to let things go."

Annie sighed slowly into the phone receiver. She had already been wallowing in her subconscious for nine years. Now that the memories had broken out, she was definitely going to wallow, consciously.

Annie congratulated herself for completing her therapy. Duncan had come through for her in his testosterone-aggressive way. They were spending Labor Day weekend together. They checked into a hotel as Mr. and Mrs.

English, then drove to a nearby Irish pub. Hours later, he was dancing a jig while he played darts drunk when he stumbled into a chair.

"Dammit, Annie, I think I broke my right foot." He held onto the chair, grimacing. "We better get out of here."

She stepped forward to help him.

"Luv, you'll have to drive—I can't use my foot." He leaned on her as they hobbled to his Volkswagen Bug parked across the street.

"I don't know how to drive stick-shift."

"You'll have to learn." He winced at each step, trying to walk without using his right foot, his left arm wrapped around her shoulders.

She helped him into the passenger seat, then came around to slide into the driver's seat. She was putting the key in the ignition when he yelped, "Wait, you have to put your feet on the clutch and the brake.

"What?"

"Put your left foot on the clutch and push it all the way down!"

"I don't know what the clutch is!"

"See those three pedals down there—accelerator, brake, and clutch! Get your right foot on the brake and the left foot on the clutch and turn the ignition key on." She thought momentarily about the foot organ she liked to play at school and got the car motor turned on.

"Now keep pressing the clutch with your left foot while you move the gear shifter into first gear."

"I don't know what a gear shifter is!"

"Christ, Annie." Grimacing in pain, he put her right hand on the round ball standing up between their seats. "This is the gear stick. You're going to shift through the different speeds when I tell you. We're going to go from neutral to first now. He moved his hand on top of hers to show her how to shift."

"Shit!" She had no idea what she was doing.

"You're doing fine. Now slowly remove your foot from the brake pedal while you slowly pull off the clutch."

"What's the clutch?"

"Where your left foot is! Dammit, Annie!"

She tried to follow his instructions, but the car wasn't going anywhere.

"You have to give the car some gas. Put your right foot on the gas pedal—now!"

"I can't do this!"

"Yes, you can. Press the gas pedal."

The car was moving slowly forward, and Annie was thankful there was no traffic.

"Ok, now speed up so we can move out of first gear into second."

"Shit."

"Move your right foot off the gas pedal while you activate the clutch at the same time with your left foot."

"What?

"Just do it, Annie!"

The car was lurching in rabbit jumps. Duncan yelped in pain with each lurch. "Shift smoothly, luv, shift smoothly!"

Annie didn't understand what shift smoothly meant. She tried to get the coordination between her feet right. What were her left and right feet supposed to do—move in opposite directions at the same time? What were gears? Duncan's voice was getting louder as he tried to explain.

"It will get better when we get into third gear, then fourth. It's hardest between first and second."

She'd been driving in second gear for a while and wondered if they could just stay in that all the way to the hotel.

"We have to keep building speed. It's time to shift to third. You do your feet, and I'll do the shifting."

Somehow Annie managed to drive them to the hotel in third gear. Duncan warned her she was going to have to start slowing down, which required she start shifting from third, down to second, down to first.

"Get your feet in the right position, luv. Left foot on the clutch, right foot on the brake."

She managed to shift down, but it wasn't pretty, and Duncan cried out with every lurch. Finally, they were at the hotel parking lot.

"Ok, feet in position, luv. Press the clutch down and keep braking," while he moved the clutch to neutral, then park. "Turn the ignition off."

"That didn't go very well, did it?" she managed to say.

"No, luv, it didn't. Let's lock the car and get to the room—I need to get ice on my foot."

In the room, he decided he would drink wine for the pain and hobbled to the dresser where he left the cooler he'd carried in before they went to

the bar and got out sangria, crackers, and cheese. He sent Annie to the ice
machine down the hall, and they wrapped the ice in a hotel bath towel on
which he rested his foot, now elevated in the bed.

Annie thought the worst was over. She took her clothes off and pulled
her blue nightgown over her head. She would be glad to lie down and get
some sleep. But Duncan was laying out the plan for the rest of the night.

"Annie, you're going to have to collect my pee and carry it to the toilet
because I can't get out of bed."

"What?"

"We can use this drinking cup." He was holding a sixteen-ounce red
plastic cup from the cooler. "Help me get my pants off." He already had
his shoes and socks off and was lying against pillows he had propped up.
"Be careful, don't hit my foot." His foot looked like a swollen mushroom
after days of rain. "Let's try this out." He directed her to stand next to the
bed while he maneuvered his penis over the rim of the cup to pee down
into it. She was surprised at how hot the pee was and how quickly the cup
filled up. He watched as she walked to the bathroom and emptied the cup.
She washed out the cup in the sink and brought it back to the table next
to the bed. He covered his body with the light blanket and leaned back on
the pillows to rest. "What a night, Annie. My foot hurts so bad. Lie next
to me. Do you want wine?"

"No, I'm going to shut my eyes. I'm tired."

Duncan kept drinking the sangria, and every hour nudged Annie
awake to come to his side of the bed with the cup. After a few trips, she
begged him, "Stop drinking so much, so you won't have to pee so much."

But he drank throughout the night, and there were hourly pee trips.

Annie noticed something different about Duncan while she was fer-
rying his pee. He wasn't sounding English. Sometime around four in the
morning, she asked what was happening to his accent. And in his drunk-
enness, he told her he wasn't English—he was from Illinois, but he wanted
to be English. That was why he pretended to be English.

"Well, wanting doesn't make it so," she sniped. She turned her head
away—the smell of hot pee was distasteful, but maybe it was his lying all
these months. And why hadn't she figured this out before? How could he
be serving in the Army, preparing to go to Vietnam if he was English? She

should have put two and two together. Was he lying about being infertile? Was she going to turn up pregnant next?

In the morning, Duncan said they would need to go to a hospital emergency room for an x-ray. He would have to call his sergeant at the base if he had broken his foot. Annie didn't think she could drive them to the hospital. Duncan said he wasn't going to let her drive—it would hurt him more to lurch the whole way. He thought he could drive after a night with his foot elevated.

The doctor x-rayed his foot—it was a nasty sprain. The doctor wrapped his foot in a bandage. They spent the rest of the weekend in the hotel room. Annie brought in food from the hotel restaurant, and Duncan apologized for getting drunk at the pub. It hadn't been a fun evening for Annie before his accident. She thought he was drinking too much and told him he was drinking too much whenever they saw each other. He said that's what they did on the base. That's how soldiers cope.

Over those two days, Duncan tried to explain how car gears worked. He said it would be good for Annie to know more about cars. She agreed but did not understand his explanations. She dreaded the idea of ever driving a stick shift with him again.

"Annie, you're never going to master smooth shifting because you're showing no interest in understanding how gear shifts work. Try, luv, try to pay attention."

"Don't try to be English, Duncan," she retorted. "And did you really have mumps in your testicles?"

"Yes. You can't get pregnant with me, Annie. Trust me."

<hr />

They planned their trip to Mexico over Thanksgiving break in a motel near the Army base. He set the agenda for the long weekend: sex in the morning and nighttime; walks or other outside activity; meals of port wine cheese, French bread, and white wine prepared in the motel kitchenette; and planning the Mexico road trip.

They would leave when Annie's college winter break started in mid-December and travel throughout the college's winter short-term, all January. This would give them six weeks to get as far south as they could, returning in time for spring term beginning in February. That's when Duncan's unit would ship out to Vietnam.

They figured they could make it to Oaxaca, two thousand miles south before they had to head back. They planned to crisscross Mexico on the coming and going. They would drive the VW Bug though Annie's feeble efforts to drive a stick shift convinced Duncan that he would not let her drive one single mile, which he never shared with her. Throughout the trip, she would pester him, "Why can't I drive? I can learn how to drive a stick shift—I promise."

She learned the truth an hour from St. Louis as their journey was ending in a major snow and ice storm when neither of them should have been driving. The storm hit the entire South and Midwest on their return. The interstates were closed with drifting snowbanks and trucks lining the roads, unable to pull their loads. Duncan thought it was an omen of bad times to come in Vietnam.

Annie tried to reassure him, "It's just a snowstorm." But her life wasn't heading to the front lines. His was, though he didn't know yet how close his high-security job typing classified documents would be to the front lines, or if incoming fire would be an issue at the base where he would live. Other officers told him he would have a Vietnamese maid to look after him; he would be drinking beer and French wines, and there were plenty of drugs.

He had already admonished Annie several times, "Whatever you do, for God's sake, promise me you won't send me a Dear John letter!" She promised she would not break up with him when they were at the airport, surrounded by brave sobbing families with their braver American sons. Parked behind the thick lines of goodbyes, giant cargo planes waited. Annie was shocked soldiers were cargo. Men, tanks, supplies—cargo. She felt lost among the families and lovers, letting go of her cargo, for the nation . . . fighting for what . . . helpless.

The dean of women called Annie's mother in late January. "Do you know where your daughter is?" The college wanted to put out a multi-state police bulletin because Annie was not back at school, and spring term was starting. The dean must have wanted that, not the college. Did the Victorian buildings and the college entry archway get together and decide to issue a police bulletin for Annie?

Mother knew Annie drove to Mexico with Duncan for the midterm break and was embarrassed her daughter was running off with "some man." Annie told her he had a name, but to her mother, he was always going to be "some man." But a police bulletin too? She resisted the dean. "I trust my daughter." But she didn't trust Annie or Duncan. She called Duncan's mother in Illinois and told her how irresponsible her son was. Annie learned this later from Duncan's mother.

The dean called Mother again a day and a half later, informing her that the college would be expelling Annie. Annie Zechman was AWOL.

When the interstates reopened, Annie returned to campus tired and red-eyed from the goodbyes at the cargo planes. She was dragging her two pieces of scruffy luggage up the stairs when two girls met her in the hallway.

"You're really in trouble, Annie!"

"I'm only three days late."

"You have to see the dean."

"Do you want me to go with you?" one of them offered.

"Thanks, but I'm fine." Annie put her suitcases in her dorm room, then headed down the steps of the old brick dormitory, long traveled by strong Midwestern women. That tradition gave her strength. She practiced what she would say. 'Classes for next term haven't started, the interstates were closed with the storms, she's twenty-one, she has a notebook filled with new poems she wrote over the midterm for her honors project, she's lost twenty-five pounds, Duncan is on his way to Vietnam, and she's back at school.'

At the administration building, she was ushered into the dean's inner sanctum by a somber-looking receptionist. Annie scanned the room: blue chairs, mahogany desk, walls of oak bookshelves, thick carpet, and three telephones on the desk. How many people is the dean calling at one time? Is this her war room?

The dean sits in her large wooden chair, squinting at Annie through thick gold-rimmed reading glasses. Her grey hair is cropped straight and short. Her lips are pursed and slick with red lipstick. Pudgy cheeks pinkly rouged. She gestures with a long index finger for Annie to sit on the chair in front of the desk.

"We were very worried about you, young lady, very worried. And your mother was frantic, frantic! Do you know you are three days late for this term? And what you put people through?"

"The interstates were closed—it was impossible to get back until this afternoon," Annie answered quietly. "I haven't missed any classes. I've been working on my senior honors project throughout the January term." She wonders if the dean can tell she's been crying at the airport. Maybe she should tell her about the cargo planes heading for Vietnam.

"We are considering expelling you, young lady." Sternness emanates from the very walls of the inner sanctum. Annie is convinced the real reason the dean is upset is that she found out Annie has been traveling through Mexico with Duncan. But Annie is twenty-one. There's nothing the college can do about six weeks of extracurricular sex. But the dean can provide moral disapproval, which she does, pursing her red lips tightly like two highway lanes caving into her mouth.

Annie is undismayed. "I understand if you have to expel me. However, I'm finished with my two majors, so I expect to receive my degree. The reason I'm staying this last term is to finish my honors project and take extra classes." She's ready to leave if they push her out.

"Well, well, well. Maybe you can stay, maybe you can stay." The dean and the college buildings standing in a red-brick phalanx begin to withdraw from the battle.

Annie says thank you, standing up to retreat from the inner sanctum, watching the red lips moving on the dean's face but not listening to her words anymore. Meyer, the sculptor professor, had done an exhibit a few months ago of eight large silver-colored metal lips (four on the top row, four on the bottom) with wagging long red tongues. The tongues were that same color red. Maybe Meyer borrowed the dean's lipstick tube to match his color palette. Maybe the exhibit was a commentary on the dean's lips. Probably not. Knowing Meyer, that was his exhibit of lips—labial. Or his dislike of idle chatter. Or his increasing dislike of teaching.

Annie walked back to her dorm room in the late January cold to prepare for her final college term. Duncan was hundreds of miles away by

70 • YANA KAZAN

now—there would be eighty-eight hundred miles between them. And no more sex therapy.

***

Annie was glad to get out of Mexico. Dysentery days, hotel rooms where bathrooms were part of bedrooms. They took showers in the rooms they slept in—there were no separate shower rooms, no shower curtains, no partitions. Maybe it was because they had so little money or because Duncan planned for there to be no partitions. Their secrets disappeared down drain holes in hotel floors, leaving distasteful smells in the air.

Each afternoon when they pulled into a new town, Duncan stopped at two or three hotels looking for the best deal. He waited in the car and sent Annie to go into the hotel and ask in the Spanish he taught her, "*¿Cuánto es una habitación para una cama doble?*"

When the desk clerk rattled off a long answer thinking she could speak Spanish, she had little idea what he was saying. She returned to the car to report what she thought the price was but couldn't be sure. Duncan would sputter, take her hand like a child, and accompany her back to her assignment to ask again about costs and view the rooms himself. Then he would make their selection—and none of the rooms had any partitions. Annie found the process annoying. Why didn't he just do it himself if that was what he wanted? She figured he wanted to treat her like a child and show her how dominant he was.

They spent most nights and afternoons when they were free from driving, strolling colorful marketplaces where Annie liked the jewelry and pottery, and Duncan liked the woven blankets and bullfighting memorabilia; searching out archeological sites; planning their afternoon main meal—he told her to call them *comida*; and drinking in bars after that. Duncan drank cerveza and tequila every night. He wanted Annie to eat the worm at the bottom of his bottles. She always refused. Whenever she could, she had ice cream. Which only added to her dysentery.

In many bars, the bathrooms were a drain on the bar floor with wood planks that surrounded the middle portion of a man's torso—she could see men's heads and legs and their pee running down to the drain. Annie didn't know where to look. When it was her turn to pee, Duncan told her women weren't allowed to go in the bar—a fight would break out if she broke the rules. She had to wait until they found a proper woman's bathroom. Annie wished she had the courage to get inside those wooden planks and drain her own fluids down that center stage. But she painfully held it in.

He planned the trip so they would arrive in each town in time to purchase tickets to the bullfights on the weekend. He read every poster detailing who was fighting. He knew about the matadors and *toros*. He chatted throughout each fight, reviewing the techniques and customs for her benefit. He was the professor of bullfighting. He hoped for good fights, for the bulls' ears to be awarded to dignitaries, for brave bulls, and courageous matadors.

Annie wanted the bulls to win. Each week she secretly hoped the bulls would gore the matadors through their fancy gold-braided jacket, black pants, and white stockings. Gore the picadors sitting on flowered horses as they lanced the bulls to test the animals' strength. Gore the banderilleros thrusting sticks with barbed points into the top of the bulls' shoulder—to weaken the animals so the matador could more easily place his sword into that one spot behind the head, like pithing frogs in the science lab. What kind of fight is it, when the animal has been weakened, when the animal's head is already drooping because he's been lanced repeatedly to weaken his shoulders?

Duncan patiently explained the horse riders must inflict pain so the bull will pay attention because some bulls don't want to fight. But they must. They must put up a good fight. That was the tradition.

There was a lesson in this. She may have to be hurt badly and weakened to fight for her own life. Is that what Flora tried to warn her about? She would think about this another day, when she was not sitting on an uncomfortable wooden plank at a bullfight in an unfamiliar town where she had to keep her wits about her because she was always one of the few women in the crowd. And worse, they could see she was not Mexican though she tried to dress conservatively, her dark hair tied behind her head and loose dress covering her knees. That was Duncan's request. But Duncan was blonde and blue-eyed—he stood out—and she was with him. Men catcalled at her, watching to see if she would flinch during the fights. When she sat stoically as she did each week, they often regaled her with raised cervezas. One man gave her a straw hat for protection from the hot sun. They wanted to know where she was from. Duncan spoke for them in Spanish while Annie played the role of dutiful wife. At one fight, a fat red-faced American man with a thin blonde wife accompanied by two plump children took seats in the front row. Halfway through the first fight, when the horsemen were lancing the bull and red blood was visibly flowing in streams over the bull's dark flanks, the couple stood up, pulling at their children. "Come along! Come along!"

The crowd jeered as they made a quick retreat. Annie sat stoically. She was rewarded with cheers from the row of men behind her, lifting their cervezas to her. Duncan drank with them from the goatskin bota he'd gotten years ago in Spain. He told Annie how proud he was to be with her, what a strong woman she was. Dr. Rickson prepared her well, Annie thought ruefully. She was a scientist, witnessing the killing of animals, hoping to draw useful lessons out of dusty killing arenas. Duncan assured her the bulls' meat was used to feed children in the local orphanage, that it was an honor for bulls to die in this way. If bulls appreciated the honor of fighting, Annie thought, why did they have to be lanced into fighting?

Early in the trip, before the weekly bullfights began, they traveled down a single-lane road from Monterrey to San Luis Potosi. Speeding south down a desolate stretch of road, four thickly mustached men in sombreros appeared across the pavement in front of the car, their arms crossed, legs spread. Where did they come from? There were no trees or structures on the landscape as far as they could see—only a few rocks spread around the desert vista. Duncan shifted down to first gear and slowed, hoping the phalanx would move off the road. He braked a few feet in front of their human line.

"*Párese aquí!*" The men were yelling for them to stop, pointing their arms to an imaginary line. "*Cuota!* Tollway!"

"What tollway?" Annie sputtered. "There's nothing here!"

Duncan muttered for her to be quiet. He reached into the pocket of his slacks to pull out money. There were words Annie could not understand in the negotiation between Duncan and the man who came to Duncan's window. Money was exchanged, and the man at the window was pointing to the road ahead. Then all four men pulled their arms up in unison like a well-practiced dance troupe and moved backward to stand on both sides of the road, two on Duncan's side, two on Annie's. They were smiling and gesturing south. Duncan whispered as he shifted into first, then second gear, "Bandits."

"Bandits? This is 1967!"

"We're lucky they let us go so easily," he said, shifting from third into fourth as the car picked up speed. He was shaking from adrenaline. "We could have been killed, Annie. You could have been raped."

But they weren't, she reminded him. But she was scared to be alone on the streets in Mexico without him. She didn't know the language and couldn't take care of herself—she was resentful she had to depend on him, resentful she was a woman.

They spent Feliz Navidad in Mexico City, eating corn enchiladas and dancing. There were decorated candies at the festival, and the candy was sickeningly sweet, even for Annie. Earlier, they watched men and women, mostly women, crawl on their knees up the steep stone steps at the Basilica of Guadalupe, clutching rosaries and praying. Annie asked Duncan why it was the women, mostly the older women, who bloodied their bodies for the church? He shrugged. He saw religious tradition; Annie saw women's issues.

They talked about the future while they drove south to Oaxaca. She wondered if he was telling her the truth about everything. He lied about being English. He told her he didn't have enough live sperm to get her pregnant, but he was talking about having a child with her. He picked out the baby's name—whether boy or girl, it would be Morgan after the English automobile. Annie hated this name. He thought she would like the name better if he explained the history of the English automobile. That didn't make her like the name any more for a child she knew they would never have.

Duncan assigned Annie the role of navigator. He explained it was her job to read maps and signs and plan excursions in Mexico.

"Map reading is not my strength. I can help, but I don't think I should be the navigator."

"You'll get better at it if you pay more attention, Annie." Before he was drafted into the Army, he was a high school English teacher—he often treated her like one of his students. She usually came through fine, he thought, when he pushed her to achieve, despite her protestations. His pushiness was not a quality she appreciated in a lover or travel companion.

When they were leaving the southernmost part of Mexico to return north after weeks of travel, Duncan gave her a new assignment: "Pick a route to get us out of Oaxaca and get us to Veracruz and after that to Tampico on the eastern coastline." That would position them for re-entry to the U.S. at Matamoros.

Annie was using Mexican maps—they were not like the automobile club maps she used when they started the trip in the U.S. The Mexican maps did not provide details about the quality of the roads. Annie planned the course the night before, after they returned from the marketplace where they marveled over intricate figures carved from radishes. Not the kind of radishes in salads in the U.S., but heavy roots that grew two feet long. Artists carved village scenes, mythical animals, and the Virgin Mary into these radishes.

They headed out after a breakfast of eggs wrapped in fried tortillas with fresh-squeezed orange juice. On the way out of town, they stopped to walk around the Tule Tree they'd heard about in the marketplace. Twice they walked around the massive trunk in amazement. Annie was dawdling. Duncan said they had to get on the road—it would be a long day of driving.

The road out of Oaxaca soon turned into an unpaved logging road that wound through the mountains. There were steep drops to ravines on both sides. At one point, a few brown monkeys dangled over the car from thick trees, interspersed among giant green palm fronds and banana trees. They passed a few Indians in white cloaks, walking single file on the narrow dirt road. There was no car or truck traffic.

"Damn it, Annie, I can't believe you picked this road." Duncan was steering around deep holes and large fallen branches.

"I'm sorry. I couldn't tell from the maps. It looked like the road was paved." She wished she could read maps better but was secretly thrilled at the sights unfolding. They were surprised to see how wet it was in the mountains—and mud everywhere from recent rain. There had been no rain in Oaxaca. Annie wondered if they would be sucked into the dense jungle, lost after tumbling down a ravine.

There was no talking until they were leaving the mountain road, heading toward the sea. Annie hoped there would be beaches along the paved coastal road—it looked like there would be from the map. But the road was bordered by wide lanes of tall grass. Still, the ocean gave off a heady salt smell when they opened the car windows to take in the air—feeding on the smell like greedy birds.

They stopped the car outside Veracruz to stretch their legs, pushing through waist-high grass to get to the water's edge—calm, smooth water. They could see Veracruz to the north. A small number of ships with black hulls—part of the Mexican Navy—clumped like dark sheep grazing in the quiet sea field.

It was nearly dark by the time they were on the road to Tampico, where they would spend the night. They were hours behind because of the slow driving through the winding mountain road covered with so much debris. Annie called out the kilometers to Tampico from the occasional signs along the road. She saw dark trailings on the road.

"What's that?" she kept asking. There were so many bumps on what should be a smooth roadway. Were they running over branches from an earlier storm?

"I'm so tired of sitting, Annie. Let's stretch our legs." Duncan shifted down and parked by the side of the road. There had been no traffic for hours.

Annie started screaming as soon as her feet touched the road. "Get back! Get back in the car!"

Hundreds—maybe thousands—of dark snakes that had been catching the day's heat from the pavement were crisscrossing the road in front of the car's headlights.

Annie and Duncan slammed their car doors closed at the same time.

"O my God, what if we get stranded here? Do you think they're rattlesnakes? If I have to pee, I'll pee out the window," she announced, imagining how to position her legs so she wouldn't pee on the window.

"I don't know what kind of snake they are." He was sitting next to her, without looking at her.

"You're lucky—men can just pee out an open door."

He gave her a withering look. "We can probably find a cup or some pottery in our bags if you have to go, Annie. You can do that in the back seat without getting out of the car."

She hadn't thought of that.

He started the car up, and they were back on the road—they could wait to pee. The snakes traveled with them. The car ran over hundreds of them from the feel of it. Annie shuddered from the thumping sounds.

"Don't you think it's strange that out of nowhere, coming south, there were bandits across the highway setting up a tollway? And now, when we're heading north, there's a phalanx of snakes?"

Duncan didn't answer.

That night in the Tampico hotel room, Duncan said unkindly, "Traveling with you is like traveling with a child."

Annie didn't say what she wanted to say, about a stick in somebody's ass. It had been a long time since they left campus—they were getting on each other's nerves. When would they have a hotel room where there was a separate bathroom, and they could restore some distance and mystery to their relationship? She checked herself before she said anything more. She realized he must be thinking about leaving next week for Vietnam.

They crossed the border between Matamoros and Brownsville. Duncan instructed Annie to go to the bank across the street and exchange their Mexican money for American money. "They're going to search the car closely. Stay away," he warned her.

"Ok." She carefully set aside some colored paper money for her collection before she asked for the exchange. She kept an eye on Duncan and the car from the bank window. Several border guards surrounded the car. They opened every door, the hood, the trunk. The little rounded car looked like a turtle being dissected in a science lab. Guards moved their hands along the interior surfaces, searching for drugs and other contraband. They felt up and down Duncan's body, his arms and legs spread widely. He was wearing a blue button-down shirt and tan corduroy slacks. She wondered if they would search her when she returned to the car. She was wearing a navy-blue dress that was too big for her now that she had lost weight from weeks of periodic dysentery.

When the guards closed the doors of the car, she walked slowly toward it. The guards were disinterested in her. Duncan later speculated she could have been carrying anything. He was worried about the pottery statuette they bought from a boy along the road outside Mexico City. The boy said it came from an archeological dig nearby. They paid thirty dollars American money for it. Duncan thought it was authentic, and Annie thought it was a reproduction. It looked exactly like the statuettes in the new National Museum of Anthropology they visited.

When they divided their finds at his parents' house later, they fought over who would take the figurine. Annie gave in. It was a fertility symbol. Anyone one who liked to fuck as much as Duncan deserved to keep the fertility symbol. He said he would keep it at his parents' house until he returned. And did it really matter anyway who kept it for the year? He reminded her they would be together after he returned from Vietnam. But Annie knew better.

Duncan gave her a gift at the airport before he boarded the cargo plane for Vietnam. "Open it so I can explain it to you." He was talking in his teacher voice. It was a tape recorder wrapped in birthday paper though it was not her birthday.

"I want you to tell me what you're doing every day on cassette tapes and send them to me, Annie. And I'll send you tapes back about what I'm doing. The year will go faster if we can hear each other's voices." He looked like he was about to cry.

"Ok," Annie nodded through her tears. She put the tape recorder in her purse.

Weeks later, she was already getting cassettes in the mail from him. She got the tape recorder out to listen to his messages. She didn't like the tinny sound of his voice. And when she tried to tape her own messages, she didn't like the sound of her voice; having to press 'start' and 'stop' and' play' buttons, and didn't know what to say. So she pretended she didn't know how to use the tape recorder.

He responded by sending her tapes in which he instructed her how to push the 'play' and 'record' buttons. "Just speak naturally into the microphone. It will sound fine, Annie. Then, simply remove the tape and mail it to me."

These instructions irritated Annie. She had no intention of sending back tapes. So, she fussed with the recorder, made pretend tapes that said, "Fuck this, shit that, fuck this, shit that." Then she wrote him a letter telling him she couldn't get the machine to work. Finally, he got the message and stopped sending her instructions.

He wanted to call her from China later in the year and told her to find a time she could be by the dormitory phone. She never found a time because she couldn't imagine what they would say for three minutes, costing twenty dollars. When she dragged her feet to find a time, he got mad and said he would call his parents—they wanted to talk to him. Clearly, Annie did not.

The dramas between them were increasing. He granted her permission to go to graduate school for one year. He would be out of the Army, and he wanted her to go with him to Germany where he was going to find a job as an English teacher in an American high school. How could she go to graduate school for one year? And she didn't want to move to Germany. What right did he have to direct her life like this? But she played along, not wanting to upset him—like she did when he proposed.

She was trying to fall asleep in their hotel room in Mexico City. She had dysentery and a sore throat so bad she could barely swallow. She explained her symptoms to the pharmacist down the street who spoke English, and he gave her medicines that afternoon. Now she needed sleep. The transom at the top of the door was open, letting fragrant flowered air in from the courtyard. Sapphire-blue tiles framed the doorway. Roosters were crowing in the distance though it wasn't near morning yet. She wished Duncan would go to sleep, but he was asking her to marry him.

She said she was too young. They didn't know each other well enough. He was leaving for Vietnam. She wanted to finish college. Everything but the truth.

The proposal extended over the next few days until it became another fight between them. Finally, she said "maybe" to end the fight and agreed to wear an engagement ring. They looked through a bag of loose brown topaz stones with a street vendor, and she picked out a round-cut stone. A shop nearby placed the stone into a gold setting and sized the ring for the fourth finger on her left hand. Almost immediately, she felt the tiny bump on one of the gold prongs. It poked into the underbelly of her finger, creating a hurtful red mark.

Annie was sure this was an omen their relationship was not a good fit. Duncan thought she would get used to wearing the ring. Did he think she would grow a callus on her finger, like he said her vagina would stop getting sore if they had more sex? Maybe that was his view of marriage: she would get used to sore spots. She removed the ring one afternoon when he wasn't watching. He didn't ask any more about the ring, but she was prepared to show him the red crevice on her finger that was hurting if he did.

After Annie's college decided not to expel her, Mother refocused their weekly calls on a new topic. "What are you going to do after graduation—it's just four months away?"

That's when the chess pieces lined up. Mother's pawn moved with, "Your best course is to get married and find a job."

Annie's rook moved with, "I'm going to go to graduate school."

Mother's knight countered: "I don't understand why you want to go on with school—I expected you to get your college degree and an MRS."

Annie's bishop explained, "I need an advanced degree to teach at a university. I'm not interested in getting married right now."

Mother's queen countered with: "Your sister is doing fine working."

Annie's queen: "I'm not Hannah."

Mother's king: "I can't help you financially. Daniel is the boy in the family—he has to be the priority."

Annie's king issued the pronouncement: "I'll be fine. I don't need your money."

There was never a checkmate because Annie was tuning out. Her mother didn't know who Annie was and she did not understand the times.

But Dr. Hill did. He watched the women in his classes—Shakespeare, Renaissance Poets, Chaucer, Creative Writing—growing up in a world unaccustomed to women pushing beyond the boundaries of their parents' rules.

Annie asked Professor Hill for advice a few weeks after Duncan left for Vietnam—before the chess games started with her mother. "I'm considering graduate school programs in English literature. Do you have suggestions?"

"I hear there's a woman department head in English at the University of Wisconsin. And they have a creative writing emphasis. Look into it." He encouraged her to consider a writing career.

"My goal is to complete a PhD so I can teach at a university and be a writer too."

"There are so many people of talent that will never make it as a writer because they don't work hard. I've never had a student like you—as productive. You have what it takes, Annie. But I'm surprised you're not going on in science."

"I don't want a career killing animals in a lab—and my math skills are too weak to go on." Her lab partner, Ruthie, already had a job offer at a research lab. The experiments were using dogs—Annie was horrified at the very idea.

There was a catalog for the University of Wisconsin's English Department in the library. No mention of women professors or a creative writing focus. Maybe they were there, she reasoned, just not featured. Duncan was reminding her in his letters that he would be back in January and they would start their life together wherever she was, so she should try to find a campus in the Midwest.

She studied the atlas in the library to see where the Midwest universities with well-established graduate programs were. She was drawn to the blue ink on the maps signaling rivers and lakes. What if she picked her next location by bodies of water? Her decision to select a college based on distance from home worked out. Maybe water should trump transportation for graduate school. It would be too expensive to move to one of the coasts to be near an ocean. She was drawn to Wisconsin and the melodic Native American names of Madison's five lakes: Mendota, Monona, Waubesa, Kegonsa, Wingra. She read about the birds that visited the lakes during migrations like tundra swans and imagined long-bodied muskies diving over the dam from the feeder creek to Lake Wingra during their migration.

She wanted to live and study near lakes, birds, and fish—no more killing frogs, turtles, and chicks in science labs. And she'd be walking and biking because she could not afford a car. Duncan's car was waiting for him in his parents' garage, but he would never let her drive it.

She submitted her application mid-spring, receiving an acceptance letter a week later. Among her friends, Annie was the only one going to graduate school—the others were getting married and finding a job. Annie would be the migratory black swan coming to Madison's lakes.

Annie's engagement ring with the offending prong rested in her jewelry box. She knew before Duncan left for Vietnam that she could not marry him. He lied about being English, and she couldn't trust him. And there was the John Donne event.

Duncan chided and cajoled her into going head-to-head in explicating a poem. Perhaps explicating poems was no different to him than shooting darts or firing a gun at tin cans on a tree trunk where he took her for practice. Annie didn't think explicating a poem should be a sporting event. But that afternoon in the cottage motel near the Army base, he directed her to open her textbook and select a seventeenth-century poet. She was tired of fighting, so she flipped through the pages and dubiously picked out a John Donne poem. It was not one of her favorites.

"How about this one?" It wasn't a long poem, so she figured they could get this over quickly.

"Fine," he said, reading through it a couple of times. She looked out the cottage window, wondering why they had to do this, telling herself to humor him.

"I'll go first." He looked ready and enthusiastic. They sat at the small table in the cottage kitchenette. He described what the poem was about, referencing footnotes at the bottom of the page, and citing relevant facts from history. When he finished, he inquired whether he omitted anything important.

"Well, there are some symbols in the poem, but probably they are not that important." Her professors taught them to look carefully at symbols and themes.

"Like what symbols?" he demanded to know. She could tell he was already irritated with her. There must be something else he was upset about.

"I think there are three symbols," she said, pointing them out. The more she pointed out, the more upset he became. Finally, he threw down the seventeenth-century poetry book and walked to the sink and began to do the dishes from their breakfast pancakes.

"You think you're smarter than I am," he blurted out, his hands covered in soapy water.

"No, I don't."

"Yes, you do! It's your superior attitude!"

She didn't know what to say. Something was going on that was different from explicating a poem. He finished the dishes, stacking them in a plastic drainer rack, and walked quickly across the small room and pulled her to the bed. He meant to have sex with her.

"No, leave me alone." She tried to push him off.

He held her down with one arm and pulled her jeans down with the other hand. She tried to resist but he was stronger than she was. There was no kissing or foreplay. He unzipped his pants and pushed his cock into her with anger. He never wore underwear when they were together. He said he could have sex more easily without underwear in the way. She tried not to move while he was grinding furiously on top of her. She did not wrap her arms around his back like she usually did. She turned her head to focus on the cheap lampshade next to the bed, then on the cottage's ceiling light, arms pressed to her sides, waiting for it to be over, hoping she felt like sandpaper because she was dry, so dry. He was raping her because of a poem? She was sure he wanted to dominate her, and she should not forget that he could.

He was done quickly. He pulled his spent cock out of her and hurried to the bathroom, slamming the door. He stayed a long time. She pulled her jeans up and rolled on her side to face the wall. When he came back to the room, she lay in bed facing the wall, silent. He did not apologize. Maybe he didn't know he'd done something wrong. He read in a chair—she could hear the pages turning. She pretended to take a nap. The afternoon was waning when he asked if she was asleep.

"No."

"I'm taking out a bottle of wine from the cooler if you want some. We're having pork tenderloin for dinner." He'd brought the meat wrapped in brown paper from the market in the cooler. "Have you cooked pork tenderloin before?"

"No, my family didn't eat pork even though we're reform Jews."

"But you eat pork, don't you?"

"Yes." She was still facing the wall.

"This is one of my specialties. Come watch what I do so you'll know how to cook it," he said as if nothing had happened between them.

She got up from the bed, making up her mind to put the rape aside for now.

He unwrapped the pork from its thick paper and placed it on a cutting board. Then he pounded the cylindrical filet flat with his right fist like it was a piece of clay. She watched him press the fleshy meat flat into submission, wondering if horny men fuck pork tenderloin when they don't have a woman around. She didn't share her musings. He was coating the flattened meat in salt and pepper from containers on the shelf in the kitchenette. Annie didn't like pepper, but she didn't tell him.

"I'm going to sauté the meat in a fry pan and pour wine on top of the meat," he demonstrated like a culinary teacher. He stopped to drink wine from the bottle, offering the bottle to Annie. She declined. He asked her to set out plates from the cabinet above the stove and cut up the cheese and fruit in the cooler. "There's a French bread in the cooler you can slice too."

Over dinner, he talked about plans for tomorrow. He was going to show her how to shoot a bow and arrow.

"Where are we going to get the equipment?"

"It's in the trunk of the car—I rented it at the base."

He was a planner and well organized. She'd give him that. If he'd left it to her to plan activities, they wouldn't have any. Annie decided while chewing her pork tenderloin during dinner that she was never going to tell Duncan that the rape after making her explicate that poem was a deal-breaker, and she was never going to forgive him. She reasoned it would still be ok to go to Mexico with him—he would be leaving for Vietnam after that, so their time together was short. She did not love him, and she did not want him to love her.

Annie's conversations with Professor Meyer were more interesting to her than Duncan's conversations. Another sign she would have to break things off with Duncan.

She met the new art professor when she was copying student transcripts for her job with the registrar's office. He came into the office to use the paper cutter. His grey corduroy slacks hung below his belly paunch. He was young, with long brown hair and smart blue eyes. His distinct brown mustache created a thick eyebrow for his upper lip.

"Hey."

Annie nodded in return

"I'm teaching sculpture. Meyer. It's my last name, but I use it for my first name." He had a low, raspy voice. She imagined he had a testosterone fuel pump in his throat.

She smiled, "Annie. It's not my real name, but that's what I use."

"What's your real name?"

"Annalise."

"What's wrong with that?"

"Sounds like Anna-lyze."

"So . . ."

"I don't want to sound like an analyzer."

"Are you an analyzer?"

"Maybe."

"Where are you from, An-neeeee?" he asked, drawing out her name.

"Texas. Biology and English majors."

"Potato chip?" He offered her the bag he was holding.

"No, thanks."

He nodded. "Well, good to meet you." Then he ambled out of the copy room.

Most nights Annie studied at the science building. She liked the animal specimens in jars on the shelves, the Bunsen burners, sinks that turned on all over the room, colored charts on the walls, the cold countertops, and the tall lab stools.

She heard footsteps coming down the hall, wondering if it was the night guard who checked the labs and would tell her it was time to go back to the dorm.

"Hey, An-neeee, what are you doing?" It was Meyer.

"Homework. What are you doing?"

"Sketching fetuses," he said. "Fe-ta-suss," he said again for emphasis, accompanied by a short guffaw. He flipped open the sketch pad tucked under his arm. There were pages and pages of drawings of fetuses with thin dark-hatching for shading.

"These are great, so realistic."

"Thanks."

"I thought you're a sculptor. Are you teaching drawing too?"

"I'm teaching sculpture and an art history course."

It was obvious he was spending a lot of time drawing from the nearly full sketchbook. "Why are you doing drawings then?"

"Drawing is important for sculptors—maybe more important than for painters, though I do paintings too." He took a seat on a lab stool at the worktable across from her.

"Why?"

"You have to know how objects are constructed to make forms. Drawing helps develop that kind of knowledge, keeps your eye sharp. Shouldn't you be hanging out with friends in your dorm?" he asked. "It's late."

"Wish I could—but I have to study a lot." She explained she was doing two majors and was a work-study student working half time to help with expenses. "I like to study in the lab—it's quiet."

"Ditto," he nodded. "Taking any art classes?"

"I have. History of art, Asian art, and modern art. And thinking about minoring in art history. I've been whittling wood pieces for a couple of years—folk art faces carved out of parts of tree branches."

He frowned. "Whittling is not art—they're fetishes." He said it again for emphasis: "Fe-ti-shishs."

She thought he should see them before making a judgment but didn't want to correct him. "I've been thinking about taking a sculpture class to do something hands-on. I like working with wood."

"Good idea."

"I'd have to sign up as independent study for only a credit or two because my schedule is so packed."

"That could work. I'd love to have you in my class, An-neeee." He got up from the lab stool and said he'd see her later—he had to get home.

———

She didn't see Professor Meyer for several weeks but knew where he was much of his time—working in the sculpture studio in the greenhouse behind her dormitory. She could see the greenhouse through her dorm window.

She attended his first exhibit in the administration building. The featured piece was a large wood frame holding eight slick silver metal lips with long protruding red tongues. Each lip was a foot wide. Some people said it was scandalous. She thought it was gross but brilliant. She overheard someone say he was eccentric. She heard one of the girls in another dorm telling her friends she was going to go to the greenhouse in her raincoat, naked under it, and ask him what he thought about her form when she opened the raincoat. They were all laughing. She wondered how anyone could do that and if she should warn Meyer.

Annie signed up for Independent Study Sculpture before she left for Mexico with Duncan. At the first sculpture class in February, Meyer invited the ten students to join him on the lawn next to the greenhouse. The landscaping crew was donating chunks of trees recently cut down. Everyone was to select a wood piece for their wood sculpture project due the end of the term. The other assignments were outlined on the course syllabus: projects in plaster of paris; wire; and a twenty-page paper on a sculptor of their choice.

For the writing project, Annie chose Giacometti. She liked his fluid lines, lumpy bodies, texturing, gauntness, and movement. His figures seemed impacted by wind—leaning into the wind or pushed by the wind. Annie wrote her paper in verse because the white space around verse seemed to match his sculptures.

Her plaster of paris project portrayed a biological life form—an amoeba she'd seen in the microscope in biology lab. She started with a rectangular piece of plaster and used a sander to shape the rounded form. She titled it, *Beginnings of Life*.

The wire project was a simple design based on her favorite whittling project: two eyes and large lips. She used the design for the wood project, sketching on graph paper to get the right dimensions, two large eyes that looked like lips, and a mouth with exaggerated lips. Annie's wood chunk was a four-foot-tall by three-foot-wide section of an oak tree. It was so heavy she had to roll it across the lawn to the greenhouse steps and push it up the steps to the greenhouse floor. Two students helped her hoist the chunk to the counter to work on it.

First, Annie stripped off the bark with chisels and wood mallets. She planned to carve two inches into the wood, large eyes that looked like lips. And a deeply carved mouth with big lips. When the lips encased the deep eye holes and mouth holes, she envisioned a head that curved like a guitar body, a feminine shape.

When Meyer saw her design, he exclaimed loudly to the entire class, "We're not here to work on folk art—too primitive!"

She had seen similar pieces in the museum in Chicago. She wanted to focus on biological parts that were major symbols of life: lips, crevices, eyes. She did not think her design was folk art. So for the next three months, she grooved and rounded, smoothed and sanded, and carved deep recesses into her tree chunk in between classes in the daytime, nights, and weekends.

In the evenings, Meyer often worked at the other end of the greenhouse, welding metal sculptures. Fountains of sparks flew, reflecting fireworks through the glass walls and ceiling in the night darkness. They frequently talked while they worked from their own stations. He made fun of her for working so hard and wanted to know why she wasn't out dating like the other girls. She said she was engaged to a soldier in Vietnam.

As Annie's sculpture got smaller from chiseling, she thought about dividing the piece into three—two eye-lips and the mouth-lips—and using a metal chain to tie the pieces to make a train of large lips. She drew what the new piece would look like, entranced with the idea that one piece could morph into a moving piece with wood and metal chain. She thought her work was credible, not folk art. She was sure her work was better than the other plaster carvings strewn around the greenhouse. Several students had given up on their wood projects because it was taking too long to produce anything. Meyer let them substitute a second plaster of paris sculpture.

One night Meyer told her that one of the girls had come to the greenhouse in a raincoat, naked. She opened her coat and asked if he was interested. He told her to close her coat and go home. Annie asked if it was Sally. It was. Annie was glad Sally had not entrapped him—he might have lost his job.

"What are you going to do when you graduate?" Meyer had just told her he was taking a new job at a university in the west—he would be moving when school was out with his wife and new baby.

She shared her latest plans. "I'm going to Martha's Vineyard for a summer writing job with a team writing a high school botany textbook. In the fall, I'm going to graduate school in Madison."

He nodded with approval.

She wondered what she would do without him to talk to. She knew he had a special feeling for her. Before his baby was born a few weeks earlier, he asked if Annie would marry him if his wife died in labor. Maybe he was joking, or it was the stress of the baby coming. She pretended not to hear what he said.

She was planning to pack up the wood lips recently divided into three pieces to travel in the car driving to the East Coast. She could finish her sculpture in the summer. When she went to the greenhouse to collect her pieces, they weren't there, and the greenhouse was cleaned out of all the students' sculptures. She headed to the main art building to see if someone moved them there. They weren't there. She called Meyer's office phone.

"Hey, this is Annie. Where are my sculpture pieces? I'm ready to pack them up."

"I took them to the dump yesterday."

"Are you joking?"

"You were obsessing. It was not artwork. It was a fetish, Annie. I took the pieces to the dump."

She didn't believe him.

"It's at the dump, Annie."

"Then I'm going to go to the dump to find it." She felt sick to her stomach.

"It will be buried under other trash by now." Then he laughed—she couldn't tell if it was an awkward laugh or a real laugh but he laughed. What kind of teacher throws away a student's project after months of work? He did not apologize. She was sure something was wrong with him—it was a feeling she had. And she had another feeling—that she was not done with him even though he was heading west and she was heading east and he had thrown a piece of her in the dump.

Annie would be graduating with majors in biology and English and a minor in art history. She'd been right to go down these roads, as disparate as they may have appeared to others, including her favorite English professor, Dr. Hill.

In the fall, he called Annie to his office and encouraged her to write a collection of poetry for a senior honors project. He said she was the best writer in his creative writing classes. So she submitted her proposal to the English department. At the end of the school year, she would present her project to a faculty committee in an oral defense.

She wrote all year, pulling in topics from her therapy with Duncan, summer job at the hospital, and travels in Mexico. She had more than enough material. All that was left was to submit the final publication and prepare for the review committee. She selected topics for shock value as much as literary value, she realized with some remorse only days before the oral review. It was too late to scale back and go more conservative.

She found a disc jockey from a local radio station to record a selection of her poems for her presentation. She thought a strong professional male voice would sound better than her softer, trepidatious voice. DJ Smithy selected three poems to tape in his studio. He liked the poem about the man who entered the hospital emergency room with the shattered Pepsi bottle in his rectum—the medical interns pulling out glass shards, wondering what the story was, and who was the woman accompanying the man looking so embarrassed. Annie worried the committee might question the literary value of this poem. She was prepared to talk about the dilemma of modern man—who among us is not a shard in the ass of life? There was the ode to her dissected frog Otto, whose heart beat for hours after the lab experiment was done, carrying his heart wrapped in a tissue in her coat pocket until it stopped beating, imagining what she would do if it beat indefinitely. The committee had to see the poetic value of a heart separated from its body while it beats on. And the poem about Duncan's peeing in a cup she emptied all night after he hurt his ankle—a relationship poem forecasting a breakup.

At the late afternoon meeting in a windowless conference room, Annie set up the tape recorder trying to avoid Professor Hill's amused gaze. She had not spoken to him about her project since the day he refused to be her honors project advisor. He agreed to work with two other students writing traditional literature papers. He wanted Annie to work with the writer-in-residence they brought to campus to help aspiring writers like Annie. But the writer-in-residence was immersed in her own writing and was not interested in Annie's work. So when Professor Hill told Annie no, she announced she would work by herself.

At the May defense, Annie forced herself to look directly at each committee member to display confidence, then said she would be playing three poems from her one-hundred-page collection they received in advance in their bound notebook. She pressed the 'play' button and sat back in the wooden conference chair, gripping the arms tightly. Out came DJ Smithy's booming baritone stating the first poem's title, then Annie's description of glass shards in a man's ass—followed by the other two selections. She felt exhilarating power—for a moment—both thrilling and terrifying.

At the end, she rose to press the 'stop' button and sat back in her seat. There was silence. Presumably, the English professors were processing the performance. Annie was glad Professor Rickson was not on the committee—he would have been shocked by this reprobate Annie. And she was glad the writer-in-residence had already left the college for a new appointment. What would a real writer have said?

The committee chair delivered the first response. "Thank you, Miss Zechman. You have assembled an impressive body of work. You write a bit like William Burroughs in *Naked Lunch*." There was head nodding. Were they saying she had written a pornographic piece of work? What should she say?

Dr. Hill went next. "You show quite a bit of talent, Annie, and I encourage you to build a career as a writer." He was smiling kindly. Perhaps he felt guilty she had no advisor to work with.

Annie never recalled the conversation after the first two comments though she was in the room an hour, and the tape was only eight minutes. She did not recall packing up the tape recorder and exiting the room but thinks they shook her hand, one by one.

Later that week, she learned that DJ Smithy showed the poems he was preparing to tape to his daughter who lived in the room next to Annie in the dorm. Though he seemed like a liberal fellow, agreeing with little persuasion to be Annie's reader, his daughter was not so enlightened. Annie overheard her whispering in the dining hall to the other girls how sick Annie's poems were. Annie's friends never looked at her the same after that. Annie concluded from this that being a writer was a hard business. You could lose friends.

Annie reported to the dean's office that she was not going to walk in graduation when she received a form addressed to Annalise Zechman to fill out. What was the purpose of walking in graduation? She didn't want the name Annalise on her degree—her name was Annie.

The dean's office notified her in writing that walking in graduation was mandatory—she would not graduate unless she attended the event. Annie mulled over leaving the college and requesting a transcript later—surely they would have to provide a transcript. But she was too tired to fight over her name.

So when the college president called out Annalise Kaylah Zechman at graduation, Annie Zechman walked resolutely up the steps of the chapel in her black robe with the black mortarboard half-cocked on her head, while the President announced she was a double major in English and biology and was awarded Highest Honors in English. She knew many of her classmates thought she was sick. What did they expect from someone who came from the city that kills presidents?

Two days later, Annie met up with her friend Theodora and her biology professor-husband to make the drive east in his car. It was a twenty-hour drive to Woods Hole, then a ferry ride to Martha's Vineyard.

The book publisher had rented a house for the botany team to share—a two-story stately white colonial that was walking distance to the town of Edgartown and the beach. Annie liked the symmetry of the house, the black front door centered between matching windows.

Their work started right away. The professor would lecture about a topic in the morning. In the afternoon, Annie would turn the information into text a fourteen-year-old could understand. The professor would clean up the text and submit the drafts to the publisher. Theodora would research information for the professor's lectures.

Most nights they piled into the car to go fishing at the edge of the ocean. Then they would prepare fish dinners the next night of whatever they caught. If they didn't catch anything, they'd go to the fish market or to clam bars for quarts of fried clams. Annie walked to the beach and around Edgartown alone as often as she could.

They were comfortably settled into a routine when Charles Henry, a friend of Theodora's, visited from Boston. He pursued Annie in all the rooms of the colonial house. She wondered why she wore her black and yellow flower culotte sundress with the two paisley-shaped cut-outs at the waist, which looked like sperm shapes she realized later, the day he came into the kitchen while her hands were deep in water preparing the bluefish for dinner. He slid his fingers inside the two fabric holes to touch her sun-tanned belly, pressing his body to her from behind, "Don't you want to be with me? I need a woman like you." He said he was a great lover. That piqued her curiosity—she decided the scientific method was best and felt no guilt having sex with Charles. She knew she was not going to marry Duncan. How could she marry someone who raped her, who would fight over who could explicate a poem the best? And what if he wanted to go to more bullfights—she was not going to more bullfights. And Annie was missing Meyer more than Duncan. How could she marry someone she wasn't missing?

Charles left after a few days. Annie was not sorry to see him leave—she did not want to be pursued, and he was not a great lover. The botany team settled back to their symmetry in the colonial house.

The ferry was on time the afternoon Annie left Martha's Vineyard at the end of the summer. Charles told her before he left that he might see her in Madison—he might take classes there next summer. Annie had not left the island since she arrived. Leaving the team to finish the final chapters, she was ready to take her land legs back. Her gazelle and lion were tired but used to running with more purpose now. There would be no herd to protect her in Wisconsin—she'd left her friends from college behind. And what if Flora was right, that more bad things were coming? Annie had added incest to Flora's list. And killing Otto—and so many frogs—that horrific day. And Meyer's betrayal—carting her wooden lips to the garbage dump. President Kennedy's assassination was already on the list—and now unbelievably two more this year—Martin Luther King, Jr., and Robert Kennedy. She would count on Flora's list as one the horrible assassinations of national leaders. At twenty-two, there were seven on her list she could not process. Years earlier, she decided that the worst things are the ones you cannot process—they're so bad you can't understand them. You have to live with them if you decide to live. She shuddered to think what life would be like at thirty.

The ocean waters swirled brown with sand beneath the ferry as it docked. She lifted her two suitcases and walked down the footbridge to the parking lot in Woods Hole to wait for the bus to Boston's airport.

MADISON

Two weeks after her twenty-second birthday, Annie was on an airplane to Madison, watching the Atlantic Ocean disappear from sight. A U.S. Treasury Bond gifted for her un-confirmation lay on the bottom of her purse to pay for fall tuition at the university. She used her last paycheck from the botany project to rent a room above Ethyl's Underwear Shop on State Street. It would be an easy walk to Lakes Mendota and Monona. The student union at the south end of the street invited Lake Mendota into a porch of piers, sailboats, canoes, food shops, and walkways.

Three pointy-busted mannequins lived in the bay window on Ethyl's first floor. Ethyl changed their underwear weekly—black underwear, red, white, pink, and sky blue. Sometimes she balanced tall peacock feathers in the corners of the window. The deep blue third eyes of the tail feathers lent an air of mysticism to her homage to underwear.

Two floors of furnished rooms—four per floor—were stacked on top of the shop. Tenants shared a common bathroom—toilet, shower, sink. Each sleeping room had a bathroom sink, twin bed, and kitchenette with small-size appliances—oven, refrigerator, sink, small row of cabinets. There was a narrow window in Annie's room, though she could see only a brick wall across from her and a slice of the alley, since Ethyl's was flanked by brick buildings.

Annie shared the third-floor bathroom with three male students. They each paid four hundred and fifty dollars monthly. Ethyl advertised the twelve-by-fourteen-foot rooms as apartments, but it was really a rooming house well located between the Capitol at one end of State Street and the university at the other end.

To earn rent money, Annie found a waitress job at Garibaldi's Italian restaurant a few doors down. Her shift was nine to three in the morning, five nights a week. After the restaurant closed at three, she and the dishwasher stacked the chairs on the tabletops and mopped the floors while the owner squared the day's accounts in his basement office. She'd get back to her place by four and in bed by five after she washed the garlic and spaghetti smells out of her hair. Most mornings, she had an English literature class at eight. It was a brisk walk down State Street and up the hill to Bascom Hall. She wore the standard female outfit—miniskirt, turtleneck, high leather boots—dangling her well-shaped legs in the biting air and walking quickly.

At work she wore a sleeveless black uniform shortened to mid-thigh, white turtleneck underneath, and high black boots. She tied her long hair behind her neck with a black cord and tried to look French. She didn't make much tip money—mostly poor students frequented the restaurant after the bars closed. They'd come in looking for a table where she was cleaning away leftover pizza, asking if they could eat the leftovers. She looked the other way and got in trouble with Mr. Louie watching from the kitchen.

"*Rapidamente*, Ah-knee! Clean-a! *Rapidamente!*" he admonished when she came to the kitchen with the tray of dirty dishes.

She had no intention of hurrying. If people wanted to eat leftover pizza, what was the harm? She couldn't afford to buy groceries either. Mr. Louie let the waitresses, cook, and dishwasher eat one meal free each shift. Annie ate hers before shift. The cook would fry a thin steak for them— she'd grab a cup of minestrone soup and spumoni ice cream if there was time. She ate quickly before making up the salad bin to pull salad plates from later.

Annie didn't like Jonas the first time they met. She rapped on his door at the head of the stairs, talking fast when he opened it. "There's a fight in the alley. Will you come with me to see if things are ok?"

His blue-pool eyes sized up her request. He stalled long enough for her to understand he would not follow. She felt embarrassed for bothering him and retreated to her room. The alley was quiet.

A few weeks later, he knocked on her door. "It's too much for me to eat," he said, offering her a large slab of chocolate cake on a paper plate.

She wondered if this was a peace offering.

"Thanks so much—I'll put it in the frig for later—I'm making a bookshelf and rearranging furniture to make this place more functional."

"Can I see?" He peered around the door.

"Sure."

"I'm Jonas," he said, making a half salute by his forehead.

"Annie."

"Do you need help?" He saw several boards on the floor for what he guessed was the bookcase and bedding piled in the corner. The bed was mid-route to a different wall.

"Thanks, but things need to stay where they are till I set up the bookcase."

"I've heard the music you've been playing—I have some albums you might like."

"O gosh, the walls are so thin. Am I too loud?"

"Nope, it's fine."

"I play the same things over and over," she said apologetically. He must have heard Otis Redding and the Rolling Stones a hundred times the last few weeks.

"I'm going away for the weekend—you can borrow some albums before I leave."

She nodded.

He was back at the door, centered between the side jambs when he turned to ask as an afterthought, "Interested in seeing a play on campus sometime?"

She thought about the blonde woman she'd seen going in and out of his room the last few weeks, figuring that was his girlfriend.

"I don't know my work schedule yet," she said cautiously, not sure what to make of his invitation. "I work most nights at Garibaldi's."

"Ok, I'll check back and see what's playing."

She'd seen his name on the mailbox—Jonas Erikson. Probably Scandinavian. He had a Northern look—blond chin-strap beard, light-colored hair, watchful blue eyes. He talked slowly and gave off an introverted vibe.

When she came home from school on Friday, he'd left a box of albums outside her door with a note: "Back Sunday night." She liked his orderly printing.

Annie knocked at his door Monday to return his albums. He invited her in, and they traded information. He worked night shift as an aide at the state mental hospital. He was a French major at the university. She was in the master's degree program in English and worked last summer on the East Coast helping her college biology professor write a high school botany textbook. She was engaged to a soldier in Vietnam. She didn't tell him she was never going to marry Duncan. He didn't mention the blonde woman.

Most nights, Jonas left for work in his white scrubs before Annie left for her waitress shift. Annie left the restaurant when the streetcleaners were washing the streets. She walked quickly past the five buildings between the restaurant and Ethyl's. Jonas's room was dark. She heard him come up the stairs a few hours later, walk down the creaky hall to shower, then walk back to his room where he slammed the door. Then quiet.

From her room, Annie could see comings and goings at the head of the stairs. On some of his nights off, the blonde woman knocked at his door. Annie knew she was there because that was the only time he closed his door—he liked to keep his door ajar for better airflow when he was home alone. She heard soft voices through the walls and water running from his sink though she could never make out words.

Usually Annie didn't see Jonas until dinner time when he came to her room to ask if he could use her phone to call a cab to get to work. The scent of his Old Spice took up residence on the phone receiver. He came by Garibaldi's some afternoons when she pulled an early shift. He'd take a table near the window, order coffee, and read *Le Monde*.

"Do you have to read the French newspaper for courses at school?"

"No." He was amused at the thought someone would make him read *Le Monde*.

Annie met the blonde girl the afternoon she finished her bookshelf project. For weeks she'd been using columns of books to hold up the shelves but decided columns of bricks would work better. She arrived at Ethyl's carrying nine bricks when Jonas and the blonde woman were at the front door. He held the door open and offered to help with the load, but Annie said she was ok—"I'm almost home."

He introduced them quickly—"Annie, this is Mary—Mary, Annie." Mary did not smile when Annie said hi which Annie didn't think much about at the time. Annie was focused on unloading the bricks which were getting heavier by the minute.

Back in her room, Annie wrapped each brick in blue and green paisley-patterned paper. She'd already wrapped three long boards in a sapphire-blue fabric. The bricks would support each shelf—a brick standing vertically at each end of the boards and one in the middle. Annie's books would fill the first and second shelves, record player on the top shelf, albums stacked on each end of the first shelf. Her collection of Mexican baskets would sit on the floor under the bottom shelf.

Annie was surveying her work when Jonas knocked at the door. She had smelled his pipe tobacco wafting down the hall, heard his guitar, and wondered with growing irritation how long the foreplay would be going on—why didn't he just shut his door and fuck Mary. Annie was castigating herself for feeling uncharitable because she was alone and Mary wasn't, when Jonas was at her door.

"Hey, can I use your phone?" He was wearing a white wool cable sweater, looking rugged and handsome. He walked to the blue and green bookshelf covering most of the wall across from the bed to check out her handiwork. "Looks good—nice how you wrapped the bricks."

"Thanks—came out better than I thought."

"I'm making a quick run north and need to call the airlines to ask about a flight." Annie nodded while he picked up the receiver.

"Thanks," he said after the call. He looked back to smile at her as he left the room.

Annie lifted the receiver to smell his diminishing scent, then rearranged the albums stacked at each end of the bookshelf—classical on the left, folk and rock on the right. Annie heard Mary leave. There was no fucking because Jonas never closed his door. He returned to Annie's room for small talk. She noticed the blue in his eyes looked different. Mostly his eyes were cornflower blue—now they looked grey. She learned in college genetics class that there are no blue pigments in people's eyes—blue eyes like her own hazel eyes are affected by colors and lights around them. She liked they had that in common—their eyes changed hues.

He left on his trip the next day.

When Jonas came to Annie's door for their first date, if this was a date, the plan was to go to a French play they talked about weeks ago. She wasn't sure what to wear because she didn't know if this was a date. Because he had a girlfriend and Annie was engaged. But Annie proceeded to dress as if it were a date. She tried on three outfits, deciding to wear a short navy-blue skirt and sweater and a black push-up bra. If this was not a date, she would not have worn the push-up bra.

Jonas wore a navy wool sweater, tan corduroy slacks, and a chestnut-colored leather jacket that looked almost orange. Annie was sure he dressed up. And there was the Old Spice scent. She didn't know if he liked how she looked—this was her first date, if it was a date, since her brief fling last summer with Charles.

They went to dinner before the play and made small talk which felt awkward because of lurking feelings which maybe were there—maybe not. It was easy to talk at Ethyl's but not at the restaurant and not dressed like it was a date. And his eyes—a strong blue—were reflecting his navy sweater.

He sat close in the theater, hooking his arm on the seat behind her and occasionally touching her shoulder. Annie told herself it was friendly touching. Duncan would not have liked her friendly touching anyone, but she was not thinking about Duncan.

After the play, they walked to a bar on State Street that featured jazzy music. A tree grew in the middle of the floor. Small blue lights positioned at the base of the trunk spotlighted darkness and mystery. Annie wondered if the tree shed leaves in response to the seasons or if the bar owner added fake leaves to create the tree's fulsome look. She'd been quiet after the play. "Is my silence bothering you?" she asked him at the tree bar.

"It is now, but it might not later." His answer was insightful, so different than Duncan's aggressive style.

There was low-key watchfulness between them and she was uncomfortable. The rules of engagement were changing. Back in his room, they talked while she stood by the window looking at the well-lit stores on State Street. He was lying on his bed—not asking her to sit by him. So she stood while they talked, and at some point, he fell asleep. She watched him breathe quietly for a few minutes, glad he trusted her enough to fall asleep. She could never fall asleep with anyone in the room. She tiptoed to her room, wondering if he'd been bored by her chatter. He woke a few hours later hearing a bus outside, wondering what time Annie left and if she was insulted he'd fallen asleep while she was talking.

Later he knocked on Annie's door asking to see the writing she'd told him about at the tree bar—her college honors project. She reached for the binder of poems standing with the classical albums next to the bookcase. He asked if he could take it to his room to read. She agreed but worried he would be shocked by the content, like her friends were, and his opinion of her would change.

She didn't know what he thought of her writing. He never asked about any of the poems. Many of his nights off from work, he fell asleep while Annie was talking in his room. She confided things she told no one else. She was not going to marry Duncan. She told him about Meyer and her summer at Cape Cod except for the part about Charles. She kept him up to date on how her classes were going. She learned to leave his room when he was struggling to keep his eyes open. She was amazed at how effortlessly he could move into sleep.

One night he stayed awake late into the night, listening and asking questions. It was a rare moment—she longed to be quiet like he was quiet. She stretched out on his bed and felt truly tired for the first time around him. She buried her head in the red and green cotton quilt his grandmother gave him when he left for Madison, and he touched her hand. From the first night, there had been no touching.

The hours of talk were spiraling them into chambers of a nautilus shell. She wasn't sure she could have a normal relationship with a man following her therapy with Duncan. And she couldn't count Charles because her time with him was so brief. Jonas was writing poetic notes to her now. He said he was fearful he would not measure up as a man after reading her poems. She realized changes were coming—she was unready and uneasy.

"Annie, I'm losing my job at the hospital," Jonas confided one night. His eyes were grey—he was wearing a grey sweatshirt.

"What happened?"

"I've been leaving one of the ward doors open for a couple of hours at night so my patients can go outside and look at the stars."

"Sounds like a good thing."

"The rules require doors are locked at all times. I thought that since I'm always with the patients, I could be outside with them."

"I would want someone to open the door for me if I was locked up all the time."

"The hospital doesn't agree. They said it's not my call. Bottom line—they no longer need my services. I have one more week."

Annie didn't know what to say.

"It's more complicated. This is where I'm assigned for my conscientious objector service with the Army."

She didn't know what that meant.

"There will be paperwork to transfer my CO service to another job. I'm going to try to go to school full-time and finish my degree while this happens because the paperwork could take a while—the Army goes slow."

Annie had just given her notice to Garibaldi's. After waitressing for three months, she had developed painful calluses on both feet. She needed a better job to accommodate classes and make more money.

A few nights later after a walk by the lake, Annie and Jonas found their way into the old stone church near campus. She was surprised the doors were unlocked. It was empty inside.

"I don't think churches lock their doors," Jonas said.

"I think synagogues do. When I had to get to Hebrew class early, I had to knock on the door until someone let me in."

"Our Gods have different rules," he quipped.

They took a seat in the center of a dark pew in the first row of the balcony, in the nave. Small sidelights along the walls across from the pews offered just enough light to find their way in the dark. They faced forward as if a service would be starting. Then Jonas leaned over and kissed Annie twice. She knew he was going to kiss her but didn't know he would kiss her a second time. They were not remarkable kisses, but she was relieved they kissed. They were going deeper into the nautilus shell.

They didn't talk about the kisses when they left the church. And after the church visit, there was a surprising long week of no touching. The next week, Jonas looked directly at her with grey-blue eyes and said, "What am I supposed to do—jump on you?"

Annie smiled awkwardly, feeling the walls of trying to resolve unspoken feelings. They began to move consciously together then, without talking about the change in their relationship. They would kiss beneath a round white Chinese lampshade hanging from center ceiling light in his room. When he installed the lampshade a month earlier, he asked Annie, "Do you think the lampshade is sexy?"

She didn't think so—how could a lampshade be sexy—but she said yes to be agreeable. She didn't ask why he always kissed her under the lampshade but was glad to be kissing him.

On a walk by the lake a few nights later, Jonas asked Annie to live with him. They had not had sex. He said he wanted them to share a bed at their new place. She didn't know if they would be sexually compatible, thinking about Duncan. She thought she would want her own bedroom, or at least a second bedroom if they needed distance. And she wasn't on the birth control pill—she told him Duncan was infertile, so she had not had to deal with pregnancy worries with him. Jonas told her not to worry. He used condoms. She offered to see a gynecologist and look into the pill. They talked about the ways they were already good together. They could talk together well. She liked his quietness and how distant he could be— his distance pushed her to move outside herself. He was not aggressive. He was her best friend. He liked her drive and talent. She brought a new energy to his life.

They each had a six-month lease, so he called Ethyl to learn how soon they could leave. He slipped a note under Annie's door with the news.

Annie—talked to our woman
Ethyl, she says we
must stay [or at least pay] through Jan.1.
Pay your rent she also
says. But then we're
free—Free—FREE.
Yes

They were celebrating in his room with a bottle of wine and chuckling over Ethyl's latest display—mannequins lounging in pink underwear on a pink silk quilt with peacock feathers lining the walls.

There were steps on the creaky stairs. Mary hesitated at the half-open door when she saw Annie sitting on the floor next to Jonas's bed. He invited Mary in. Jonas took her coat. She was dressed in a stylish tan dress with stockings and heels, hair tied back in a scarf. She said she was attending Bible school and was in the area.

Mary sat on the edge of Jonas's bed. She smoked a cigarette, apologized for not knowing much about wine and not really liking it, talked about problems with her car, and how her daughter was doing in school. She looked frequently at Jonas for help in this awkward conversation, but he smiled as if this was a normal get-together. Annie wanted to be alone with him but knew it was not possible. She disliked the moments of silence and smoke fumes, so when Mary lit her second cigarette, Annie made up the excuse she had to study for an exam and left.

Annie heard the door to Jonas's place close, the faucet water run, and French music playing. Mary stayed the night, leaving early in the morning. Annie wondered who was taking care of her daughter. Maybe Mary planned to stay the night and pre-arranged everything.

Jonas did not come to see Annie the next day, and Annie resolved to stay away from him. She'd been right to keep her distance—they would not be living together or having sex. How could they now? They did not talk the rest of the week.

Mary came to see him again, and Jonas closed the door. Annie played "Sittin' on the Dock of the Bay" continuously to block out sounds from his room but heard Mary leave at one in the morning. Annie was in bed with the door unlocked when Jonas knocked on her door and came in to join her on the bed. He held Annie and said Mary would not be back. Annie wasn't sure she believed him. The next night Annie had sex with Jonas. It was not like sex with Duncan. There was no pain—and Annie's noisy head voice turned off—leaving a welcome new quiet. She was surprised at the simplicity of their connection. They were inside the nautilus, together.

Annie was uneasy. She was used to looking for the back door whenever she entered a house, in case she needed to exit. Hypervigilance and mistrust were gifts from Grandpa. Was there a way out if things went south with Jonas, and what did she see in him, really? She liked his handsome Northern looks. The way his eyes changed colors. His no-frills style. How simple their time together was—walks, reading in the library, quiet talking, stopping for ice cream. For the first time, Annie's internal life felt uncomplicated, and she could breathe. She wasn't afraid of him, but she feared her growing attachment.

They were playing chess and within the next move or two, one of them would checkmate. Annie was prepared to play it out, thinking there was no way out. One of them would prevail. Jonas sighed as if he was emitting a mantra and folded the board in half so the remaining chess pieces tumbled over the top of the board.

"That's enough," he said quietly.

Annie thought that was the most intelligent, interesting move of all— no wins and no losses between them. They played far enough to share their strategies. That was the kind of man she wanted to live with, in her mind and heart. They picked up the sixteen black and white pieces spilled around the floor of his room and carefully re-nested them into their box.

Annie moved into his room. They threw their extra things in her room and started the search for a new apartment. Duncan was weighing heavily on her—she had not told him she was involved with another man. He planned to come to Madison in a few weeks to live with her. She could not let him come—he would find out about Jonas living down the hall. Jonas would hear the fighting through the walls. She knew there would be fighting, and Duncan would push her to have sex. She was sure of that.

So she did the one thing Duncan made her promise not to do. She wrote the Dear John letter. She waited to send it until a few days before he was ready to leave Vietnam because she worried about his safety if she told him sooner. She apologized for writing this way, telling him she knew they were not well suited for each other before he left for Vietnam but was afraid to tell him then. She tried to tell him in Mexico, but he wanted her to take more time to think their relationship through. She apologized again. She worried for him, wanted him to be safe, and knew he would find another woman who would be better for him than she could be.

Duncan warned Annie he would never speak to her again if she ended their relationship this way. True to his word, a box arrived at Ethyl's days later containing the gold necklace with the round charm with her name inscribed she had given him to wear by the cargo planes at the airport. She knew he had never taken it off. There were other personal effects in the box but not a single word from him.

Annie deeply regretted breaking her promise but was sure she had done the best thing for them. She wondered how he was taking it. Did he really love her? Would he be lost without her? Surely he recognized the distance between them, how difficult it had been to communicate. She was not sending tapes on the recorder. She was not trying to share her voice or listen to his.

Annie smelled the gold necklace to see if there was a scent of Duncan. It felt alien, cold, and metallic. She placed the necklace next to the identical necklace she wore in her jewelry box. The two round charms engraved with "Annie" settled like shrunken heads side by side in their casket. She was glad Duncan lived through the year and re-entered civilian life. He had taken care of her in his own way, despite the rape in the Ozarks she could never forgive. She was taking a risk with Jonas now—Duncan would not be here to help her.

They wrapped themselves that cold evening in his grandmother's quilt like butterfly babies in a cocoon. She knew cocoons were not the resting place they seemed to many. Old caterpillar bodies are busy digesting themselves from the inside out, fluids breaking down into cells used to form new bodies. She and Jonas were not resting—she imagined they were turning into something new.

On any other night, their kissing would have escalated to sex, or they would have grown tired and gone to sleep. But their kissing spiraled into a milky way of nerves inside lips and stars welding currents in their brains— was it her brain, his, or some new brain? There was a distinct scent that was entrancing and addictive—maybe the smell of the air in his lungs. She wondered if he smelled the air in her lungs—she never experienced this before.

She would look back on this night—their hours of cocoon kissing—with longing for more and trepidation. Would she find this place again with him or anyone? Would he kiss like this with someone else? Would losing him be one of the bad things Flora tried to warn her about? She was not prepared to live without him now. She sent Duncan away so easily—heartlessly. What if Jonas sent her away? Duncan would say she deserved it.

* * *

It was ten degrees below zero outside, and Jonas was feeling edgy. His room was hot from radiator heat.

"Let's get a donut." He stood to stretch his legs and shoulders. Annie was studying for her final exam in Victorian literature. She'd been rereading passages for nearly an hour, struggling to recall what she had just read.

"Is anything still open?"

"There's a place on the other side of town. We have time to walk there."

"Ok." She pulled on an extra sweater and her high leather boots, wrapped herself in her green Air Force parka, and tucked the thick mittens that were warming on the radiator in her coat pocket.

They headed down Ethyl's two flights of stairs. The pre-Christmas window display featured the plastic ladies in red—bras, garters, and bikini panties. Festive greenery lined the display window floor, and white lights sparkled like snowflakes from the ceiling. The ladies were bald; they never wore wigs.

"The window would get more attention if Ethyl put pubic hair on the ladies," Annie remarked.

Jonas chuckled and pulled her to him while they headed south down State Street. Foot-high snow lined the sidewalks on both sides. The snowplows had not come by in a while. Annie positioned her feet inside footprints from earlier walkers. At some point, they turned toward the lake, engraving their own footprints on pristine snow.

"Let's walk out here," Jonas was saying.

"On the lake? I thought we're going to get a donut?"

"We can get there this way." The temperatures had been below freezing for weeks. Jonas was already several feet out on the ice, testing it by stomping his thick boots left, right, left, right. The sounds were dimmed by the ice. The lights from the city blinked around the curving lake line. Small houses and trees shadowed against the lights. Before them, the lake was an expanse of white, fading into the night frost.

"What if it isn't frozen thick enough out there?"

He was walking ahead, gesturing for her to come along.

The cold was already snaking from her feet to her thighs. There was no liner in her boots. She was always cold in Wisconsin, unused to the weather. She admonished herself to keep walking—that would be better than complaining—and if she was moving, she wouldn't freeze in place.

He was breathing in the night air slowly, meditatively, while they walked.

"How can you breathe? It's too cold to breathe." She didn't wait for him to answer before she followed with, "Where's the donut place?"

He pointed to the faraway bank, but all she saw were flickering city lights and homes surrounding the lake. And ahead, more frozen lake.

Was it a mile, a half mile? She couldn't assess distances in the dark. She was trying to skate her feet forward, surprised at how bumpy the ice was. In the daytime, the surface looked smooth from the shoreline. The lake must freeze unevenly, making lumps, she figured. They scuffed along, traction coming from a thin snow layer on top of the ice.

"How much longer?" They must have walked an hour already. She couldn't imagine a donut shop close by. Maybe he has in mind scraping together snow with his hands and making an ice donut for her when she's ready to die on the ice.

"Not much farther."

The houses were small in the distance. She was shaking uncontrollably. It had been a long time since she could feel her feet or thighs.

Finally, he turned toward land, a row of houses ahead. They made their way up a narrow street where they saw the shop's sign, "Open until eleven." It was nearly that according to a round black clock on the far wall of the shop. Jonas ordered a coffee for him, cocoa for her, and two donuts from the four sad-looking donuts on the tray on the counter. She was grateful for something to eat though the donuts were greasy and tasteless—probably made that morning or yesterday. She decided not to complain. She was worried about the walk back.

"You're not going to make me walk back on the lake, are you?"

"No," he smiled. "We'll walk back through town."

"You mean there was an easier way to get here?"

He smiled without answering.

The walk back was longer than he remembered. At least that's what he said. But it wasn't as cold, away from the lake ice they walked across earlier. It was after midnight when they neared Ethyl's holiday window.

"Next time you want to walk across the lake, tell me so I can dress appropriately," she sniped.

He nodded. She struggled to peel off her thin boots with painful tingling fingers and bring her dead feet to life. He curled up in the bedspread ready to go to sleep.

Annie was struggling to finish the term. They were her first graduate-level courses and she didn't like any of them. She came to the university hoping to study creative writing. She lined up for registration in Bascom Hall with hundreds of students. Coming from a women's college, she was surprised to see the number of men lining up. It was the Vietnam era—men were flocking to universities to avoid the mandatory draft—every male between eighteen and twenty-six could be drafted.

The advisor's office called students to come forward alphabetically. Annie realized she would be last to register. A woman with a clipboard advised them to stay in line because they didn't know how long it would take to move through registration.

Waiting students started out standing but eventually sat on the floor, leaning against the walls on both sides of the large hallway. Annie met students who moved to Madison from Eau Claire, Chicago, Minneapolis, Boston, Baton Rouge, New York, and Los Angeles. From time to time, students who had been called into an advisor's office threaded their way back through the line of students flanking the walls muttering, "I can't believe that class is gone."

The waiting horde called out, "Which classes are closed?"

And they would hear: "Shakespeare is closed. Chaucer is closed. American Lit is closed."

One by one, Annie put an "X" through her top choices on the course catalog she was holding, wondering what would be left. She had already learned there was no creative writing program or even a course to take. If she wanted a master's degree, she would have to take literature courses.

Seven hours later, the lone Z finally entered an advisor's office. A tired man in a blue button-down shirt looked her up and down quickly over his tortoise-shell eyeglasses. "And what would you like to take?"

"What's left?"

"Not much. Sorry, you're last today."

"Yeah, Zs don't fare well on days like this."

"Next term we'll flip, and you'll be first," he said to offer her hope.

"That will be good." She wondered if she'd even be there next term. She wasn't sure she could afford a second term of out-of-state tuition.

He suggested options: "How about Victorian Prose and Middle English? I see you've taken previous courses in Chaucer and Medieval Literature at your college. And your prior Latin and German courses would be helpful in Middle English. You could add in Eighteenth-Century Lit? You need three courses to be full-time."

"Are there any other choices?"

"Not really." He removed his glasses to wipe his eyes with a tissue.

"Well, ok, whatever I can get."

And with that, Annie was registered. Her next stop was the university bookstore where she purchased more books than she ever imagined would come with a course. Each course required hardbound, expensive books—hundreds of dollars she didn't have.

Classes started the following week. The reading was heavy and odious. She wasn't interested in the content. By October, the realities of a Wisconsin winter were setting in. By November, it was clear that waitressing wouldn't cover her expenses and the bunions on her feet were red and angry. She thought about dropping out of school.

"What do you think I should do?" she asked Jonas.

"Stay in school. Don't go to class. They don't care if you go to class."

"You're right. They don't take attendance."

"Do the reading, turn in the papers, and show up for the tests. It will be better next term when you can register first. And find a new job—where you can get off your feet."

That sounded like a good plan.

When Annie was done with her first semester—papers submitted, tests done—she'd gotten two As and a B+—so she and Jonas celebrated at the bakery down the street with chocolate eclairs, agreeing they were a work of art. Large oblong pastry dough baked crisp but not too crisp, filled with rich chocolate custard, topped with chocolate ganache icing. Afterward, Annie suggested they walk to their favorite pier by the lake. They pulled their wool caps low over their ears, zipped up their parkas, and donned thick gloves. Annie was excited about what she was about to do—she had not told Jonas.

When they reached the pier and walked out on the planks over the water—frozen and immobile—Annie removed her gloves and reached into her backpack to pull out three culprits of her misery. She looked at the gold-printed titles one last time, then with as much force as she could muster, hurled three Victorian prose books onto the ice. She didn't know if the books would land on top of the ice and rest there or disappear into the ice. Surprisingly, the Victorian era disappeared quickly, perhaps cushioned in ice pockets that had formed below the surface. It didn't matter to Annie—they were out of sight and off her back. She had never thrown a book away—what she learned from the elaborate prose and tedious poetry was those writers were pushing back on the rationalism of the previous era. They were turning to romanticism and mysticism in religion and the arts. She could be one of them—begin a new era next term with courses she liked, in a new apartment with Jonas.

"Thanks for encouraging me to stay in school—I don't know if I would have made it through the term without you," she said as they walked home from the pier. She was feeling energized by the afternoon's events when they got home. They undressed and got into bed, and she rolled on top of him to have sex which seemed a fitting end to her Victorian era.

TEN BEFORE THIRTY • 111

The sun was shining when the latest snowstorm let up. A thin layer of snow lined the windowsill. Jonas cracked the window open last night when it was too warm to sleep. He'd been up for hours reading, waiting for Annie to wake up.

"How about walking around the Capitol?"

"Ok—after I run down to the bathroom."

He nodded and put his teacup in the sink, making up the bed after she left. He watched her walk down the hall in a t-shirt that barely covered her bare bottom—he thought about having sex before their walk.

Back in the room, she pulled a sweater and jeans on while he put on a lightweight jacket—no sex now—he'd been thinking about a snow quest for a while—this was the perfect snow for it—light and fluffy. He removed his shoes and socks, then opened their apartment door and gestured for her to walk ahead of him.

"What are you doing?" she said, pointing to his bare feet.

"Don't worry." He was giving her that don't-ask-questions look.

They headed down Ethyl's two flights of stairs and emerged on the ground floor to a thick snowy landing. He was quiet and bemused. His feet sank into the snow. He pressed ahead down the narrow walkway on State Street, fitting his feet into indentations made by other people's shoes.

"Is this some new Zen exercise?"

He ignored her. She walked behind, watching his feet slip into the pockets of snow. All the way up State Street, past shops, around the square of the Capitol, then back down State until they were back at the steps of Ethyl's. There was no talking. Annie's mind was filled with questions. Why was he walking barefoot in the snow? Was she supposed to take her socks and boots off and join him, to be a good partner? She didn't think he would want that. He knew she was never going to put her bunions into Madison's snows. It was his challenge. Did he want her to witness his feat—why ask her to come along? She knew he would not answer her questions.

───── ◦ ─────

By living together, Annie and Jonas would reduce the nine hundred dollars they were paying at Ethyl's and find an apartment for five hundred dollars or less. They agreed to move farther from the university so the rent would be less—they had their eye on a neighborhood close to the Capitol. They agreed to lie to landlords about being unmarried if they needed to, given the law about cohabitation, and they searched for a two-bedroom apartment because Annie wanted a room of her own in case they needed more space between them.

The afternoon they looked at the top floor of a four-story brick apartment building on Pickney Street, Annie realized Jonas was better at scoping out places than she was. The tenants had strung blankets and bedsheets from ropes attached to the ceiling throughout the apartment to divide the place into quadrants. They'd fashioned a narrow corridor to walk through the rooms to get to the one bathroom. Jonas walked through the apartment slowly taking it in. Annie had already dismissed the place when she saw the maze before them.

"This will work," he said with a satisfied smile.

"What? We'd have to walk up four flights of stairs. And there's not enough room," she protested.

"We'll pull down all the blankets and sheets. The bones are fine. The rent is right. It's two bedrooms. The stairs should not be an issue—exercise is good. We'll be living in the penthouse."

She was doubtful but they signed the four-hundred-and-fifty-dollars-per-month lease.

The day they moved, Ethyl was setting up her New Year's window. She was taking down the red Christmas display and setting up a black underwear display. She put up a sign, "Welcome 1969! Twenty percent off all items."

Jonas and Annie looked back at the plastic ladies dressed in black lace.

"Happy new year, girls."

A week after Jonas and Annie moved to the penthouse, she made good on her promise to see a gynecologist. She gave herself a pep talk in the waiting room, rubbing her cold tingly hands. 'All you have to do is take off your jeans, cover up with the white sheet, get on the table, put your feet in the metal stirrups, and open your legs. The doctor has seen a million vaginas. Pretend you're a scientist.'

The nurse called her name, telling Annie to follow her to the examining room.

"Take off everything from the waist down. Here's a cover-up. The doctor will be in soon."

Annie sat at the edge of the examining table, trying to remember to breathe.

"What's going on today?" the doctor said cheerfully entering the room.

"Hi. I'm here to see if I can be on the pill. I've never had a gynecological exam—I'm really nervous."

"Ok, good to know. We'll do an exam and go over your menstrual history. Are you sexually active?"

"Yes."

"What type of birth control are you using?"

"My boyfriend uses a condom."

"Not the most reliable method." The doctor frowned.

"I worry all the time about being pregnant because I can go a couple of months without a period—it's been like that since I was eleven."

"You may not be ovulating on both sides."

"And I'm so hairy—I've been reading about problems women can have with their ovaries that can cause hair to grow on their faces." She was embarrassed to tell him about the hairs around her nipples she'd been plucking out.

"Some women can have problems in their ovaries that cause an increase in the male hormone and increased facial hair can be a result. Also problems keeping their weight in check."

"Sounds like me."

"Scooch down on the table. Let's take a look."

Her feet were in the stirrups. The metal speculum that looked like a duck's bill disappeared quickly inside her like a duck dipping into the lake. There was no way to run away with her vagina propped open like a construction site. She wished there were women doctors doing these exams. She hoped the hair on her legs hadn't grown back—she shaved last night so she would look smooth. She even shaved off the "J" she'd grown on her left thigh. She'd been shaving her dark leg hair around the J for weeks.

114 • YANA KAZAN

Jonas didn't care if she shaved it off—he was not as impressed with the hair tattoo as Annie was.

"Well, have any of your other girlfriends grown your initial on their thigh?" she asked last night.

"No one else," he responded dryly.

"Just relax," the doctor was telling her.

She tried to relax while her right hand covered her belly in sympathy for her inside parts that seemed like foreign countries—vagina, cervix, ovaries, fallopian tubes, uterus. She never liked their names—couldn't there be better names for women's parts? Most names in the human body come from Latin and Greek. Vagina is Latin for a sheath for a sword—too militant. Clitoris is Greek for *kleis*, a key to gain entrance through a door. Too game-like. She tried to remember to breathe while she thought of replacement names. He was telling her he was taking a cell sample to screen for cervical cancer—this was a new test recommended for women. Since she's so young, this would be a baseline test for her.

"Ow!" She felt an uncomfortable pinch in one of her countries.

"All done. You did great, Annie."

The speculum was thankfully closed, and he withdrew the duck's bill.

"Just need to check the rectum for any abnormalities in the muscles between your vagina and anus." He said anus. Old French for ring. He slid his gloved finger through the ring, up her ass. Can he tell she hasn't had a bowel movement for days? She's always constipated. Jonas keeps telling her to eat more salads. You can't hide any secrets when there's a finger in your ass. She never liked it when Duncan put his finger in her—he thought it would make her feel good. He was hoping she would agree to anal sex. She told him she would think about it.

"Everything looks good. Get dressed and let's talk about your options."

Annie pulled her clothes on quickly.

"I think it would be good to start on the birth control pill—it's highly effective, at ninety-eight percent. And your periods will be regularized."

"Ok."

On the way home, she filled the prescription at the drugstore, chastising herself for being such a coward and not eating salads.

Her relief at getting through the exam and starting on the pill was short-lived. The pills poured hormones into her, and she was getting headaches that worsened every day. "I don't know if I can be on the pill. My headaches are getting worse, Jonas."

"Get off them. We'll find something else." He was still using a condom because the doctor said it would be a month before the pills would protect them. She was glad he was concerned about her, but he'd been hoping they could have sex without worrying about getting pregnant.

"What did you and Mary use?"

"Mary was on the pill," he said matter-of-factly.

"Oh." Of course, she thought—it was so much easier fucking Mary. She wanted to ask about condoms. When did he first use one? Who showed him how? Did any girlfriends put it on for him? She knew he had girlfriends before Mary. Should she put it on for him? Would that be sexy? He probably didn't trust her to do it right. And she was sure she'd laugh from nervousness, thinking how funny a penis looked standing straight up with a rubber hat on like a buoy or swimming pool toy—something that could float. He never turned away from her when he opened the package, slipping the rubber ring over his penis, and slowly rolling the sheath up, calm and focused. She looked away when she thought she might giggle— she was sure laughing was not sexy.

Annie returned to the doctor a month later to tell him about the headaches. He explained the pill was a high-dose mix, and research wasn't clear yet on what the dose levels should be. He pulled out a report from his desk drawer to show her. The pill she was taking contained 250 micrograms of levonorgestrel and 50 micrograms of ethinyl estradiol, but new research was looking at pills with only 100 micrograms of levonorgestrel and 20 micrograms of ethinyl estradiol. Researchers were thinking it would be possible to reduce the pill's potency without being less effective at preventing pregnancy.

"I don't think you're a good candidate for the high-dose pill, Annie— I'm concerned about the headaches. A barrier method would be better—a diaphragm." He showed her the dome-shaped silicone cup. "You insert it before sex or several hours before. It's eighty-eight percent effective when you spread a thin layer of spermicide around the cup's inside lip. They come in different sizes so we need to do another exam to see what size works best for you."

She agreed this might be a better option—and walked resolutely back to the exam room giving herself another pep talk to get back in the stirrups. He inserted three different-sized diaphragms to see which fit best to cover her cervix. Latin for neck.

"The medium-size seems best, Annie."

Of course. She didn't imagine she would have a giant cervix or a small one either. She imagined her cervix was like an average-sized country—France.

Annie stopped by the drugstore on the way home to fill the prescription for the diaphragm and spermicide. It felt overwhelming—hundreds of dollars she didn't have for doctor bills, birth control pills, the diaphragm, spermicide, the pills she couldn't use. She didn't want to complain to Jonas. And what if he felt the diaphragm during sex? One more thing to deal with.

She showed Jonas the diaphragm, wondering if showing him would take away the romance and mystery. They agreed he should still use a condom so together they would put up enough protection. They agreed this was an irony, arming like warriors for lovemaking.

The first time she inserted the diaphragm in the bathroom, carefully slicking smelly sperm-killing jelly around the lip, she imagined saying to him, 'Oh don't pay any mind to the round slicked up dish covering France,' while she tried to nonchalantly take his penis inside her without laughing with embarrassment, hoping the rubbery dish did not dislodge under humping and emerge like a jaunty beret on his penis when they were done. He said he didn't feel the diaphragm in France.

Annie's second semester was going better. The same advisor registered her. "Hey, Zechman, you're first!" He was smiling and wearing the outfit he wore in the fall—blue button-down shirt, tortoise-shell eyeglasses, brown leather loafers. She got the three courses she wanted—Shakespeare, American Literature, Modern Novel—and quickly left the hall filled with hundreds of students, including so many men trying to avoid the draft.

Their new apartment felt luxurious after Ethyl's rooming house. Jonas built them a desk that spanned the entire wall in one room. Annie used thumbtacks to attach artwork to the walls, including pictures of Meyer's metal skeleton sculptures. On the opposite wall, they set up bookshelves made with wood planks and bricks.

Off the office room was the living room, and off the living room, a small porch room with glass windows on two walls. The living room hosted a wall of windows that looked down on the neighborhood's treetops and rooftops, and up to the clouds. Their small bedroom was at the opposite end from the porch room. Off the bedroom, there was a good-sized bathroom with a claw-foot tub and spray attachment for sit-down showers. Each room with an outside wall had a column-style cast iron radiator.

The bedroom radiator sat low and humble—painted discreet grey—under the window next to their bed. Jonas left a narrow space between the bed and wall so he could get out easily on his side of the bed. The radiator was her favorite thing in the apartment, after the desk he built. She discovered she could curl one of her feet along the inside rim of the radiator's rounded chambers enabling her to push her body closer to Jonas's during sex. When she was on the bottom, her left foot well positioned could leverage her body higher; when she was on her side facing him, her right foot helped steady her. She doubted the engineers who designed the cast iron hearths imagined their full functionality. She never told Jonas the radiator helped them have better sex.

Annie found inexpensive Indian bedspreads and made curtains for the living room and bedroom windows.

"I like them, Annie. Good job."

She didn't know if he meant that. She was sure he preferred the spare look.

Annie worked half-days in the university's entomology department on the other side of Bascom Hill, at the head of the agricultural side of campus. The dairy store managed by graduate students was next door. She could get ice cream every day for lunch for twenty-five cents. She enjoyed the long walks to campus from Pickney Street. Living with Jonas that winter, spring, and summer was the happiest time of her life. She had thought very little about Flora's list since she met Jonas. She wondered if it was easier to process the bad things with a confidante now.

They were vigilant about suiting up before sex. Annie inserted the diaphragm lined with spermicide every time, and Jonas gloved his penis in a condom. She had missed two periods. She didn't tell Jonas she was going back to the gynecologist.

The doctor was visiting France with the duckbill cranking her wide open. "From the look of it, you're pregnant, Annie. You may be having a tubal pregnancy, an ectopic pregnancy." He delivered the news peering up through her spread legs. He explained a fertilized egg can attach in the fallopian tube, not the uterus. He would do a test; it would take a couple of days for the results.

"What happens in an ectopic pregnancy?" she asked, trying to pretend this was a normal conversation despite the fact that her medium-sized vaginal O was staring him in the face with a shocked expression.

"We might be looking at surgery, but let's wait to see what the tests say. I think you should start taking vitamins in case you're pregnant, and it's not an ectopic pregnancy. Ok, we're done here. You can put your clothes back on." The duck bill was back on the tray.

It felt like a long walk to Pickney Street. Jonas told her weeks ago he would never bring a baby into the world because the world was too fucked up. She'd been more optimistic; she was willing to take the risk. Or maybe she was more selfish. She wanted to be a mother someday. But they agreed they were too young to have a baby, and they were not worried. His sperm would have to be like Attila the Hun to get through their killing field—the condom, the diaphragm, the toxic jelly.

Jonas was making scrambled eggs in the large frying pan, cutting in small pieces of leftover potatoes and tomatoes, when she told him. He reacted like he always did to difficult news—a momentary surprised expression quickly covered with outward calm. They talked quietly while they ate, and he did the dishes after dinner, processing the news while Annie sought solace in a hot bath.

That evening they walked like a team on a mission to the library to read about ectopic pregnancies and abortions. Annie felt sick to her stomach reading about the procedures. How would she ever come up with a pep talk to get her countries through this? Maybe it was pregnancy making her nauseous. There was no talk of marriage. This did not trouble Annie because she didn't think they were ready for marriage though Jonas made a joke the week before when he asked if she would still wear lace underwear when they were married. She assured him she would.

The doctor called her at home. The report was negative. Annie and Jonas celebrated with sundaes at the ice cream shop on State Street. She ordered two scoops—dark chocolate plus black cherry—with extra hot fudge, whipped cream, nuts, and a cherry. Jonas ordered two scoops of butter pecan—with hot fudge, whipped cream, nuts, and a cherry. He gave his cherry to Annie.

They ran into a friend at the ice cream shop who wanted to know why they were so happy. They didn't tell him. But Annie was not as happy as Jonas. She wanted to finish school, and they didn't have any money to have a baby, but she wanted to have a baby with Jonas. She was harboring a growing fear he would not stay with her or stand by her.

⎯⎯⎯ ◦ ⎯⎯⎯

Annie and Jonas stretched out on two large grey concrete blocks in the park by Lake Monona, side by side. It was late spring and a warm Sunday morning. They watched the clouds swirling, holding hands across their stone beds.

She'd just reread *Romeo and Juliet* in Shakespeare class. The sleeping potion Juliet took made her look dead when Romeo found her on her stone block. In his grief, he drank poison because he didn't want to live without her. When she woke from her stupor, he was dead. So she stabbed herself in the heart, not wanting to live without him. Their bodies lay on side-by-side stone blocks.

Professor Smith reminded the class that Romeo and Juliet were teenagers—Shakespeare might not have written the same story if they had been adult lovers. What would she do if she woke up and Jonas was dead in their bed? Would she kill herself? She was sure she would not, but maybe she would later if she couldn't cope without him.

The clouds looked like white caps on ocean waves crashing above them. She had a dream last week she was chained to a rock and vultures were circling, waiting to feed on her. She woke sweating, thinking it was a dream about vulnerability, her flesh parts too open to hurt.

"A storm is rolling in," Jonas said, pressing her hand in their safe bridge across the blocks. They were resting—not comfortably because the stone was not comfortable—but they were not ready to leave their stones yet.

What would it be like if lightning struck them right then—if they died together? Would they be buried side by side? Her family would claim her body, his family would claim his. They would be separated, and there would be nothing they could do about it. She would rather be buried next to him, with a fine quote they both liked etched on an arching, conjoining headstone. Or be cremated and their ashes sprinkled in a rock garden near one of the lakes. But who would bury them, who would find them a final resting place? She turned her head so Jonas would not see her free right hand swipe away the tears that were starting. His eyes were fixed on the whitecaps above them. He asked her last week if she would bury him in his favorite blue work shirt with the ivy he had drawn on the pocket—a vine with green leaves drawn with permanent marker. She said she would. The air felt like a light comforter on their bodies. She was wearing a blue t-shirt, tan shorts, and brown sandals. Her dark hair spilled over the back of her cement block. He was wearing his blue work shirt with the ivy vine on the pocket, tan corduroys, and work boots.

"I feel married to you, Jonas," she said without thinking, feeling the energy surging between their joined hands.

"Yes."

She smiled. She loved the word, yes.

* * *

Their first summer together they signed up for sailing lessons at the university's marina on Lake Mendota. She wanted to see what was beyond the point where the land shaped like a loaf of bread ended and get out on the lake where she could sail topless and wouldn't get a tan line. Jonas never said why he wanted to sail, but she figured it was his Norwegian heritage.

They attended orientation together. The instructor handed out a booklet about the program. The boats for beginners were one-sail, two hundred and fifty pounds, white with blue trim. Larger two-sail boats were for more advanced sailors. He enumerated the safety rules—wear life jackets, watch the red flag which would be raised to call you back when the weather was getting too dangerous to sail, and who would come rescue you if you got stuck out in the lake without wind. Before you could take a boat out, you had to pass a written test on the rules and a sailing test with an instructor.

Annie spent several lessons learning how to tie knots, figuring out where the wind was coming from, and poring over pictures showing tacking patterns. The tacking pictures reminded her of geometry theorems—this did not bode well. She tried to visualize how ducking under a fast-swinging mast and re-securing the sail was so important that it was going to be on the final test. Surely there was an easier way to sail than tacking—the importance of the zigzag concept did not make sense. And what was that about heading directly for the pier and suddenly turning the sail to avoid ramming the pier, with the ducks and students watching?

While Annie was trying to process information about wind patterns, Jonas passed the written test, passed the beginner's sailing test, and was in intermediate sailing, crewing in two sailboat races. It was the Norseman in his bloodline, she concluded. He liked rough winds and could envision tacking triangles getting him somewhere. She had Russian Jews in her bloodline—who knew what they were up to when his relatives were sailing to America from Norway? Most of hers must have been hunkering down in eastern European ghettoes, clueless to the telltale ribbons signaling changes in airflow.

<hr />

It was weeks later, with clouds menacing in a charcoal sky, when she realized she was in love with Jonas, and this was always going to be so. She had moved her chair from their shared desk to the living room's expanse of windows to look out at the green carpet of tree leaves below and the ominous clouds above. Her legs rested on the radiator. They had been living in the new apartment since January. In this quiet moment, she realized what Jonas meant to her, and she was never going to be the same.

He came home late afternoon, shivering from a wild sail in the lake, clothes wet from the boat's capsizing. He was crewing in his first advanced sailing race. She started a hot bath while he peeled off his clothes, balancing them on the ledge of the sink. Annie sat on the toilet seat to keep him company, hugging her legs to her chest, admiring his body.

He stretched out in the hot water, submerged to his head. The boat had heeled too far in the choppy waves and wind changes, dipping the sails in the water and throwing the crew out of the boat. The three of them managed to climb back in and right the boat, with Jonas standing on the keel. The marina ran the red flag up the flagpole, ending the race due to rough winds.

He was in a happy mood soaking in the tub. When he stood to wipe off, he wrapped his blue towel around his waist and stepped to the rug, reaching his hand out to hers. He pulled her to the bedroom and they had sex—his skin damp from the bath—while she used the keel of her radiator to push closer to him and their bodies heeled together.

She couldn't know that day the fatefulness of her predicament. Once she became aware of the depths of her feelings, Jonas seemed to become aware too. And he started to pull away over weeks—in little ways at first, as if he was trying to adjust the sails between them. As he pulled on a cord here or there, she started to lose her balance. Her past began to haunt her and old dreams stirred. Wars in Hitler's Germany, trains assaulting her in the night. She cried out in her sleep, and Jonas would wake her from frightful places. She wished she could go backward in time, regain equilibrium. She tried to focus on his flaws, but his flaws didn't matter—she didn't expect perfection. She didn't want perfection. She had crossed over and there was nothing she could do but hope he would not hate her for loving him. In the weeks that followed, she could not contain her outbursts and tears—about Jonas, school, what they would do when their lease was up. He left the apartment when she was upset, thinking she needed time to herself. When he left, she grew more disconsolate, pacing the floor, writing notes in her journal, and crying.

He returned to red-rimmed eyes and wet tissues stacked in the wastepaper basket. He wished he had not come home. He planned trips in his notebook—to France, Spain, islands south of India. And he played songs about the road—Dylan's low scratchy voice chanting prophetically about lone travelers who leave their lovers. His backpack was parked ominously near the front door. In it he kept a dark green wool turtleneck sweater, a map of France, and a small notebook and pen. That was all he would need in his next life, without Annie.

Annie rationalized it didn't make sense to try to have a love relationship when there was a war on. Why was she even trying? She felt guilty when she thought about the brothers and sisters, husbands and wives, and mothers and fathers suffering. She felt guilty women were not being drafted while so many men were being killed and maimed in a war they didn't understand. The television news flooded the airwaves with scenes of young men and women protesting the war, dragged to police vans, blood streaming from their heads, eyes, arms, and hands. Police billy clubs pummeled and boots kicked protesters in flimsy tie-dyed shirts and sandals. Tear gas shrouded the nation. Napalm shrouded Vietnam. Tear gas and napalm were new cloud formations in a war world.

But guilt was only useful if it got someone to take action, and what actions could Annie take? She tried to push the guilt out of her mind, shaving her legs smooth before she wrapped her limbs around Jonas, rolling with him in fluids and soft panting, while the demonstrators marched across the nation like military troops in tie-dyed uniforms. Music blasted harsh and jarring—guitars screeching like incoming bombs, drums beating rapid gunfire, howling lyrics—to help their generation cry out warnings. There were quieter messages too—folk songs with truth-saying to expose the underbelly of the war. Parents couldn't decide whether to pack their sons off to Canada or advise them to be a man and serve their country like Jonas's father when Jonas told him he was applying to be a conscientious objector at nineteen because he couldn't kill anyone. At the very time their generation was trying to deal with their biological imperative—find a mate, or two or three and try to build a life and contribute to your community—there was no ignoring the larger reality: it was war time in Vietnam and in the streets at home.

Jonas started to help with draft counseling in Madison, working with a group of young men trying to evade the draft. There were counterculture brochures that offered a menu of ways to get a medical waiver: ruptured spleen, poor eyesight, flat feet, asthma, allergies to bee stings, eat two dozen eggs the night before your physical exam so your albumin count would be high, arrive at the draft board in diapers or yell at the wall to demonstrate your mental instability for service. Whatever you could do for a medical waiver.

Annie blamed the war for sucking the life out of her relationship with Jonas. She felt like a reporter of skirmishes on their personal battlefield. A month earlier, Jonas's father sent him a one-sentence note from northern Wisconsin: 'When are you going to be a man and join the Army?' Earlier that week, the police stopped Annie and Jonas on their nightly bicycle ride: "Where are you going, folks? We need to see your ID. Do you have four dollars on you?"

Jonas and Annie fished in their pockets for money. The police were arresting people in the student neighborhoods who did not have four dollars on them under a vagrancy law no one but the police seemed to know about. And there was the latest warning posted on the co-op grocery bulletin board on Mifflin Street—high school boys would be coming to town to rape the hippie women. The local police put the word out—they would not intervene.

Annie blamed Vietnam for Jonas's growing anger. She was sure there could be no loving between them through anger. But Jonas said it wasn't the war. "There's no chemistry anymore, Annie," he said flatly one afternoon.

She lurched as if a train locomotive had smashed her caboose heart. She tried not to let on. She wanted to protest, "You're wrong, you're wrong!" Maybe he was in denial because he was depressed, and it was her job to break through the barbed-wire fences he was building. But she was depressed too. She was crying so much, at nothing, at everything. Her antelope and lion were stuck in quicksand, desperate to get free. Jonas was not going to help her. He was as lost as she was. They were lost separately, even as they wrapped their legs around each other and rolled in their fluids, looking for respite, for a while yet.

That was when Charles came to Madison. Comfortable and familiar, the charismatic medical student Annie met a year ago in Martha's Vineyard. Annie was hoping Jonas would be jealous when he learned about Annie and Charles, but she didn't want to tell Jonas about that, not yet. Charles arrived with his girlfriend, Eva, to take a summer six-week course at the university.

The four had their first dinner at a Chinese restaurant, sharing dishes on a Lazy Susan in the center of the table—beef and broccoli, sweet and sour shrimp, orange chicken, and lemon chicken. Eva poured the tea, and Charles regaled them with stories about dissecting cadavers in school and how he met Eva, his brilliant classmate.

"It was love at first sight—I fell in love with her long red hair and sexy one leg," he said loudly enough for the table next to them to hear.

After that proclamation, Charles whispered to Jonas, knowing Eva and Annie could hear, "You should stick with Annie. She's going to do well in life," implying he knew a lot about Annie.

Jonas nodded though Annie knew he would be put off by this invasive advice.

Charles put his arm around Eva's small shoulder, sharing with the table, "You can't believe what a great fuck Eva is, with one leg."

Annie and Jonas exchanged glances of discomfort and looked to Eva to see how she was reacting. Eva did not seem embarrassed. Annie was thinking Eva was too smart for Charles. But maybe she was so relieved to have a boyfriend she was willing to put up with his boorishness. Was he putting this on for them, for Annie?

By dessert, the conversation turned to what summers in Madison were like—the weather, the lakes, the sailing.

"Would you like to go sailing with me tomorrow?" Jonas asked Eva. He liked her quiet demeanor.

"I'd love that."

The four agreed to meet on the pier by the student union at noon.

Dinner concluded with fortune cookies. Jonas got, 'A new voyage will fill your life with untold memories.' Annie, 'Land is always on the mind of a flying bird.' Eva, 'Meeting adversity well is the source of your strength.' And Charles, 'People are naturally attracted to you.' They laughed at the synchronicity of their fortunes.

The cold lake water was moving with mild chop and moderate wind. Jonas helped four-foot, eight-inch Eva into an orange life jacket that engulfed her small frame. Jonas and Charles conferred over where it was best for her to sit in the boat, and she entrusted her crutches to Charles and Annie who would be waiting on the pier. Not that they had a choice. Jonas didn't invite Charles and Annie to go along.

Eva tucked her hair under a wide-brimmed straw sunhat. A thin crimson ribbon held her hat on. She was concerned about getting too much sun. Her skin was smooth like pale, bleached china.

Jonas pulled the tether rope into the boat. Charles saluted Jonas at the helm, "Godspeed, captain." Then the brisk northwest wind spiraled quickly up the invisible inside track of the single fluttering white sail, pulling Jonas and Eva through the water toward French Bread Point. Before long, the boat disappeared.

Charles paced nervously along the pier. "How long do you think they'll be gone? Does Jonas know what to do if the winds come up high?"

"It's great sailing weather—steady winds today. Jonas is a really good sailor," Annie assured him. "He has Norwegian bloodlines. Can Eva swim?"

"She can do any damn thing." He seemed insulted Annie would ask. Then he turned his attention from the lake to look closely at Annie. "It's been a long time. You look good, babe. How are you and Jonas doing?"

"Honestly, we're having problems. I don't know if it's the war and the craziness or what." Her words trailed off.

"I'm sorry. He seems like a nice guy, but different."

"He's quiet. That's one of the things I like about him."

"I thought you were engaged to an Army guy in Vietnam?"

"Yep—ended it last December when Jonas and I decided to live together—Jonas was my neighbor." She was hoping Charles would offer her advice about Jonas.

Instead, he moved to another topic. "Did I ever tell you I fucked my sister for a few years before we went to college?"

"What?" Annie was unable to cover her surprise. "Are you kidding?"

Charles seemed pleased to have Annie's full attention. "It was something we both wanted—she's my twin sister—we think alike."

He could not be telling the truth. He could be outrageous, for attention. "Isn't that incest?"

"It isn't incest if we both wanted to do it. We talked about it—we both wanted to have sex but didn't want to have to worry about the girlfriend/boyfriend thing in high school."

TEN BEFORE THIRTY • 127

"Didn't your parents find out? Did your sister have some psychological problems to deal with after that?"

"We hid it from our parents. They were never home. They traveled a lot and left us to fend for ourselves. She's fine. She's studying to be a psychiatrist now."

This seemed so normal to him. She wondered if Eva was sharing shocking stories with Jonas, and if she was, what he was thinking. She decided to change the subject. "Well, what about you? How's medical school?"

"Great. I was lucky to meet Eva. She helps me with all my classes. I love her so much." He played with the crutches lying next to them on the pier with his feet.

Annie figured Eva was the brains of the operation. Charles would never make it without her. He would probably drop her when he finished school because he'd meet some other woman.

"What are you doing for work these days?" he asked.

"Working for an entomology professor, typing pages of insect names in Latin. Good thing I took four years of Latin in high school. I'm the perfect person to type scientific names and think about bugs," she chuckled. "And I don't have to talk to anyone."

"Good for you—some people wouldn't like to be describing insects all day. You never struck me as the squeamish type. I remember you cleaning the bluefish."

She smiled, remembering what he looked like naked. Tall and handsome, disarming without clothes—his game-playing stopped when he was naked. "What courses are you taking here? Don't med students take the summer off?"

"We have the summer off, but the school advises us to strengthen our resumes—think ahead to what we might need for our residency. Eva and I thought it would be good to take courses we could both use—so we're doing a course in histology."

"Like microbiology?"

"Not really. Microbiology deals with microorganisms—histology deals with tissues. In school, we studied the big structures in anatomy—the ones you don't need a microscope for. This summer, we're looking at the tissues you need a microscope for—muscle and nervous tissue. I don't know what I'm going to specialize in yet, but this seems like a good area to get stronger in, especially if I end up going into cancer. Eva wants to be a pathologist. How come you didn't keep going on in science—you were working on the botany book last summer, right?"

"Yep, but I couldn't stand killing animals for research, and that's what it looked like I would have to do if I went on. So, I decided to work on a master's degree in English—hoping to get into the doctoral program. I'm almost done—the master's exam is in six weeks."

He nodded. "A lot has happened in a year for both of us. You're smart, Annie. You're going to be fine with or without Jonas."

She didn't think she'd be fine but didn't want to say that, so she nodded like she was agreeing.

He'd been keeping his eyes on the horizon while they talked, scanning the lake for the returning sailboat. Annie felt comfortable with him. She was glad he was not coming on to her. He seemed more settled than last summer. "Don't worry about them—it will be a while yet."

"Been meaning to ask, is this the lake where Otis Redding died?"

"No—his plane crashed in the lake on the other side of the Capitol—Monona—1967." She played "Dock of the Bay" all the time during her last months at college and last summer at Martha's Vineyard. She wondered if he remembered her playing that song while they were having sex.

She was in her dorm getting ready to leave for Mexico that December with Duncan when she heard the news: the plane sank nearly fifty feet into thirty-four-degree lake water in Madison. They kept hearing news reports on the radio while they were driving south. And just a few months later, when she was deciding where to go for graduate school, she kept thinking about the Madison lakes, feeling drawn there.

"I'm going to close my eyes for a few minutes." She was tired and worried about Jonas.

"I'll stretch out too." He laid next to Annie on the pier. There was a comfortable, welcome silence between them.

She dozed off until she heard Charles stirring.

"I think I see them."

She sat up—the sailboat was skimming in quickly in the good winds. Charles and Annie stood side by side, old lovers watching the boat get closer, waving to their new lovers. They could see the crimson ribbon on Eva's sun hat. Eva was waving back and talking with her hands animatedly to Jonas as they neared the pier. Annie wondered what they had been talking about.

Jonas lined the boat up next to the pier and threw the rope to Charles to tether it to the post. Then Charles reached his long arms into the boat to scoop up Eva, setting her on his right hip like a child. He carried her several feet to her crutches lying on the pier.

"Thanks for taking me out, Jonas. It was such a treat." Eva looked back to Jonas from her holster on Charles's hip. She looked white and angelic, smiling broadly.

"Good sail," he answered in his spare style.

As they left the pier, Jonas and Charles talked about hitting the bars that night. Eva was too tired to go out. No one invited Annie.

The next day, Jonas told Annie he was planning to hang out with Charles that evening. This buddy thing was not what Annie imagined when Charles came to town.

Jonas could see that Annie was upset but didn't know why. "Why are you upset?" he asked in exasperation, with his hands on his hips.

Annie could not believe how clueless he could be. "He used to be my lover!" she blurted out.

"What?" his eyes widened. "When did that happen?"

"Cape Cod. He was friends with Theodora and came to visit." She could still picture him ambling into the kitchen, watching her prepare the bluefish for the dinner party that night. He lined up his tall body behind her, wrapped his right arm around her waist and nuzzled his head against her neck. "I'm an incredible lover, Annie. You should give me a try. Let's do it."

His bravado was surprisingly inviting. She'd left Meyer weeks ago, unsure what to do about her feelings for him. She wasn't going to marry Duncan. Why not have sex with Charles? So she wrapped the fish in foil, placed it on the top shelf of the refrigerator to marinate, and let Charles lead her upstairs to her bedroom. When the sex was over, she concluded it was warm but unexceptional—he was a glib penis with a big ego. They'd had a good conversation about whether he would be a good doctor. He assured her he knew a lot about body parts, especially women's. They talked about their futures after dinner and took a long walk through Edgartown. She told him it was one of the first ports for the whaling industry in the

1800s—the white clapboard mansions were built by sea captains for their families. The next time they had sex, Otis was singing to them from the dock of the bay. The next day Charles returned to Boston.

Annie was satisfied she shocked Jonas. But learning of their liaison didn't have the effect she was hoping for. Jonas and Annie were slowly unbuckling at the hip no matter what.

Charles and Eva left town in early August when Annie was in the middle of her master's exam, trying not to sink her academic dreams. Charles whispered in her ear when he was leaving, 'Don't worry, babe, you'll be fine.'

Annie didn't think she would be fine but was glad he had something special to whisper to her. Jonas didn't ask what Charles said.

That next week Jonas and Annie met two friends for a late dinner. Afterward, they walked by the lake because it was too hot to go home yet. "Nice night for a swim," Jonas said.

It was nearly midnight—no one around. They peeled off their clothes, piled them on the small beach by the lake, and made a dash for the water. Annie hit the water first, Jonas right behind her. She had never swum in the lake at night. The water was cold and exhilarating. They waded out until the water was up to their shoulders. Jonas pulled Annie close with her legs tucked around his waist. He wanted to have sex. She wanted to swim, but he was inside her before she could say anything. She wondered how he could get hard in cold water and whether the water would be squishing inside her as they got their rhythm going. Her eyes were closed in the dark, and when she opened them, there was a yellow highway of light beaming across the water. Jonas pulled out of her and held her close while a bass voice shouted staccato-like across the water.

"Come. Out. Of. The. Water. Come. Out. Of. The. Water."

"It's the cops, the damn cops," Jonas said angrily.

The two couples who had been several feet from one another since they splashed into the lake moved into the lane of light, then breaststroked their way back to shore like a phalanx, feet walking the sandy bottom. Two burly policemen aimed large flashlights at them, scanning up and down their bodies like they were directing airplanes to a landing strip. Annie wondered if they would be billy-clubbed and arrested, naked.

"Get dressed," the officers blared in unison.

Annie ran to her pile of clothes and pulled her t-shirt on first to cover as much of her body as she could, then pulled on her shorts. She rolled her bra and panties into her hands because she thought it would take too long to put them on. She wished she had a towel because her clothes immediately stuck to her wet body.

The four were dressed and standing in a line in front of the officers.

"Who are you, and what are you doing here?" The officers trained their flashlights on their faces.

"Students," Jonas said. "We wanted to take a short night swim."

Annie wondered if she should give a fake name if they asked for a name.

"The park is closed. Can't you college people read the sign here?"

The four of them said nothing.

Then it was police slow-talk-like-they-are-dummies-time again. "You. Need. To. Leave. Right. Now," accompanied by flashlights lighting up their bodies.

Jonas turned first to leave, and the three quickly followed while the officers lit their fleeing backs. The couples said awkward goodbyes when they reached the street.

Back at their hot penthouse, Jonas was quiet while he showered the lake off his body. It was her turn next. She was thinking about algae and other lake organisms in her vagina, wondering whether any sperm that might have swum out of him could live in the lake temperature. She didn't think he finished anyway. But she wasn't sure and wasn't going to ask him.

There were two options to complete the master's degree: after two semesters of courses, complete a thesis paper, or take a cumulative exam. Annie chose the exam because she thought it would be faster. It never occurred to her she might demonstrate her skills better in the thesis option.

In April, the English department provided instructions for the exam. It would be four hours long, given once in early August. Students should prepare by reading sixty titles that covered all genres of literature on the list in the packet of instructions. Annie scanned down the list with disappointment—she had read only ten of them. She imagined she should prepare for a 'Name That Tune' exercise—match author to title to genre to plot. Memory was not her strong suit—she was best at analyzing and synthesizing.

What she hadn't figured on when she chose the exam option was her mental state. Her tumultuous relationship with Jonas, rising death toll in Vietnam, fighting in the streets between the police and students, race wars, women's movement, worries about getting pregnant, worries about paying rent. Nothing was stable—why was she reading worthless books, preparing her for nothing? She did her best over the summer to read and take notes, hoping to recall what she was reading through the thickening fog of distractions. Jonas often found her huddled on their bed when he returned from work, reading and tearful.

"I can't remember what I'm reading anymore. I hate this."

He didn't know how to help.

She recognized her predicament. Flora was probably shaking her head on the other side, wondering if her great-granddaughter was going down for the count. What an ignoble end, going down reading sixty of literature's best works when so many others were being pummeled with billy clubs and tear-gassed into submission.

Annie walked resolutely up Bascom Hill to the large classroom that August morning to face the exam. She felt defeated before she picked up her pen. She barely slept the last few nights, passing the hours reading and crying quietly on the living room couch, while Jonas slept a few feet away in their bed. They had not had sex in weeks. She figured it was her fault. How attractive did she look with puffy eyes and damp tissues stacked next to her hips, books piled around their mattress on the floor. She'd only gotten through thirty-eight titles. When she opened the test pages, she realized she was right—it was 'Name That Tune', a memory test. Her odds were not good.

A week after the exam, she received the English department letter explaining their four types of recommendations: level one was passing with an offer to enter the PhD in English program with full tuition coverage and a teaching assistant position; level two was a recommendation to enter the PhD program with no financial assistance; level three was a recommendation to complete the master's degree with no recommendation to enter the PhD program though continuing was permissible; and level four was no approval to complete the degree. Annie's performance qualified her for level three. She felt lucky to pass, given her state of mind. When people asked how she had done, she said she finished her degree, but it was not a pretty finish.

A week after the exam, Annie flew to Texas to visit her mother and sister. Her birthday was coming, and she wanted a break from Jonas. Their apartment lease was up mid-September—they needed to think about next steps.

Each day the thermometer outside her mother's apartment door exceeded one hundred degrees. Annie slept in the spare twin bed in Hannah's room. Hannah was living at home after college while she worked to save money to get her own place. Annie did not share with the family what her life was like with Jonas. They didn't know she was living with a man. She did share her mediocre performance on the master's exam. They understood the crossroad Annie was at, done with school and trying to figure out what to do next.

"You're too thin," Mother remarked the first day Annie was home.

"I like to be thin." She did not tell them she lost her appetite because she was depressed.

They celebrated Annie's birthday a few days later at a restaurant. The dinner special was roast beef, peas with onions that resembled eye lenses, and tomatoes that still had their roots attached. Annie separated the roots on her plate, wondering why the restaurant didn't remove the roots. She separated the eye lenses and slid them into a corral she made with a pea fence on the side of her plate. She didn't like peas. Dessert was chocolate cake with thick fudge frosting. Cold water killed the over-taste. This was the biggest meal Annie had eaten for weeks. She was thankful she was done with reading and crying.

After dinner and back at home, Annie picked up her A-Marine Band harmonica from the bookshelf in the bedroom and started to play, "Old MacDonald Had a Farm," toot, toot, toot, toot, toot.

"Be quiet, Annie. I'm not feeling well," Hannah snapped at her.

"Are you sick?"

"It's the weather—it's too hot outside."

"Hannah, it's cold in the apartment from the air conditioning." Toot, toot, toot, toot, toot.

"I need to sleep—be quiet!"

Annie responded by playing "Row, Row Your Boat."

Hannah clutched her head with both hands. "I have a terrible headache. Stop making noise, Annie. I mean it!"

"This isn't noise," Annie protested. "This is music. Row, row, row your boat . . ."

Hannah pulled the blanket over her head.

"Why don't you get earplugs?" Annie kept playing more tunes.

"Shut up, just shut up."

Annie smiled and moved to her next tune. "It's 'Taps.' I'm playing 'Taps' for you." Then she sang the tune in case Hannah didn't recognize it.

Hannah yelled, "Shut up," and held her head in pain.

Annie threw the harmonica on the bed, picked up her bathing suit, and marched in her best twelve-inch band high-step to the bathroom to change clothes. Then she marched out of the bathroom wearing her one-piece sapphire-blue suit humming a rendition of "On Wisconsin," toot, toot, toot, toot, toot . . .

It was traditional for Annie to take a birthday swim. It happened every August, though she never planned the swims. Tonight the half-moon was just a sliver cupping the apartment roof when Annie got to the pool. The June bugs were waiting. If she stepped on any, their thick red-brown beetle bodies would deflate on the concrete and cling to her feet, so she tried to avoid them. It was still ninety degrees though it was well after nine. She was thinking that Dylan Thomas had written a poem on his thirtieth birthday as she splashed down the four curved steps of the pool into the turquoise water, remembering his opening line, *It was my thirtieth year to heaven* and the line, *My birthday began with the water.* Annie's water was bathtub warm. The lights surrounding the pool were blinking like eyes. During the day, she had walked to the shopping center, seven miles round-trip. Her body felt stiff. She sat for a bit on the bottom rounded step up to her neck, muscles soaking in the warmth of the water.

TEN BEFORE THIRTY • 135

Then it was lap time. She started to count laps as she swam across the large pool back and forth. She lost track after twenty-five. She swam mostly a slow, steady breaststroke, switching to a trudgen crawl, a side-stroke, or frog-kick on her back every few laps. She didn't like to splash in the water, so the regular crawl with a flutter kick was out. She liked side kicks under the water and smooth steady strokes. She wanted to be one with the water. She worked on her style each lap, trying to dip her moving arms into the water smoothly, breathe evenly, and kick under the water for strength but no splash.

At the end of her swim, she did seal dives and treaded water in the deep end. Finally, acrobatics—sculling on her back with knees pulled to her chest, raising her right leg like an erect penis with a balletic pointed toe. And raising both legs, toes pointed, sculling hard to hold her body steady. Newly twenty-three, Annie stood on her head on the pool's bottom, lifting her legs triumphantly and pointing her toes, legs opening to a shapely Y, closing to the prayer-position with pointed toes. She imagined centuries were passing inside her gait upside-down, and she could walk miles in the water.

While she'd been swimming laps, she was thinking—that warm water like this must feel like amniotic fluid to a fetus, what the ideal proportion should be between frosting and cake, how lucky she was to have a pool to herself, about skinny dipping and sex in the lake with Jonas, whether her dad and Flora could see her from the other side and were wishing her a happy birthday, and whether it mattered to anyone if bad things happened to her. She wondered if she would be alive next August and if she would still be living with Jonas.

He called earlier to wish her a happy birthday. His low voice was comforting but far away. "You've been gone too long, Annie."

What did that mean? There were bubbles in the conversation that seemed to hold something important for them, that they were afraid to break, aware of a tension, but not knowing if it was a good or bad tension. And what if the skin of those bubbles shrunk so thin they gave way—what then? So they shared several silence bubbles between short bursts of words catching each other up—she said she was going to dinner with the family, and she walked the dog, and he couldn't walk on the hot pavement, so they had to jump from lawn to lawn. He said he was going sailing, and she was gone too long. By the end of the call, she was pretty sure their silence bubbles were not good bubbles. How could they be? Tears had been starting in Annie's eyes all day, and they were not from sweating in the heat.

Mother had been reminding Annie that today was their day. Mother celebrated every birthday with Annie—it could never be Annie's birthday alone. No doubt, Annie had been sitting uncomfortably low in her mother's birth canal, waiting impatiently to get out. Didn't the doctor cut the cord to give them both their lives back? That separation was not part of her mother's memory, but Annie celebrated the birthday separation.

Annie had little to say to her mother and Jonas earlier. So she plunged alone through the warm pool for more than an hour that evening. The water coated her skin in slime from the oil of earlier swimmers. When she finally emerged from the pool exhausted, mindful to avoid the June bugs loitering on the cement walkway back to the apartment, she imagined the slime would not wash off as long as those microscopic remnants of skin remained. So there would be some time when she would carry the slime with her, waiting for the cells to slough off—and that seemed like a good thing.

It was quiet in the cold apartment. Hannah had gone to sleep, or perhaps she was pretending to be asleep when Annie came through the room to head to the bathroom to take a shower and wash the chlorine out of her bathing suit. She was glad to climb into the twin bed and stretch out. She went to sleep with Jonas on her mind. Did he miss her? Why did he say she was gone too long?

<hr />

She returned to Madison, nervous to see him. She took a taxi from the airport. He greeted her at the door, eyes deep blue, handsome and tan from sailing. He hugged her like he was glad to see her. She was glad to see him. She'd been writing him long letters she would never send. He was energized and agitated. "You've been gone too long. We need to leave town."

"Why?"

"It's time to take a trip. There's a bus at three-thirty. We have a few hours to get ready."

He was giving off that Zen intonation when something has to get done, but Annie isn't supposed to ask questions. She's supposed to know—or better yet—she's supposed to be. This was not one of the games Annie was good at.

"Where to?"

"North. Hudson Bay." He mapped out the trip to Canada while Annie was in Texas, eleven-hundred miles—twenty hours of travel.

"How do we get there? What about money?" Her Texas bags weren't even unpacked. "What do I need to take?" Was he seriously wanting to leave the same day she returned from Texas? Maybe he was joking.

"Bus and train. I have money. We can share my sleeping bag. We'll camp and do hotels. We don't need that much. We'll just be gone over the weekend."

Annie told herself to say yes, not be negative. They would be to-gether—that was all she wanted. So she threw clean clothes and toiletries into her backpack. The sleeping bag was already rolled tightly in its own bag, tied underneath his backpack.

When they headed out a few hours later, she was wearing open-toed sandals with no socks, jeans, and a t-shirt. He wore hiking boots, socks, and carried a sweater. It was so hot in Madison, Annie imagined it would be warm, even far north.

They walked the few blocks to the Greyhound Bus Terminal with their packs on their backs. Annie was excited to be going on a trip with him. He was smiling when they boarded the bus. They'd be going through Green Bay, and then Escanaba, he explained, looking at the map. He said she looked good. He held her hand.

It was dark hours later on the bus when Annie, exhausted from the early morning flight from Texas, rested her head in Jonas's lap. She was home. Wherever he was, that was home. She felt happy for the first time in weeks, resting on his lap while he stroked her hair. She thought about the day they'd stretched out on the stone blocks next to the lake and felt married. She felt that way again.

The bus pulled into Escanaba's small station which was only a desk with a few wrinkled brochures and two bathrooms—men's and women's—inside an old Victorian house. Annie went to pee. The bathroom looked like it had not been cleaned for a decade. The toilet didn't flush. Annie tried to hover above the seat—not touch it—and pee quickly. She pinched her nostrils closed to keep from vomiting from the stench.

"Is the men's bathroom as bad as the women's?" she asked Jonas when she came back to the ticket desk.

"Yep."

The bus headed to Sioux Ste Marie, then Sudbury after they crossed into Canada, then north to Cochrane. That's where the road ended. Next they'd catch the Polar Bear Express for the several-hours train ride to their destination, Moosonee. The train carried passengers along with canoes, trucks, and other cargo.

Annie wanted Jonas to tell her what he did while she was away. She hoped they would talk about how to improve things between them. He was in a pensive mood. He didn't want to talk. They closed their eyes and tried to sleep. It was an all-night-and-next-morning ride.

The train was the only way to get to Moosonee—there were no roads in. The train stopped along the way to let people off and on. People came out to signal the slow-chugging train to stop, and the train stopped to let them on. When the train plowed through lush green fields, people ran out from small cabins to wave.

Finally, the conductor called out, "Moosonee, Moosonee." Annie and Jonas collected their packs and jumped down the train's metal steps to a dirt road. They walked down the road toward the few small buildings that made up the single main street. They had read the population was less than one thousand and most were native Cree.

"Do you think we'll see moose walking up the street?" she asked Jonas.

He didn't answer her.

She'd been cold on the train, mad at herself for not realizing how far north they were going. She should have brought a jacket or sweater. Why didn't he tell her to bring practical clothes? When she complained about being cold, Jonas said they would find a place to buy whatever she needed. Sure enough, just up the dirt road was the largest building in town, the trading post. Annie bought a thick black wool sweater and socks. Jonas didn't need anything; he'd packed his green wool turtleneck sweater.

After the trading post, they found a nearby rock promontory overlooking the Moose River. It was one of the rivers that flowed into James Bay ten miles away.

"Can you believe it? We're standing at the Gateway of the Arctic," she said with excitement. They were sharing a loaf of bread and cake purchased at the trading post. Jonas smiled. That's when Annie felt something pinching her crotch. She looked around the rocky area where they were sitting to see if there were ants or a nest they might be sitting near. She didn't see anything. She kept turning away from Jonas, trying to scratch so he wouldn't notice. The itching was intense.

They planned to spend the first night at a motel across from the trading post. The next day they would head to a park to camp out. She couldn't wait to get to the motel to take a hot shower and lather her crotch with soap. The soap didn't help. She woke throughout the night to scratch what was now an incessant burning itch. Maybe she developed an allergy to something in the air or picked up an allergen on the train. She asked Jonas if he was having itching. He said no.

The next morning, they traveled by water taxi to the provincial park operated by the town. Though there was open water now, they read that in a couple of months, all the water around the islands would be frozen. Then heavy trucks would carry people across the waterways on the ice. The park was spread across five islands in the river estuary. The shallow waters were an autumn staging area for migratory, Arctic-breeding water birds—geese and ducks especially. The guidebook indicated there would be tent sites at the park.

The boat dropped them at a bare-looking campground that provided a few tents to put a sleeping bag in. It was unseasonably cold, the boat driver said. Annie and Jonas hiked around the island and ate the bread and cheese they purchased at a café that morning. Since there would be no light at the camp, they planned to be in their sleeping bag before nightfall. They met another couple—other than the four of them, the island seemed deserted.

There was a single pump for water—cold water. At dusk, Annie snuggled close to Jonas in the sleeping bag, and before long, their bodies created a thick humidity inside the bag. Jonas didn't seem to notice. He always slept easily. Annie tried not to scratch her crotch, but she was itching so. Her head outside the bag was cold while her body was sweating inside the bag. The outside temperature was dropping hourly. She wished she'd bought a wool hat at the trading post.

It was after midnight when Annie heard footsteps and saw flickering lights. The footsteps were moving around their tent. Annie's heart thumped so loudly she was sure it would wake Jonas. They were told there were no park staff on the island. It couldn't be an animal because there was that flickering light. Jonas was sleeping soundly. She wondered if someone was coming to rob or kill them. Whoever it was, was looking around. She tried not to move or make a sound. She was desperate to break out of the restrictive sleeping bag, feeling claustrophobic, tied to Jonas, who was in no position to defend either of them as long as they were prone on the ground. And she was itching so badly.

Whoever it was, whatever it was, moved away, and she only heard bird calls in the distance for the next sleepless hours.

The next morning, they were stretching out, weary and irritable. Jonas because Annie was complaining, Annie because she hadn't slept with the itching, the cold, and the visitor to their campsite.

"Did you hear the footsteps last night?" she asked.

"No. Maybe it was an animal."

"It had a flickering light and was moving around our tent." She was sure it was not an animal.

Jonas looked doubtful. Maybe she imagined the lights. Anyway, nothing happened to them.

They washed in the water pump area not far from their tent. The other couple was at the water pump too. The woman was in her underwear, washing her short dark hair in the frigid water. A thermometer mounted on a nearby fence post was pointing to the thirty-two-degree mark. Annie was shivering. Was she supposed to wash her long hair in this freezing water? Take off her clothes? Pretend she's the warrior woman this other camper obviously was and Annie was not? And what would she do about her crotch? Did the other woman have an itching crotch?

"I'm itching so much, Jonas. I don't know what to do."

This wasn't the camping adventure he imagined. Annie was doing nothing but complain. They packed their things and headed to the shore to wait for the boat taxi driver who told them he'd be back the next morning for them. He said they were expecting an early winter—the water would ice over soon. Annie's body was shaking from cold, and she was trying not to scratch in front of the driver.

Back in the safety and warmth of the weather-beaten motel, she tried lathering up in the hot shower and used Jonas's razor to shave off her pubic hair. She could see how red and raw her skin was. She wanted to ask Jonas to examine her but was afraid to ask—he already told her what a pain she was to travel with. And they hadn't had sex for a month.

The shower helped, and she was warm. "You look like a girl without your pubic hair," he said. "Let's take a nap."

"My hair is still wet," she said, twisting her hair into a bun on top of her head and pinning it in place with a tortoise-shell clip.

"It'll be ok." He got a dry towel from the bathroom and spread it on one of the pillows.

She climbed into the motel bed, resting her head on the pillow with the towel. She was glad waning sunlight was filtering through the thin curtains. She liked to see him undress. He took his clothes off and dropped next to her. They talked about what time they would need get up to catch the train the next morning and whether to pick up food to take with them. Then he rolled on top of her, and they had quiet, comforting afternoon sex—so welcome after weeks of not touching each other.

After a short nap, they found their way to the small, mostly empty café for a light dinner. Neither of them was very hungry. They shared a bowl of thick pea soup and greasy fried cod. He drank a cup of coffee and dunked a hard roll in it. She spread butter on her roll and drank a cup of hot tea. She had never liked pea soup but didn't tell him—she didn't want to complain anymore. It was thankfully warm inside her belly. It was a short brisk walk back to the motel. The air was clean and fortifying. Annie usually did most of the talking when they walked together, which Jonas seemed to enjoy. But she was not feeling like talking, and he seemed glad for the quiet.

The next morning, they pulled their packs on their backs and walked down the wide dirt road of Moosonee to board the train heading south. They would transfer to another train headed to Toronto, then bus to the US through Detroit and on to Madison through Milwaukee. Dark-haired children escorted them on their walk, dancing around them down the worn path. As they boarded the train, Annie paused on the steps to look back at the children, wondering what their lives would be like, thinking of the harsh winds that would be coming soon and the heavy trucks driving over the ice to the islands around them. She said a quick prayer, asking God to protect the children.

142 • YANA KAZAN

Then she followed Jonas to their seats on the town side of the train so they could continue to watch the children out of their window until they were out of sight. The train blew its whistle and slowly swayed south.

⸺⸺ ◆ ⸺⸺

It was a long day and night of train rides, bus rides, and walking with their packs. Annie and Jonas were quiet when they finally climbed the four flights to their apartment. She was glad to be home—she was sore from the trip, tired from sitting, and raw from scratching.

She pulled her clothes off as soon as they opened the front door and climbed into the bathtub, holding the shower hose on her back, then aiming the shower spray at her vagina. The water didn't hurt. She felt numb. After her shower, she dressed in clean clothes and started collecting their dirty clothes and towels, filling up three pillowcases to take to the laundromat down the street. She had devised a system that worked well for laundry—balancing pillowcases filled with laundry on her bicycle seat and walking the load to the laundromat.

She was searching the apartment for coins for the laundromat when she noticed the cigarette butt in the wastepaper basket next to their bed. Small. White. Sickening. It was garbage, but it wasn't her garbage. Jonas didn't smoke, and neither did Annie. No one was in their apartment while they were away, so the cigarette butt must have been there before they left for Canada. A butterfly was taking flight in her heart. She had an inkling of what Jonas may have meant by her being gone too long.

She watched the laundry swirl in the soapy froth of three washing machines. She'd brought a book to read, but the words were swimming on the page. She was thinking about the cigarette butt, what she would say, what he would say. The washing machine bells were tolling for Annie. She loaded up three dryers and listened to the clothes of Texas and Moosonee thumping loudly, thrown around the metal tubs shot with hot air until their clothes and towels quieted with dryness. She had ninety more minutes to think about the sickening evidence in the wastepaper basket.

She packed up the pillowcases and arranged them on the bicycle seat, leading her steed back to the apartment, feeling the heat from the pillowcases warming her belly as she leaned into their warmth. Up and down the four floors to their apartment three times because she could only carry one heavy pillowcase at a time. Jonas had gone out after they returned home, and he was home now. They were making dinner when she asked, "Whose cigarette butt is in the wastepaper basket next to our bed?"

His deep blue-pool eyes looked startled. The seconds were passing and he wasn't saying anything. Annie's butterfly was fluttering ominously in her heart.

She asked again, "Whose cigarette butt is in our wastepaper basket?"

"Mary was here."

"When I was in Texas?"

"Yes."

"Did you have sex with Mary in our bed?" she asked though she knew the answer. The butterfly morphed into a starling, beating rapidly, almost out of control in her heart chamber.

"Yes." He was not defending himself.

Annie never would have known if he'd thrown away the cigarette butt. Maybe he wanted Annie to find it. Or he didn't care.

Annie was hurt at her very core but tried not to let on. He was unapologetic and mute. Was she supposed to accept that he was free to have sex with anyone he wanted to? Yes, they were having a rocky time, and she went away to think about things. And it was the times—everyone had multiple partners. And they were not married. But she felt married. Living with him had been the best year in her entire life, even in their bad times. She was still rationalizing that he didn't owe her any loyalty when they agreed to table the Mary conversation until they were more rested. They went to sleep exhausted from the trip, the laundry, the cigarette butt. The laundered clothes felt clean, but she was still itching horribly. Maybe the allergy would go away now that they were home.

The next morning, Jonas left the apartment early after showering with the bathroom door closed. Usually he left the door open. Annie was in bed pretending to be asleep. He didn't tell her where he was going. Maybe he was rushing off to see Mary. Maybe he would return after they fucked and tell Annie he was in love with Mary.

When he came home, he dropped a small brown paper bag on the kitchen table. She wondered if he picked up chocolate eclairs as a peace offering.

"I have crabs. I went to the doctor, and he gave me this medication for pubic lice. Did you have sex with someone in Texas?" He was talking quietly, looking intently at her.

"What? Are you kidding? I didn't sleep with anyone in Texas!" Was he making fun of her at a time like this?

"This is serious. We don't want parasites in our apartment."

Annie grabbed the medication out of the bag and ran to the bathroom to get the salve on her crotch. He followed. They both stood with their pants around their feet in the bathroom, slathering on the smelly gel.

"We have to take our clothes to the laundromat and wash the bedding again," she said practically. "It was that women's restroom in Escanaba. Now you know what it feels like!"

He helped pull the bedding off the bed and pull their towels off the hooks in the bathroom, filling four pillowcases with laundry. It took both of their bicycle seats to hold the heavy pillowcases. They walked their bikes side by side to the laundromat, joined in their mission to kill the parasites in their lives. They pretended to read books they brought with them, glancing up from time to time to watch the soapy water through the washing machine portholes, then listening to the heat pounding the dampness out of their clothes. They were a team again, she thought, looking for a silver lining.

That night there was blissful relief from itching. Annie was so happy she got out her box of crayons and colored a picture of brown crabs on a big piece of paper and wrote in red letters at the top, "Jumping Escanaba crabs, gather here." She balanced the sign between the pillows on their bed. From then on, the Escanaba crabs were the metaphor for their trip. It was the first time they laughed together, really laughed since she'd left for Texas.

Annie didn't know what to think about Jonas and Mary—there was no medical salve to take away the pain of betrayal. Did Mary think it was wrong to have sex in their bed? Did Jonas? Did he tell Mary he was breaking up with Annie? Did he have sex more than once with her? There was only one cigarette butt, so maybe it was only one time. Did Mary find Annie's radiator and leverage her leg to get closer to Jonas during sex? Did Mary leave the cigarette butt in the wastepaper basket hoping Annie would see it? Annie could not ask him the questions multiplying in her mind. She knew she would have to live without answers. She figured he was hoping she would forget or forgive. Maybe he didn't care if she did either. She kept asking herself what was wrong with their relationship? There was a feeling of foreboding—something really bad was coming for Flora's list.

———— ⚬ ————

In Annie's dreams, fogs were developing inside her lungs, lifting up and out to the walls and ceilings of their apartment. She tried to explain the fogs to Jonas. He wasn't responding to her poetic notions anymore.

The apartment lease would be up in a few weeks, so they looked for another place to live. They found a first-floor duplex near the public library on the other side of the Capitol. They agreed to stay together and agreed Annie could get a cat. She'd been talking about getting a cat for months. Jonas was more of a dog person, but it didn't matter if it was a dog or cat—he made it clear he could not commit to taking care of any animal then. Annie assured him it would be her cat, her responsibility. As soon as the lease was signed on the new place, which had a small yard nestled among the other 1920s-built homes in the West Dayton Street neighborhood, they went to the animal shelter to look at cats.

At one of the open cages, a handsome mid-sized male black cat, young but not a kitten, looked into Jonas's eyes confidently and crept up his extended arms which made a two-lane bridge between the cage and Jonas's chest. The cat was selecting Jonas. Annie continued to walk around the shelter looking at other animals, especially females. But Jonas kept saying quietly, "That is the one." So Annie selected the black male cat who selected Jonas. They brought the black cat to the new house in a box the shelter gave them. Annie named him Black Cat Zechman.

The first-floor flat had a large front room with three bay windows. A long hallway led to a small back room they set up for their bedroom. It held their double bed and two bookcases. A bathroom branched off the hall. The little bedroom opened to the kitchen. The kitchen was big enough for a small table and two chairs, and a torn tan easy chair left by the prior tenants nestled into the corner next to the refrigerator. Stairs at both ends enabled them to enter through the front and back doors. The cat could go in and out of the back-door landing to play in the yard.

They covered the eight-foot wall opposite their bed with brown butcher block paper, and Annie printed quotes on it in different ink colors so they could go to sleep and wake to words in color.

One quote she made up—in French because it sounded more meaningful in French—printed in purple ink: *Il y a cette motion la . . . Il y a toujours cette motion la.* *["There is only that movement, there is only always that movement."]*. Movement separated the living from the dead, life was a verb.

She printed a passage from Yevtushenko's "I Fell Out of Love with You" in red ink:

> *You should start saving love right at the beginning*
> *From those passionate 'Forevers!', those childish 'Nevers!'*
> *'Do not make promises!—the trains were bellowing,*
> *Do not make promises!—mumbled the telephone wires.*

Simone de Beauvoir's quote went in the far-right corner in turquoise ink: *One is not born, but rather becomes, a woman.* Next to that, in mustard-colored ink, de Beauvoir's lover Jean-Paul Sartre: *If you're lonely when you're alone, you're in bad company,* and *We are our choices.*

In the left corner in green ink, the proverb Saul gave Annie when she was fifteen:

> *Every morning in Africa, a gazelle wakes up.*
> *It knows it must run faster than the fastest lion*
> *Or it will be killed.*
> *Every morning a lion wakes up.*
> *It knows it must outrun the slowest gazelle*
> *Or it will starve to death.*
> *It doesn't matter whether you are a lion or a gazelle.*
> *When the sun comes up, you better start running.*

E.E. Cummings scrolled along the bottom of the wall in orange, *It takes courage to grow up and become who you really are.*

Anais Nin took a middle space in navy blue: *We write to taste life twice, in the moment and in retrospect.* Another middle space in navy went to Sylvia Plath . . . *everything in life is writeable about if you have the outgoing guts to do it, and the imagination to improvise. The worst enemy to creativity is self-doubt.*

Red ink along the top of the wall went to Yossarian from *Catch-22*, *The enemy is anybody who's going to get you killed, no matter which side he is on*. And another Yossarian in green ink: *Insanity is contagious.*

And Woody Guthrie called out in black ink, *Take it easy but take it.*

Annie left spaces on the wall for new quotes to come in time.

———————⬤———————

They settled into the new house with the new cat, and life started to feel normal again. Until Jonas mentioned he was invited to Mary's house. He invited Annie to come along.

"Are you sure? Is that ok with her?"

"It's fine. Mary knows I'm living with you and she's married," he reminded Annie.

Annie wanted to say that didn't stop her from sleeping with you when I was in Texas, but she didn't say it.

When they arrived at Mary's, her husband was away on a business trip. Clearly, Mary didn't know Annie was coming. The lights were dim, and there were two wine glasses on the table. Then the awkward small talk commenced. Sometime during the evening, before Annie excused herself to have an involuntary cry in Mary's bathroom after Leonard Cohen started singing about being up at four in the morning in New York City, Annie received the message from the universe that Jonas would be leaving Annie for Mary. The universe didn't explain what Mary would do with her husband, but the dry cracker Annie was eating to try to act normally was advising Annie to prepare for abandonment. And L. Cohen was underscoring the message.

Eating cheese and crackers from a small blue plate, Annie tried to distract herself from the growing tension in the room by focusing on Mary's hair. The last five inches of her head hair were blonde, but the four inches close to her scalp were brown. There was an even line of color separation around her head as she was letting her natural color grow in. It created a halo effect though the halo was not at the top of her head but the bottom. Annie did not want to conclude that Mary's halo was slipping. Annie concluded too that Mary's pubic hair must be brown not blonde. The only person in the room who would never know for sure was Annie. Mary and Jonas would know, and Mary's missing husband.

While Annie dabbed her eyes with cold water in the bathroom so Jonas would not know she'd been crying, she told herself she had no reason not to like Mary other than the fact that she had sex with Jonas in their bed. And here was Mary in a new seduction scene months later.

When they left Mary's house, Annie felt cold. The fall nights were bowing already to the coming winter. She had become an unwilling witness to Jonas's other love. She didn't understand why he didn't see what she saw. He told Annie that this was not a seduction scene and chastised Annie for jealousy. Annie agreed she was jealous, and this was not an attractive quality. She told him he was naive and too trusting. She was willing to take the blame for how badly things were going in their relationship. She was convinced he was giving up on her because she had too many flaws. And now he could add jealousy to her flaw list.

A voice inside kept trying to speak to her: 'He's not an antelope or lion like you.' Annie heard the voice, and it stopped her cold—for a moment. She had not figured out who Jonas was yet—was he fighting for survival like she was, for himself and for them? And if he wasn't, why wasn't he? Should she talk to him about this? No, he would give her his Zen look and keep his distance. The last thing she wanted was more distance from him, despite Mary's efforts to come between them.

She turned to music for answers, especially to L. Cohen. He'd been talking to her since she found his novel, Beautiful Losers, in her college library. He was coming to the university's Homecoming next week, It would be an anti-war celebration called Bring Them Home from Vietnam. Jonas and Annie couldn't afford to go to the concert, but they walked to the fieldhouse around seven-thirty when the concert started hoping to hear him singing from outside. Jonas thought they might be able to get inside after the concert and try to meet him.

One of their friends went to the concert. Cohen told the audience a group called the White Panthers offered to be his bodyguards but he turned them down because their name sounded like a Disney character. Maybe if they were called the Snow Cobras, he said he might have said yes.

During the concert, Cohen decried the death around them—from Vietnam and so many musicians. That September, Jimi Hendrix died in his sleep. Soon after, Janis Joplin. He dedicated a song to Janis.

Jonas and Annie never got inside the fieldhouse but standing outside still felt like something.

Annie and Jonas were sitting in a café down the street from their new flat catching a late breakfast when she asked him about becoming a conscientious objector.

"Ok, but give me a minute." He started to write dates and words on a paper napkin with his black pen, and took a few sips of coffee. "I applied at nineteen. I figured I would be drafted soon. I was going to school up north, but they were starting to draft guys from school."

"I thought you can't be drafted if you're enrolled in college?"

"Every state has a monthly quota to fill. If they need more guys, they can draft them from college."

Annie was surprised to hear this. She started thinking back—three years ago—1967—that's when Otis Redding's plane crashed into Lake Monona. She was getting ready to go to Mexico with Duncan. That seemed so long ago.

"Then how did you get CO status and end up in Madison?"

"First, you should know CO status isn't only a Vietnam thing. The Supreme Court has permitted alternatives since World War II and before. You always had to make a case you were a pacifist."

"What's the definition of a pacifist—do you have to be religious?" Jonas never talked about religion. He'd never gone to church since they'd been together except the time they kissed in the stone church.

"I wasn't religious then—or now. And pacifism was never based on religious beliefs. And you don't get CO status just because you apply—it's not a given."

"What's the decision based on, then?"

"There are three kinds of status you can request—noncombatant where you do an approved alternate service—or if you don't want any part of the military, they offer a prison term in places like Fort Leavenworth—and there's mental illness—they can classify you as mentally ill."

"What? It's hard to see prison and mental illness as options," she said with incredulity.

"Yep, I wasn't sure what to do—thought about going to Canada like so many guys, but alternate service seemed the better way to go."

"What did your family think?"

"My father said being a CO is unpatriotic. He told me to wait to be drafted and then go." His face clouded over when he mentioned his father.

"What about your mom?"

"She let my father do all the talking."

Annie shook her head, frowning. Jonas got up to get more coffee from the carafe on the café counter. She knew his parents didn't think much of her. Jonas told them he was living with a girl who moved to Wisconsin to go to school here. They said a girl from New York was trouble. But she wasn't from New York. People in his northern town assumed most students were coming to Madison from New York, bringing liberal thoughts and ruining the university and the state.

When he was back at the table, she said, "Maybe if your parents met me, they'd like me."

"They would like you, but they'll never change their minds about the war, especially Dad."

Jonas told her that one of his professors up north cautioned him to think about his career, that some employers might not hire him or might even fire him later if they found out he was a CO. But that reasoning assumed he would be returning from the warfront in one piece. "Around that time, two guys back from Vietnam came to talk to a group of us on campus. They told us what was going on in gruesome details—warned us not to go. I made up my mind they were right. It's insane, Annie. More than six thousand Americans were killed two years ago—and more than eleven thousand last year—projections are sixteen thousand for this year. And even if you live through it, the number who get injured is three times the number dead."

Duncan never laid out the statistics for her before he left.

"I could accept dying if I could understand the reason for putting my life on the line for my country—but I couldn't and can't accept our reason for being in this war."

Annie had never heard Jonas talk at length about something so personal.

"To make a long story short, once I knew I couldn't agree to fight in good conscience, I moved forward with my application."

"What was the application like?"

"There were several questions—I wrote six pages. They accepted my application—then there was a hearing to answer questions before the local draft board. After the hearing, the board would issue their decision, and whatever the board decided, you had to go with it—no appeals permitted. And if they reject your application, you have to enlist in the Army or do a two-year prison term."

Annie imagined Jonas at nineteen—they met when they were twenty-two. "I'd like to read your essay."

"It's in a box at my parent's house. Will try to find it next time I'm up there."

"What was the hearing like? What did you wear?"

"Suit and tie," he said smiling. "The hearing was in a room in the courthouse in my hometown."

"Were you nervous?"

"Kind of. I tried to guess the questions I might get—the board was made up of five men my father's age—all World War II vets. I had heard applicants got a lot of what-if questions."

"What are those?"

"Scenarios—what if you were facing World War II and not Vietnam— would you have fought to prevent Hitler from invading the U.S.?"

She grimaced. "Did you have an answer for that?"

"I rehearsed an answer—something like "Yes, I would have fought in that war, but the circumstances of Vietnam are so different since the entry of nuclear weapons. War now is raising the possibility of destruction of the entire planet, and the issues of Vietnam are not as clear as when Nazi Germany was threatening the survival of civilizations of entire countries."

"Wow, good answer." She would never have thought of the nuclear weapon part. "I can't believe you still remember your answer."

"Yep." He seemed to enjoy talking about this.

"So what questions did you get?"

"Actually, the hearing didn't go as I imagined. I was the only applicant that day, and they had other things to talk about on the agenda. They rushed through the meeting which was fine with me. My application was on the table in front of them. I recognized one of the board members—a doctor in my town. He was nodding off—you know, falling asleep."

"What?"

"Yep, the lead guy shuffled my papers and said everything looked in order and asked if they were in agreement to approve. They all nodded except for the doctor who was asleep. Then the head guy stamped approval on my application with a rubber stamp."

"Oh my gosh . . . amazing!"

"Then the lead guy said I could leave and wished me good luck. I left the courthouse and that was that."

"How did you end up in Madison then?"

"Since I heard it took time for applications to get through military channels, rather than wait for official orders for my alternative service site, I decided to move to Madison to start looking for a site myself —the requirement was you had to do service at least one hundred miles from your home location. When I got to Madison, I found the job as an orderly at the state mental hospital. So I applied for approval there, and it met the Army's requirement."

"A CO is in the Army then? You're technically in the Army?"

"Yes, I have to complete two years of approved service or go to jail for two years. I finished my first year at the state hospital. That's where I met Mary—she's a nurse there. You know the rest—after I lost my job, I found my orderly job at the private retirement home."

Jonas tucked the envelope he was writing notes on in his pants pocket and got up to get more coffee. This was the first time Annie realized he was in the Army.

Jonas worked at the private retirement facility for six months when the Army sent a letter to their new address on West Dayton Street. The letter said the Army had been searching for him since he left his approved service at the state mental hospital. His employment at the new institution was not an acceptable site. They would not be counting the months he worked there toward his required service. They concluded Jonas had absconded from his service, and they were preparing to have him arrested and relayed to federal prison for draft evasion.

The next day, a man identifying himself as Mr. Smith called. Annie answered the phone. He said casually, "This is Pete Smith. Is Jonas Erickson around?" Annie thought Mr. Smith must be their friend, Jesse Smith's father. Annie told him Jonas wasn't home, but she would have Jonas call him.

When Jonas called Mr. Smith back, he was informed that Mr. Smith was from the FBI and Jonas would be relayed to federal prison.

Jonas protested: "Sir, I'm working on my public service." He explained there was a public ward at the private retirement facility, and he was an orderly, exactly like at the state mental hospital.

"Not at that retirement facility you're not. Had you requested the Army's approval, which was your responsibility, Mr. Erikson, you would have learned that that institution is not on their list of approved sites."

"Is there a way to have the public unit of the retirement facility added to the Army's list?"

"No, there is not." The rest of the call covered the details for Jonas's jailing.

"You have to hire a lawyer, Jonas, to sort this out," Annie insisted after the call.

Jonas found a lawyer to take his case for three hundred dollars. The lawyer agreed to call the colonel overseeing COs in southern Wisconsin. The lawyer requested a last chance for Jonas, reminding the colonel that Jonas put in a year at the state mental hospital and did not realize the last six months at the retirement facility were not approvable. The colonel begrudgingly agreed to give Jonas a second chance, with the stipulation Jonas be assigned to a location outside Madison. He assigned Jonas to a hospital in Bruchen run by the colonel's Army sergeant friend. It was that or federal prison.

Jonas had two weeks to get to Bruchen. Annie and Black Cat would hold down the fort while Jonas figured out how many months would be required to complete his service. It was looking like twelve to fourteen more months. Annie would get two jobs if needed to pay the rent at their Madison place. Jonas went to the barbershop and had his hair clipped close to his head and beard shaved off, so he would look like a new military recruit for his Army sergeant boss. Annie cried when she saw him shorn. He didn't look like himself.

It was the start of their second winter together. He packed the few belongings he would take to Bruchen and left Annie crying like she had never cried when Duncan left for Vietnam. Annie didn't walk him to the Greyhound station, and he didn't look back at her crying from their front porch.

———————

In Bruchen, Jonas rented the first-floor flat in a large Victorian house within walking distance of the hospital. There was no heat in the house. This seemed preposterous. How does a house in Wisconsin have no heat? He purchased a small electric space heater for the one room he would sleep in. He slept in a sleeping bag on the wood floor of the small den with French doors he could close off from the rest of the flat. No bed, no couch, no chairs.

A strange visage came with the flat—Mabel the landlady. She had a penchant for peeking in the windows in various drunken states. She flailed her arms outside his windows like women in Greek plays, with loud, crazy chatter, hitting the windowpanes for emphasis. Maybe she was the drunken chorus sent by the gods to rail at Jonas's life and choices. Annie dubbed her Mad Mabel.

Jonas didn't see a need for window coverings. He didn't care who looked in because he was not looking out. He was there for one military mission: mop floors and clean bedpans at the hospital. His French degree completed months ago at the university was useless, he told Annie. The Army didn't care about his skills. They wanted him to mop floors and change bedpans. That was the job designated for COs.

After his first week on the job, the Army sergeant who ran the hospital told Jonas he was bringing an unacceptable, offensive attitude to the hospital. "You better get your attitude in order, young man. That's an order," he snapped one morning as Jonas mopped the floor near his office doorway. Jonas had been reading an Alan Watts book on his lunch hour. The nursing station where three portly nurses cloistered during the day had taken offense to the abstract shapes of a man and woman on the blue paperback cover. They reported the offensive book to the sergeant, who ordered Jonas to stop reading dirty books on his lunch hour. "Find better ways to spend your time, young man. That's an order!"

Worried for him, Annie visited Bruchen though Jonas did not ask her to. She arrived on the bus. Jonas met her at the station which was a drop-off site at a coffee shop. They hugged and Jonas lifted her backpack on his back, and they walked hand in hand toward his flat. They'd barely left the coffee shop when two Bruchen police officers slowed their black-and-white car next to them, calling out, "Hey, what are you doing, folks?"

"Walking," Jonas answered in a low voice.

"Do they know you?" Annie whispered.

He shook his head no, his eyes straight ahead while they kept walking.

"Come over here, little lady," one of the officers gestured with his second finger that looked from a few feet away like a plump sausage. "You," he motioned to Jonas with his sausage finger, "stay over there." Over there meant the sidewalk they'd been walking on.

Annie walked warily to the curb. The officer on the passenger side looked her body up and down. "Are you visiting this fellow?"

"Yes." She thinks they must know him from the way they're looking from him to her. Have they been tailing him ever since his sorry ass came to their town?

"Do you know that *co-hab-i-ta-shun* is illegal in Wisconsin, little lady?" The officer says the syllables slowly like he's a kindergarten teacher. The cop sitting behind the wheel lets out a guffaw and brushes his thinning blond hair over his bald spot with his hand. "We can come in the night and see if you've had *sex-u-al in-ter-course* and arrest you if you have." He slowly enunciates these syllables too. Both cops are smiling broadly, mouths curved like bananas, teeth yellow.

Jonas comes over to the car as the car starts to pull away from the curb.

"Remember what we said, girl," the sausage finger man calls out. His banana mouth has lost its curve; it's set straight and menacing.

"What did they say?" Jonas is upset. His voice sounds hollow, as if there is not enough breath in his throat.

She tells him what they said, wondering if she imagined this. But who could imagine dividing up the syllables in *co-hab-i-ta-shun* and *sex-u-al in-ter-course*?

There was no sex that night though it had been weeks since they saw each other. There was little sleep that night too. She was surprised he had no furniture—they were resting prone on sleeping bags on the thin rug in his den room. She was uncomfortable but did not complain. He had acclimated already to sleeping on the wood floor.

Annie was sure the banana crime-fighters would be blasting their way through the front door any minute with a sperm detector. And Mad Mabel would be behind them, like a frightful witch in the *Wizard of Oz*. Annie was cold in the heatless house—and scared. Was this where Jonas had to live for a year?

It was Annie's third night in Bruchen when two police officers—different officers than the ones the other afternoon—did arrive with red blinking flashlights. They pounded on the front door and entered the flat using a key Mabel had given them before Jonas could open the door.

"I called the police!" Mabel shrieked at Jonas and Annie like a banshee. She was right behind the officers, wearing a red-flowered housecoat and unlaced men's brown leather boots.

"Quiet it down, Mabel," one of the officers barked.

The officers held their flashlights in front of their faces like spears. "There's a power outage, folks. We need to check the house." The implication was, Jonas caused the power outage. As if their single electric heater whining on and off, trying desperately to stay up with the below-zero weather outside, was causing the power outage in that sorry neighborhood in Bruchen. The officers looked with surprise at the empty flat. No furniture in the living and dining room, no table and chairs in the kitchen. Two sleeping bags with head pillows on the floor in the den, two backpacks against the wall, a few books on the floor, and the little heater furiously whirring because cold air was pouring into the room with the French doors open during the search.

Mabel was gesticulating both arms like an orchestral composer gone mad. They could smell the stench of alcohol on her breath.

"There's nothing to see here. They have power," the officers concluded. They backed out of the flat, red flashlights still shining to light their path

TEN BEFORE THIRTY • 157

out. Annie's pounding heart returned to normal after a few minutes, and Jonas looked defeated. This was the America they were living in, with so many of their generation dying in Vietnam. No love was blooming in this sickening frigid air.

When Annie returned from Bruchen, she had to face facts. The Army owned Jonas, and he would be gone for at least a year. She needed a roommate to split the costs for their apartment in Madison—she couldn't afford to pay Jonas's part of the monthly rent, one hundred and twenty dollars. Her job didn't pay enough for living expenses, school tuition, and care for the cat. She wanted to live with Jonas—she would give up everything to join him—but he told her he had to do his service alone, and Bruchen was no place for her.

That week Annie pinned a roommate-wanted ad describing the features of the apartment on a bulletin board at the drugstore near the university, the drugstore where Annie filled her diaphragm prescription. Nineteen-year-old Mona Golden from New York answered the ad.

Mona arrived the next day to look at the place. She was tall and pretty, long cinnamon-colored hair, soft fawn eyes, well-spaced broad features. She liked the house and asked when she could move in. She wanted to take the living room in the front of the house for her bedroom because she liked the bay windows facing the street. That would leave Annie the small bedroom down the hallway at the back of the house.

Annie agreed though she didn't know how well this would work. There was no door between Annie's bedroom and the hall that led to it, and no door between the bedroom and the kitchen. The front room did have a door that closed it off from the rest of the house.

Annie agreed Mona could move in. There was something Annie liked about Mona, and Mona could afford to pay her half of the rent. And Mona did not seem concerned when Annie told her Jonas would be visiting some weekends from Bruchen and did not mind that a cat would be living with them.

Mona set up her bedroom like an exotic lounge. A large mattress on the floor covered with an Indian print coverlet and several colored pillows. A tapestry-looking wool rug of purple and deep reds on the wood floor.

She covered the bay windows with colorful Indian print curtains. Several pots of incense took up positions on the windowsills, and bottles of dark patchouli oil squatted on a mirrored tray on the antique wooden dresser in the center of the wall opposite the bed. A large mirror in a curved oak frame above the dresser reflected the room.

Mona's room of textures and color was a contrast to Annie's room of bookcases and wall of words. Mona also came with a penchant for cooking midnight meals, late-night sleep schedule, and sex partners.

Annie found a second job at a department store wrapping gifts before Christmas. Her schedule was regimented: entomology department day job on campus and evening job at the department store, completing the day by nine in the evening. In-between time she spent walking to and from—she didn't have a car.

Mona usually didn't go to sleep until early morning, following nighttime sex, late-night cooking, incense burnings, and late-night showers. She went to her classes at the university in the afternoons. Annie bought earplugs to try to sleep, but there was no way to cover the smells. Mona cooked vegetable stir-fries with pungent sesame oil. And she wore patchouli oil.

The cat waited by Mona's door to scoot into her room as soon as the door opened. He took a position on the patch of wooden floor between her bed and the purple rug, stretching on his belly like a crocodile to stare at her. She stared back or tried to ignore him. Undeterred, his lemon eyes fixed on her. Mona thought there was something godly about the cat. Annie wondered if this was an aggressive move by the cat to get her to move out so his friend Jonas could return.

The cat stepped up his confrontations with Mona. After long-staring, he would rise from his crocodile sprawl and back his body to the target of choice and spray urine to mark it as his. He never marked territory in the other rooms of the house. Mona wasn't happy about this, and Annie didn't blame her. Annie told Mona not to let the cat in her room, but the cat always found his way in. Mona retaliated by marking the territory he tried to claim with patchouli. More urine, more patchouli. Neither was winning.

Mona was a more enlightened woman than Annie. Mona wanted the freedoms the men she knew had; this meant daily sex on her terms. She enjoyed the hunt and was good at it. She was a nude model in the university art department and had the pick of men with her exotic Rubenesque body. Most days she went out looking for a penis, she found one for the night.

When Annie woke in the morning to get ready for work, she scanned the hallway on her way to the bathroom to see what shoes lined the wall. Mona made everyone take off their shoes before they entered her room to keep her purple rug clean. Mona's black boots or her Birkenstock sandals, depending on how cold it was outside, lined the hall like parallel-parked cars, next to male lace-up work boots, moccasins, running shoes, huarache sandals, or platform shoes. On snowy or rainy nights, wet parkas, scarves, and gloves lined the hallway too, thrown on the floor. Some mornings Annie ran into a naked man walking out of Mona's room on his way to the bathroom. Usually, he would cover his penis with his hand and mumble an apology.

Mostly, Mona's men did not return for a second visit. Annie didn't know if Mona explained they would be a one-night stand or if it was the man's decision. Mona was well organized and kept an inventory of the men who cycled through. The number exceeded fifty when she told Annie about the list. She rated men by the size of the penis and the man's sex performance. The men didn't know they were on a list in Mona's top dresser drawer. There were skinny penises, fat ones, giant ones, short ones, limp ones, and battering rams. Whenever a man did come back, and Annie knew his rating, she had a hard time looking him in the eye. It was embarrassing to know too much about a penis and a performance.

One of the battering rams let himself into the house one afternoon—the front door was unlocked. When he discovered Mona was out, he headed down the hall to Annie's room.

"Let's fuck," he said to Annie, who was in bed reading, as he started to pull down the zipper to his pants.

"Get out."

"What, you don't need a good fuck?"

"No, get out!" she said more emphatically.

He turned to her word wall and took out a red pen from his jacket pocket and wrote, "Kilroy was here." Then he swaggered down the hall, opened the front door, and slammed it loudly when he left, his battering ram intact.

When Annie needed a ride to take the cat to the animal hospital to have his testicles removed so he couldn't impregnate the female cats in the neighborhood and would hopefully stop marking territory in Mona's room, Mona told Annie to ask the battering ram for a ride. He was the only person they knew with a car. He agreed to give Annie and the cat a ride. Maybe he thought he would get a good fuck for the transportation from Mona or Annie.

"I can't believe you did that to the cat," he exclaimed on the way home from the procedure, looking with disdain at Annie. The cat was resting inside his carrier box. "What kind of woman cuts the balls off a male of any species?"

"A woman who knows there are too many animals without homes." She supposed in his worldview, there could never be too much sperm spewing on the earth from the males of every species.

He shook his head in disgust.

Annie told Mona what he said about the cat's balls. In a hushed voice, though they were alone in the house except for the cat, Mona told Annie that the battering ram raped her. She decided at the last minute she didn't want to have sex, but he wouldn't take no for an answer. And he turned out to be so big that he hurt her. Mona gave him the highest rating for penis size and girth on her list but lowest for performance because it was rape. Even if she wanted to fuck him in the future, which she said she would never want, he was too big.

Annie felt uneasy when the battering ram put his Kilroy on her wall like he was marking territory in her bedroom. Hearing about the rape only added to her dis-ease. And the word wall was getting too much attention from Mona's men as they made their way through her bedroom on their way to the kitchen for post-sex stir fry. The paper wall would have to come down.

Mona and Annie were making stir fry for dinner when they started the conversation about the number of lovers people should have.

"I think men should have hundreds, thousands even," Mona said.

They chopped mushrooms, tomatoes, yellow and orange peppers, broccoli, pineapple chunks, carrots, and bean curds at their small kitchen table. Brown rice steamed in a covered pot on the stove. Sesame oil and soy sauce sizzled in the wok, waiting for the vegetables.

"That seems too high." Annie tried to imagine how much time it would take in a life to fuck thousands of times. "Maybe it would work for men if they came really fast," she offered wryly.

"Yeah. If they come in like ten seconds, easy to get a big count. But even if it takes a man one hour to fuck someone, and he fucks one thousand times, that's only one thousand hours of fucking. And that is only like twenty-five weeks of total fucking . . . like if a man fucked forty hours a week like a job." Mona was tallying it up in her head. "A thousand would not be that big a deal if he fucked consistently for like thirty years."

"You're good at math. I can't do that without a calculator. But we're talking about one thousand different partners, not like a man fucking his wife for his whole life. Would our fucker be able to find that many different partners?"

"I know some who would," Mona said confidently. The vegetables were steaming in the wok now.

"Well, what about women? What do you think a woman's number should be?"

Mona thought hundreds. Her reasoning was after hundreds—for herself anyway—she would be able to be independent of men, and that was something she wanted.

Annie thought less than fifty but more than five. She thought she could be independent of men no matter what her number was. And she didn't want lovers who would be done in ten seconds either.

"What do you think the rules should be for counting? Only penis penetration or do fingers count too? And do you count rapes? What about double-counting—do you count someone again after you've gone through a long period of abstinence?"

Mona thought full penetration was the right definition—and penises, not fingers. Annie agreed. She did not bring up the coke bottle she heard about at the hospital where she worked one summer in college. Privately, she thought you might have to count objects inserted in your vagina, as disgusting as it was. Rapes should count even though that seemed unjust. And it would not be fair to count penises after periods of abstinence. To count, a new fucker had to be a new fucker.

"Does it matter if there are orgasms?" Mona asked Annie. The stir fry was almost done. The green vegetables were shiny.

"Don't overdo the vegetables. I don't like it when the broccoli gets mushy," Annie reminded Mona, who was stirring with a spatula while Annie washed the cutting board and knives in the sink.

Mona nodded. "Let's give it one more minute. I want to be sure the carrots are cooked enough. What's your answer to orgasms?"

Annie shrugged her shoulders. "I don't think they should count. I don't think most women have that many, at least not with a man. Maybe with a vibrator or some other way."

"I agree. Hand me your plate." Mona carefully divided the stir fry between their plates and added a scoop of brown rice next to the mixture. "Wow this is great," Mona said, after she tried the first spoonful of vegetables.

"Yeah, really good."

"Should we count the different sex positions we've done?" Mona asked.

"Why?"

"Because that's part of being independent of men, or being like a man."

"How so?"

"Positions are important. I don't want to always be on the bottom, where a man is controlling me. Or he's coming at me from behind. I feel more powerful when I'm on top. Then I feel like I'm fucking him, like I'm a man. I like that."

"I never thought about it that way. Do you feel like you give up power if you go down on somebody?"

"I don't know. If he makes me go down on him, like pushes my head down and I don't want to, then definitely I've given up power."

Annie agreed.

"Do you have a favorite position?" Mona asked. She got up to scrape the rest of the brown rice from the pot to her plate.

"Not really." Annie was thinking about the sideways position where she used the radiator in her last apartment to get closer to Jonas. That was a favorite. But her favorites were not positions. What she really liked was clasping hands tightly with Jonas during sex like they were a force together. And holding their arms high above their bodies. And wrestling. She liked showing him her strength, and she wanted to feel his. She wasn't sure that was sex, but they only did this when they had sex. Maybe they were supposed to be wrestling partners, not romantic partners. Maybe that was what she wanted most from him, someone to spar with, someone to match energies with safely, a foe she respected, someone she trusted with her body. That was sexual, the attraction between them. She wasn't going to share this with Mona.

"Do you have a favorite position?"

"I like to be on top."

By the time they were done washing and drying the dishes with a towel, they concluded they could almost be done with sex for the rest of their lives since they had nearly made their counts. Annie was at three, Mona more than fifty. They agreed they should raise their numbers because they were not done with sex.

Annie reflected later, when she was trying to fall asleep, that they never talked about love. Was sex different if you loved your partner? How many people you fuck should you love?

———— ◆ ————

Annie was perched on a wooden bench in the bus station in Milwaukee, shivering from the cold even though she was wrapped inside the folds of her new Air Force parka. It cost twenty-eight dollars at the military supply shop in Madison. The fake fur fringe around the hood tunneled into a narrow air hole when she needed to close off the invading wind. She liked the orange lining, the green outer coat of slick nylon, and the deep pockets.

She was waiting for the bus to Bruchen. A bushy brown-haired woman in a thin wool coat had crossed the terminal floor and was standing in front of her with her legs spread in a power position. She scrunched up her ruddy cheeks and spit a long gob of rainy hatred into Annie's face, followed by the epithet: "All you students should be lined up and shot dead with rifles!"

Before Annie could speak, not that she knew what to say, the spitting monster receded like a sea creature to hide among the bus station fish.

There was menacing in the air but who was the enemy, Annie wanted to ask someone, anyone. There was no one to ask. The motley sea creatures lining the pews of the station were bowed in sleep, in boredom, or in resignation.

Annie walked quickly to the women's room to wash the spit off her face. When she returned to her pew, she pulled her parka hood close around her so she could look out, but no one could look in.

* * *

Jonas was visiting in Madison and barefoot the afternoon he lifted the heavy pot of boiling soup Mona was making for lunch with real chicken and small thin noodles. He held the metal pot away from his body because it was so hot. He carried it quickly down the back stairs and dumped the soup into the snow. It was five degrees below zero.

She raced after him yelling, "Jonas, stop! Are you crazy?"

The soup made a yellow staining puddle in the snow, steaming briefly.

"Why the fuck did you do that?" Mona demanded to know in a loud, high-pitched voice.

Jonas didn't answer. He walked slowly back up the stairs with the empty pot. He was smiling like the Buddha.

Annie had been complaining to Jonas about how much she missed him, how crazy Mona was making her, coming through her bedroom at all times of the night with her men to make a meal cooked with smelly sesame oil after sex. How Mona was borrowing her clothes without asking, how she'd cut the buttons off Annie's long green wool vest without asking.

Annie figured Jonas was trying to stand up for her in the only way he could—by throwing Mona's chicken soup in the snow. Mona didn't understand what Bruchen was like. Mona didn't understand how trapped and defeated Jonas felt. Mona thought he was crazy. Annie didn't think he was, but she didn't think he should have thrown the soup in the snow. He would not apologize to Mona. The cat ran down the back stairs to lick the cooling soup in the snow.

* * *

Two weekends a month, Jonas returned to Madison to see Annie and the cat. But he had another reason now—Jayce Uelzen. He'd seen her at an art exhibit on campus before he left for Bruchen. He walked across the room

TEN BEFORE THIRTY • 165

to introduce himself. He told Annie that Jayce was the most beautiful woman he had ever seen.

"I'd like to meet her." Annie was curious to see what the most beautiful woman in the world looked like.

"Yeah, good idea." He was surprised by Annie's open attitude.

He invited Jayce to meet them for coffee the next weekend he was in town. She looked like pictures Annie had seen of Queen Nefertiti in an art book. Broad exotic features, plump lips, silken skin, curved brown eyes. She was bigger than Jonas's women, and this irritated Annie—how could Jonas tell Annie not to gain weight, and here was the most beautiful woman in the world who weighed thirty pounds more than Annie.

Over coffee, Jayce told them she'd grown up on a dairy farm in central Wisconsin, one of twelve children. She loved horses. She was studying to be a doctor, and she talked softly and slowly.

Annie liked her and wished she didn't. Annie could see that Jayce liked Jonas the way she held eye contact with him. But Jayce liked Annie too. The two women made plans to meet on a weekend Jonas was not in town.

Jonas called Jayce and wrote to her from Bruchen. He did not tell Annie—Jayce told her. He set up a date the next time he was in Madison to go to a play with both of them. Annie figured he asked Annie to come along because Jayce would not go unless Annie went. Jayce told Annie she respected that Jonas and Annie were a couple and would not go out with him alone.

When Jonas put his arm around the back of Jayce's seat at the play and not Annie's, Annie recognized the move. Annie couldn't pay attention to the play. The play was between the three of them—Queen Nefertiti would take Jonas from Annie; she was sure of it.

After the play, Jonas accused Annie of being jealous. "Jealousy is not an attractive quality," he reminded her sanctimoniously.

"You're right. It's not attractive. Don't take me on any more dates with your girlfriends." She was angry and her belly hurt from the tightness of the evening.

He sighed slowly, his long breath a white flag to halt the battle for tonight. "Let's go to bed. I don't want to fight." He took his clothes off and climbed into bed naked. He fell asleep quickly leaving Annie to fret alone through the night. That was how it was many nights—Annie trying to fill the spaces in their bed with her voice. He was usually silent, breathing steady, avoiding her on his way to sleep. She talked on, thinking he might be awake, or might hear her in the in-between state of awake and sleep. If he did, he never responded. She railed alone at the night and the times.

Jonas invited a couple he met at the hospital to join Annie and him for dinner on a weekend Annie visited Bruchen. Jonas and Annie tried to pretend life was normal by going to the grocery to prepare. They bought food, paper plates, and plastic utensils because Jonas's only provisions in his kitchen were a coffee cup and a few bowls.

They set up the food on the floor in the bare living room next to the den with the French glass doors. Annie thought an indoor dinner picnic on the floor would work fine. They were spare. Life was spare.

The couple knocked at the front door. There were introductions and excuses for the plan to eat on the floor. It seemed normal, even fun, Annie thought. The blue paper plates and utensils were set around in a circle on a white sheet neatly folded on the floor. There was a bottle of red wine in the center of the sheet and a few lit candles on the windowsill—the window Mad Mabel liked to peer through. They hoped Mabel would leave them alone tonight.

The picnic was going well and they were cutting slices of the cherry pie when Jonas stood up to stretch. The three of them sat cross-legged looking up at him. Annie noticed how thick his tan work boots were. With arms outstretched to the ceiling, to the night sky, to the full moon he remarked about earlier, he emitted a loud, angry, animal howl Annie had never heard from him before. They were startled but no one said anything. He turned quickly to pick up his parka, pull his black wool cap over his head, and close the door behind him as he left the house.

The couple looked at Annie with surprise. She heard herself saying, "Don't worry, he probably just needs to get some air." Annie did not intend to follow him. Her job was to host his guests. She made small talk, encouraged them to have more pie. Minutes passed, then an hour. It was growing late, and Jonas had not returned.

The couple helped Annie clean up. They asked what they could do. Annie told them not to worry. He had been under a lot of stress, and he'll be back. They thanked her awkwardly for dinner and left.

It was late when he returned. "Are you ok?" she asked. She knew she asked a stupid question because he had told them in one horrific animal cry that he was not ok. He said nothing. No excuses, no apologies for leaving Annie to fend for herself. They got ready for bed, sliding into their separate sleeping bags on the rug on the wood floor of his den with the French doors closed, while the electric heater whined. He fell asleep right away. Annie went over the evening in her mind, wondering what she could have done differently, wondering how she could help him, knowing he would not let her help him.

———— ◆ ————

Back in Madison, Annie was having trouble holding onto her face. She could feel her face de-imaging like a Picasso painting. She'd been watching mirrors, searching for signs of wholeness when she walked past them. She wondered if people could see her face sliding around when they met her. And if they did and asked what's up with your face sliding around, what should she say?

Annie was meeting Roberta for the first time in person. Roberta had been a patient in Jonas's ward at the state mental hospital. She looked at them over coffee across a small table in the student union. She looked intently, barely blinking, for a long time into Jonas's eyes. Her hands kept rubbing her face as if to tear away a mask, and the movement was the exact impulse Annie was feeling on her own face. Roberta had slate grey eyes and an acne-spotted, shiny face. She stopped rubbing her face and smiled at Annie. She didn't seem to realize that Annie and Jonas were a couple. Maybe she was wondering where Mary was—she knew Jonas when he was with Mary. Annie felt her own face thankfully emerge from the ice. Roberta's eyes darted from Jonas to Annie and back.

"Annie's trying to be a writer," Jonas was telling Roberta.

"I'd be interested in what you're writing," she said.

Annie smiled and thought about the attractive spine Jonas told her about—Roberta's strong back, muscular shoulders, and inner fierceness.

Jonas was telling them he had no need for sanity. He read that in Kerouac. Annie wondered how he could speak so cavalierly about sanity. Jonas said there are no more myths left. What was he talking about?

Annie decided to leave them talking in the student union. Later, Jonas told Annie that Roberta advised him Annie was mentally ill. The fact that Roberta would be on lithium for the rest of her life meant she was coping with her illness, but she pointed out Annie was not diagnosed and not in treatment, so Jonas should be worried. Annie could not dispute the fact that she was struggling in a firestorm of jealousy and worry. Was that mental illness? What was the difference between sanity and insanity? And was Jonas on solid ground? Annie tried not to feel insulted but she did. Even if her face was sliding around in puzzle pieces, loosely associating, and frozen sometimes, that was none of Roberta's business. Maybe Jonas should fuck Roberta and decide for himself who was mentally ill.

Though Annie knew this cold March had to give way to warmer seasons soon, it felt menacing now—still so many cold days to come. Roberta had been calling the house for Jonas lately. Annie kept telling her Jonas was in town only some weekends, and he had no phone in Bruchen.

Annie was just home from work, glad to be out of the cold, when Mona picked up the ringing phone—"Annie, it's Roberta."

Annie walked over to take the receiver from Mona. "Annie, you have to come over. There's no one else to call. I'm having an episode."

"Jonas isn't here, Roberta."

"I need you to come. Now." She gave Annie the address and apartment number.

Annie didn't want to go, but she pulled on her parka and boots.

"Mona, she's having an episode. I have to go over there. If I don't come back, she has probably killed me," Annie called out wryly.

"Don't go! Call her back. Tell her you can't come."

"It'll be ok. I was kidding." But Annie didn't know what an episode meant. And why did Roberta call—clearly Roberta didn't like her, and she thought Annie was mentally ill. But Annie walked the two miles to

Roberta's apartment in the cold, then up two flights of stairs, knocking on the black-painted wooden door.

Roberta opened the door breathless. "Thank goodness you're here. I'm so cold. I have to get in the bathtub. Come with me."

Is it normal to be invited immediately to the bathroom? No, Annie reasons. But maybe it's normal for Roberta. Jonas probably wishes he could be here to see Roberta stripping off her clothes.

The white bathtub is an old claw-foot model with shiny silver faucets. Roberta tests the water with her fingers. "It has to be hot, really hot," she says. She stands in front of the tub, naked, one leg resting on the side of the tub. Then she gets inside the tub, cupping her knees to her chest, shivering, and describing the pressure inside her head. "I'm afraid I will have to go back to the hospital. I can't go back. I won't go back." She rocks from side to side in the hot water.

"Have you been taking your meds?" Annie thinks to ask.

"Yes, I just take lithium now." She says she's seeing scary images. She's afraid. She talks about a recipe for meatloaf they must try out when she gets out of the bath. She winces at demon faces. She chatters about swimming and diving and how long she can swim under the water, longer than anyone she knows. Jonas told Annie that Roberta was a competitive swimmer in high school. She tells Annie that she turned into a cat once. The hospital staff fed her in bowls. She lapped milk and water from the bowls they put on the wide windowsill in her room. They petted her like a cat along her back, and she liked it so much, meowing with pleasure. Then one day, without any warning, she became the Virgin Mary. She told the staff she was going to have a baby named Jesus. The Virgin Mary ate her meals from a plate with a fork and knife,

Annie tried to make sense of Roberta's chatter. Sometimes there was silence, and Annie wondered if she was supposed to talk. But it became clear that Annie was not supposed to say anything during the silences. Roberta told her to shush. She needed quiet. Roberta told Annie she was there to make sure Roberta didn't drown. If Roberta's head went under the water, Annie's job was to pull her head back up.

"You'll pull my head out of the water, won't you?"

"Yes, of course. I used to be a lifeguard at a summer camp."

"That's good, that's good. But if I slide under the water, it won't be like I'm trying to swim under the water. I'm a good swimmer, but I won't be able to save myself if I go under the water."

"I understand. Don't worry. I'll save you."

When the water grew cold, Roberta opened the left faucet to add steamy water. Annie sat next to the tub on the white toilet lid. After a time, she was getting stiff from sitting and stood up to stretch. She thought she must have been there an hour already, but she was not wearing a watch.

"Don't leave me, don't leave!" Roberta cried out. Big tears spilled down her face.

"I was just stretching. I won't leave."

Roberta confided she would spend the whole night in the bathtub if she had to, to wait out this episode.

"Is there anyone I can call for you? A doctor? Family? Friends?"

"There's no one." Roberta's body rocked from side to side.

Annie wished Jonas had a phone in Bruchen and she could call him. Whenever he called Annie at night, he found a payphone at the nearby coffee shop or he called from the hospital during the daytime. It was so late now—he would be asleep.

Roberta's athletic body was boy-like, narrow hips, flat chest, small nipples. Her skin had a grey hue. There were acne marks on her back, but the deepest marks were on her face. She had straight dark hair and slate grey eyes. She was a handsome woman. But she was chattering on so. Annie feigned interest in the chatter, trying occasionally to interject words, a question here and there. It didn't matter to Roberta. She was lost in her episode. Annie thought she would petrify on the toilet seat—it had been hours since she arrived at Roberta's.

Then without warning, Roberta decided it was safe to get out of the tub. She pulled the plug, and the water drained down. Her heavily wrinkled skin was a mixture of grey tones on the top half of her body, pink on the lower half. She was shivering. She said she was exhausted. Annie wondered if this was from the hours of sitting in the tub or the energy she put into the choppy waves of chatter.

Roberta wrapped herself in a large blue bath towel and headed to her bedroom to retrieve a flannel nightgown. The red-checkered gown was

TEN BEFORE THIRTY • 171

several sizes too big, and she pulled at the voluminous folds to tuck them around her tightly, holding the tucked-in material with one hand.

"Now we have to make meatloaf." With one hand, Roberta gestured for Annie to follow her to the kitchen. Her other hand held the nightgown folds around her small body. Now she was pulling out items for the meatloaf like she was on a mission: box of saltine crackers; hamburger meat, milk, eggs, and ketchup from the refrigerator; and boxes of seasoning from the cupboard above the oven. She took out a large glass bowl from another cupboard and a metal baking pan. And a large spoon to mix the ingredients.

"Can I help?"

"No, I need to do this." Roberta threw ingredients into the bowl. Her exhaustion minutes ago seemed to have dissipated while she mixed the meat with the other ingredients. After everything was blended, Roberta pressed the thick mixture into the baking pan. The preheated oven was ready for the pan. "The secret to this recipe is the crackers. You crush saltines all over the top," she explained with excitement.

Annie had never seen anyone cook with such intensity.

Roberta put the meatloaf into the oven and motioned for Annie to sit on a chair at the kitchen table. Roberta tucked her legs underneath her flannel gown, hugging her body with her arms. She was drinking water from a cup. "This is my favorite cup. My aunt bought me this when we went on a trip in 1960 to Massachusetts. Look, it's a giraffe."

Annie saw the brown and yellow giraffe markings on the wooden cup. They must be painted on. The handle was the giraffe's curved neck with the head fixed to the top of the cup—the giraffe's ears were peeking above the top of the handle. "Nice, really nice," Annie said. "I've never seen a giraffe cup before."

"It's an heirloom," Roberta said. "Meatloaf is my favorite food." She explained the different types of meatloaf she liked to make—with oatmeal or cornmeal mixed into the meat, but she liked saltine crackers too.

The smells of the cooking meatloaf were wafting through the kitchen. When the oven buzzer signaled the meatloaf was done, Roberta thrust her small hands into tattered oven mitts and retrieved the pan from the oven. She had already pulled out two plates and forks from the cabinets. She cut large slices of meatloaf from the pan and dropped them into the plates, bringing the plates to the table. "Let me try it first," she said. "It might be too hot." She blew on the meat and set her giraffe cup close in case she needed water to cool her tongue down. "This is the best!" she exclaimed. "Try it! Try it!"

Annie tried the meatloaf and agreed it was really good. They ate their meatloaf without any more talking. It was a fitting end to this night, Annie thought.

Roberta stood up. "I'm going to go to bed. It's ok for you to leave. I'll do the dishes tomorrow. I have to get into bed right away, or the visions will start up again."

"Are you going to be all right?"

Roberta nodded confidently and headed down the hall to the bedroom clutching the nightgown folds around her like a cocoon. Annie followed her. Roberta collapsed on the bed, pulling the flowered bedspread under her neck. Her grey eyes were already closed. She turned her body toward the wall, away from Annie standing next to the bed. Annie heard regular breathing and, thankfully, no more talk. She waited a few minutes to see if Roberta would stay asleep, smelling the faint aroma of meatloaf. She headed to the front door, took a last look around the apartment, and zipped up her parka, wrapping the blue-and-black-checkered wool scarf around her neck that Jonas gave her. She closed the apartment door, checking to make sure the lock engaged behind her.

Annie walked the two miles home at midnight, thankful she had a clear head. Streetlights and a high thin moon lit the cold path. The cat greeted her at the door. Mona was in her bedroom with the door closed. A pair of black men's boots were balanced against the wall next to Mona's black boots.

"Is everything ok, Annie?" Mona called out.

"Yes, thanks."

Annie climbed into bed, relieved to stretch out. The cat lined up against her thigh. What would Jonas have done—Roberta would have preferred to have him there, not Annie. Would Roberta have wanted to have sex with him after the bath and not make meatloaf? Or would she have made the meatloaf and begged him to stay the night? Who would Annie call if she had an episode, though she didn't understand what an episode was, really. But if horrible images were frightening her, she thought she would call someone like Jonas. He would open the door to the night stars, and that would make Annie feel better. And Annie would want him to stay the night.

⸻

Annie was waiting in her bedroom that Friday for Jonas—he was coming for the weekend. The bus usually arrived around six. It was a ten-minute walk from the station. Mona was entertaining in the front room. There were several seconds of punctuated sex cries. Annie piled pillows around her ears so she wouldn't have to listen.

Annie heard the front door open, and then he was standing at the doorway to the bedroom. "Hi babe, how are you?" he said, reaching for her hand as she jumped up to hug him. She started to cry, relieved to see him and overwhelmed because so many things had been changing, for her, for him. The cat swirled figure-eights through their legs. Jonas balanced his pack in the corner, removed his work boots, and stretched out on the bed with Annie and the cat. He expelled a big breath, slowly, like it was finally safe to breathe.

They talked quietly while the cat nested between them. Then there was quick knocking on the doorframe of their bedroom. A strange man was saying, "Sorry" and rushing the few feet through their bedroom to the kitchen. Mona was in the bathroom; Annie could hear the shower water. The stranger was opening the refrigerator door, and Annie heard kitchen drawers opening. Maybe he was looking for silverware.

The toilet flushed. Then Mona rushed through the bedroom on her way to the kitchen, wearing her purple kimono with the silver and gold dragons stitched on the arms and back. "Sorry," she said, smiling at Annie and Jonas lying on the bed with the cat. Her patchouli trail followed her into the kitchen. Annie knew a sesame oil trail would be tracking through their bedroom next, while Mona and today's Romeo made a sizzling stir fry.

Annie and Jonas talked about what they wanted to get done that weekend. Jonas needed to find legal documents they had packed away in boxes during their move. Annie needed to search through letters of inquiry to start another job search. She knew Jonas wanted some respite, however brief, to pretend he was home. But neither of them felt like they had a home anymore. Bruchen was no home. The house in Madison wasn't their home either.

The next morning, Jonas asked Annie if she was with him.

She was thinking, 'No, I'm not with you,' but couldn't get the words out. She could have come out fighting, for him, for them, but she was giving up. She heard his need to fall away from her. Her heart ached from sadness and fear. Her saying nothing was an answer to him. She knew that.

In the afternoon, they walked in the cold to the library, leaving the house to Mona. Jonas sauntered like it was a spring day. Annie sped up and Jonas slowed down. It hit Annie that Jonas was not going to help save either of them from the death grip tightening the harness between them. She was dying by his side, and he refused to acknowledge that.

So she took off running. She would have to save herself. She ran past stores flying like a monster train puffing loudly, sucking the unwelcome cold air into her lungs, kicking her legs faster and faster through the streets, crying and letting tears freeze on her cheeks. She looked behind her—he was nowhere to be seen. Maybe he walked back to the house or ducked into a coffee shop. It was a mile later when she slowed down and stopped. Her legs were shaking. She didn't know why she was running. She hated their situation but hatred was not going to take her where she wanted to go. The demons assaulting them could not run as fast as she could, she thought.

She walked back to look for him. He was still walking, slowly. He did not question her. He looked numb. He was tolerating her like he was tolerating his CO service. She could barely stand to think that he was just tolerating her, that she was an unwelcome duty.

They returned to the house he had found for them in the fall, that she shared with Mona now. Annie couldn't stand this house. She hated the walls and the doors and the cramped space and the boundaries and the people—she hated her tiny bedroom, the dirty dishes in the kitchen sink, the smell of sesame oil. Jonas treated her like she was a patient.

"Take off your clothes. Get into bed."

She smiled that he was so patronizing. She thought, "Fuck you," as loud as her brains could blast a silent vibration. The cat curled between them—the cat never took sides when they argued.

"We both need a nap." He was trying to breathe quietly, tread lightly. Annie was too keyed up to sleep. He fell asleep and she stewed. Later they walked to a nearby café and shared a salad. It was a long day. He knew she was running from him—she had no choice. He was pushing her to run from him.

Annie was surprised when Mona asked Jonas for advice about men the next morning. They were having a cup of tea at the kitchen table. Last night's man had left in the middle of the night, after sex. "Why doesn't anyone want to be my boyfriend? Why do they fuck me and not come back?" Mona asked Jonas.

He looked at her thoughtfully. "The answer to the riddle is, close your legs."

Mona was not insulted. "You might be right," she said.

He left mid-afternoon for Bruchen. He was tired. They had become inmates. Annie thought of calling him back as he headed out the door to walk the few blocks to the bus station. Maybe they could still clear the air—but what was the use? There was nothing but silence to counteract the frustration, fear, and growing distrust between them.

Later, Annie talked with Mona to see if there were ways to hold down the late-night walk-throughs to the kitchen. Annie needed more privacy and quiet. Mona agreed to enter the kitchen by going around the outside of the house and coming up the backstairs rather than going through Annie's bedroom. They concocted a barrier between the bedroom and kitchen—a thick tie-dyed bedspread that would hang from the ceiling across the doorway. At least there would be the illusion of privacy and not as much kitchen light spilling into Annie's bedroom.

It was still a bother to hear the kitchen sounds and smell the cooking oils when Mona was making stir frys late at night. But the penises stopped lining up each night because Mona was giving up on sex—she was going to become a born-again virgin. This was a blessing for Annie. She had been listening to too much fucking for months.

***

Annie needed a better-paying job. She knew students dancing at a bar downtown who were making good money. One was dancing topless. Ron's sister was a Playboy Bunny in Lake Geneva. Mona was a nude model in the art department. How hard can it be, Annie thought, to take your clothes off? That's what so many women have to do to make ends meet. The choices for the women Annie knew were slim—teacher, nurse, dancer, waitress, secretary, retail—while the men went to Vietnam. Did the men and women of her generation have good choices?

Annie filled in the application for the Midwest Talent Company to see if she could earn money dancing while she figured out options. The application asked for her age, health status, weight, height, and reason for applying as a dancer. She wrote: "I like to dance, and I'm trying to save money for school tuition."

She walked to the post office to mail her application. Two days later, the Midwest Talent Company called on the phone.

"We received your application, Annie. We'd like to have you come for an interview."

Annie was flattered they called so quickly. She needed money to pay bills. Mona said she could cover rent next month if Annie couldn't, but Annie didn't want to sink further into debt.

"The interview is in Green Bay," the woman told her. "That's where our office is. It's only two and a half hours away. You can take the bus if you don't have a car. We'll reimburse you for the ticket." Annie didn't have a car—she would take the bus.

The woman and her husband will meet Annie's bus, and Annie can stay with them overnight. They do this all the time for their dancers. This sounds plausible. Annie has heard this is a real company that hires dancers.

Annie decides to go to Green Bay for the interview. It's afternoon when she catches the bus to Milwaukee, where she will transfer to the bus to Green Bay. She carries a small pack since she plans to be gone one night. She tells Mona she'll be back tomorrow after the interview.

Annie counts the number of farms the bus passes out the window. She thinks about her choices. She worked hard to get her master's degree, but she still can't find a good job. So many unemployed and underemployed people in Madison have advanced degrees. Her PhD friend is washing dishes at Garibaldi's. Annie doesn't want to go back to waitressing. It feels like the world doesn't want her generation to succeed. Maybe her best asset is her body, not her mind, and she should accept that. Breasts and vaginas count—she learned that as a girl.

The bus pulled into Green Bay. The woman on the phone told her to look for the blonde woman wearing a navy jacket, standing next to her dark-haired husband. Annie sees them from the bus window. Mr. White's hair is straight and slicked back. Mrs. White has gold buttons on her navy jacket. They look like they're in their forties. They look ok.

"We're so happy to meet you, Annie," Mrs. White says warmly. "Our car is over here. We're going to head to our home. We run our business out of our home."

This whole thing seems bizarre, but life is bizarre, Annie reasons. They could be inviting me to their home to murder or fuck me. But probably not. They own a business; this is just a business taking advantage of women like me. And I'm going to be ok with this because this is what women have to do.

They pull into the driveway of an upscale two-story house painted navy blue, with white trim windows. Inside, they take her parka and offer her a soda. They invite her into the office. Mr. White—he tells Annie to call him Mr. Michael—sits behind a large wooden desk. Mrs. White—Cecille—sits in a chair to the side of the desk. Mr. Michael has Annie's application on the desk.

"Let me explain the kind of business we're running. We hire women like you, smart and working their way through school. We pay good wages. We send you on the road to smaller towns where you will be dancing in bars. Your job is to dance, and in between dances, mingle with the customers and get them to buy drinks. You will pick another name because our dancers have found that anonymity is important."

This is not the job Annie imagined. She thought there would be a stage and a dressing room where she could read in between dances. Now she's going to have to walk around and talk to people. And she doesn't even drink—how is she going to get people to buy drinks? What is she going to wear when she's talking to people?

"What towns are you talking about?" Annie asks, leaving her string of questions to talk among themselves in her head.

Mr. Michael explains there is a tour of towns. The girls travel by bus. He names towns in Wisconsin, the Dakotas, and Minnesota.

"You'll be in each town for a couple of days, sometimes just one day. My company pays the hotel bills and travel. You'll be traveling for several days, and then you can be back in Madison for a week or two. And then you'll go back on the road. Do you like to travel, Annie?"

"Yes." This is sounding like a truck-driving gig—she takes her body from town to town like a delivery service—but she won't have to do any of the driving.

Mr. Michael tells her they need to see how she dances. He stands up to put a record on the player on a corner table. He cues Annie to start dancing when the music begins.

"Right here?" She wonders if there is a room with a stage in the house.

"Here is good." There's a large rectangular blue rug next to his desk, so she thinks he must mean for her to dance on the rug.

A Rolling Stones song with a driving beat comes on. She shuffles her legs back and forth and side to side, making crossover Y patterns to the left and right. Her arms pace out short, controlled movements to the music. She's concentrating on her dance—there's no smiling. This is business.

Then he says matter-of-factly, "We need you to remove your t-shirt so we can see how you will look in our costume."

Annie quickly shifts into dead mind to accommodate this news. Had Annie been alone with Mr. Michael, she's not sure what she would have done, but she feels comfortable with Cecille there. Annie stops dancing and removes her t-shirt, then goes back to her dance.

Mr. Michael asks if she would be comfortable going topless. He explains she will make more money if she dances topless, and he wants to see what they have to work with. So Annie removes her bra, dancing on only in her jeans.

"You're going to need some tightening up," he says, frowning. "Once you dance for a few weeks, you'll be tightening up your abs." Annie is surprised Mr. Michael thinks she could be in better shape. But she agrees, she could be looking better. Thankfully, he doesn't comment on her small breasts.

Mr. Michael says her dancing could be improved too, but she can start the next night. She puts her bra and t-shirt back on with them watching. Cecille says Annie will stay with them tonight, and will be teamed up with a more experienced girl named Barbara. Barbara is working on her bachelor's degree in business at a northern Wisconsin university. Barbara and Annie will dance at a bar in Green Bay the next day. They'll meet the following morning. Barbara will help Annie find the right music, costume, and theme for her dance. Cecille and Mr. Michael will name Annie—they have to find a name that is different from the other dancers.

That night Annie somehow falls asleep in the house of the Midwest Talent Company, hopeful this could work. This is the best she can do, she reasons, feeling the weight of her exhaustion and lack of opportunity—and the plight of so many women she knows.

The next morning, Mr. Michael and Cecille drive Annie to an upscale hotel in downtown Green Bay. Barbara is waiting in the lobby. Annie signed a temporary agreement to join Midwest Talent as a dancer over breakfast.

Barbara is a confident, fit, chatty blonde, a few inches shorter than Annie. "Come on up to my room—we have a lot to talk through."

In the room, Barbara asks her questions, "What are your goals in life? Do you have a boyfriend?"

Annie explains she's trying to go back to graduate school but needs tuition money. And she has a boyfriend in the Army, and she's trying to manage expenses on her own while he's away for another year.

Barbara says she's two classes short of her business degree, but she's not sure she will finish. She's been dancing for a year, making good money.

"Do you like it?" Annie asks.

Barbara says she doesn't mind it. She likes the money. While she talks, Barbara pulls out costumes wrapped in tissue paper from a large box. She holds the costumes up, trying to figure out which will look best on Annie.

"You look pretty thin, Annie. We need to find something that will fit you well. Why don't you try some of these on, and let's see what fits?"

Annie nods and starts trying on costumes with Barbara watching. They're all bikini tops and bottoms that can work with one another despite their different colors. There's a bright pink top and bottom. And a top and bottom with hues of neon blue. Annie likes a purple and gold bottom that goes with a gold top covered with sparkly gold sequins. A tassel made from multiple purple silk ringlets waterfall from each nipple. The stitching in the costume pieces is excellent. Clearly, a real seamstress has stitched these.

From across the room, they looked flimsy to Annie, but up close, they're made for action, she thinks sardonically.

Barbara shows Annie how to take off the top easily, plus pasties that attach to your nipples when you dance topless. Barbara has a collection of wigs to change her appearance. Annie can borrow any of them—tuck her long hair inside a wig for tonight's performance until she gets her own wigs. Barbara picks out a blonde curly wig for Annie to wear. Annie likes the idea that no one will recognize her, not that she knows anyone in Green Bay.

Then it's time for themes. Barbara's theme is to enter the stage in a cowgirl outfit to a rowdy country-western song. She plays poker with two men who are plants in the audience while she takes off different pieces of clothing as she loses quickly in the game and keeps dancing. She made up this routine herself.

Annie is impressed—it's so complicated—play poker, dance, interact with the audience, smile, remove clothes. Barbara says with some satisfaction that after trying a few different themes, this is her biggest moneymaker, and it goes well with her latest stage name, *Sassy Flush*. Annie is having a hard time visualizing the cowgirl-poker theme. It sounds more like a strip show than dancing.

"What theme ideas do you have?" Barbara asks.

"I thought I was just going to dance. I don't really understand what you mean by theme."

"You know, like a western theme, a school-girl theme, a cheerleader theme." Barbara throws out scenarios, but Annie isn't seeing herself in any of them. Annie had imagined she would be a go-go dancer in a cage, and she could ignore the audience and dance mindlessly.

Barbara says impatiently, "Let's talk about music then—we'll come back to themes later. What do you like to dance to?" Annie likes rock groups but mostly folk songs. She throws out names—Bob Dylan, John Prine, Ritchie Havens, Linda Ronstadt, Rolling Stones.

Barbara laughs at the idea of Annie dancing to most of those singers. "You have to find tunes that are going to be sexy, Annie. Maybe the Stones will work." Barbara starts flipping through several records stacked in a box in the corner of the hotel room and picks out some for Annie. Annie doesn't even know all the songs. But she figures she can fake it and dance to any music in her purple and gold costume.

Barbara seems to have given up on Annie in the theme department because they never come up with a dance character for her. Annie is trying to figure out how she's going to carry this off. Her little voice inside which has been mute for weeks, feeling like she has lost her life with Jonas, is making pitiful attempts to talk to her: 'What are you thinking, girl?'

Annie reminds the voice. 'I need to do this; this is all I'm fit for right now.'

Barbara says she needs to take a nap, and Annie should take some time to get in the right frame of mind for tonight. Barbara will introduce her to the crowd and let them know she's a new dancer, and they will catcall, so Annie should expect that. This will be a good introduction to the dancer's road. Barbara is smiling with encouragement, "You can do this, Annie. It's a good gig."

Annie nods but she's not so sure. She decides to go for a walk to clear her head while Barbara takes a nap. Outside the hotel, the wind is blowing hard, but the air feels good. Annie walks down Main Street trying to visualize tonight. Her purple and gold costume. The tassels. Blonde wig. Dancing to songs she doesn't know. A new name. Trying to entertain catcalling men. Her mind feels like it's on slow. She comes to a river where there's an old Black fisherman sitting on the pier. His hair is shockingly white. He nods hello. No one else is around, so he must mean her.

Annie says hello. "How's the fishing?"

"Not much action," he says.

"What's this river?"

"The Fox. You must not be from around here."

"From Madison."

"What are you in town for?"

"I'm supposed to be an exotic dancer for the first time tonight—at Flanagan's bar down the street." She says she's not sure she wants to do this.

"Then why do it?"

"I need the money—the job market is so bad in Madison."

"Not great around here either. I used to stoke boilers on the steam locomotives for the Milwaukee Road Rail —got injured and couldn't work that job anymore—went on disability."

"Sorry to hear that."

"Tried to get on with another railroad after I healed up some—ever hear of the Green Bay and Western?"

"A passenger train?"

"Freight."

"What do they carry?"

"Mostly refrigerated foods and paper products. Wisconsin is big on paper, you know."

"Didn't know that."

"Yep, a leader in paper—toilet paper, napkins. Was hoping to get work on the new diesel trains but they weren't hiring Black guys. Lucky to still have my disability."

"More time for fishing," she says, wanting to find a silver lining.

"Yeah, but I wanted a second chance—you know what I mean? Kept hoping my body would heal better if I had a new job to look forward to—didn't want to stay on disability."

She nods, tugging her jacket collar tighter around her neck in the wind. "No one wants doors to close."

"Ain't that the truth. They say when one door closes, another opens. But sometimes doors just stay closed—if they were ever open in the first place." He reels his line in closer to the pier.

Annie is thinking of the doors closed to her as a woman—and his closed because he's Black and aging.

"It's getting cold out here in the wind. Better head back. Enjoyed talking to you."

"Me too. You shouldn't have to dance in one of those bars if you don't want to." He looks concerned.

"I think it will be ok."

He gives her a military salute, "Wishing you well, Captain."

She smiles—she likes being called Captain. Maybe the Whites will call her Captain.

Barbara is not in the room when Annie gets back to the hotel. She's left a note written on hotel stationery on the desk. "I'm in the restaurant downstairs. Come join me."

Annie's purple and gold costume with the sequins is resting on the bed. She fingers the silk tassels—so soft, so pretty. She decided on the walk back that she cannot put this costume on tonight. She folds the costume carefully into tissue paper and places the box on the chair by the desk. She finds paper in the desk drawer and writes a note "I'm sorry, Barbara, I can't dance tonight. This isn't for me. Thank you for all the help you gave me today."

Annie walks out of the hotel quickly before she changes her mind and heads for the bus station. She makes up affirmations to repeat to herself. 'I'm not defeated. I'm going to keep moving. Be a Captain.'

On the bus to Madison, Annie recognizes the route—the bus will be going near Bruchen. When they get close, she walks up the aisle with her backpack and tells the driver to let her off up ahead.

"I can't do that. You can't get off in-between towns."

She recognizes where she is. "Just let me out, up there," pointing to an intersection on the highway she recognizes. I'm going to a friend's house, just past the hill. Please let me out. I'll be fine." Reluctantly, he slows the bus and lets her out.

Annie is strangely exhilarated. She finds her way to town, then to Jonas's house, feeling surer of herself than she has in a long time. She knocks on his door, wondering if he will be home, wondering if he will realize how far she has fallen when she tells him where she has been.

He opens the door with surprise. She decides to spare him the details of Green Bay. He will think she is going to great lengths to get back with him, to make him feel sorry for her. She spends the night and heads to Madison the next morning.

There are repercussions for ducking out of Midwest Talent. They remind her she signed a contract. For two months, she receives preachy motivational newsletters filled with homilies about loyalty and perseverance, probably written by Cecille, designed to keep the dancers in tow. Annie wonders if a lawsuit is coming. She wonders what Barbara thought. She probably was not surprised since Annie could not even come up with a dance theme.

But Annie did come up with a theme. She was at the library taking a break from looking at job ads and reading about tassels—she could not get the purple tassels out of her mind. She read that in the Torah, the Lord instructed Moses to tell the Israelites to make tassels on the corners of their garments to help them remember the Lord's commandments and to keep tassels as a sign of holiness. She imagines coming to the dance floor in a short religious robe with tassels sewn on the arms of the robe and gold tassels sewn onto the bra and bikini pants under the robe. Her theme would be sharing with the audience that she had been instructed by the Lord (maybe she would have to say 'master') to remember the Ten Commandments. And then she could remind the audience, in good humor, about the commandments she intends to honor as she swings her different tassels and removes her robe. She isn't sure what music would go with the theme—something Slavic and upbeat, with instruments like zithers, lutes, and kettledrums.

Annie tried not to laugh out loud in the library while she imagined her theme. Cecille and Mr. Michael should be glad she was not going to be part of their dance family, a reprobate among the troupe. She was thankful the old fisherman snapped her back to reality, and now she knew the Lord wanted her to wear tassels to remember what is important.

She had forgotten her father's white woolen prayer shawl until that afternoon in the library. When she was a girl, her father showed her how he wrapped the tallit with its twined and knotted fringes attached to four corners around his shoulders when he went to the orthodox shul. She could not go with him because women and children were not allowed to sit with the men. Did her father pray to be a better man when he wore it? She didn't even know if he was a good man. She only knew that other people said he was a good man. She wondered if he was looking down on her, upset that she liked the purple tassels on the dancer's costume, worried for his lost daughter. Where did his tallit go after he died? She never saw it again. She realized at that moment that his tassels were with him—the tallit would have been draped over him before the casket was closed.

The oppressive winter months were passing. For the first time in a long time, Annie could select a small rock from the driveway and kick it down the sidewalk to her destination. Today, the destination was the state employment office. She started with a kick as hard as she could down an imaginary centerline on the sidewalk, then ran forward to kick the rock forward when it slowed. While she was kicking, she was thinking about ways to pay her mounting bills. Her bank account was down to ninety-five dollars.

She pushed in the heavy glass door at the employment office. It was just down the street from the office where she applied for food stamps yesterday. The clerk there told her to check out the jobs at the employment office. "Good morning. What can we do for you?" the woman behind the counter asked.

"I'm here to see what jobs are available. I'm having a hard time finding work," Annie offered with no hesitation.

The clerk handed her forms to fill in. Questions about her educational level, years of work experience, and the type of jobs she was looking for.

Annie took a seat on a nearby chair to fill in the forms. When she finished, she handed them to the clerk.

"We'll call you when the counselor is ready to see you."

Annie returned to her seat. She fingered the rock she put in her coat pocket so she would have it to kick back down the sidewalk on the walk home.

"Miss Zechman?" A thin red-haired woman called her name.

Annie stood up like she was in elementary school. "Here."

The counselor looked her up and down and motioned her to follow to a small office off the open waiting area. Annie took a seat in the wooden chair next to the desk. The counselor reviewed her application. "What sort of jobs have you been applying for?"

"The clerical jobs I've been applying for are telling me I'm overqualified. And the two teaching jobs I applied for have not called me back. I need a job. I'm out of money."

"Well, one of the things I'm seeing is your educational level—don't put your master's degree on your application, dear. It's best to minimize your educational level for clerical jobs."

"Don't I need to be truthful on the form?" Annie asks, wondering if it's okay to lie on the form that asks you to sign and date it and swear you're telling the truth.

"It's not a lie if you *understate* your education," the counselor explains. "It's best to say you've had a few years of college."

"Are there professional jobs I can find now that I have a master's degree?"

"Honestly, there's an oversupply of people in Madison with degrees— even people with doctoral degrees are finding it difficult to find good jobs.

You're part of the baby boom population—there are just too many of you," she says matter-of-factly.

Annie knows this is true. The dishwasher at Garibaldi's has a PhD. And women with graduate degrees she knew were dancing topless at bars downtown.

"I'd like to send you out for a temp job with the state, Annie. One of their transcriptionists is out on maternity leave, and it looks like you have good clerical experience—you've already worked as a transcriptionist at a university hospital."

Annie nods her head, "That sounds good, thank you."

The counselor calls their office to tell them she's sending over an applicant and gives them Annie's name. "Go to their office tomorrow morning to complete a formal application and have an interview, and don't tell them you have a master's degree. Just indicate you have a few years of college."

"Ok, thank you so much," Annie says, slipping the address for the job interview into her jacket pocket with her rock. She leaves the office optimistic for the first time in a long time. She positions the rock in the center of the sidewalk and kicks it down several blocks of sidewalks and street intersections all the way to her house.

The state unemployment office is five miles away on the outskirts of town. Annie will catch the seven-fifteen morning bus to get to their offices by eight for her appointment. She keeps pulling at the hem of her best dress, white with embroidered blue and green stitching around the collar. She's worried her mid-thigh dress is too short. She's wearing sandals which she hopes aren't too casual, but she doesn't have any other shoes to wear—she only has winter boots. She keeps checking her watch to see if she'll make it on time. The bus ride is taking longer than she thought. There are so many stops along the way. It's almost eight when she gets off at the bus stop across from the large brick and glass office building. She enters the double-wide doors and takes the elevator to the third floor, looking for the Appeals Office in the unemployment division.

"I'm here for a meeting with Mrs. Walters," Annie says to the clerk sitting behind a long wooden desk. The clerk tells her to take a seat, gesturing to a row of chairs in an alcove by the elevator doors. Annie barely settles in her seat when Mrs. Walters walks toward her with her hand outstretched, "Annie?"

Annie stands to greet her.

"Let's go to my office, dear. I've looked at your application the state sent over." Their conversation is brief. Annie has been worried about lying on the form, but the employment office is right—Mrs. Walters doesn't ask any questions about her education level. "You've had good clerical experience, and we'd like to consider you for the position. You'd be joining our typing pool to transcribe unemployment compensation cases which come to our legal office for appeals. All the appeals are taped. You'll be wearing a headset and transcribing tapes. You'll also be typing legal documents containing our lawyers' decisions on each case. These are official documents that cannot have any errors. So, it's very important that our typists are one hundred percent accurate."

Annie listens intently and nods.

"We're going to ask you to take a typing test for speed and accuracy," Mrs. Walters continues. Here's the page of text to type." Mrs. Walters leads Annie to a desk where there's a blue typewriter. A black metal stand is set up next to it to hold documents. Annie balances her purse on the floor and sits down to wait for instructions. Mrs. Walters sets the clock next to the typewriter to start the time. Annie is nervous that Mrs. Walters is going to watch her type—she'll see that Annie does not follow proper style. When Annie moved from Pennsylvania to Texas, she missed the high school typing class everyone else took. So Annie created her own method which served her well in high school and college. Mrs. Walters says, "Go," and the clock starts. Thankfully, Mrs. Walters walks back to her own desk. Annie types the text as fast as she can. The topic is an unemployment compensation case. When Annie finishes, she turns the clock off and takes her paper to Mrs. Walters.

"Seventy-five words per minute, three errors. Great job, Annie. Can you start tomorrow? Our hours are eight to five. An hour for lunch."

"Yes, I'll be here tomorrow, at eight. Thank you so much." Annie is already thinking about how early she's going to have to catch the bus to be sure she gets to work on time.

Annie's first day at the new job goes well. The women in the typing pool show her how to use the headsets and pull tapes from their common bin of incoming tapes—and where to put her finished work. The reasons people are appealing their unemployment compensation cases are diverse. Annie will be listening to all of it on the tapes—injuries that won't heal, muscles that won't work, backs that can't bend, arthritic joints that have gone rigid. Annie is looking forward to the stories—this is something she does not know much about, and this will be so much better than typing up lists of insects with their Latin names like she did for the entomology department.

On the second day of her new job, Annie runs to catch the seven-fifteen bus. She's just yards behind the bus at the stop when it pulls out in a haze of grey gassy smoke leaving Annie running behind it.

"Dammit!" He must have seen her in his mirror—why didn't he stop? The next bus won't be here for thirty minutes. She's going to lose her job on the second day because she's late. She decides to hitchhike to try to get to work on time. Cars are parked along the curb, and no one will see her if she's on the sidewalk with her thumb raised. So she walks up the street past the bus stop and steps in between two parked cars to stand in the street, putting her thumb out to let drivers know she's looking for a ride. A car slows. 'Oh shit—cop car,' she mutters to herself. There are no good interactions with police in her neighborhood.

The officer parks his car next to one of the parked cars along the sidewalk and gets out. "What are you doing, missy?" he says to Annie, eyeing her up and down.

"I just missed the bus, officer, and need to get to work on time."

"What are you doing in the street? It's illegal to hitchhike in the street."

"No one can see me if I'm standing on the sidewalk, officer. There are all these cars lined up." She points to the cars lining the street.

"That's no excuse. Let me see your license." Annie gets her Texas driver's license out of her purse and hands it to him. She shakes her head in disbelief.

"Officer, do you have to give me a ticket? I have no money."

He looks at her impassively and hands her the ticket with a warning to stay on the sidewalk. Then he gets back in his car and drives away.

All this has taken so much time that Annie is going to wait for the seven-forty-five bus. She will just be late. She will tell the office there was so much traffic that her earlier bus was late. What's another lie when she already lied about her education on their application?

The more Annie thinks about her hitchhiking ticket and the money she has to pay, the angrier she gets. She decides to contest the ticket. She writes a letter to the court explaining she could not follow the hitchhiking rule because no passing car would see her if she was hitchhiking from the sidewalk in that location. She receives a court date a few days later in the mail.

Annie arrives for traffic court in a pink miniskirt, black shirt, and brown sandals and takes a seat at the back of the filled courtroom. At least fifteen cases are on the docket before Zechman. The bailiff calls each case before the judge. Running a yellow light. Running a red light. Failing to make a full stop at the stop sign. Parking illegally. Failing to signal. Speeding. No one yet for hitchhiking illegally.

Judge Whitman looks like he's at least fifty. His black robe matches the color of his thinning hair. He snarls and berates every one of them as they explain their reason for being in his courtroom. "I wouldn't want my kids to be on the street with you! What are you doing even driving? What kind of lame excuse for a man are you? Do you think I'm going to fall for that? I wasn't born yesterday."

Annie listened for nearly two hours to Judge Whitman berate people. No one has a voice. The court reporter has been furiously typing the exchanges. A bored-looking newspaper reporter sits at a small desk in the corner of the courtroom with a sign on it that says "press." He has not been taking notes.

Annie is last on the docket. The courtroom is nearly empty when the bailiff calls out, "Zech-MAHN, Annie Zech-MAHN" like he is the town crier.

Annie's legs shake as she moves to stand before the bench. The judge sits several feet above her in his thick wooden seat. He looks at her with disdain like he has looked at everyone who has come before him.

"What are you here for?" Judge Whitman asks in an accusatory voice.

"Hitchhiking in the street, your honor," the bailiff answers for Annie.

"What? That's a dumb thing to do," the judge snarls.

Annie gathers her voice to explain. "I had to step into the street, your honor, because there was a row of cars parked against the curb, and no passing cars were going to see me if I didn't stand in the street to try to catch a ride. I was late for my new job."

Out of the corner of her eye, Annie sees that the newspaper reporter has moved from his chair where he has sat idly all morning to hear the dialogue between Annie and the judge.

"Well, that is a really stupid answer, MISS Zech-MAHN, the judge says. Is it MISS Zech-MAHN?

"Yes, it is, and it is ZECH-man, your honor." Mona advised her to add "your honor" to every sentence she says.

He snarls, "My five-year-old could come up with a better excuse than that. How do you plead?"

Annie is thinking she should plead not guilty when the judge admonishes her, "You better plead nolo contendre, Miss Zech-MAHN. Do you know what that is?"

"Yes, your honor," but she is thinking not guilty is the correct answer.

He seems to be reading her mind. "That is what you will plead, or I am going to send you to jail. Do you want to go to jail?" He peers down at her intently now.

"No, your honor." But maybe she should go to jail and let the state of Wisconsin pay for her meals, and she can write a book about her experiences, and she wouldn't have to go to her new job anymore. But she thinks better of it and decides to plead no contest.

"Come over here, MISS Zech-MAHN." The judge gestures for her to come closer to the bench, wagging his index finger like a metronome. The court reporter moves forward to stand by the bailiff who is watching, expressionless.

Annie moves closer to Judge Whitman's throne. She knows her face is flushing red but not from embarrassment—from anger.

"I'm going to give you an assignment, MISS Zech-MAHN. You will write an essay entitled, 'Why Pretty Girls Shouldn't Hitchhike.' The essay is due at my office within twenty-four hours, or I will send the police to your house to pick you up and take you to jail. Do you understand?"

Annie musters her courage and says, "I will write an essay on 'Why People Shouldn't Hitchhike' because, before the eyes of the court, there should be no difference between men and women."

Judge Whitman leaned back in his throne and boomed his outrage. "You *will* write an essay on 'Why Pretty Girls Shouldn't Hitchhike'!" Then he adds, "Why didn't you just stand on your head in the street, Miss Zech-MAHN, and wave your legs around to attract attention? Is that the outfit you were wearing that day?"

"Yes, your honor, I was wearing this outfit that day." She wanted to tell him this was her favorite outfit. She said again what she believed to be true: "Before the eyes of the court, there should be no difference between men and women."

The judge was done with her. "You will turn in an essay on 'Why Pretty Girls Shouldn't Hitchhike' and have it at my quarters by five tomorrow, or my officers will arrest you." With that, he slammed his gavel on the desk where it reverberated loudly and rose from his throne, flouncing out of the courtroom to his inner chambers. The bailiff told Annie she was free to leave. The reporter was writing down notes on his tablet.

Annie's legs were shaking when she left the courtroom, and she was angry at what happened to everyone who stood before the judge that morning. Her legs were her own gavels, pounding the pavement walking home. There would be no kicking the rock home that afternoon.

"How did it go?" Mona asked.

Annie filled her in.

"I told my friend Nancy about your going to traffic court today. She knows a woman who slept with Judge Whitman to get off a drug case. He's a hypocritical son-of-a-bitch, Nancy said. She said, 'Don't get into it with him.'"

It might be too late. Annie sat down that afternoon to write her essay. She put the judge's required title at the top of the page, still wanting to resist the assignment. She mused about opening the essay with a paragraph about pretty girls having a vagina, setting up the paragraph to describe the perils and challenges of having the bad luck of being born female. If she was a man, she wouldn't have to worry about hitchhiking. Is that what the judge wanted to hear? She shook some realism back into her head and decided not to say anything about being pretty or being female in her essay. Is the judge even going to read her essay? She wrote the shortest, most plebian essay she'd ever written, following the template she learned in high school. Open with a thesis statement, follow with three paragraphs—main idea in the introductory paragraph followed by two examples. Last paragraph, summarize the main points. Done.

The next afternoon she walked to the courthouse to drop off her essay, fearful of what might happen next. She wore jeans to cover her legs in case he called her into his office to inspect her outfit. What if he entraps her, like she has heard has happened with other women? She is prepared to fight, but he's a strong foe. When she arrives at his office, the receptionist asks why she is there.

"I'm here to turn in an essay assigned by Judge Whitman in court yesterday."

The receptionist takes the envelope with Annie's essay in it and thanks her. She places it in a large basket on the counter and tells Annie she can leave.

Annie counts each step from the wide courthouse doors to the walkway.

A few days later, Nancy calls to tell Mona and Annie to look at the newspaper—there's an article about Annie's case. Annie and Mona don't get the newspaper at their house, so they walk to the public library to read the court reporter's article. It reports that Annie Zechman was directed to write an essay for the court on 'Why Pretty Girls Shouldn't Hitchhike.' Annie is mortified. Why did the reporter have to write about her? What is Judge Whitman going to say?

A week after the newspaper article comes out, Annie receives a handwritten note in the mail from her former advisor in the English Department. "I'm glad to see you're using your writing talents to write essays, Miss Zechman." No doubt he is amused, but Annie is not amused.

Weeks later, Annie receives a packet of letters in a manila envelope from the courthouse. There is a message on Judge Whitman's stationery: "The court has received these letters from people around the state who have read the newspaper article, Miss Zechman. You have a fan club." He didn't sign his note or mention her essay.

Surprised, Annie sits on the floor next to her bed to read the letters. One says the state should pay for karate lessons for her to learn how to defend herself. Other letters advise her to be careful. A letter writer from northern Wisconsin will be praying for her safety. Others applaud her for pushing back on gender fairness issues. Annie is amazed so many people are thinking about her plight, no one is berating her, and most of the letter writers are women. They understand what it means to have a vagina and no car. Annie hopes the case is closed, but she has a sense this is not the last run-in with Judge Whitman.

Jonas was losing interest in Annie for cause. He told her he fell in love with an independent woman, but that woman is gone. Annie filled in the rest of his thoughts for him. She'd become cloying and weepy. She has no decent skills to sell in the open market. She is in financial trouble all the time. She has nowhere she wants to be but by his side. She can't tell anymore who the critic is—him or her criticizing herself.

She cannot continue like this. Her job with the state is only for the summer. What then? Her master's degree in English is getting her nowhere. She read about graduate level courses in administration. Maybe she should try those.

A month later, she walked into her first course, the *Politics of Education*, the only course available in the evening. There were fifty-nine men in the lecture hall. She took her place at the back of the room, and several men turned around to stare at her. No one spoke to her for weeks. One assignment was to figure out the relationship between a number of people in a network, based on clues the professor gave them. He called it a sociogram. She worked hard to figure out the relationships, drawing lines that demonstrated different types of linkages, unsure if she identified the correct set of connections. She established five different connection lines, depicted by colored lines drawn in crayons.

Professor Brown asked them to pass their completed assignment down their rows. As she sent her sociogram forward, the men in the class kept putting her assignment on the top of the growing pile. Theirs were black and white; she heard snickering about her coloring job. She kept her eyes fixed on the professor's riser at the front of the room, ignoring the audience. When their papers were returned the next week, Professor Brown had colored a large A in red crayon at the top of her paper and written her a note: "Loved the coloring job!"

The next assignment was to write a paper on an important political issue impacting higher education. She wrote a paper on "The Politics of

Confrontation," discussing student unrest in Madison in the context of Vietnam, racial injustice, and the women's movement. She defended student activists and the violence in the streets as the last and only recourse that powerless populations have.

Three weeks later, Professor Brown was at his podium when class began. "Thank you all for your papers—there were many excellent ones, but one stood above the group, Miss Zechman's. I have sent a copy of her paper to the president of every campus in the university system."

He had not said anything to her about her paper before his announcement. Now he was walking down the aisle of the lecture hall to personally hand her paper back to her. There was a large black A at the top of the page. "Congratulations," he said, smiling at her.

After she was outed like this, several men congratulated her. Three asked if they could form a study group. By the end of the term, she felt she had earned her A and had a new goal: to transfer from the English Department to complete a doctoral degree in education policy and administration by the time she was thirty, whether Jonas loved her or not. Maybe then the bad things Flora warned her to prepare for would come to an end, or at least she would be better prepared to deal with them.

Annie worried about Jonas in his dark, cold outpost in Bruchen. He'd been returning less often to Madison, and she thought that sending their cat to stay with him for a few weeks might lift his spirits. Someone she knew was driving to Bruchen the next weekend—Annie asked if she and Jonas could catch a ride and if their cat could come along. She would stay a day in Bruchen and leave the cat with Jonas. She didn't ask Jonas if he was ok with the cat staying with him, but he never said he didn't want the cat. Later she would ask herself over and over why didn't she talk this out with him? Why didn't she think more about the best interests of the cat?

Her day in Bruchen passed quickly, and she took the bus back to Madison, leaving the two men in her life behind, Jonas and the cat. Things were strained between Annie and Jonas, but she thought they would get through it. Maybe the cat would help.

Weeks passed and the cold weather was finally lifting, though the evenings and mornings were still below freezing. Jonas was talking about heading north for a concert on a hill somewhere and other trips he wanted to take. Annie decided to surprise him with a weekend visit. The bus arrived early afternoon. She walked from the bus stop to his flat. No one was there. Annie knocked on Mabel's door—something didn't look right. She could see furniture in his flat through the window but he didn't have furniture. Where was he? Where was the cat?

"Hey girlie, I evicted him," Mabel said, with a grunt and dismissive right hand holding a beer can. "I don't know nothin' about a cat. New tenants just moved in."

Annie had more questions, but Mabel already closed the door. She never liked Jonas, and she didn't like his hippie girlfriend either.

Jonas had not told Annie he was no longer at the house. Where was he? Where was the cat? She felt like there were nails in her stomach. She hurried through the neighborhood calling for the cat. Maybe he was hiding in the shrubs. But it had been so cold at night. If Jonas had been gone for days, the cat would have had to fend for himself and might have frozen to death. She'd arrived a couple of hours ago and already missed the last bus to Madison. She knocked on more doors but no one answered. Why was no one home except Mabel? Annie tried not to cry. She told herself to keep her wits about her. Her heart felt like it was beating in her hand, not her chest. It would be dark and freezing as soon as the sun went down. She had no money. She didn't think there were any hotels in Bruchen. She would have to hitchhike back to Madison.

It was late afternoon when two men in their twenties picked her up in a black truck. They had her sit between them in the front seat. She felt uncomfortable, so she said as little as possible to them. They asked if she wanted to stop at a bar and get a drink. She said no and asked them to let her out of the car. She was afraid they wouldn't. They let her out in the middle of nowhere as the afternoon was morphing to dark. She was frightened she would be lost out there and freeze like the cat. And then a van came down the empty highway. She put her thumb out, hopeful. A family of five with a large white dog picked her up in their tan van. They were headed to Madison—she could ride with them the rest of the way.

They were angels in the cold. She would not die that night. She kept telling herself she was ok. She was safe.

Jonas called her several days later, unaware she had been in Bruchen.

She yelled into the phone, trying not to cry. "Where have you been? I came to find you. Where's the cat?"

"I went north. I waited on the hill, thinking you might come find me."

"What? I didn't even know what concert you were talking about. How would I find a concert on a hill with no information? Where's the cat? Why didn't you tell me Mabel evicted you?"

"I don't know. I left town and let the cat out so he could find his way."

"How could he find his way? It's been freezing every night. He doesn't know the neighborhood. Mabel said she evicted you. When did that happen? Where are you living?" This was the craziest conversation they'd ever had. Annie wanted to go on and on at him, but there was only the silence of bubbles now between them, empty fragile bubbles waiting to be punctured.

"I don't know what to say, Annie. I got a single room in a house near the hospital. I was evicted. The cat never came back."

"Why didn't you tell me? I would have found someone to give me a ride to Bruchen to get the cat." The tears rolled down her cheeks. She was sure the cat had frozen, alone and scared. Jonas was in no condition to take care of anyone. He was barely taking care of himself. He'd been sending her all the signals she needed, and she ignored them. She never should have taken the cat to Bruchen.

There was no apology from Jonas. "I was waiting for you, Annie, on the hilltop."

What was he talking about—this magical thinking wasn't thinking. She couldn't blame him because she was just as irresponsible as he was. "I can't talk anymore right now." She hung up the phone.

Mona heard her sobbing in the bathroom. She had never heard Annie crying before. "What's wrong, Annie? Are you ok?"

Annie sobbed through the door, "The cat is gone. Probably dead. Jonas put him outside and left town after he got evicted."

"Oh my God, I'm so sorry, Annie. Is there anything I can do?"

"It's my fault. I shouldn't have taken the cat to Bruchen."

"It's not your fault—Jonas shouldn't have left him."

He told her he could not handle the responsibility of a pet before he left for Bruchen. She did not listen. This was on her. She emerged from the bathroom with tissues covering her nose, eyes puffy. She retreated to her bed, rolling on her side to face the wall and pulling her legs up to her chin under the blanket. She said prayers over and over for the cat, asking for his forgiveness. Like she did for Otto the frog.

Mona and Annie moved in the summer to the second floor of a large house on Mifflin Street, in a neighborhood of old houses and apartment buildings with painted murals and the co-op grocery. Annie was glad to leave the duplex meant for her and Jonas—she was trying to put Jonas behind her. There were three bedrooms. Mona's friend Sally from New York would join them for the summer. Mona let Annie take the largest bedroom because Annie had the smaller room in the other flat. The large bedroom had a porch outside it. Annie loved waking up in the new bedroom and walking out on the front porch. There was room for all her things and a door to shut out the noises and Mona's cooking smells in the kitchen at the other end of the apartment.

There was a new man in Annie's life. Bowie was a Marine, back a year from Vietnam. Six-foot, seven-inches tall, he looked like a 1970s Madison postcard: straight blond hair hanging a foot below his black cowboy hat, brown cowboy boots, and blue-striped bell-bottom pants. She met him a few weeks earlier at the Nitty Gritty bar. He invited her to meet him later that week in a café for breakfast.

"I'm attracted to you, Annie. I'd like to have an affair with you, but I'm not going to play games. You can decide if this is something you want—I'm fine with whatever decision you make. Also, you should know I'm bisexual though I'm mostly with women. One more thing—I won't be having sex with anyone else when I'm with you." He said this over three sunny-side-up eggs that ran yellow yolk slime all over his toast. And a cup of dark coffee.

Annie liked his frankness. A few days later, she agreed to give a relationship a try. She told him she was still in love with Jonas, but he was going his own way. Bowie was fine with that. He told her he was half-dead; she said she felt half-dead. They appreciated the irony of coupling skeletons.

The first time they had sex, Bowie sang the last verse from "Maggie's Farm," Bob Dylan's war cry, in a low and quiet voice. She didn't know if he was singing to her all the things he was never going to do but decided it would be best not to take it personally. Maybe he was singing to find a good humping rhythm or distract himself so he would last longer. She wondered if he sang with men. He had not been with a man he said since Vietnam.

There were a lot of good things about Bowie: he didn't care how much Annie weighed, he didn't criticize her, her shorter frame lined up against his taller frame comfortably when they were naked, and he covered her cold calves with his large feet to keep her legs warm. There was a downside too: a serious drug and alcohol problem, courtesy of Vietnam. He dropped acid most days before he walked to his job at the post office and drank alcohol every night.

He was drunk the night he told her all the men in his squad of twelve were killed in a battle north of Da Nang. He stood tall in the middle of the smoke, gunfire popcorning around him, screaming for them to kill him too. A Marine chopper swooped straight into their hell—they were not going to leave the dead and wounded behind.

"They shipped me to a mental hospital in Italy. I tried to kill one of the nurses with my bare hands, so they kept me tied to a bed for months. They didn't know what to do with me. They said I couldn't leave the hospital if I was going to kill people. Their last option was a lobotomy. When I heard that, I willed myself to stop fighting, and they let me out—I'm on disability benefits for the rest of my life."

On the walk home from the bar, he stepped into the bushes to vomit. "I'm sorry, Annie," he apologized between retching.

"It's ok. I'll wait over here."

When he finished, he wiped his hand across his mouth and they walked home in silence. He brushed his teeth with the brush he kept at her house, and they had sex. He did not sing "Maggie's Farm" that night—he did not sing at all.

He stayed in Annie's room most nights during the summer though he had a small rental near the university in a State Street rooming house. He rarely stayed there—he didn't want to be alone. That summer, Mifflin Street was a place and time for lost people to stick together. No one wanted to be alone though everyone was alone.

Annie started a list of protests when she moved to Madison because she wanted to pay attention to what so many were sweeping under the rug. The list was growing longer and more troubling every month.

The spring before she moved to Madison, students planted 435 white crosses on the grass on Bascom Hill. The headstone sign said, "Bascom Memorial Cemetery, Class of 1968," and they chanted to passersby, "Pray for the dead, and the dead will pray for you." The university removed the crosses the following morning but everyone had seen the pictures. Annie thought about the overnight cemetery and those dying in Vietnam every time she climbed the hill to go to class.

In the second semester of her master's degree program, Black students led the 1969 strike to boycott classes, take over lecture halls, and block building entrances until administrators addressed their demands around racial inequalities. The governor activated the Wisconsin National Guard for two weeks. Annie would not cross the lines to attend class—she worked on coursework at home.

Two months after the Army sent Jonas to Bruchen, there was the January 1970 damage to the Army Research Center on campus. The next day, a firebomb damaged another building. Days later, firebombing at the Primate Lab, and attacks on other buildings.

In February, protesters ran through campus breaking windows and confronting police when five members of the Chicago Seven were convicted of crossing state lines to incite riots. The Chicago Seven had been arrested during the protests at the 1968 Democratic National Convention in Chicago.

The next week, the march from the Library Mall to the Engineering Building to protest General Electric recruiting on campus—students broke windows when met by police.

Then the Teaching Assistants strike mid-March over collective bargaining—there were signs decrying Dow Chemical recruiting students on campus too—Dow made the napalm used to burn down forests and bushes to eliminate any cover for enemy guerrilla fighters. The volatile petrochemical mixed with slimy gel burned the earth in Vietnam—and any people it spilled on. The Wisconsin National Guard was called to campus and classes were shut down for a month.

Annie was weaving her way through the crowd on Bascom Hill to get to class when the pulsing crowd pushed her to the bayonet phalanx and a bayonet pointed inches from her chest. She looked with shock into the unblinking eyes of the young man on the other side of the bayonet. She did not want to be here. She was tired of fighting. She backed slowly from the bayonet to the safety of the inner crowd and found her way to class. Chairs were overturned—demonstrators had gotten there first, and class had been disbanded.

When the demonstrations moved to the streets, one of the bay windows at Annie's house was cracked by a tear gas canister thrown by police. Walter Cronkite broadcast the news that night across the street from their house. Mona fled for a safer neighborhood. Annie stayed with the cat, determined not to be pushed out of their home. People she didn't know knocked on the back door to get water from the kitchen faucet for towels they held under their noses in the tear-gas fray. It was the police against the students all spring. Nearly 900 campuses that spring participated in the nationwide protests to United States expansion of the Vietnam War into Cambodia.

Then the unthinkable Monday in May. The Ohio National Guard was called to Kent State University. The wooden ROTC building was burning to the ground, with more than 1,000 demonstrators surrounding the building. Ohio's governor called protestors 'the worst type of people in America and said every force of law would be used to deal with them.' The Guard and university officials assumed a state of martial law would be declared to move control of the campus to the Guard. At Monday's noon rally, nearly 1,000 guardsmen occupied the campus and the shooting began. Many guardsmen fired into the air or the ground but some aimed into the crowd of unarmed students—firing more than 60 shots over thirteen seconds. Four students were killed and nine wounded. The guardsmen said they fired because they were in fear for their lives. Annie posted a note on the bulletin board on her bedroom wall: UNNECESSARY.USE. OF.FORCE. KENT.STATE.

Madison's unthinkable came three months later at three forty-two in the morning. A Monday, like Kent State. Annie heard the blast thunder in her bedroom. She ran to the porch to see her Mifflin Street neighbors at the curb, looking to the sky to see if there was smoke—and to each other, for answers. Mona and Sally stumbled to the porch, rubbing the sleep from their eyes, "What happened, what happened?"

"It has to be a bomb on campus," Annie said with tears in her eyes.

The New York Times reported Monday's act as the most destructive domestic terrorism the nation had seen yet, amid the dissent and despair over the war. Robert Fassnacht, a physics post-doctoral student who grew up in Indiana was working all night in his basement lab so he could go on vacation with his wife and three young children before classes started in a few weeks.

Four student protestors targeted the Army Math Research Center in Sterling Hall using homemade explosives stashed in a stolen university van. The blast largely missed the Army Center but took out most everything around it, killing Robert, injuring four others, and damaging 26 buildings.

Mona's friend who lived a quarter mile from the blast told her the locked back door of her house was blown open from the force of the bomb. The church tower windows on University Avenue and Van Vleck Hall were blown out. A nurse Annie knew said the blast caused some cardiac ICU patients at the hospital to jump out of bed, tearing out their IV lines, and some surgeries needed to be redone.

The university chancellor called for fortitude. He said the university was doing everything they could to ensure the safety of students. But what about the safety of the nation and soldiers in Vietnam?

Annie's mother demanded that Annie come home. She said it was too dangerous to live in Madison. Annie refused to leave. But others did leave —or did not return to school in the fall.

The bomb changed everyone. You knew you had to rail against the war but you were guilty too—for killing your own.

Annie doubted that Flora would want her to put political actions, as horrible as they were, on her bad things list. But how could Annie not? She still could not process President Kennedy's assassination when she was in high school. Or Martin Luther King, Jr.'s assassination in April 1968, when she was in her final weeks in college. Or Robert Kennedy's assassination months later when he was ramping up his campaign to run for president and Annie was working in Martha's Vineyard.

Annie looked up the definition of assassination—murder by a sudden or secret attack, often openly, and often for political reasons. How could anyone feel safe in a nation in the gunsight of a rifle? Feel safe in a crowd? Have their voices heard through the fog of tear gas and shattering glass? Annie added assassinations to Flora's list.

Just weeks after her hitchhiking debacle and day in Judge Whitman's courtroom, Annie was riding her bicycle early Sunday morning to check out the new house she would share with Mona and three new roommates in September. It was on East Dayton Street, not far from her old apartment with Jonas on Pickney Street. She would do some cleaning in the house before they moved in. She was scantily dressed—cut-off blue jean shorts, yellow t-shirt, barefoot. The key to the new house swung from a little key chain in the pocket of her shorts.

She was biking on an empty street two blocks from the Mifflin Street apartment. She heard the siren behind her and pedaled to the side of the road, thinking an emergency vehicle needed to get around her. The police car was stopping behind her. A large burly officer got out of his car. The car's lights flashed red.

"Didn't you see the red light, girl?"

"There was no traffic, officer. I slowed at the light but didn't think I needed to stop since there was no traffic."

"Well, you were wrong, girl. You need to stop at red lights. I need to see your ID."

"Officer, I'm riding a bike. I don't have a driver's license on me."

"I need an ID."

"I wasn't aware you have to carry a driver's license when you're riding a bike. I live two blocks away, on Mifflin. If you follow me home, I can get my driver's license," she offered.

"No, you can't. I'm taking you to the station. Lock up your bike over here." He gestured to a nearby stop signpost. She locked her bike to the post.

"Get in the back seat," he says, opening the door to the car, his red emergency lights still flashing.

TEN BEFORE THIRTY • 203

Annie cannot believe she has to get into the police car. Is she being arrested?

The officer, who has a red face and fingers that look like bratwurst on a giant dinner plate, squeezes his meaty body into the front seat. Annie reminds herself to be quiet; be glad he has not handcuffed her. He drives her the short distance to the police station. Annie feels small and vulnerable, barefoot in her shorts and t-shirt. She knows she looks like a hippie girl, and this is not a good look to Madison police.

Bratwurst-man walks her into the station and tells the officer at the desk she's being arrested for running a red light.

Annie speaks up, "On my bicycle, officer, with no traffic anywhere."

The second officer looks impassively at her. He tells her to move to the next room where they'll be fingerprinting her. In the fingerprinting room, an officer tells her, "Stand this way, over there." She's supposed to line up behind a line marked with yellow tape on the floor. She sees a large bulletin board across the wall from her. There are several photographs on the board of university students. She recognizes several of them.

It's sinking in—they must be picking up students and developing files on them because of the war protests. An officer takes her picture. He presses her fingers one by one into a black ink pad and rubs her blackened fingers onto empty white squares on a piece of paper for each fingerprint. Her five right-hand fingers are blackened and pressed onto the paper in their own squares.

They tell her to move to another room. A burly woman officer arrives. She barks out orders: "Remove your shirt, pull down your shorts, panties down, bend over."

Annie protests, "The male officers are watching." She can see them out of the corner of her eye.

The female officer hisses, "No one is watching!" She pulls blue surgical gloves on her hands.

Annie sees bratwurst-man duck quickly out of sight. The female officer spreads Annie's butt cheeks. She looks between Annie's breasts. Annie's breasts are so small she can't imagine what the officer thinks she is hiding. The officer hands Annie a large checkered frock that looks like a housecoat. "Put this on," she snarls. "Keep your bra and panties on—we're going to take your shirt and shorts."

Annie is barefoot, and the concrete floor feels cold.

"Don't I get a call? I thought I get a call," Annie asks.

"You'll get a call when you get a better attitude, girl. You need to cool off." Meat-man has stepped forward now that Annie is wearing prison garb—the checkered housecoat.

The woman officer puts the key chain into a small tan envelope and licks it closed. Annie thinks she looks like a military sergeant—no makeup, no earrings, no smiling.

"Why can't I keep my key chain? Do you think I'm going to try to hang myself with this half-inch key chain?"

The officer stares at her coldly. Clearly she sees no humor in Annie's quip. Officer Bratwurst sees no humor either—his face is red and he has sweat blobs across his forehead. Annie can't understand how he can be sweating when she's so cold.

"Don't I get my call?" Annie asks again.

"You'll get a call when you calm down, girl."

Annie thinks she's calm. Isn't being sarcastic a sign of being calm, she asks herself.

The female officer leads Annie down a long dirty-white hall with dark smudge marks on both walls. They come to a row of jail cells on both sides. Annie hears clanging on the bars and a woman's voice catcalling. Annie wonders if they're going to throw her in with women who will attack her. The officer points for her to enter empty cell # 20 in front of them. The number is posted above the cell. It's a small cell where she will be alone. There's a metal toilet in the corner. No toilet paper. A plastic mattress. Graffiti words on the walls but no graffiti pictures. Annie's feet are so cold. Maybe it is the fear settling in.

The officer slams the metal door closed, and Annie is left to ponder her crime sitting on the plastic mattress. Is her crime no identification on her bicycle? Running a red light at an intersection where there is no traffic? Why did they have to look up her ass and between her breasts—for contraband? She doesn't know what legal is anymore. And all those pictures of students on the bulletin board, students who have been fighting back, demonstrating against the war, against unjust race and gender treatment at the university. Is their crime trying to have a voice? She knows now that all of them have clean asses and sat in cells like this one.

She shivers, wondering how long she will be in here. None of her friends know where she is. Jonas is in Bruchen. Mona is out of town for the weekend. Sally returned to New York. Bowie left town for a concert. Who can she call if she gets her call? Roberta? Mary? She's sure none of Jonas's women would come save her. Maybe Jayce would, but she has not seen Jayce for a long time and doesn't know her number.

It is hours before the female officer comes to open cell #20. Annie is huddled on the plastic mattress with her legs tucked up tight under the oversized house dress.

"Time for your call," the officer barks into the cell.

"She can call me," someone catcalls from a cell down the hall. "Let's see her!"

"What happens if someone isn't home?" Annie asks.

The officer snaps at her. "You get one call. If someone isn't home, that's your call. You don't have to make bail. You can go to traffic court tomorrow, Monday morning."

Annie tries to think this through. Should she go to traffic court in her prison dress, barefoot, and stay in jail tonight? It will be Judge Whitman's courtroom. And even if they let her put her own clothes back on, she'd be showing up in his courtroom in shorts, a t-shirt, and barefoot. And she will go last because she's a Z. He will recognize her from the essay debacle for sure. And he will throw the book at her. What will her university advisor think when there is another newspaper article, which there will be if Whitman turns her case into a spectacle which he will. And the bored reporter will no doubt write another article.

Annie decides it is best to try to make bail—just pay the money though she is sure there has been an injustice done. She follows the woman officer down the hall to a room where there is a black phone mounted to the wall. Annie decides to call the Nitty Gritty where she knows the bartenders. They will be there on a Sunday night, someone will be there, and they can get a message to someone. She doesn't know the number for the Nitty Gritty. The officer hands her a wrinkled phone book to find the number.

"Read me the number, and I'll dial," the officer snaps.

Annie waits nervously as the officer dials, wondering if she will have to spend the night in jail, wondering if they will put her in with the other women she has heard for the past few hours yelling insults to one another. One of them keeps yelling out, "Where's the new girl? Bring in the new girl!"

The line rings, rings, rings. The officer hands the phone receiver to Annie.

"Nitty Gritty," a male voice says.

"Don't hang up, please don't hang up. This is Annie Zechman. I'm in jail and need someone to help me make bail. They need $25.00. Can someone come over and pay the bail and pick me up? I'll pay you back, I promise."

"Annie, it's Jake. Don't worry. We'll find someone to come over."

"Oh, thank you, Jake. Thank you so much!"

The officer who has been listening takes the phone from Annie and hangs it up with more force than she needs to. She walks Annie back to cell #20. The door clinks shut behind her. Someone yells, "Put the new girl in here with us. We want to see her!"

Annie sits on the edge of the plastic mattress, tucking her legs underneath her housedress, trying to stay warm. She feels numb. It's at least an hour before the female officer comes to get her. "Someone is paying your bail. Follow behind me."

Annie's small feet pad behind the officer down the hall. Annie thinks it's best to say nothing. The officer pulls out of a large, locked drawer the envelope with the small key chain in it and the envelope with her clothes. She hands Annie her t-shirt and shorts. The officer watches with a bored look while Annie steps out of her prison shift and puts her clothes back on. The officer hands her the key chain. They walk side by side to the front desk where Annie sees Jake, the Nitty Gritty bartender and Andre the harmonica player in the band that plays there all the time. They are trying not to laugh. They paid the twenty-five-dollar bail before Annie arrived at the processing desk.

Annie takes a place between her rescuers. Andre whispers for her to be cool. One of the officers is signing a paper and tells her to sign, which she does without reading it.

"You're free to go," the officer says with no affect. She does not see Bratwurst-man. His shift must have ended hours ago.

The three walk to the car to ride the few blocks to the Nitty Gritty.

"Are you ok?" Andre asks when they get to the parking lot.

"I don't know—but thank you so much for coming. I'll repay you as soon as I can. Don't drop me off at home. I need to get my bike—the officer made me chain it to a stop sign two blocks from my house." She directs them to the signpost and gets out to unlock the chain. She decides it's best to walk next to her bike, on the sidewalk, escorting it home, lest Officer Bratwurst is secretly following her to see if she is going to illegally ride her bicycle with no ID.

Back inside the Mifflin apartment, she heads for the shower. She needs to stand under hot water and let the water splash inside her ass cheeks to seek out contraband she might have picked up in cell #20.

Mona found the five-bedroom house on East Dayton Street. It was a quick walk to the Capitol and Lake Mendota. Mona handpicked the roommates: Ezra the folksinger with his white dog; Liza the long-haired blonde who told them she would hardly be there because she would be sleeping at her boyfriend's house—she needed a place so she could tell her mother that she had her own place; Joseph the transcendental meditator; Annie; and Mona.

Annie had the least money of the roommates because she was in graduate school, paying for tuition and working part-time. Mona assigned the smallest bedroom on the second floor to Annie. Only a twin-size bed fit in it, with a small dresser and standing lamp. There was no closet.

Annie paid the least rent—fifty dollars per month. Sammy, a friend of Mona's, paid to house a second refrigerator in the kitchen to store drugs he was selling. His refrigerator had a lock on it. Annie and Ezra objected to their house being a front for Sammy even though they received house money for it. But Mona convinced the roommates he needed to deal drugs like marijuana, downers, uppers, peyote mushrooms, and LSD to pay his way through medical school—his parents earned too much to get student financial aid, and his parents wouldn't help him with school costs. Sammy's face was smooth, and his mouth turned up—as if his skin had been pulled taut—into a smile that looked like a shark. Everyone called him Sharkface.

The roommates fought over the primary refrigerator. Joseph was a vegetarian and didn't want his food to touch animal products. So they set up a separate shelf for his vegetables. They labeled it the cootie shelf, and the shelf above it, the beastie shelf. Mona made small placards to tape inside the refrigerator to keep the sections straight.

Joseph spent hours daily meditating. Annie asked him for a mantra because she wanted to meditate too. He said she would only get a mantra if she went through the official transcendental meditation program. She wanted a mantra without going through the program. He said no—she should do it right. Bowie told Annie to pay Joseph no mind—he didn't think she had to go through the training. "Just pick a syllable you like," he said. But she didn't want it to be FA or LA, which is what she thought about first. So she went with OM which she knew other people used and that's what Mona and Bowie used.

Joseph spent a lot of time in the bathroom. He said he needed to soak in the tub. Annie and Mona took turns knocking on the door. "Joseph, get out of the tub. We have to pee." He was probably performing mantras under the water. They could hear the water sloshing. "Stop masturbating so much," Mona liked to call out. She knew that made him mad.

When Joseph emerged from the bathroom, it was always filled with steam, and his face was red. He had no use for any of them. His parting shot typically was, "I'm going to meditate now, and you have to be quiet for at least an hour. I said one hour!"

Mona would yell out, "Aye, aye," give him a military salute and within fifteen minutes her stereo would be blaring Richie Havens, not because she didn't respect Joseph but because she forgot about Joseph.

Joseph would yell, "Turn that thing down. I'm trying to meditate."

It seemed like the whole house was meditating day and night. Annie figured they were pulsing a protective energy field around the house, though there was good and bad energy—animal and plant foods fighting in the refrigerator, and Sharkface pulling drugs out of the locked refrigerator to take to customers at locations far from the house. Mona told him he wasn't allowed to have any strangers come to the house—it was a security thing—and he followed the rules.

Annie was alone when she took a half-LSD pill one night to see what it was like. Sharkface gave it to her. He told her to take only half a pill and be sure there were people around in case she had a bad trip. She felt herself shrink like Alice in Wonderland to become a giant girl in a miniature dollhouse. The paper she was writing on for a school report turned into papyrus, and the words became thousands of years in depth and meaning. The words on the papyrus were truly profound—the words were entering a history book of the world. She was certain she would win the Nobel Prize for literature with her human three-dimensional history. The phone was ringing. She picked up the receiver and heard a voice but could not answer. She had become a receiver but not a sender; she could no longer respond. She left the house to walk to the Nitty Gritty to listen to the band playing that night. On the street, she perceived she was walking slowly, and slowly had a dimension. She came to a traffic stop but couldn't recall what the red and green lights meant. She knew one meant to walk, and one to stop, but which was which? Cars were moving in slow motion down the road like giant horses. A police car strolled by. She felt terror. The horses continued past her. She took a chance on a traffic light color and walked slowly across the street. The giant horses stopped to watch. She was sitting in the Nitty Gritty in the corner watching red lights flicker from the bass player's guitar. Bowie's friend Stan, a medic in Vietnam, came over to talk.

"Hi, Annie. How are you doing?"

She tried to talk but no words emerged. She couldn't get up. Stan found her a ride home.

The next day she told herself to never take acid again, not even half a tab. She'd lost her voice. She was prey. That is not how her gazelle and lion should live.

It was three in the morning when Bowie showed up—the bars had closed. Mona was getting ready for bed, walking naked down the hall from the bathroom.

"Annie's asleep. Why don't you come in my room—you can sleep here." Mona's bedroom door was open. She was standing in the doorway while he looked at her voluptuous body.

Annie was awake. She'd heard Bowie laughing across the hall and figured he would stay in Mona's room and have sex with her.

"Nope, gonna wake up Annie—she's my woo-man."

He turned away from Mona's doorway to open Annie's door, flipped on the light, and told Annie to wake up. He put down his pack, picked up the book she'd been reading before she went to sleep, and asked her to read to him. He wasn't fully drunk—he was happy. They went to sleep in a bit. Annie woke to the alarm clock at seven to get ready for work. Bowie reached over her body, picked up the little clock on the windowsill and hurled it out the window. Annie clambered quickly out of the mattress on the floor to rescue the clock in the yard. She couldn't afford to buy another clock. She got ready for work, and Bowie went back to sleep in her bed.

Annie and Bowie spent most late afternoons in bars near the Capitol—after he finished work. He drank beer and read science fiction books and Annie brought a book along too. Lately she'd been excusing herself to go for a walk, knowing he'd still be there when she came back. The bars were depressing—dark and dingy. She wasn't sure she could keep seeing Bowie though she enjoyed so much of their time together. Like his foot wash at her house the other day. He stuck his feet out of the shower, and she sudsed them generously, pressing bubbles between each toe. He laughed and the floor was wet with soap while a marauding puddle of water advanced down the hall. Joseph got mad because they were making noise when he wanted to meditate.

And she enjoyed the afternoon at the lake. He dripped wine from his bottle on her belly and licked the wine off her. She laughed and laid back in the sun with him.

In her dream last night, Annie and Jonas were hanging from a wire like spiders spinning webs. The webs were separate and the patterns distinct. They were trying to meet in midair, weave together. But it worked for only a moment, as long as it took the string to harden from liquid body juices. Annie woke from the dream with Bowie sleeping on the rug next to her bed.

He said it was time to leave Madison. He wanted to go to Seattle to find his father who he had not seen since he was a child. He asked Annie to go with him. She said she needed to stay to finish school. But he knew the truth. She couldn't spend her life in bars watching him drink himself to death. He was bent on self-destruction, and Annie was trying to pull herself out of her own depression.

Bowie painted a picture of a man with skyscraper buildings coming out of a cracked skull. The caption said, "In the city there is a desert made by people who always take and never give." He gave it to Annie before he left town.

Two weeks later, they walked to the Greyhound station.

"Are you sure you can't join me?" he asked again.

"I can't, Bowie. I'm sorry."

He was wearing his black cowboy hat, white t-shirt, and blue-striped bell bottoms. Lately he had stopped singing "Maggie's Farm" when they had sex.

He leaned his tall frame around her and held her for a long time.

"Love you, girl. You're going to be fine."

She didn't think she was going to be fine but didn't want him to worry about her like she worried about him.

And just like that, her disabled Marine took "Maggie's Farm" with him on the bus to Seattle. He flashed the peace sign from the window.

⁕

It was late fall when Jonas moved back to Madison. It had been a year since he left for Bruchen. So much had happened. He'd been storing most of his things in the Mifflin Street duplex attic. Annie brought his things to the East Dayton house for him to pick up when he was ready. Guitar. Kitchen things. Bedding. Clothes. Books. Was their private war over? Annie was afraid to hope.

In the end, their divorce came in phases, small visits marked by the exchange of things. One day he called to ask if he could get his sixteen-ounce mug back, the one with Paul Bunyan on the front, the blue ox, Babe, on the back. She wished she could keep the mug but it was his.

She tried to tell him that her hands were feeling grey, that her eyes were growing distant from her face, that her mind and her body were all moving on their own like they did not belong to her anymore. But all she said was she would return his mug.

The wind that day was blowing hard and loud. She pulled the fur hood on her parka about her neck, trying to stay warm. He would meet her at a coffee shop down the street. He was sitting in a booth.

"Hey, how are you?" he said. His eyes, looking grey-blue, read her dissonance.

"Okay, how are you?" Her hazel eyes, looking green, searched desperately for an old connection. But he had carefully severed most of their connections. He was remote and quiet.

"Here's Paul." She took out the mug wrapped in paper towels and handed it to him.

"Thanks."

There was a quick smile, then small talk. Her heart was breaking because he did not love her anymore. He said he was staying at Michael's farmhouse outside Madison until he figured out where to go next.

She wished he would come home to her, but she would not tell him that. And there was no room for him in the house with the five roommates anyway. Her room was tiny. There was no closet even in the room. And she was determined not to cling. He would tell her he is a dead man if she shared her thoughts. She doesn't want to hear he's a dead man.

There is a second visit two weeks later. "Meet me in the alley. You know, the alley that looks like a French street."

At seven in the morning, they meet to decide what will happen to them in this season of separation. It is like a morning duel, to kill a relationship off, she thinks. It's Saturday. She washes her hair early that morning, winds curlers into her long hair, and sits for a long time on the floor waiting for her hair to dry. Last night she dreamed about Otto the frog. In the dream, she reached for a pen in her coat pocket and brought up the tissue holding his heart. Jonas was next to her, asking, "What's that?"

She says, "It's nothing," a Kleenex she cried into or an ink blotter or a piece of bubblegum inside the tissue. She pressed the paper wad into her hand with Otto's heart in it and walked to the edge of the lake, and threw it out on the ice. Jonas was bending down to tie his walking boots. She tells him that was Otto the frog.

He looks at her, "What? Who?"

She says, "I killed him." She turned away and walked along the frozen lake. Jonas followed her. After the dream, she mused it was so long ago that Jonas followed behind her or next to her.

That morning she dressed quickly, pulled her black boots over her jeans, and walked to the French Street alley with its narrow grey-brown buildings and cobblestones along the edges. She turned the corner—it seemed like such a long time since she had seen him, really seen him. He was watching her come toward him. He looked so handsome. There were birds crying out. She dug her hands into her pockets.

"Hi," he says.

"Hi." She shuffles her boots in the snow at the curb. The buildings stood so lean.

"How have you been?"

"Fine." She drifts into a myriad of thoughts she wasn't sure she should share with him. Her colleague at work died. Muriel was a little person. She had four normal-size children. What would they do without their little mother who was so strong?

Jonas talks about his new girlfriend and plans to travel. Annie tells him Muriel had a heart attack. He shuffles his feet. They were ready to leave at hello. Growth was like that, dissonant and distancing.

She put out her hands, and he took both hands in his, held them briefly. He said he would come by later that day if it was ok to pick up his books and clothes and guitar and colored pens. He's going to stay longer at Michael's farmhouse.

She's afraid she will not be able to breathe if she stands there any longer but does not tell him. Then her legs start walking away without her brain telling them to. She's sure that something or someone else must be moving her legs for her. She turns to watch him for a moment from a few feet away. She waves—then whatever is driving her legs tells her to 'run, run, Annie.' And she runs from their French alley, around the corner, passing the shops that line the next street over. She knows she will be leaving town soon, her heart broken, but she can't tell him that.

He watches her go quietly; he lets her go quietly. She doesn't think his heart is broken. Like hers is.

Mona started to date Michael when they lived in the Mifflin apartment. She complained to Annie she couldn't give him a high rating in her notebook though she found him very sexy. He never kissed when they had sex, and that seemed strange. Mona was worried she might have bad breath. "Will you smell my breath—is there something wrong with me?" she asked Annie.

Annie smelled Mona's breath. It smelled normal. "I'm not going to kiss you to see if that smells."

Mona laughed. "I'm glad I don't smell. But even if he's not going to kiss me, his performance isn't very good. He doesn't last very long."

"How long?"

"I don't know—a few minutes? It doesn't seem very long." Mona thought she could help Michael by spicing things up—wearing lace panties, no bra, and short dresses that barely covered her vagina. This did not help. He was losing interest, and Mona was looking silly.

"Your breasts are too big to go without a bra," Annie advised her. "You know what you're going to look like when you're forty if you don't start wearing a bra?"

It was weeks later when Michael stopped seeing Mona sexually, but he kept hanging around their house. He liked being friends with Mona and Annie.

After Annie and Mona moved to the East Dayton house, Michael stopped by for a visit. Only Annie was home. He complained he was getting shaggy—he needed a haircut. His long brown hair was silky like Prince Valiant's in the comic books. "I'll cut it for you," Annie offered. "I used to cut hair in my college dorm."

"Cool," he smiled.

Annie set him up in a chair in the middle of the kitchen floor like he was a small island. She stood behind him. She borrowed the sharp hair scissors from Mona's dresser drawer. Annie pulled up sections of his long hair one by one to determine the length for each section. What should have been a ten-minute haircut lasted nearly an hour. She pondered every section of hair, drawn into the strength and silk of the fibers. She felt him relax under her fingers, the combing and brushing out. They discussed Annie's obsession with Jonas.

"How can one person feel so much attraction and the other person claims not to?" she asked while she snipped small slices of hair, matching the new swath to the others, judging the symmetry she was trying to achieve.

"People are different, Annie. You have to accept that. You can feel one thing, and Jonas can feel totally different."

Michael's words were helping her understand her separation from Jonas. Michael's hairs were lined up now, but Annie hesitated to put the comb and scissors down, enjoying the feeling of his hair in her fingers. "I think we're done," she finally said quietly, ruffling both hands through his scalp a last time.

He smiled and moved his chair back to the kitchen table while Annie swept up the hairs on the floor with the broom in the corner of the kitchen. "That was so great, Annie, so great. Thank you." Later Annie would hear Michael telling his brother that Annie had given him the best haircut he ever had.

Annie and Michael decided to deliver a Christmas tree to Kit, their friend who had just moved in with a Jewish fellow. Kit had never done the holidays without a tree, but she couldn't get a tree for fear of hurting her boyfriend's feelings. Annie and Michael figured Kit would not turn down a tree if one showed up on the porch. They waited until eight on Christmas Eve, after the tree stand closed. Only a few scraggly trees were left on the lot, so it didn't feel like Annie and Michael were stealing. They selected the biggest scraggly tree that fit into the bed of Michael's truck. The dusting of snow from last night's storm gave the tree a festive look in the dark.

"She'll be so excited," Annie exclaimed. "Let's just drop it on the front porch, ring the bell, and take off. She'll never know who brought it."

When they arrived at the house, they pulled the tree off the truck and gouged a new trail in the snow to the front porch. They rang the bell, then ran back to the truck. While Michael was starting the motor, Annie saw the porch light come on and someone open the door.

"Hurry up, they'll see us!" They had parked on the curved driveway, out of sight of the house. The motor was turning and turning.

Michael groaned, "I think we're dead."

"Shit, what are we going to do?"

Kit was heading up the driveway in her parka. They were going to be caught red-handed. So they got out of the truck when she stood in front of them, "Surprise! Merry Christmas!"

Kit was delighted. "I can't believe you brought me a tree! I've been so worried about not having one." Joel was heading toward them too.

"Come inside," Kit said. "It's too cold to stand out here. You have to have something to drink with us."

Michael and Annie exchanged glances of recapitulation, then followed the couple to the house. Michael explained they might have to spend the night because his truck won't start. There's only one extra bed upstairs, Kit tells them. Of course, they must stay. Michael offers to sleep on the couch downstairs, and Annie can take the bedroom.

"Oh, we've been friends for so long, we should be able to share a bed," Annie says.

Kit sets up the tree in the living room and Joel helps. They have hot apple cider and Christmas cookies Kit baked and then it's time to turn in.

Annie and Michael leave their clothes on when they get into the double bed. Annie is wearing an intricate bead necklace she made weeks ago with small garnet and black beads.

It's a cold night. It seems like the right thing to do to turn to one another. Michael turns to Annie's parts—her shoulders, arms, breasts—when her necklace breaks, and they hear the tiny beads scampering around the wooden floor. This must be an omen, she thinks. And he's not kissing her. He's petting her like she's a cat. He's surprised she's soft. He tells her he has always thought of her as hard. "I can see what Jonas sees in you," he says.

The mention of Jonas shocks her. Jonas is living at his farm now. She thinks to say at that very moment, "I can't sleep with you, Michael, because—"

He finishes her sentence, "because of Jonas."

She lets it stand. It is not because of Jonas. Jonas would be fine if she had sex with Michael—he would probably like her to have sex with Michael because he's a fan of Michael. It's because Annie knows too much about Michael's penis from Mona, and Annie doesn't want to deal with penis issues tonight. She turns away to go to sleep that Christmas Eve knowing she spared them both from humiliation if he couldn't have an erection. She owed him that much after the magical haircut they shared. And they were friends.

The next morning, Michael helps Annie pick up the beads that scattered around the bedroom floor. He rolls them into a small piece of paper he carried in his jeans pocket to roll marijuana in. "Now don't go and smoke this," he chuckled as he passes her the bead package.

⸻

Annie was having troubling dreams about directions. Train station dreams. Airport dreams. She runs from counter to counter asking ticket agents when her plane or train is leaving.

"Tell me your destination, and I will tell you when your train leaves," the agent says.

"I can't recall my destination," Annie says, embarrassed and grasping for help.

He wants to help: "I can't tell you when your train leaves if you don't tell me your destination."

Annie covers her face with her hands and starts to cry. The agent tells her to sit in the corner by his desk and see if she can remember. "It will come to you," he says in a calm voice.

Then Annie notices another train pulling out of the station. It's Jonas's train—she sees him standing by the open door on that train. There are other trains radiating from many tracks, crowded with people. But Annie does not know her destination. So she continues to sit on the floor near the agent's desk, trying to remember. After a while, she goes back to the ticket counter to ask to see a map. Maybe if she can see the names of locations, it might jog her memory, and she will know her destination, and then she can board her train.

The man at the counter shows her a map but it does not help. Annie is always going to be lost and left in the train station while people she loves leave for their trains. She does not know that is a destination—that living in the train station is a destination, that being lost is a destination.

⸻

The Judge Whitman incidents unwittingly set off the Zechman justice gene in Annie. She wanted to be a lawyer and fight for justice—more than she wanted a career in higher education research. Her brother was applying to law schools. He told her to apply too so they could start school at the same time, and open a family law firm when they finished. Daniel applied to two schools and was accepted by both. Annie applied first to the University of Wisconsin so she could stay in Madison. With a 3.8 grade point average in her master's degree, she thought she would be admitted. But her test scores were average and she was female, two strikes against her. When one of her male friends was accepted with a 3.0 grade point average, Annie headed up Bascom Hill to the law school to ask why she was not accepted. An administrator explained their ten percent quota on females—he said she was not in the top ten percent of the applicant pool.

On the walk down the hill, she mulled this news over—wasn't a quota illegal? If she questioned it, like bringing a lawsuit, there was a risk—she'd seen that with the student movement, the way people treated students who railed against Vietnam or the women's movement or racial injustice. They were labeled troublemakers, and who would hire them down the road?

She called Saul to tell him about the quota. He wanted to file a lawsuit, but Annie was tired of fighting. She would have to leave Madison—go someplace where she can work and save money for school.

Jayce had left Madison for Houston when she didn't get admitted to medical school in Wisconsin—she was taking classes in biochemistry to raise her grades and try to get into medical school in Texas. If Annie came to Houston they could share an apartment. So Annie applied to the University of Houston and Texas Southern University. The University of Houston turned her down. Only Texas Southern accepted her. Saul was doing legal work for a Black militant group fighting racism and he told her she'd be one of the few white people and one of the few women at Texas Southern—she would learn a lot and would be unique. "It's a good thing to be unique in law, you can do this, Annie!"

Annie felt like she was trying to find a life path with only half of her wits left about her. No doubt the Wisconsin law school was right: she did not measure up to the other women around the nation. She had a decision to make—move to Houston and go to Texas Southern, or stay in Madison and pursue the PhD program in higher education administration. First, she needed to save money for tuition.

Theodora invited her to come to St. Louis where she was in graduate school. She could get a job and rent the extra bedroom in her apartment and nurse her Jonas heartbreak there. "You'll be ok, Annie. No man is worth it. You need to put some distance between you and Jonas, and save money for school."

Reluctantly, Annie packs up the two dress cases she still has from her college years and buys a one-way bus ticket to St. Louis. She's almost broke and feels hopelessly broken. She doesn't try to see Jonas before she leaves.

On day two in St. Louis, Annie finds a temporary job at a café near Theodora's apartment. She will make sandwiches and ice cream sundaes and work the coffee machine. She won't make enough from this job to pay for groceries and rent, so she applies for food stamps at the government office five miles from the café. She chains her bicycle, which she brought with her on the bus from Madison to a signpost outside the food stamp office. She stands in line for two hours.

Annie finishes filing her papers and leaves the building to head to the café for her shift. She only has a short time to get there, or she'll be late for work. Her bike is gone—lock, chain, and all. Folks are milling around in front of the barbershop across the street.

"Have you seen my bike?" Annie asks, gesturing to the signpost. There's headshaking. No one is going to reveal whatever it is they have seen. Annie is the only white woman around. She's trying to figure out how she's going to get to the café—she can walk it, but she isn't wearing comfortable shoes. Her flimsy sandals will give out. And she'll be late for work. There's nothing to do but start walking down the four-lane street with cars streaming by, hot tears flooding her eyes.

She's a few blocks from the food stamp office when she hears the rumbling motor. She looks back to see a long black car that looks like a hearse with glistening blue wings. Five Black men are yelling out the rolled-down car windows, "Come on, baby, come over here." The car brakes screech to a stop ahead of her, then backs up slowly to line the hearse next to her. They want her, they yell. Both doors on the curb side swing open, and one of the men is heading toward her. She doesn't know if this is a joke. Should she play along? Should she run? Her heart is pounding, but her mind has switched into slow-motion mode.

Out of the corner of her eye, she sees a red city bus barreling toward them though there is no bus stop here. The bus brakes noisily and opens its door right behind the hearse. There's a quick thick smell of gaseous exhaust coming from the bus. The man just inches from her rushes back to the car, which peels away with screeching tires and more catcalling, "Get you next time, girl!"

Annie runs to the bus and jumps onto the first step breathless. She looks up to the very round face of a middle-aged Black man. He's not smiling. She starts to cry on the top step as she fishes through her purse, stalling because she knows there is no money in it. "I don't have any money for the fare—I'm sorry." She's shaking, adrenaline coursing through her body.

"It's on me, lady. Go take a seat." He still does not smile. He closes the bus door and pulls back into traffic. Annie sits next to an old woman reading a book who evidently has seen nothing of the drama through the front window of the bus. Annie tries to collect herself. From time to time, she sees the driver watching her in his rearview mirror.

When Annie gets off the bus by the stop across from the café, she exits from the rear. She knows the driver is watching. Later she wishes she had gotten his name or bus number so she could write the city about his heroic act. She didn't know if God or her dad or Flora sent him, but she said a prayer for the bus driver and his family that night.

The next day, Annie applied for a better job at the nearby university hospital as a medical transcriptionist. Her high school Latin came in handy for typing medical terms, and she already worked as a transcriptionist at the university hospital cancer ward and unemployment compensation office in Madison.

Theodora helped Annie find another bicycle to get around town. Every day, Annie rode to her hospital job through the park on a street that passed the back side of the city zoo. The giraffes lived on that side of the zoo, and their necks craned high above the fence to watch as she rolled by, waving and hallooing to them loudly. Morning was a crisp, fresh time, before the sultry summer air thickened during the day. Annie had made up her mind—she might have a broken heart, but she was going to keep moving no matter what. She couldn't know then there would be no bus driver to save her in Litchfield, Illinois.

———— ◦ ————

Now that Annie was living in St. Louis, she was talking more to Meyer, her sculptor professor from college. He was encouraging her to go to law school and get over Jonas. His three-month art exhibit in a St. Louis gallery was over and he was transporting the sculptures and paintings that didn't sell to his studio in Denver. He would drive all night when traffic would be light. His station wagon would pull a low-down trailer filled with his artwork.

Annie offered to keep him company. A road trip could be fun, and they would have a lot of time to talk. She would fly right back to St. Louis so she could be at work on Monday if Meyer would take her to the airport when they arrived in Denver.

Annie was alone in the apartment when Meyer arrived Saturday late afternoon—Theodora was out of town. The gallery helped him pack up the trailer. He knocked on the door, telling Annie to hurry. "I'm double-parked on the street." She looked out the window to see the brown station wagon with the trailer behind it in the middle of the street, next to the line of cars parked in front of her building.

"Ok, I'm ready."

"Do you want to have sex before we go?" he said, laughing.

She gave him a withering look. "We're not having sex." They had never had sex before. Why would he even ask this?

"I thought it couldn't hurt to try. It would help my driving—you know, I wouldn't be so tense."

Annie hoisted her small pack over her right shoulder. "Let's go." In the car, she buckled her seatbelt and asked what route they were taking.

"Interstate 70 through Missouri, Kansas, Colorado—about twelve hours. I can't drive too fast with the heavy load behind us. We're not going to stop except for meals and gas. But we can stop if you decide to have sex along the side of the road."

Annie chuckled and checked her watch. "We should be able to be at the airport in Denver in the early morning—plenty of time to catch a flight home."

Clearly, he's been thinking about having sex with her. Annie knows his marriage is in trouble. He told her he needs a friend. He already has a girlfriend in Denver. And his wife has a new boyfriend.

The miles pile up behind them now that they're out of the city. She asks questions about the business of art. How do galleries work? How does he make such tall metal sculptures in one piece? What does it take to weld metal? Where does he get the supplies? How does he create such smooth finishes? They talk about art. He tells her about his girlfriend, his wife, his sons. What graduate school in art was like. How disappointed his father was when Meyer told him he was going to be an artist. He doesn't like his job in the university art department. There's too much paperwork and committees that waste his time. He just wants to do art. He asks Annie why she wants to be a lawyer. He wants to hear all the things that are wrong with her boyfriends. He wants to know who has the biggest cock and how big it is. Did she ever measure it? And who has the biggest bank account? What does she like to talk with them about?

It's foggy that night. Their headlights seem to be hitting a solid wall in front of them.

"Damn it. Damn tumbleweed!" There's wind with the fog, and large plant balls coming at them like soft bombs. He can't swerve with the trailer behind the car. She's never seen tumbleweed so big. "It's Kansas, Dorothy," he says, guffawing. "There are big balls here."

He slows the car near a deserted-looking building in the middle of nowhere. "I have to pee. Don't go anywhere," he says, opening his car door.

She watches him disappear behind the small building.

He returns to the car and leans from side to side, stretching his back outside her door. "Do you need to go? We may not stop for a while."

She opens her door and steps out.

"Go behind the building." The headlights are facing the building so she has enough light to see. She pulls down her jeans and squats next to the building to pee, pulling out a piece of Kleenex from her pocket to wipe herself.

When she returns, Meyer asks if he can kiss her. She says yes. He kisses her several times. They are not great kisses, but they're warm. He's gruff, the way he kisses. She wishes he was not so gruff.

"My neck is sore. Can you rub it while we drive?" He shows her where it's hurting.

She slides closer to him on the front seat and rubs the back of his neck while he increases speed on the highway.

He asks about Jonas. "Why didn't things work out? You two seemed so tight."

Somewhere in Kansas, she gives him the short version. "It was a combination of things—Vietnam, he lost interest, he had other girlfriends." She wondered if that was true.

He nods—he's heard that story before. "What's your family like?"

She gives him the short version for that too. "I left home early. I'm different from my family. I'm the black sheep. I was sexually abused by my grandfather and didn't tell anyone because I knew no one would believe me. So I left for college and never went back, really."

"I'm sorry." He didn't know what to say to that.

They talked about friendship between men and women. "I don't think a man can be friends with a woman. Men will always want to have sex with the woman," he postulated.

Annie disagreed. "I have had lots of friendships with men who didn't want to have sex with me. Platonic relationships."

He snorted at that word: "Pla-ton-ic. That's bullshit, Annie. I'm not talking about you. I'm talking about men. Men are always going to want to fuck you. They're not going to be your friend."

"I don't agree. Maybe you want to fuck everybody, but not every man wants to fuck every woman."

He snorted a low gravelly laugh. "I'm right, Annie. You know I'm right."

They fought about this driving through Kansas bombed by more tumbleweed balls. Annie gave him examples from literature of men and women who were friends.

"That is story time. Those writers made it up, Annie."

"I think we could be friends. I think we are friends."

"No, I cannot be friends with a woman."

"What about your sister. You're friends with her, aren't you?"

"Yes, but she's my sister. You're not my sister, Annie."

He pulled into an all-night café and gas station. "We can get early breakfast here."

Annie headed for the women's restroom while Meyer put gas in the car. She washed her face in the sink. Then she joined Meyer at a booth near the door. The café is empty.

"What do you want," an aging waitress with bushy pumpkin-colored hair calls out from the counter by the kitchen. She doesn't even walk to the table.

Annie shouts back, "Pancakes and bacon. Orange juice."

Meyer shouts, "Black coffee, two eggs over easy, toast with jelly." He looks intently at Annie. "You don't look tired at all. I'm beat."

Annie doesn't feel tired. "You had to load up the car before we left, and you're doing all the driving."

"I don't sleep much at night," he tells her.

She smiles sympathetically.

Pumpkin-head brings their plates to the table, and Meyer pays her right then.

He dips his toast in his runny eggs and drinks the coffee, "Eat up. We have a long way to drive."

They're back in the car feeling better after hot food.

He asks her about the best book she's ever read, and he tells her what books he likes. She's surprised he reads about anthropology, religion, and history. She figured he would read mostly art books.

"Hey, I have a gift for you, Annie." He pulls a small box from behind his seat.

"What is it?"

"Open it." He flicks on the overhead light inside the car so she can see the sculpture. It's a clay rendition of a red penis climbing out of a grey clam. It's mounted on a thick wooden frame. The title was printed in gold-colored ink, "The Secret of the Clam."

She didn't like it but wasn't sure if she should tell him.

"Do you know about clams? Why I think about you when I think about clams?" he asked.

She rolls her eyes at him. "No, why?"

TEN BEFORE THIRTY • 225

He flicks off the overhead light. "Clams live in a shell with no brain—they have a retractable foot that looks like a tongue or a penis. Clams are males when they're young—when the water gets warm enough, the clams release their sperm, and maybe their sperm meets up with eggs out in the water too, that are produced by larger, older clams that have turned into females. But maybe they don't. Do you know what it's called when a sperm and egg manage to meet up in the water?"

"No, what?"

"A mulberry. When the cells of the eggs start to divide and turn into a cell ball—they call the ball a mulberry. And that's it, Annie, it's like reproduction by chance." He chuckled, "You could learn something from my clam sticking out his penis."

"Does that mean you're a young male clam or an old male turning into a female?"

"Good question," he smiled approvingly. "I think I'm still a young clam, Annie, putting it out there, not knowing if the water is warm enough to make a miracle connection."

"So if I'm a young male that is turning into an older clam female who will put eggs out there, you're saying this all works when the waters are the right temperature to meet up?"

"Yes, after the amazing gender changeover there is a lot left to chance. Then comes the mulberry, Annie," he chuckles.

"I'll remember all this the next time I look at the mulberry jelly at the grocery."

"Good. Get some jelly and think about it, Annie."

"I can't believe you're so interested in clam sex."

"I'm interested in every kind of sex," he said laughing. Then his mood went somber. "Annie, I don't want to be alone. I don't want the divorce but it's coming. I get suicidal when I'm alone."

She didn't know what to say. He always seemed so strong and confident. She wondered if the clam gift was a message about some sort of future with her—if he'd been thinking about their relationship.

The hours passed into early morning. At dawn they watched the first striations of pink, mauve and gold paint the prairie canvas, and half an hour later, the sun lift its perfect bowl above the phalanx of mountains ahead.

"Glorious, Annie. This is glorious."

She agreed. Their easy talking was slowing as they realized their time was coming to an end. And then he was driving on the airport road to drop her off.

"You don't look like you've been up all night," he says. He's tired and looks tired. "I'm glad you came with me, Annie. It's so fun to hang out with you."

"We're friends—I'm glad I kept you company."

"We can't be friends, Annie. You know why. But there are those miracles of warm ocean water. Think about it." He leans over to kiss her.

She exits the car and waves as she heads into the airport. His clam sculpture is tucked into her backpack. He watches until she passes through the sliding glass doors, then pulls the station wagon and trailer back to the road.

It was two weeks since the road trip with Meyer. Theodora was back in town. They were reading a magazine article listing twenty ways to make money. "Listen to this one," Theodora says while they drink orange juice. "You take a trip on an airplane. You travel with two pieces of luggage and get the claim checks for them. A friend meets you at the airport and collects your luggage. Meanwhile, you look around the baggage area for your bags which you're never going to find. You file a claim with the airline, but the airline is never going to find your bag. You list the contents of the missing bags, and the airline pays you two hundred and fifty dollars per bag or five hundred dollars for the two."

"What, you can get five hundred dollars?" This might be the way to pay for law school tuition. Annie rationalizes this is a logical next step—because of her treatment as a woman—quotas for women, her male friend getting into law school when his grades were lower than hers—she has to fight back anyway she can—this is what it means to be independent—you have to live by your wits, do things that make you feel uncomfortable. So Annie and Theodora decide to carry out the plan next week.

Annie leaves Theodora's apartment with her two large dress cases—one nested inside the other. Annie takes a city bus to the outskirts of town to get to the interstate, where she will hitchhike from St. Louis to Chicago's O'Hare airport. She will stay overnight in Chicago to visit Michael's brother and his wife, then catch a return flight to the St. Louis airport the next day where Theodora will pick up her bags. Annie's been hitchhiking in Wisconsin the last few years to save money. She's never had a car of her own. She's been telling herself, if men can hitchhike, so can she. She dresses that day as manly as she can—baggy t-shirt, baggy jeans, long hair pulled back with a tie, no makeup. She looks plain on purpose.

She's standing at the entrance to the interstate connecting St. Louis to Illinois when a red Ford Mustang stops. She tells the driver her father is dying of a heart condition, and she has to get to O'Hare to catch a flight to Texas. The driver looks like he is in his late twenties. Blond, blue-eyed, clean-cut. There's an embossed emblem of a mustang horse on the inside glove compartment and a wood-look plastic grain accentuates the entire car—Annie's never been in a Mustang before. The driver seems okay. She never asks his name and does not give him her name.

Mustang-man says he works on the docks in St. Louis. He's heading home to Illinois. He'll give her a ride part of the way. She says she's trying to save money to go to law school in the fall. She places her luggage trunk in the back seat of the car. There's small talk for the first hour. Then they stop at a gas station near Litchfield. She had seen the Litchfield sign. Mustang-man heads to the men's room, and she goes to the women's room. Then they're back in the car. She struggles to keep the chatter going, feeling tired.

He turns off an exit road.

"Is this as far as you're going?" she asks, seeing cornfields ahead. The stalks are eight or ten feet high. He slow-brakes the car by the side of the cornfields and places his right hand on her left forearm. His hand feels like ice.

"How about doing something for me now?" he says without a smile. At the same time, his left arm reaches over his body and pulls a gun from under the center console of the Mustang. His left hand is now holding a large black gun an inch from Annie's forehead.

She's buckled into her seat belt, adrenaline suddenly fueling a thousand top-speed thoughts through her head. Is he going to shoot her? Is this a joke? Should she make a run for it? Where can she run? Into those dense cornfields? If she makes it to the cornfields before he shoots her in the back, is he going to track her down with the gun and shoot her in the cornfields? He looks fit—no doubt he could outrun her, and she's wearing sandals, not even running shoes. And what about her luggage in the back of the car? Is she really about to lose her life? A little inside voice is answering her. 'Stay calm, stay calm.' All in a split second.

She hears another voice she doesn't know she has saying, "You don't want to do this; I have to get to Chicago." All while the voice inside her head is telling her to remain calm, telling her not to run, advising her it is too risky.

He isn't talking. Maybe he doesn't have voices in his head. The gun is pointed an inch from her head. The road is deserted. No one is going to see or hear anything. The cornfields stretch for miles. He parked far enough down the road that if she darts out of the car, she will never be able to get back to the highway before he chases her down.

She has a last thought about jumping out of the car and hiding in the cornfields when he says coldly, "Pull your jeans down." He's holding the dark gun barrel in front of her forehead and she imagines herself bleeding with a bullet wound from the center of her face.

She never remembers unbuckling her seatbelt, but she must have. She decides in those slow-motion moments to do what she has to do, and some new force takes over for her as she splits into two people in an instant. Her right hand covers her eyes, leaving a small air space where she can hover, in courageous fear, while he opens his pants.

She never closes her eyes. The gun never leaves his left hand. She wonders if he is left-handed or right-handed and if he is a good shot with his left hand. She pulls her brown baggy jeans down with her own left hand and then her white panties—they are her favorite—they have a lace panel in the shape of a V on the front panel. She's cold, shaking, and hovering in her narrow eye space. That space between her hand and her eyes is the space she needs to continue to live.

He moves across the front seat to get on top of her. She is still sitting in the passenger seat. She is thinking ahead. What is he going to do when he's done? Will he shoot her and leave her dying in the cornfields or push her out of the car? He paws clumsily at her right breast. She shoves his hand away in disgust—a reflex. Surprisingly, he does not continue with her breast but fumbles with his pants with his one free hand.

Annie notices through her eye space that he's wearing boxer shorts. What kind of rapist wears boxers? And they have blue patterns that look like bluebirds though it's hard to see peering through the spaces between her fingers. She can't lower her hand to see better because her spirit will have no place to wait—and above all, she must protect her spirit.

Then she catches a good glimpse of bluebirds—and the tiniest penis she has ever seen—it is limp. Her fear increases tenfold. 'Oh my God, now he won't be able to do it, and he will kill me because he's impotent.' All the while, the real penis, the firm gun penis, is at her head. Maybe a big blast from his gun will satisfy him more than whatever snort he's going to get out of that penis for the twenty seconds he ends up being inside her. He did something inside her she thinks, but she is not sure what.

She wishes she could focus on what is happening to be better prepared for what is coming, but she is hovering in that space between her hand and eyes, trying to hold her spirit there, trying to keep breathing. The fear is so thick she can barely move.

It is a fast rape. She fights the feeling that this is not real. She doesn't know if the killing part is next. Will it be a fast killing like the fast rape? Surely, there will be more pain. And no one will hear her dying in this cornfield, with the corn so tall, lining the narrow road like fences for as long as the eye can see.

He rolls back to his seat from between her legs, and without his permission, she quickly lifts her white panties and brown jeans back into place, using both hands. Her spirit is uncovered and she is trying to be ready for the next assault.

He starts up the car. She doesn't know where the gun is. It is no longer pointed at her forehead, but it can't have gone far. He must have it in his left hand. Maybe he is waiting to surprise her with a bullet to the side of her head.

"Do you want to get out of the car, or should I keep driving?" he asks.

She's incredulous they are having this conversation. Should she get out in the deserted cornfields? What if he shoots her as he drives away? He is acting as if he has done nothing wrong.

She plays along, trying to stay calm. "If you would take me to the intersection of the highway and this road and let me out, I would appreciate that."

"Ok." She's sure now that he has put the gun next to his left side where she can't see it. They are leaving the cornfields.

At the highway intersection, she gets out of the car and pushes the seatback forward to retrieve her luggage from the back seat. She doesn't know if he is looking at her. She is too afraid to look at him. She says nothing. She closes the back door and the passenger door. Then the red Mustang with the limp penis and hard metal gun pulls away to travel down the highway alone.

Annie is alive and trembling, nausea sweeping over her in waves. Her legs are weak. She is shaking next to her shabby packing case in her loose yellow t-shirt and baggy brown jeans. Her clothes must be disheveled, so she tries to put herself in order.

Just minutes later, a dark blue sedan stops. Annie has not put her thumb out, but she is a young woman standing next to luggage in the middle of nowhere. Her heart is pounding in fear. What if it is a man? But it is a woman, thank God, it is a woman. The woman says, "I don't usually stop for a hitchhiker, but I thought I should stop when I saw you. Is everything ok?" She looks like a military woman with close-cropped hair.

Annie wants to tell her she is not okay, but her inner voice speaks up to tell the same story she told Mustang-man. Her father is having heart surgery, and she needs to get to O'Hare. That is why she is distraught. The woman nods her head sympathetically. Maybe she thinks Annie is off one of the nearby farms though there are no farms Annie can see close by.

The woman thankfully chatters for the rest of the ride about her business. Annie's mind is on autopilot. The woman goes out of her way to take Annie directly to the airport, and Annie thanks her profusely. She wishes she could thank her properly. Later she will mention this woman in her prayers, telling herself there must be a God because she is still alive, and someone sent this military woman to rescue her.

While they were driving toward the airport, Annie decides she cannot visit her friend in Chicago that night. She decides to fly to Madison to seek safe haven—Jonas.

Hours later, she deplanes in Madison. There's the sky, and she's breathing Wisconsin air. There are two rainbows arching overhead. It has just rained. This must be an omen but of what? The man she loves is in Madison, but he's the man who has hurt her by leaving her. And now she's been raped. And she was nearly kidnapped weeks ago. Surely, Jonas will not turn her away now. She gets into a taxi to head for town. The rainbows are obviously for someone else on the plane, not for her. She trusted the red Mustang. She let her guard down.

The taxi drops her off at the Nitty Gritty bar because she isn't sure where to find Jonas. She has not changed her clothes yet. There's a big crowd at the Nitty Gritty. It feels safe to be in a room with a lot of people. Annie pretends nothing has happened as people she knows come up to say hello. It's been months since she left town.

Michael, who rents the farm where Jonas is renting a room from him, sees her. "What are you doing back?" She tells him she was hitchhiking to Chicago to see his brother and she was raped, so she came back to Madison to see Jonas.

Michael is shocked—how can Annie be talking so normally? She must be kidding, but she wouldn't kid about something like this. "Are you all right?" he asks, grabbing for her hand, to hold her hand.

She says she is. But she's still processing what happened hours ago in a slower, more methodical part of her brain. She's telling herself everything is ok. It was a fast rape, it was not a painful rape, she got off easy, there are no bullet holes in her head, no beatings, he didn't force her to carry on with him for hours. She had almost convinced herself it had not even been a rape. But there was a gun at her forehead, and she keeps seeing the metal hole of the gun barrel and how thick the metal rim was. And how tiny and limp his penis was. And the bluebirds.

Michael asks if Annie wants a ride to the farm. She says yes. Even if Jonas isn't there, she can stay in his bed. Jonas is there when they arrive. She tells him what happened but spares the details. It's late, and she's so tired from the day. He is still home to her.

She undresses while Jonas leaves to brush his teeth. He gives her a black and green checkered flannel shirt to put on which she gratefully pulls over her naked body. She takes her white panties to the bathroom after Jonas finishes and washes them in the sink. She's trying to decide if she should throw them out or ask Jonas if they could burn them in the yard. She wonders if there's a ritual she should go through to dispose of panties after a rape. She doesn't know what to do and doesn't want to ask for his opinion. So she asks him for a bag. He goes to the kitchen and comes back with a small brown lunch bag, the kind children carry to school. She carefully places the panties, still wet from being washed in the sink, in the lunch bag and folds the bag into her purse. She will transfer the lunch bag to the back of her underwear drawer in St. Louis and figure out what to do with her panties another time.

Jonas is quiet, kind, and guarded. Her rape is not going to change his mind. He wonders if she got herself into this mess so he will feel sorry for her. They had not parted on good terms. She wanted to stay in Madison, and he advised her to go. He was trying to be rational: "Look around, Annie, there aren't any jobs for people with graduate degrees. Leave and save yourself."

She knew that was true but believed he wanted to be free of her, to see other women. They climbed into his bed. He wrapped his arms around her. She knew he didn't know what to say, and he would be quiet. That is one of the things she loved about him, that he could just be quiet.

She left the next day to return to St. Louis, focused on the luggage plan. Theodora met her plane at the airport, and Annie handed her the baggage claim checks. Theodora carted the two packing cases off to her car. Then Annie looked in pretend-vain for her bags. After a respectable amount of time. Annie headed to the claims office to pick up the papers to fill out that ask her to list the contents of her bags if her bags didn't turn up. The agent assures her the bags will turn up.

They do turn up, of course, in Theodora's car. On the drive back to the apartment, Theodora is saying how easy this has been. Annie shakes her head. "Not so easy."

"What do you mean?"

Annie tells her about the rape. Her voice tone is flat as if she is telling Theodora she bought a pair of shoes on the trip.

Theodora, usually unflappable, is shocked, and her voice gets emotional. "Are you ok? Are you ok?"

Annie nods she is, but she is not. She does not tell her details. She's never going to tell anybody about the secret space between her hand and her eyes she created for her spirit which gratefully stepped up to take control when she split into two beings, about the sick bluebirds on his boxer shorts, about his tiny penis with so many flaccid wrinkles, and how powerless she felt—waiting to be shot in the cornfields after he finished with her.

When they got back to the apartment, Theodora phones her husband, who is working in New York. He is more emotional than Annie or Theodora. He is angry at them both. He yells at them for taking such risks and ends his tirade with, "That's what the two of you get for doing something illegal!"

Theodora's lawyer friend comes to the house and advises Annie to report the rape to the police. She won't. There's the airplane scam—and her past. They always bring the woman's past up in court cases. If she'd had sex before, especially with multiple partners, she must have been a willing partner this time. That's how it is. And if she goes to the police, she will have to tell her family. She can't do that, even if she hardly ever sees them. It would hurt them too much, especially her mother. Annie is sure she has to be quiet about this, like so many other things.

Annie thinks the better idea is old-style justice. She tries to recall numbers on the Mustang license plate, where he said he worked along the docks, and other identifying information. She believes she can find him. She can put together a women's posse, big women who will carry weapons like clubs with nails on their heads, and they will find him and beat him until he is dead. She does not want him beaten up and living—she wants him dead, and she wants his bluebird boxers bloody.

The lawyer says, "You can't go kill him; rape is not considered a crime worse than murder."

Annie disagrees. "It is as bad as murder. It's definitely as bad as murder."

Theodora tells Annie to see a doctor in case Mustang-man is diseased.

Annie is convinced God is retaliating for the airline scam. 'Ok girl, if you want to commit crimes, there's going to be a price to pay.' That's when Annie prays for forgiveness. She decides she will not put in the request for reimbursement from the airlines. She will tell them she found her bags. And it begins to dawn on her what it's going to be like to live the rest of her life as a woman. She isn't going to be able to live the Jack Kerouac life, seeking adventures along the highway of life, and ever feel free again. And she cannot judge a person's character by looking at him, by talking to him.

She was wrong about Mustang-man and so many other people. And she knows what powerless is, knowing the reality of the barrel of a gun.

Waiting for this to sink in, Annie passes the time dreaming about the women's posse, envisioning Mustang-man's death over and over. The next Wednesday, on garbage day, Annie calls in sick to work. She pulls the brown lunch bag with her favorite white panties in it from the dresser drawer in her small bedroom. She doesn't open the bag because she doesn't want to see her old panties. She takes the bag to the garbage bin outside the apartment and waits for the garbage truck. It usually arrives between nine and ten in the morning. The truck is on time. Annie stands by the apartment door so she can watch the metal tongs of the truck lift the garbage bin and dump the contents into the rumbling maw.

Flora's list grew by four that year—Annie added the final breakup with Jonas, the near-kidnapping on the street after her bicycle was stolen, and the cornfield rape. Then Annie received Jayce's letter. Jayce moved to Houston a month earlier to pursue her dream of medical school. She started a paper route job and was raped in a dense fog at four-thirty in the morning on her third day of work. A young Black man dragged her into the bushes, punched her in the face, and warned her to be quiet. She told Annie she felt uncomfortable saying he was Black. Was she racist because she shared his skin color? She did not go to the police and would not give up her paper route—she needed money for rent and school—but now she was fearful and nervous all the time. She asked how Annie was faring without Jonas and trying to get into law school. She was not giving up her dream to go to medical school. She said they should both be strong. Annie wrote her back and told her how sorry she was and about the cornfield rape. There were more letters talking about the irony of them being raped the same month. They didn't know if they were racist. They both mentioned the race of their attacker when they talked about it. Why weren't they just men, not white and Black men? Annie added Jayce's rape to Flora's list. She reasoned it wasn't right for Annie's to be a really bad thing and not Jayce's too.

Another for Flora's list came weeks later. The handsome doctor Annie worked with invited her to go on a bike ride over lunch. Her job was transcribing radiology reports dictated by the doctors on tape recorders—his was the voice she most enjoyed hearing because he left her flirtatious messages on his tapes.

They met at the bike racks. She was wearing her pink miniskirt, white blouse, and sandals; he was in blue scrubs. She'd been looking good these last few weeks. She'd been sitting by the apartment swimming pool to develop a deep tan while she tried to sweat away the memory of bluebird shorts, gun barrels, and cornfields. She wondered after Jayce's letters if all women have to accept a common fate: low-paying jobs, closed doors, and rape.

They rode through the hospital parking lot toward the park. Her doctor was several feet ahead. Annie saw the large old car with wide metal wings backing out rapidly from a parking space toward her. She knew it would hit her. Time slowed. She heard herself cry out in anticipation of the impact. At the same moment, she heard her doctor yell, "Get out of the way!" It was too late. The car hit with a sickening metal-on-flesh thud. Her right foot felt demolished though the skin was intact. She fell to the pavement. Three men in the car jumped out with cans of beer in their hands.

"Let me have a look. Let me have a look," they yell, trying to grab her foot.

"Leave me alone," Annie protests, trying to protect herself from further assault. The doctor is by her side. He says he's a doctor and he will help her to the emergency room. The men are apologizing. There is no exchange of car insurance information or names. Annie leans on the doctor's left arm for balance as he walks her bike, along with his, back to the hospital, up the concrete driveway to the emergency room. She hops slowly on one foot, the damaged foot flailing like a swollen fish corpse. The emergency room doctor knows Annie from her rounds picking up transcription tapes. He says he will x-ray her foot and leg for free. Her foot looks like it's the circumference of her thigh.

"Good news, Annie. Amazingly, no broken bones, but you have extensive tissue damage. I'm going to give you a tetanus shot—the metal car bumper was rusty. You need to keep your foot elevated as much as you can for several weeks. Tissue damage can be a long heal, longer than bone."

Weeks of elevating her socked right foot follow while Annie types patients' charts from dictation. Her doctor leaves messages on tape to cheer her up but no more flirtatious innuendos.

Annie concludes God is delivering swift justice. He must have sent the car to slam into her foot to prevent her from seducing the married radiologist.

That's when Texas Southern University sends a letter: she has two weeks to let them know if she will be attending their law school, and a down payment on fall tuition money will be due then. Annie tries to figure out how to make this work. Can she get to Houston in her condition? She's barely able to walk, doesn't have enough money to pay the tuition, and is fragile from the rape. Was Jayce's rape an omen? The two women planned to share an apartment in Houston. Daniel was starting law school, and he's the boy in the family, her mother just reminded her—he has to support a family someday. Annie is on her own.

She makes three decisions. Tell Theodora she's leaving town. Inform Texas Southern she cannot attend law school at this time. And give two-weeks' notice to her job at the hospital. Her swollen foot, sad vagina, broken heart, and empty bank account made the decision that Annie Zechman is in no shape for law school. Furthermore, the tribunal is calling for excommunication to Dallas at her mother's house. The tribunal will reconsider her prognosis at a later time.

EXCOMMUNICATION

The tribunal sends twenty-four-year-old Annie Zechman to the city she struggled so hard to get out of in high school, the city that kills presidents. She has left what she cares about most—a life with Jonas. She does not explain to anyone her excommunication by tribunal. The only shoe she can ease her slow-healing foot into is an open-backed wooden clog with a blue suede upper. She clunks like a horse when she goes up and down the stairs to her mother's second-floor apartment, no matter how lightly she tries to tread.

"I hope it's ok to stay for a while," Annie says to her mother. "I'll look for an apartment as soon as I get a job. And I'm going to get braces for my teeth."

"It's fine to stay with us. We love you. We're happy you're back." She doesn't say anything about Annie's idea to get braces.

Annie sits cross-legged on one of the black leather chairs set around the table at the open end of the narrow galley kitchen keeping her mother company while she's making dinner—stuffed peppers. Annie plays with the small blue plastic chicken among the other tchotchkes on the metal bookcase next to the table. When she presses the chicken's pronged feet against the table, a small yellow egg falls out of the chicken's butt.

"Where did you find this chicken? I love this."

Her mother laughs. "I don't remember but I like it too. Do you like stuffed peppers?"

"Not really, but I'll eat the insides—not the peppers."

237

"I love peppers," Mother says. She's already mixed the beef and onion in a frying pan and added spices and rice. She uses a spoon to fill the peppers with the meat mixture. The six peppers look like green bowls stacked side by side in the glass baking pan. "Do you think you'll eat one or two?" She's trying to decide if four are enough for the four of them tonight.

"One."

"Then we'll be good. I'm worried about your foot. Does it hurt when you walk? When do you think you'll be able to wear regular shoes?"

"It does hurt if I've been walking a long time. The doctor says soft tissue heals slowly. I don't know about other shoes—I'm just glad I could find these to wear."

"I'm sorry I can't give you any money to go to law school. You know I have to help Daniel."

"I know. I'll handle things on my own." Annie tries to assure her mother she'll be fine, but she feels like a wave breaking on a shore—some of her waves are swelling strong and steady, hitting the beach with purpose; others are half-formed and flaccid.

"And I can't get you a car to get around—we don't have the money."

"I know, Mom—I'll find a job soon." Hannah is working and just bought her own car. Annie already got into it with Hannah when Annie arrived two days ago. Hannah refused to share her bedroom with the twin beds they slept in when they moved to Texas nine years ago. Annie reminded her she wouldn't be there long—she'd find an apartment as soon as she found a job. Hannah told her to sleep in the den. Daniel's twin bed was in the den, along with a long wooden desk that spanned one wall, bookshelves, and a reading chair. Annie said it didn't make sense to sleep in the den because she would still have to use the bathroom off Hannah's bedroom, and there was no closet in the den. Hannah told her to sleep in the den, and she could knock on Hannah's door to get access to enter the bedroom and then the bathroom.

Annie's sore foot was walking on eggshells at the house. Her tribunal reminded her to accept what she could not change; this is what excommunication requires. So Annie set up her things in the den and used her suitcase as a closet.

The job search kicked off the next day. Annie saw an ad for airline stewardesses in the newspaper and sent in her application. She got a call back within a day.

The morning interview with the airline was going well—Annie was already imagining flying around the world in a snappy colored costume and studying French or Spanish. Once she had a few years of flying experience, they said she would be a good candidate for their administrative training program with her master's degree. Annie was reveling in the idea she would have actual destinations from airports she would fly through—she would have places to go.

"So, Annie, is there anything that will affect your appearance in the next several months?"

Their question didn't make sense. Was this their way of asking if she is pregnant, which she knows is illegal to ask in an interview? She explains she plans to put braces on her teeth soon because she has impacted wisdom teeth, and her dentist recommends braces after he removes her wisdom teeth.

"Our policy does not permit stewardesses to wear braces, but we would welcome you to reapply when your braces are removed."

Annie is surprised at the change in the tone of the interview. The polished-looking interviewers—a man and a woman—both with perfect teeth, stand up to usher her out. Annie's horse-shoes clop on the terrazzo floor. Then she deplanes their offices.

"Bye-bye."

"Bye-bye."

"Bye-bye."

Annie emerges to a steamy Texas heat though it is still morning. The airline offices were cold from air conditioning. She's trying to remember where she parked her mother's grey sedan. It doesn't seem right that stewardesses can't wear braces. Is this a safety issue? If the plane goes down, would she have a hard time saving lives with braces on her teeth? She knows this is about brand—their women need to look good in a snappy outfit and smile with great teeth. There are no male flight attendants. Are the pilots—mostly men—able to wear braces?

In the car she turns the air conditioner on high. The tribunal is telling her to shake it off, to process this later. She borrowed the car for the day to check out jobs, and that's today's mission. Next on the list, the local school district office. Before she left the house, Mother asked if she liked chicken cacciatore—that's what she is making for dinner tonight.

"I like chicken but not the sauce. I can move the sauce to the side."

"I wish you would eat more—you're too thin. Be careful driving." Mother handed her the keys to the car, and Annie clunked down the stairs toward the carport, thinking what it would be like to do meal planning every morning like her mother does. Annie didn't like to think about what she would eat for dinner in the morning.

By the time Annie drove through heavy traffic to the school administration building near downtown, it was early afternoon. She asked at the main desk if she could talk with someone in the research office. She had read about the school district's impressive research operation. The secretary made a quick call.

"Someone will see you," she smiled at Annie. "Go up those stairs over there, then all the way down the hall to Room 205—the deputy superintendent's office."

The deputy superintendent had already come out of his office to meet Annie at the head of the stairs. She apologized for dropping in without an appointment.

"No worries. Follow me," he said, walking to his office.

She took a seat in a chair next to his oak desk.

"So, what can I do for you today?" he said amiably. He was in his late fifties, balding, long-sleeved, striped blue shirt with sleeves rolled up informally—no tie, top button of his shirt opened.

"Thanks so much for seeing me. I'm interested in getting into education research and hoping you can help me determine how to prepare for this type of career," Annie explains. She sees his PhD in a bronze frame on the wall next to the desk—in psychology. "Here's my resume if it would help to see my background. I've completed all the coursework for a teaching license except student teaching at the University of Wisconsin and completed my first PhD level course in educational administration. I've just relocated back to Dallas."

He scans her resume quickly and asks if she's comfortable writing.

"Yes, my master's degree is in English—I've written many academic papers and worked on school newspapers in high school and college." She asks what type of background is needed to work in education research.

"Have you ever written a grant proposal?" he asks, leaning back in his chair.

"No, I haven't." She feels like they're not on the same wavelength and tries to get the conversation back on track. "What type of topics are your researchers focusing on?"

He continues to flip through her resume. "Do you think you could learn how to write a grant proposal?"

"Well, yes, I think I could write any type of document." She wonders why he's not answering her questions about a research career.

"So tell me how you would learn how to write a proposal." He leans forward over the desk.

She starts making up a plausible answer. "Well, I'd identify people who write grant proposals—like at the universities and the city or county offices and meet with them to learn their processes. I'd review their documents, read books and articles about grant writing, and from that figure out how to write proposals." She realizes he must be intending something with his questions.

"We're adding a new office of grants, Annie, and just hired an experienced fellow from Chicago who will be joining us in a few months to build out the office. We're interested in hiring a writer now to get us started. We could consider you for this role, see how you do if you're interested in something like this."

Annie was flabbergasted and nodding her head, yes, she could do this. Yes, she would like to do this. Her tribunal would like her to do this. Her ailing foot would like her to do this. Energy inside her belly is bubbling up hopeful.

He smiles at her, pulling out a form from the desk for her to fill in. "Good timing you came in today, Annie. Fill this in at the front desk and leave it with the secretary." He stands up and escorts Annie down the hallway to the stairs. She tries not to clunk too loudly on the concrete floor.

Two hours after Annie walked into the school administration building, she has completed the application and has a full-time professional job. They classify her as a Resource Teacher-Grants, thanks to her academic degrees. She will start Monday at eight in the morning. The salary added to the letter of agreement will enable her to qualify to buy a car.

That night the family celebrates with chicken cacciatore, green salad, fruit salad, and ice cream. Annie skips the salad and fruit salad and scrapes the sauce from the chicken. She makes everyone a sundae with chocolate ice cream from the freezer, Hershey's chocolate syrup, and walnuts. While she tries to fall asleep later in the den, she reviews the day with her tribunal. She wishes she could call Jonas to share the news.

The next morning, Annie asks her mother for a ride to the Ford dealership. She told the family during dinner last night she was going to look into buying a car so she could get to work. They said she was moving too fast. She said she was not moving fast enough. Her mother agreed to give her a ride but reminded her she could not help her financially.

"I know. I think I can buy a car based on proof I'm employed—using my letter of offer."

A salesman greets them at the Ford dealership. "Howdy folks, how can I help you today?"

Annie says she's looking for a small stick shift car—no frills, easy to drive. And she will need financing—she's starting a new job.

The salesman points out a small white car mid-way down the first row on the lot. "What about something like this? It's new. Got most everything you want on it."

"May be."

They walk to the car, looking through the windows. It has black-and-white checkered upholstery. "Do you want to test-drive it?"

"Yes, but I don't know how to drive a stick shift," Annie says apologetically. "I still need to learn."

"How about I drive you around the lot and down the street so you can check it out. Come on, Mom, you get in too." Annie's mother gets in the back seat, and Annie gets in the passenger seat. "What do you think?" the salesman asks while they're driving.

"Nice." Annie likes the drive and the upholstery. Mother says it's the right size and she likes the black-and-white checkered squares too, but there isn't air conditioning and she thinks it will be too hot in the summer. Annie doesn't care about air conditioning. It will be too expensive to add as a feature. And she's prepared to be uncomfortable in her exile though she is not going to tell them that.

"If you want this car, Annie, I'll teach you how to drive a stick shift," the salesman offers.

"That would be great."

TEN BEFORE THIRTY • 243

They go inside the office to talk about price. The finance officer looks at the school district job offer and says they will not require any money down. They agree on the price and draw up the paperwork. The salesman tells Mom she can leave now—Annie's going to drive herself home.

"Are you sure you can drive this, Annie?" Mother looks worried.

"Yes, go home. I'll be there soon," Annie tries to sound as confident as the salesman. Mother's grey sedan pulls out of the lot, and the salesman starts the driving lesson. It's an hour of explanations and practice shifting. Annie does a lot of jump-frogging around the lot. The salesman is thankfully much calmer than Duncan was when Annie was trying to drive his car in St. Louis.

"Ok, Annie, you have enough skills to head for home," the salesman says. Annie is not sure she's ready. "You'll get it. Just go slow," he says.

Annie thanks him for his help. She's barely breathing as she shifts from neutral to first gear as she slowly steers the white Pinto with twelve miles on the odometer out of the lot toward her mother's apartment several miles away. She manages to shift gears without frog-jumping by talking to herself out loud through each maneuver. She parks the Pinto in front of the apartment building, standing back when she gets out of the car to look back at her first car which will take two years to pay off in monthly installments. She clumps up the stairs in her clogs and announces with satisfaction that she can drive a stick shift.

A week later, Annie drives to the nearby community hospital to answer an ad for a part-time receptionist in the nursing station. The hospital likes Annie because she has worked as a medical transcriptionist at two hospitals. They hire her for eight-hour shifts on Saturdays and Sundays, doing receptionist work, setting up the nurses' schedules, and arranging for funeral mortuary pickups when a patient dies. To be at the hospital at seven in the morning, she will be heading out at six fifteen every weekend, clunking down the stairs while everyone is asleep. Her grant writing job will pay for the car and for rent at an apartment; the weekend job will pay for her braces. Exile is working—the tribunal is making good decisions, if only Annie will follow them.

The oral surgeon extracts nine teeth in preparation for braces—four impacted wisdom teeth, four incisors, and a baby tooth nesting above an adult tooth. There are hurting, gaping holes in her mouth and holes in her gums where they dug the teeth out. The next week, the orthodontist glues metal bars onto the teeth that remain, threading wires between the teeth to pull and push the teeth to close up the holes. Annie must wear a headpiece at night to put more pressure on her teeth, the orthodontist explains. There is a shocking amount of discomfort in her mouth. She is sure that no man would want to mess with her with gaping holes in her mouth and braces, and this is a good thing. She will get comfortable with discomfort, she will heal, and men will leave her alone.

Annie moves out of her mother's den after two months using money saved from her paychecks. She finds a furnished one-bedroom apartment near Southern Methodist University to be closer to the school district office. A few days a week she drives forty miles to Denton to take graduate-level courses at the university in the morning, then fifty miles to the south to work all day on grant proposals, then twice each week after the day job to teach courses from seven to ten at night at a community college—freshman composition and sophomore literature—another part-time job she has found. Then there's the drive to her apartment to start the round of trips early the next morning. And on weekends, the hospital job.

She pushes herself to keep going. One morning she runs off the road between Denton and Dallas after she misses a detour sign in the middle of nowhere. There are no other cars around and she manages to get back onto the main road. This is a wake-up call. She'd been imagining a car wreck coming soon, rubbing her tired eyes to stay awake, picturing her teeth smashed, wondering how she will avoid a metal mess of braces glued to her teeth if she lives through that.

Annie enjoys the teaching portion of her week the most. At the beginning of each class, she asks her students to arrange their chairs in a circle. She leads discussions about reading literature, how to communicate through different types of writing, and how to capture thoughts in writing. There are a number of returning Vietnam veterans in her classes. Young, distracted, hypervigilant. She asks one of them what his goals are in taking her class.

"Return to life, ma'am, " he said with no affect.

The education administration courses she's taking at the university early mornings are not difficult. She's getting good at proposal writing during the day, having taught herself to write proposals during her first six weeks on the job. She's been churning them out quickly in computer education, legal education, bilingual education, and counseling.

Exile is heady because exile is so productive. Her foot has healed enough to put away the clogs and wear regular shoes. Her vagina is on hiatus, not sad. Her heart is still broken, but she's too busy to dwell on Jonas anymore though he writes to her. And her bank account is no longer empty.

To pass the time in exile, the tribunal tells Annie she can take up with Mason, twenty-two years older than she is. He had a vasectomy years ago which makes sex easy. Annie is not interested in putting her diaphragm inside France. And Mason is so handsome and Southern that an affair is clearly in order. He does not mind the braces on her teeth—he thinks she looks like a teenager. This is a little creepy, but she doesn't dwell on that. She knows she will not get too involved with him because they're so different—she knows she will leave town eventually, alone.

She thinks it will be safer emotionally to take up simultaneously with a second man. There's a handsome computer man who likes her. They have sex one weekend—or try to—when Mason is out of town. She discovers that Colton wears body shirts that extend over his crotch and snap closed. He explains he likes his shirts to lay close to his body and look unwrinkled. When Annie goes to stroke his penis before sex, he feels smooth like a woman. She doesn't know if she's supposed to unsnap his onesie. Would this be sexy? He takes his own clothes off while she takes off hers. He turns out to be impotent when they try a few times to have sex. He reassures her this has nothing to do with her—this is a longstanding problem.

Since sex is not going to be their main activity, Colton tells Annie his favorite activity is bridge, and they're going to be a formidable couple. He can't wait for them to play with his friends. They meet his friends after they put their clothes back on after a no-go at sex. The deck of cards is on the dining room table. Drinks are poured and ready. Colton's shirt is smooth and unwrinkled. He introduces Annie as his new girlfriend. Mason would not like this, but Mason isn't there.

Colton has taught Annie the basics of the game in the car driving over since she's never played bridge. At the bridge table, she is not paying attention to the cards that have been played. Colton whispers multiple times to pay attention to the cards that have already been played. Annie did not understand she is supposed to memorize played cards so she will make better choices when new cards come up.

The Colton/Annie team is not doing well. Colton keeps raising his eyebrows at her, then pointing his eyes downward. Annie knows he is signaling her to pay attention. She does not like this so she excuses herself to go to the bathroom to take a break. She's in there a long time, looking at herself in the mirror, examining her braces, and looking through the medicine cabinet to see what his friends have stocked. There must be a lot of itching going on based on the number of anti-itch ointments on the shelf. When she comes out, Colton is waiting by the door.

"What are you doing? We came to play. You're not even trying."

"This is not a game I'm ever going to enjoy, Colton. I'm not going to spend my time off trying to memorize everyone else's cards that have been played."

"Fuck!" he says under his breath. Irritated, he heads back to the game table. She hears him saying Annie has a headache and is having a hard time paying attention. He says they have to leave.

That was their last date. Mason came back to town the next night, and Annie concluded that two men is too many.

Two years were nearly up. Annie felt like a migratory bird being pulled back to spawning grounds in the northern lakes. She applied for a fellowship to finish her PhD at the University of Minnesota. She reasoned it would be close to Madison, and she didn't think she would be able to find tuition money to finish a program in Wisconsin. Mason applied to the Minnesota program too. He was hoping to stay with Annie and move up north with her.

TEN BEFORE THIRTY • 247

Things with Mason were comfortable. There were dates most weekends. Usually dinner followed by sex, and he stayed over at Annie's apartment. Annie had to leave for her weekend job at six in the morning, so he left for his house when Annie left. Sometimes they added Sunday nights too. She didn't have time during the week to see him except for occasional lunches at work.

The snake situation was a turning point in their relationship. Annie was going to be late for work if she didn't get up—she was still tired, naked in her bed, waking up alone. She heard something—a muffled sound—coming from the window air conditioner. Finally out of bed, she was making a dash for the closet on the other side of the room to get her robe when she saw the snake jumping at the wall under the air conditioner. A foot long with black stripes.

She stopped dead in her tracks, then backed up to the bed, hopping up on it. She kept her eyes on the snake, trying not to panic. The snake kept flinging its body at the wall. Each time he hit the wall, there was a loud thump. Annie figured he got into her second-story apartment through the air conditioner—would he slither to the bed and jump up on it with her? She couldn't get to the closet to get clothes without running by the air conditioner wall.

She jumped off the bed and closed her bedroom door, running to the kitchen to call Mason.

"Hi babe, what's up?" Annie never called him during the week.

"Mason, there's a snake in my bedroom!" She was talking loudly.

"What?"

"There's a black striped snake in my bedroom, jumping at the wall. I don't know what to do. I'm naked. I don't know how I'm going to get my clothes on. Can you come over?"

"I have to get to work, Annie. I have a meeting. Do you think it's a garter snake? They're harmless."

"I thought garter snakes are green. This has black stripes. I'm too scared to go back in there. I'm naked—I can't get to the closet."

"Call the police. They'll send someone over. Don't tell them you're naked. Go back in the room and get what you need from the closet. I don't think the snake is going to bother you. Just keep your distance. Call me after you talk to the police."

248 • YANA KAZAN

"Ok."

She called the police and told them she didn't recognize the kind of snake she just found in her apartment and she was too scared to try to catch it.

"We'll send an officer." They took down her address.

"How soon?"

"Give us fifteen minutes, ma'am. Our station is close."

"Ok, thank you so much."

Annie had to go back into the bedroom and get to the closet for clothes. She opened the door a crack to look inside. The snake was still jumping at the wall. She walked quickly on tiptoes to the closet, hoping the snake would not see her. She held a large frying pan she picked up in the kitchen in front of her breasts like a shield in case the snake came after her. She got to the closet and pulled clothes on while the snake kept jumping at the wall. He was probably more scared to be in her apartment than she was she kept telling herself.

The doorbell rang—it was sooner than fifteen minutes.

She ran out of the bedroom, closed the door, and let the officer in.

"Morning, ma'am. I'm Officer Sanders. I hear you have a snake in your apartment." He was a tall blond man with thick black glasses.

"Yes, in my bedroom. I think he got in through the window air conditioner. He's been jumping and jumping against the wall by the air conditioner. I don't know what kind he is." Annie was talking fast while she walked down the hall.

"Let's have a look." He had a gun in his holster. Annie was hoping he was not intending to shoot the snake. He opened the door. The snake was coiled against the wall, probably exhausted from flinging himself against the wall. "I don't know what kind that is. I'll take him to the station so we can figure out what kind he is."

Annie suggested he could put the snake into a glass jar or a paper bag.

"Let's try the paper bag."

She ran to the kitchen to get a grocery store bag. "Will this work?"

"Yes, that's good."

"I don't want to see you catch him—try not to hurt him. I'm going to wait in the living room." She waited in the living room, pacing around the coffee table.

The officer came through the living room holding the bag. "I got him."

"You won't kill him, will you?"

"No, we'll let him go once we identify what type he is."

"Ok, well thank you again so much."

"Ok, ma'am, you be careful now."

Annie locked her front door and called Mason to fill him in.

"You did good, Annie. I know it was scary."

"Oh my God, it was. I'll call the station in a bit to ask what kind of snake it was. I need to get to work now."

"Ok, talk to you later."

Annie wondered if there were other snakes outside the apartment building climbing the wall toward the air conditioner unit. Would she feel safe tonight in her bedroom?

She called the station on her lunch hour from her office.

"Nothing to worry about, ma'am. It was a garter snake. Sometimes they get into air conditioning units."

"Thanks again for coming to get him."

Annie was surprised Mason didn't come to her apartment when she called him. If a snake had been in his bedroom and he called Annie, would she have run to his house? Probably not. They had a relationship of convenience. That was how they wanted it.

A week later, they both received letters from the University of Minnesota. Annie was accepted—Mason was not. She knew the university was looking for women to enter careers in administration—she figured that's why she got in. She was relieved Mason wasn't going with her. Finally, she had a ticket out of town—a destination.

Weeks later, Annie turned in her resignation to the school district. She told her landlord she was moving. She turned in her resignation to the college where she'd been teaching. She secured copies of her transcript so the university courses she took would transfer to the PhD program in Minnesota. She made an appointment to have her braces removed at the orthodontist.

Annie packed up the white Pinto just paid off from her two jobs. Her trusty steed was filled to the brim for the trip north. She kissed Mason goodbye. She said goodbye to her family. She was headed nine hundred and forty miles north, back to real life. She was going to see Jonas again—Madison wasn't that far from Minneapolis. And Mona would be there too.

Exile was in the Pinto's rearview mirror, and Annie's tribunal had been quiet lately. Annie was back in the driver's seat, driving stick shift. She had not added any bad things to Flora's list for a while.

THE FINAL COUNT

A nnie deliberated on traumas while she drove to Minnesota. Trauma seemed a better word than bad thing. When they were saying goodbye, her mother told Annie to try to be happy and not to wallow. Her mother had told her years earlier to stop wallowing. Annie had gone to the dictionary to be sure she understood what she was *not* supposed to do.

There were three definitions. Annie was certain her mother did not know this. According to the first definition, Annie was a large mammal lying in mud to keep cool, to avoid biting insects, and to spread her scent. According to the dictionary, the mammal might be a hog or water buffalo. She wondered why Noah Webster was saying it was a hog and not a pig. A hog weighs more than one hundred and twenty pounds, the pig less. So, weight was evidently linked to wallowing. Maybe Annie was the water buffalo of her family.

According to the second definition, Annie was a wallowing boat or airplane—rolling and lurching in heavy weather. What was wrong with that?

In the third definition, wallowing was indulging in an unrestrained way in something that created a pleasurable sensation, basking and luxuriating. Maybe her mother thought she was enjoying feeling sorry for herself, getting undeserved pleasure from traumas. That was probably the definition Mother meant.

It was a blustery day as Annie's car sped through Oklahoma like an airplane lurching in choppy clouds—wallowing for real, she noted to herself. She was seat-belted to her black-and-white checkerboard front seat like a large bovid. She grazed thoughtfully on peanut butter and apricot jelly sandwiches on rye bread her mother had packed in a large plastic bag. Radio reception was only picking up sad country-western tunes. Dolly Parton singing about Jolene, begging the other woman not to take her man just because she could. Charlie Rich sorry for losing his head and letting his world slip away from him.

Annie didn't mind wallowing—all three definitions. Aren't you supposed to identify the crises you live through? Roll with them? Get the bites from them off in the mud? Then move beyond them if you can? That was the hard part, moving on.

Driving through Kansas and Missouri, Annie reviewed the trauma list she carried in her purse in case she thought of one to add or sometimes remove. Her understanding of what traumas are had changed since she was a girl. Now she understood they were a mix of emotional undoings, injustices, and shock—to her entire being. The times she couldn't think straight, went numb, could not emerge from easily. The list swirled like uncontrollable tumbleweeds through her mind. Her father dying. Incest with her grandfather. Date-rape with Duncan. Stranger rape with Mustang-man in the cornfields. Helpless to save Fran from sexual assault. Jayce's rape in Houston. Mother's betrayal, breaking her word—and Meyer's taking her sculpture to the dump. Hit by a car. Losing Jonas. Losing her cat. Nearly kidnapped from the street twice. Killing animals in college. Strip-search in jail. Three national leaders assassinated. Communities torn apart from war and racial injustice. More than ten and no doubt more were coming.

How to process these—how others thought she was supposed to process things—and why she was not supposed to wallow seemed more troublesome. Was wallowing writing about traumatic events? Was it ok to write about them once but not several times? Was wallowing talking to friends or strangers about them? Talking to family? Going to therapy? Should Annie mention traumatic events, if she even did, just once to people? Were double, triple, or quadruple mentions wallowing?

There must be something else at play she mused as she pulled into a gas station. Like when you don't come home married to the right person after a certain age, it must be because you have been too busy wallowing. Or if you've been fucking around with too many men that are not of your caliber, this is because you have been wallowing and let your guard down, and low-caliber men invaded your life.

She knew now that traumas are deeply distressing experiences—and it was her job to figure out what to do with the dark tumbleweeds in her head. The Pinto sped by the large *Welcome to Minnesota* sign leaving Iowa in the rearview mirror. She imagined that the large white letters on the green background carried a personal message: *Welcome to Minnesota, Annie Zechman—no wallowing.*

Annie made the drive in fourteen hours. She headed first to a hotel near the university where she had made a reservation for two nights. The next day she searched for an apartment in Dinkytown, a student neighborhood near the main campus—renting a one-bedroom furnished apartment on Fourth Street. On her second day in town, she moved her things from the Pinto into the apartment, feeling hopeful. She was out of Texas and on course to finish a doctoral degree. The coursework she took in Madison and Texas would transfer to the program in Minnesota. She wished Jonas was with her, but she tried to put him out of her mind. He wasn't worried about her—she was sure of that.

The next day, twenty-one doctoral fellows were ushered into a university meeting room on the St. Paul campus with a dozen faculty members. The department head described the program. Then he asked the students to pick a track—elementary/secondary education or higher education. They were to stand by the faculty lead for each track positioned at two ends of the room. She wished they could play Red Rover, her favorite game when she was a child. She imagined an elementary education line versus higher education. Each line locking arms and players one by one trying to plow through the opposing line as a test of strength. Whoever lost had to go to the other line. Eventually, one line would dominate as they demolished the weaker line.

This musing was her way of stalling. No one told them in advance they would have to pick a track. She was still standing alone in the center of the room.

"Miss Zechman—Annie—which track are you joining?" the department head called out.

"I don't know. I'm interested in both—the way the elementary/secondary and higher education systems work together." She wondered if they would ask her to leave the program now. The department head said they could tailor-make a plan with her. She nodded and stayed in the center of the room, trying to breathe normally.

The next decision was selecting an advisor. She had heard you can't get through a doctoral program without a decent relationship with an advisor. Your program of study must be approved, dissertation topic approved, and dissertation committee approved. The advisor was supposed to get you through this. And she had heard how politicized it could be, especially for the women graduate students.

A phalanx of faculty wearing suits and ties—all white men—formed a line like a dance troupe at the front of the room. One by one, they described their research interests so the students could decide who would be the best match for them. Annie heard special education, organizational theory, politics of education, policy, sociology of education, social psychology, and research and statistics. She did not hear systems theory.

A fast-talking sociology professor was announcing he usually takes all the minority students because that's his area. Annie guessed he meant people of color and women. She decides she's not going with him. The research and statistics professor is quiet and mild-mannered. He's carrying a man-purse over his shoulder, which Annie likes, and her weakest area is math, so it might be a good tactic to align with him. So she picks Professor Browning. No one else picks him because they're afraid of statistics she learns later.

The program has already registered them in three required courses, and they will move through the program as a cohort. One of the required courses is a year of research and statistics with Professor Browning. There was groaning at this news.

On the drive back to her apartment after orientation, Annie carried out one of the decisions she made during the drive north. She would try to do right by a cat that needed a home, still feeling remorse for not protecting her cat in Bruchen. When she drove to campus that morning, she passed a pet store on Snelling Avenue. So she stopped that afternoon to see if there were cats. One scraggly grey kitten was huddled into the corner of a large cage in the center of the store. The clerk said her brothers and sisters were adopted over the last few days. This female was the runt of a litter of four. Annie thought it was fate—one sad soul left for her. The kitten seemed uninterested in Annie, but Annie figured the kitten was depressed and Annie must adopt her. She carried the unfriendly soul to the car, and they drove to the apartment.

Annie named her Miss Kitty after the strong dancehall woman in the television show, *Gunsmoke*. Someday Annie might get a dog and name him Matt Dillon after the marshal on *Gunsmoke*. And get another animal she would name Chester after Matt Dillon's sidekick.

That night in bed Annie took stock. She was signed up for classes, the university was going to tailor-make a program with her, she found an advisor who did not seem too invasive, she had an apartment and funds in her fellowship to cover tuition and books for two semesters plus a stipend for living expenses, the braces were off her teeth and her teeth lined up straight, she was out of Texas and closer to Jonas in Madison, and she had a cat roommate. Miss Kitty was laying comfortably now on the bed.

Annie congratulated herself. Excommunication had done her good. More traumas were no doubt coming—she was twenty-seven and Flora said they would be coming till thirty. Annie knew she was stupid for paying Flora's dream any mind—life brought bad things for everyone. Why count them, why dwell on them? Flora's dream had imprinted in her mind when she was young and Annie wasn't willing or able to let it go.

Annie's life quickly spiraled into days and nights of going to class, studying in the library, studying at home, and hanging out with Miss Kitty. There was no place to park her car near campus so walking and taking the bus were the best ways to get around. Within weeks, Santos from her cohort was her new best friend. He grew up in South Texas with parents from Mexico who spoke no English. He offered to babysit for Miss Kitty when Annie went to Madison.

Annie met Mona's ex-boyfriend, Oliver, on a weekend visit to Madison. Mona still liked him, but he'd broken up with her. Annie didn't know the particulars of their relationship and didn't know about the girl code—she learned later from Mona that girlfriends are *never* supposed to take up with their girlfriends' prior men. But by the time Annie learned this, she'd already taken up with Oliver, and Mona was angry about it.

Oliver had many good qualities. He was a good walker, had a springer spaniel dog, wrote intelligent and insightful letters, was witty, and played great tennis. Annie asked herself if Oliver's good qualities were enough to keep seeing him after a few months because there were qualities she didn't like. He would not agree that flossing teeth was important. He didn't see the need to do laundry very often, wearing the same track pants most of the time because they were comfortable. He taught at the free high school in Madison for low pay and told Annie he was more ethical than she was because she was selling herself out to the establishment. He let Annie pay for everything because he had no money and didn't see anything wrong with that.

"It's not fair to criticize me for working when you're fine with my paying for everything. You're not more ethical than I am because you work practically for free," Annie argued.

"I am more ethical, Zechman." He liked to call her by her last name, and that was not very romantic—they should have been pals not lovers, but he wanted to be lovers. Annie wanted to take walks, play tennis, and have an excuse to drive to Madison to see Jonas.

Their relationship derailed the night they went to see *A Clockwork Orange* at the university theater. Annie and Oliver were sitting mid-row in the center of the full theater. A few minutes into the movie, young men were bringing their violence to the home of a wheelchair-bound author and raping his wife to the song "Singin' in the Rain." Annie felt the sudden thunderstorm inside her gut and urge to vomit. She tried not to watch the screen, squeezing her eyes closed while she tried to hold the acid storm inside her. In a panic, she stood up and pulled her coat around her, pushing past the feet and knees of people in their row to get out. She fled to a bench in the lobby waiting for the adrenaline to stop pumping. She was not going to be a bystander to violence. She hoped Oliver would come see if she was ok. But the minutes stretched to hours while Annie waited.

He streamed out with the rest of the crowd after the movie, seeing her on the bench along the wall of the lobby. "What happened? Why didn't you come back?"

TEN BEFORE THIRTY • 257

"I couldn't watch the rape scene. I felt sick." She was surprised at how angry she felt.

He shrugged.

She thought he was clueless or didn't care or both. What if she was having a ruptured appendix or a heart attack? Wouldn't he come check on her? They headed into the crisp Wisconsin evening. It was a couple of miles to his apartment by the lake. They were both tired. He stuck his hand out to hitch a ride for them, and a car stopped immediately. Two men.

Annie pushed back, "I'm not going."

Oliver was already opening the back car door. "Annie, come on!"

"I'm not going—you can take a ride. I'll walk."

Oliver waved the car on and walked next to her in his long bounding stride.

She talked to herself while they walked in silence. 'I'm not going to open myself up to another rape. I'm sick of being prey. I have to take care of myself. I'm my only advocate. He doesn't experience the world the way I do. I'm fearful and distrustful. Why isn't he going to protect me?'

He tried to make small talk, not knowing she was busy with head talk. He was tired and wanted to get home. He still had to walk the dog. He was angry at Annie for making their night longer.

That night Annie decided Oliver was not the partner for her but did not tell him. And she did not tell Mona who was still in love with Oliver. Maybe Oliver would lose interest if Annie stayed remote and go back to Mona. But Annie wanted to keep seeing Oliver for a while yet because being with Oliver got her to Madison, and she could stop in to see Jonas.

Weeks later, Mona called Annie. "I just heard on the news that Jonas and his girlfriend were riding their bikes, and a drunk driver hit them. She died, Annie. Jonas has a broken collar bone."

Annie's heart thumped in her chest. She didn't know if she should come right away to Madison. Jonas would never call her. "Do you think anyone is with him?" she asked Mona.

"I don't know. I'll try to check on him and call you back."

Annie drove to Madison the next weekend. She found Jonas sitting alone in the small studio space in a warehouse where he made wooden children's toys to sell at craft shops. There was a figure-eight bandage around both collarbones. He was sitting still and barely acknowledged Annie as she walked toward him. "Mona called me. I'm so sorry, Jonas." She wanted to reach for his hand but didn't think he would want her to touch him.

He nodded.

"Can I do anything?"

"No."

"Are you in a lot of pain?"

"The pain doesn't matter. I had to tell Linda's parents their only daughter died. They're the ones in pain."

"Can I sit with you?"

He didn't say anything. On his work desk was a wooden pterodactyl bird on a leather cord that looked unfinished. She was sure he was not doing any work. She remembered their conversation a month ago. She stopped to see him on her way back to Minneapolis after she'd left Oliver's house. She asked if he thought they should be back together. She still felt such closeness—in the cells between them. She felt it whenever she was around him. Didn't he feel this too?

"I feel like Dick Tracy with holes in my body—I'm a shell of a man. And I'm seeing someone new, Annie. Someone I like. Stay away from me, Annie. I hurt everyone who is with me."

And now weeks later, Linda was dead. His corn blue eyes looked ash grey and Annie knew she could not help him.

Oliver offered to come to Minneapolis more weekends, so Annie didn't have to drive to Madison. They agreed she needed better birth control. She didn't like the diaphragm and couldn't go back to birth control pills. When she called the university women's clinic to ask about options, they suggested an IUD.

"I thought that is only for women who have had a baby."

"We will put them in for women who have not."

"Will you use anesthesia, or is there something I should take before the appointment?"

"No, we don't use anything. You'll be fine."

Annie's appointment was on a cold Friday in December—they advised her to take a weekend to recover. She walked to the clinic. Mona was coming in on the bus from Madison in a few hours to make Annie chicken soup.

The nurse tells her to remove her clothes below her waist, cover up with the wrap she hands her, and wait on the examining table for the doctor.

In a few minutes, he walks into the room. Balding, old, a pale grey mask of a face. His blood evidently is visiting other parts of his spindly-looking body—not his face.

"Miss Zechman?"

She nods. At least he pronounced her name correctly.

"Feet in the stirrups. Scooch down," he directs her.

She hates this vulnerable position—buttocks hanging off the end of the table, vagina squarely in his sight like a defenseless animal. She catches a quick glance of the IUD in his hand—it looks like a small fishing lure. With no warning, the ghostly doctor plunges the lure up her vagina into her cervix. Annie imagined it would feel like putting a diaphragm in, how the rubber cup slowly grabs the edges of her tissue and spreads its round walls around her inside form. That is not how it felt. She catches her breath at the force of the insertion and the instant pain.

The doctor has already turned away and left the room. Annie holds on to the narrow metal table she is half-laying, half-sitting on, several feet in the air. She feels herself passing out, falling over the right side of the table. The nurse who just came into the room catches Annie midair and gets her back onto the table.

"Hold the table, hold on. Take some deep breaths." The nurse takes Annie's right wrist to take her pulse. "Keep breathing. You're okay. Just a little shock." In a few minutes, the nurse asks if she can get up on her own and get her clothes back on.

After a few more deep breaths, Annie says, "I'm ok," but she doesn't feel ok. She eases slowly off the examining table to plant her feet firmly on the cold tile floor. She shuffles to the nearby chair where she has piled her clothes and pulls her underpants and jeans back on, pulls on her thick socks, and zips up her boots over her socks. Then she pulls on her parka to try to put layers around her body. She is shivering in small tremors.

"Take a seat in the waiting room and rest a bit before you head out to be sure you're ok," the nurse says. "The pain will go away eventually, but it could take a while. And you can take aspirin, dear."

Annie nods. She was not prepared for the pain of insertion and this new pain in her belly. She takes a seat in the waiting room. She doesn't know if she would feel better with her legs crossed or stretched in front of her. Neither position makes a difference. Maybe the winter air will help. She stands up and slowly walks out of the clinic. She doesn't have enough cash for a taxi. It's getting late, and she already missed the bus that passes her apartment building. She pulls her parka hood tight around her head and hunkers into the wind, feeling the piercing in her lower belly for the thirty-minute walk home.

At home, she and Miss Kitty curl up in bed like wounded animals. Mona arrives later. She starts right away making chicken soup in Annie's small kitchen. Annie wonders if all this pain is worth fucking any man. She hates being a woman. She hates her woman's life. None of her lovers have to deal with this.

⸺●⸺

The second semester was going better. The IUD knife was piercing less after weeks inside her. It was January 22, 1973. She was listening to the news on the radio, lying on her sofa with the cat curled on her chest. The Supreme Court struck down a Texas statute banning abortion, and this effectively legalized abortion. Anonymous Jane Roe was an unmarried Texas mother who claimed Texas violated her constitutional rights by banning abortion. The reporter said he would come back with more information after he announced the other breaking news: former president Lyndon Johnson died from a heart attack at his Texas ranch. Then the news switched back to the Supreme Court. The seven-to-two vote meant that a woman's right to choose an abortion was protected by the privacy rights guaranteed by the Fourteenth Amendment to the US Constitution.

Annie wept—for the changes underway, the hope that women would have their bodies back. The cat's citrine eyes fixed with some alarm on Annie's chest, shaking as if an earthquake had erupted inside their apartment. "Kitty, abortion is legal," Annie sobbed to the grey cat who seemed to be listening carefully.

Annie remembered Sharon. The day before cheerleader tryouts in high school, the most popular girl on the senior cheerleader squad was close to death in the hospital from an infection. She used a wire closet hangar to abort the fetus inside her. And Annie remembered Fran, her flute partner in the band. Before Annie moved to Texas, she heard why Fran left school so abruptly—her stepfather sent her to Michigan to have his baby. At fourteen.

Finally, help was on the way. Public opinion was changing—the decision to have an abortion should be made by a woman and her physician.

That night there was a special news report. Annie learned that for the country's first 100 years, abortion was not a criminal offense—it wasn't even considered immoral and was not politicized. In the 1700s and early 1800s, they called abortion the termination of a pregnancy after "quickening," when the fetus first made noticeable movements. Inducing the ending of a pregnancy before then didn't even have a name, but not because it was uncommon. Women in the 1700s often took drugs to end unwanted pregnancies. In the 1800s, some states passed a law making the use of abortion drugs punishable by up to three years imprisonment, and other states followed, although female monthly pills, as they became known, were common for decades after. That's when abortion became a serious criminal offense. Doctors in the American Medical Association, a newly established trade organization, decided abortion practitioners were unwanted competition. So doctors tried to eliminate their competition. And the Catholic Church joined the condemnation of abortion procedures. The newscaster explained that by the 1900s, all states passed laws against abortion but rarely enforced them. And women with money had no problem terminating pregnancies if they wanted to. It wasn't until the late 1930s that abortion laws were enforced. Subsequent crackdowns led to the reform movements that finally succeeded in lifting the abortion restrictions in California and New York—even before the Supreme Court decision in *Roe v. Wade*.

Annie was amazed at the changes in just a couple hundred years. And amazed that President Johnson would have a larger headline in the *New York Times* the next morning than the landmark court case. There were no women reporting the news—only men.

The third memorable event that week: President Nixon and the Secretary of State took the final steps to end the Vietnam War.

Were these events signs Annie could go back to Jonas? Now that abortion was legal, the war was ending, she was in school with a career goal, trying to pull herself together, hoping she would be able to take care of herself and her cat from now on? She didn't know how to forget Jonas. She still didn't want to live her life without him. Why was she still so fixated on a man who no longer loved her?

With all the late-night library sessions, meeting Santos for catch-up dinners, and Annie's walking time between campus and home, Miss Kitty was alone a lot and didn't like it. Her aggressive soprano meows assaulted Annie in a medley of accusations at the front door every night. And to add an exclamation mark, she started to pee on Annie's bedspread. To up the ante, the cat left two brown turds that resembled Tootsie Roll candies on the bed one night. Annie recognized the cat was upset and fighting back the only way she could—with pee and turds in the bed they shared.

On April Fool's Day, Annie visited the same pet store in St. Paul—seven months after she found Miss Kitty there—to see if there were kittens for sale. There was a chubby black kitten among a group of kittens who Annie immediately recognized was her Chester. She snuggled the little bear cub into her arms and paid the clerk thirty-five dollars. The cat rode confidently on her lap to the apartment in Dinkytown. Annie unlocked the front door, greeting Miss Kitty with her peace offering. "Look, you won't be alone anymore. This is Chester." Annie plunked the black kitten on the floor while Miss Kitty sniffed him. She did not hiss at the interloper but did not look pleased. Annie expected a fight or two between them over territory, but there was no fighting. Miss Kitty immediately seemed to communicate with the kitten: 'This is my place. If you follow the rules, you'll be ok. We're going to be stuck together. Our mom is gone most of the time.'

There were no more pee or turds in the bed. And no rapid-fire meow rounds at the door when Annie came home. They were a new pride—Miss Kitty, Chester, and Annie.

TEN BEFORE THIRTY • 263

Annie's fellowship was ending after the second semester. She would have to find a job to pay her bills. She interviewed for several positions on campus. The most promising opportunity was as a teaching assistant at an innovation center at the university. The TA would advise thirty adult students who wanted to complete their bachelor's degree—using a variety of methods to assess learning they had acquired through a number of avenues and documenting that learning to the satisfaction of the faculty.

Annie was hired. The project director told Annie later he had to make a choice between a male candidate and her. He picked Annie because she had better legs. Annie didn't call him on his sexist comment because she needed the job.

She started work two weeks later. That's when she met the tall, blond-haired student completing his PhD who also worked on the staff. He was several years older than Annie. He confided during a two-day staff retreat that he was separated from his wife, and this was his third marriage.

"Really?"

"I married everyone I dated."

"That's extreme dating," she said wryly.

"Do you think that's a character flaw?" he said smiling.

"It might be—maybe more than one." When she talked to him, she had to look up—he was twelve inches taller.

He sought her out during the retreat. Annie reminded herself to keep their relationship professional—there must be qualities he was hiding that contributed to three broken marriages.

A month later, he asked if Annie wanted to have an affair with him.

"No, you're married."

"We're separated."

"What does that mean?"

"We're agreed we are heading toward a divorce."

Annie ignored three yellow caution flags the universe was waving—he already had three marriages, he was probably a liar, and he was a work colleague. She focused on four green flags instead. Why not have an affair? He was warm, funny, and interested in what she thought. She was tired of being alone. She wasn't seeing Oliver very much. And Jonas had retreated into his own world.

After they started having sex, she learned Mitchell's wife still shared a house with him. He explained it was just a convenience; they shared two Afghan hounds that were their babies, and she was unstable mentally and couldn't handle living alone. They were in therapy to get them through the upcoming divorce. He would be seeing Annie at Annie's house because she could not come to his house. Annie accepted this reasoning, not wanting to add to his wife's mental issues.

He was at Annie's house a lot. He liked to cook for her. This required her to be at the house when he was cooking and sitting down for meals. These were not things she wanted to do.

Mitchell's favorite menu was pot roast with rosemary, potatoes, salad, and a small dessert. Annie's preferred meal was a large dessert, no salad, and beef that was not soft and stringy. She never cared for the briskets her mother made, flaking pieces of beef cooked for hours. So she was not inclined to applaud the meals Mitchell made. She preferred to eat one thing at a meal—keep things simple. And she didn't like rosemary.

Cooking started late afternoons with sex. Mitchell would get up afterward and head for the kitchen. Annie was glad to stay in bed, resting in the warmth of after-sex, wishing she could have chocolate cake and ice cream and not be called to the dinner table like they were having a family dinner. Maybe she wasn't ready to be a family with him or anyone. Maybe she didn't want to eat pot roast and pretend she enjoyed sitting down with a plate and silverware and good manners and thank him for preparing the meal. Then he wanted her to help with the dishes and clean-up. Something must be wrong with her—most people would be happy to have someone cook for them.

This afternoon after sex Mitchell headed to the kitchen, and Annie read a book in bed. As soon as Mitchell got out of bed and put his pants back on, the cats jumped into the warm spot he left. There was cooking going on for hours. Finally, Annie got up to go to the bathroom.

He followed her to the bathroom, calling through the closed door, "When will you be ready for dinner?"

On the way to the bathroom, she'd seen he set the round kitchen table with full regalia: plates, her best water glasses, napkins, silverware. She was surprised one of the cats wasn't sitting on a plate, but maybe he had shooed them away. She bet his Afghan hounds would never try to sit on the dinner plates, she mused as she sat on the toilet seat.

He called out again through the door, thinking she had not heard him, "When will you be ready for dinner, babe?"

She wanted to say never. She was in a black mood. Sex had not made it any better. She had so much studying to do for school. She would have to wash up, get clothes on, comb her hair, sit at the table like a normal person, talk, and eat pot roast. The woodsy aroma of rosemary had been punctuating the air for hours. Tones of pine and lemon made her wish she was walking in the woods, not preparing to eat stringy beef.

"Give me fifteen minutes." She heard him head back to the kitchen. He was cloying lately, and she felt irritated. She blamed herself. She was antisocial, demented, and ungrateful.

Annie's apartment, the lower floor of a two-story duplex she had moved to months ago, was always cold. The windows and walls leaked air. The cold pushed through the window seams. The only comfortable place was in her bed under stacks of blankets. The cats usually slept on piles of clothes in the small closet off the bedroom. The pride was trying to stay warm that long Minnesota winter.

When Annie complained about the cold, Mitchell had a solution. He turned on her heating pad with the electronics housed inside a soft flannel casing, and nested it between his naked belly and hers, turning the dial as high as they could stand it. Then they had sex. They both liked heating-pad sex though her IUD still pinched her sometimes. She kept asking if he could feel the IUD in France—her preferred term for her inside parts. He said France was a great place to visit. Heating-pad sex would get them through the winter and she would put up with cooked meals.

Mitchell was two years ahead of her in school. He was finishing up his dissertation and applying for a faculty position at a Canadian university. He asked Annie after heating-pad sex one afternoon if she would go with him if he got the position. She agreed to think about it.

It was a Friday afternoon, weeks later, when Mitchell brought her three pieces of fancy dark chocolate candy and a pink rose. "I'm leaving for an interview in Montreal on Sunday. I have to prep, so I won't be able to hang out tomorrow. I'll be back Tuesday."

"Ok," she nodded, sharing one of the candies with him. She made him a cup of tea and put the rose in a thin glass jar she pulled from the cupboard.

"Thanks for the rose. It's so perfect."

"Glad you like it." He was standing behind her hugging her close to his body.

"I can pick you up at the airport Tuesday," she said, looking up to him as she leaned against him.

"Yeah, ok."

They kissed a few times at the back door. She wished him good luck. He squeezed her ass and told her to take care of herself. Then he ran through the late spring snow for his car in the driveway—she had not had time to shovel from yesterday's storm.

Annie spent the weekend studying. There was no call from Mitchell telling her what time his flight would be arriving. This seemed strange, but maybe he was feeling nervous about the interview and forgot to call. She checked on the afternoon flights from Montreal to Minneapolis on Tuesday—only one flight would be coming in—that had to be his.

Annie drove to the airport on Tuesday and stood at the back of the waiting area by the gate for the plane's arrival. She was excited to see him, wondering how the interview had gone. He had planned to stay an extra day to check out housing options for them.

Annie spotted him among the passengers streaming into the waiting area—he was so tall. Before she could move forward to greet him, a dark-haired woman had run up to hug him. And he hugged her back. Annie quickly pressed her body against the wall behind a nearby column. She recognized Katharine from a picture Mitchell had shown her—it was his wife.

The two of them swam with the crowd of passengers and greeters through the waiting area. Mitchell never saw Annie. What was going on? He knew she would be there—she said she would. What were the chocolates and pink rose four days ago for? Were they a goodbye gift and she missed the cue?

Annie waited by the wall long enough to be sure Mitchell and Katharine exited the airport. Annie would be horrified to see them now. As the shock wore off, anger arrived like a bomber plane on a battlefield. Annie replayed every conversation they had recently in her mind. Did he break up with her and forget to tell her? Was he afraid to tell her? Did he say something, and she wasn't listening? Did she fail to read the cards? Was this retribution because she didn't like pot roast and rosemary? Was Katharine prettier than Annie? Did they have better heating-pad sex? Did Katharine threaten suicide like Mitchell told Annie she had been doing, and he was trying to save her life, and he thought Annie was stronger and would be fine on her own?

Annie called Santos when she got home to fill him in.

"Calm down, Annie. There has to be an answer. You know what I have always thought—he's a loser—he never deserved you. Do you want me to come over?"

Annie liked hearing that, but it didn't make her feel better. "I'll be ok. I'll see you tomorrow."

The next day she called Mitchell.

"Hello."

"Hey—I was at the airport to pick you up. You didn't see me there." There was a long silence. She figured he was gathering strength to formulate his lies.

"I got the job, Annie. I'm going to Montreal. Kat is going with me in the fall. We decided to give it another try. Our therapist suggested Montreal would be a new opportunity for us to pull together like a team. I owe her this."

Annie took several breaths, like she was underwater struggling for air. How come he never told her about their couples therapy? How come he was calling Katharine, Kat? Why did he ask if Annie would go with him? Annie was supposed to go with him. She was supposed to learn French. She was supposed to get a new passport. She was supposed to be his fourth wife because he married everyone he dated. All this was going through her mind during the silence on the phone. There was no 'I'm sorry' from Mitchell. Maybe Kat was sitting in the room with him. She probably was, petting the heads of their silky Afghan hounds, knowing nothing about Annie who Mitchell had been cooking for and having heating-pad sex with this dismal cold winter.

The next weeks were mania weeks. Annie was obsessed to see Mitchell. Surely if he saw her, he would see how much he cared for her. She called him on the phone, but he did not pick up, and he would not return her calls. Santos told her to accept the way things were and leave him alone. She rode her bicycle by his house—crazy ride-bys on the off chance he would be on the bike path. She ran into him on purpose at the bike shop one day. He stammered uncomfortably the dates he would be leaving for Montreal and quickly left the shop. Annie kept calling his house. She was possessed by the injustice of the breakup. Her bomber plane kept flying one-sided missions.

<hr />

Annie could not get up in the morning and run her customary three miles anymore. She felt suicidal. Her namesake, Andrew, killed himself at twenty-three. She was almost twenty-nine. What was she waiting for? She was crying hard the afternoon she walked into the bathroom to survey the options in the medicine cabinet. There were not enough pills to take. Should she buy hard liquor and a couple of bottles of aspirin and drink it all down? Would that do it? Should she use a razor, slit her wrists?

Annie's eyes were swollen from crying. Was she looking in the mirror to see how bad she looked—or to see if her spirit would come out and say something to her sad skeleton? Santos would be disappointed if she hurt herself. She hadn't told him how truly lost she felt lately. Jonas didn't love her anymore. Mitchell was leaving without her. Meyer said he could never be her friend—he would only want to fuck her. Mona couldn't help though she would want to. Oliver wouldn't know what to say. And she would never tell her mother anything that was seriously going on with her—her mother would tell her not to wallow. She could not bear to hear that now.

She decided to call Meyer. He would tell her to pull herself together. She had never called his home before, but she was desperate. She wondered if she could even talk, her voice thick from crying.

"Hello," a calm female voice was on the line.

Annie managed to ask if Meyer was there through her constricted throat.

"I'm sorry, he isn't here right now. Can I take a message?"

It must be his wife. Annie knew they were still talking about divorce. Her voice was serene, angelic even.

"No message, thanks." Annie quickly hung up. Who will tell her not to kill herself now? His wife's voice distracted Annie. She decided to lie down and think about ways to commit suicide—other than liquor and pills. The two cats joined her in bed. She had become prey and did not care that marauding hunters were coming for her. Her gazelle and lion lay collapsed in the open space of their savannah, surrounded by tall beige grass. Anyone, anything could maul them now.

Annie called the university mental health center. They told her to make an appointment to see one of their doctors. The intake form asked her to write down why she was here. The only pen she had with her was her green Sharpie. In thick dark green ink, she wrote: "I'm suicidal. My ability to pay attention is slipping. I feel like my face is turning to concrete when I talk to people. I have no purpose. I don't know if I should drop out of school. I can't study." She noted how many I's she had written. She was probably narcissistic too.

The health center assigned her to a psychiatrist. He saw her that afternoon. He looked like Sigmund Freud—fulsome salt-and-pepper beard, portly belly. He sat in a large wooden desk chair on wheels. He did not stand when she entered the room.

"What's going on, Miss Zechman?" His German accent gave him a Hitleresque quality. At least he didn't call her Frau Zechman.

While she was trying to explain why she was there, Freud rolled around in his mobile tank from time to time, entering her safe space, then rolling backward. Annie felt unsafe like she had entered a roller psycho-battlefield—and there was no chair for her moves. She was the pawn stuck immobile—he had the power of movement. She left her session angry. She walked back to the sign-in desk. "I can't see this doctor again. I'm scared of him. Is there someone else, preferably a woman?"

The clerk made an appointment with Dr. Wilson, the only female psychiatrist on staff. At the assessment visit three days later, the doctor heard her out and cut to the chase. Annie could meet with her once a week over six months plus join a support group of women students who met twice a week. Annie would have an intervention three times a week. The doctor offered to put Annie on an antidepressant medication. Annie didn't want medications, not yet. The doctor explained new thinking in psychiatry about adverse childhood experiences—children who experienced four or more of these experiences were more likely to suffer from depression and anxiety—it was good Annie came in for help.

Dr. Wilson's grey hair was pulled into a bun at the top of her head by several black bobby pins. She had such thin skin that Annie could almost see blood under her skin. She had a quiet voice that Annie had to strain to hear. During the weekly sessions, they talked about how Annie could be more motivated to finish her doctoral degree, improve her eating and sleeping habits, what was going on when her face froze, why her vagina was unpleasant to think about. Annie had never brought up her vagina—vaginas were not on the intake form. But Dr. Wilson said Annie needed to get comfortable with being a woman—she would have to keep fighting for recognition because there was so much discrimination. The doctor herself was one of only a few women in medical school and the only one in her class who went into psychiatry.

The doctor wanted Annie to get to know her body better. Her first assignment was to visit her vagina for thirty days and write in a journal what she saw and changes she noticed. The doctor explained this was a get-acquainted activity. The second assignment was to purchase pornographic magazines and look at other vaginas to see how hers compared to them.

Annie was dubious. Was a vagina journal the path to better mental health? But she wanted to get better, so she pulled her pants down daily to examine her genitals with a magnifying mirror and compared her parts to the pictures in the magazines purchased in plain brown wrappers at the drug store. She felt embarrassed though she was alone, wondering what God, if there was a God, thought of her examining her crotch. How many men explored their penises and testicles with a magnifying glass—and if they did, wouldn't they do this as teenagers, not when they're nearly thirty?

Annie stopped the assignment on day fifteen. She told Dr. Wilson her vagina looked comparable to the women in the magazines, but she couldn't see how this was helping her cope better with life. The doctor responded by giving her a new assignment—get a hand vibrator and practice masturbation.

TEN BEFORE THIRTY • 271

Annie told Santos about her therapy. A few days later, he gave her a box wrapped in birthday gift wrap though it was not her birthday. Resting on top of a red velvet cloth was a flesh-colored dildo, longer and with greater girth than any man's penis she had ever had sex with. She was mortified at the thought of this silicone blob inside her though she admitted it looked real. She didn't want the dildo in her house but didn't want to insult Santos by telling him. He'd gone to the sex shop on a side street in St. Paul to find one he thought Annie would like.

She was afraid to throw it away in the garbage. What if the garbage can tipped over and the dildo fell out, and the garbage men saw it? She wrapped the rubbery penis in sheets of newspaper one morning, put the package in her backpack, and dropped it in the trashcan in the women's restroom at Bridgeman's café after lunch.

Santos asked her one day where it was. She lied: "I don't know—haven't seen it in a while."

All this attention to having orgasms by herself was making her feel worse. She was crying so much—without Mitchell in her bed to distract her with the heating pad, she felt abandoned. Maybe the crying was because her father died, because she was molested and raped, because no man was going to understand her, because they were going to lie to her, because they were going to leave her.

Annie heard about another type of therapy—an emotional type of therapy. Maybe this would be better than a vagina journal and masturbation. She needed help—she couldn't go to work and cry at her desk every day.

Annie explained to the new psychologist, Dr. Conklin, that she was crying for no reason at work, when she was driving, when she was reading. She told the doctor about the breakup with Mitchell—it was dredging up every bad thing that had happened in her life.

Dr. Conklin began each session by having Annie go into a restful state through deep breathing. When Annie was in a restful state, the doctor introduced scenarios. In one session, the doctor asked Annie to pretend Mitchell was in the room and say goodbye to him.

"But he isn't in the room," Annie protested.

"Pretend, Annie. This is an exercise."

"I can't—he's not in the room. I don't want to say goodbye."

"Then pretend your mother is in the room. What do you have to say to her?"

She took several breaths and stared at the wall, trying to picture her mother. "I'll never forgive you for not supporting me, for lying to me."

Dr. Conklin tells Annie to hit the pillows on the couch. Annie hits them, but she feels foolish, like she did keeping the vagina journal. "This isn't working."

"Let's try this. Lie on the floor and get into a position that is like your inside person."

The white shag rug was evidently used for this assignment, Annie figured, stretching out on her back, comfortable, breathing evenly.

The doctor watched her for a few minutes, then said, "I don't believe you. Most people curl into a fetal position."

"Well, this is who I am. My outside—that you see—may be tied up, but that's not my inside. Inside, I'm all right. It's just when I try to interact with the world that I'm not."

The doctor looked doubtful. Annie got up from the floor and sat back on the couch, smoothing her hair down while she waited for the doctor to say something. Dr. Conklin said they were at the end of their time, and she would see her next week.

At the next session, Dr. Conklin tells Annie after a few minutes of deep breathing to imagine she is in a restful place. "Are you in a restful place?"

"Yes."

"Where is it?"

"In a clearing in a forest with a lake nearby."

"Keep deep breathing, slowly. Now you notice someone or something is coming into the area. Who or what is this?"

"It's a man."

"How do you feel about this?"

"Not good."

"What is he doing?"

"He's coming to hurt me." Annie realizes at that moment that she can never enjoy the lake or the forest or any place alone because of the risk that a man will come to that place and hurt her.

After several weeks of seeing Dr. Conklin, Annie decides to leave this type of therapy. "I can't do this type of therapy right now. I'm too upset all the time. I think this is helping—I've learned some things about myself, but I can't afford to be so dysfunctional and crying all the time."

Dr. Conklin explains there is often a period of rawness as emotions come up for many patients. She encourages Annie to come back to this approach another time.

While Annie was seeing Dr. Conklin, she continued to see Dr. Wilson and attend the women's support group. The six women in the group were all trying to finish doctoral dissertations. How does that happen, that so many women are being sidelined with mental problems, Annie wondered? Their conversations revealed how much several women hated their fathers or wished their fathers loved them or wished their fathers held them more. Annie was glad her father died if that's what fathers do to daughters. Annie wondered where the bad relationships with the mothers were—why so much focus on fathers?

Many of the women cried when they shared their 'I can't talk to my husband' or 'my father didn't love me.' Annie didn't share she was molested and raped. She didn't share she felt run over and conflicted about her bad choices in men. She shared without tears she was having a hard time finishing her dissertation. Everyone nodded sympathetically because they were having that problem too. Who knows how many real secrets the group withheld?

The therapist leading the group told them many women were afraid of achieving and subverted their success goals. She asked them to think about this. Annie wondered if she was subverting herself, and if she was, what could she do about it?

She didn't think all this therapy was helping very much, but she was glad to have a safe place to go twice a week—where it was okay for people to know she was weak. There was a psychiatrist listening to her, offering medications if she got worse. And there were women like her in trouble, wallowing.

Mitchell left for Montreal with Katharine without talking to Annie. Their last real conversation was the day he brought her chocolates and the pink rose. Did he know that would be their last time together? She was never going to trust gifts again. She learned about the dark side of gifts in high school Latin class. How the Greeks built a huge wooden horse and hid soldiers inside it during the war between Troy and Greece. How the Greeks pretended to sail away from Troy after they built the gift horse. The Trojans pulled the horse into their city as a victor's trophy. Late that night, the Greek soldiers crept out of the horse and opened the city gates for the rest of their army, which had sailed back under cover of night. The Greeks entered the city and destroyed Troy, ending the war. That trickery was a lesson—look carefully at a gift. Annie wasn't expecting deception with Mitchell's chocolates and rose. She was Troy. She felt like a fool.

In her months of bike ride-bys near Mitchell's house, hoping for a confrontation to clear the air, she thought about how much she'd given up in the year she'd been seeing him. He wanted help on his dissertation research, so she helped him. When she needed to study, he chided her for not giving him more time. So she went to the movies he wanted to go to and stayed up most of the night to study while he went to sleep. He wanted to have mealtimes which Annie concluded was him showing off his culinary skills, not about breaking bread together. And she kept in the IUD—the knife—so he wouldn't have to use condoms, so they would not have the sex stressors Annie had with Jonas. She tried to be a good partner and for what?

Annie was ready to give up on sex. Her relationships were not worth the pain. She made the appointment at the university women's center to have the IUD removed.

It was early fall—the warm air was comforting. Annie was worried it would hurt to have the IUD removed. She would tell the nurse she tended to faint based on the insertion so someone could catch her if that happened again. She dreaded seeing the ghostly doctor who inserted it.

The same nurse came to the waiting room after Annie signed in at the front desk. She led Annie to the examining room, giving her the same instructions. "Here's the cover-up. Remove all clothes below your waist. The doctor will be in soon."

Annie quickly slid out of her sandals, removed her jeans and underpants, and wrapped the white cloth cover-up around her hips. She sat on the examining table taking deep breaths, trying to remain calm.

There was a knock on the door. "Can I come in?" the male voice said. "Yes."

A young dark-haired doctor entered the room. "Hi, I'm Dr. Smith. I understand you want to remove your IUD today."

"Yes, it still causes me pain at times—I've never gotten used to it."

"I'm so happy to be doing this. I worry about IUDs for many women."

"Is this going to hurt? It hurt so much going in."

"No. You'll feel a tug, but you will feel so much better with it out, I promise."

Annie has her feet in the stirrups, and he asks her to scooch down. There's no nurse in the room. The doctor pulls the IUD out quickly. Annie is so busy doing deep breathing to stay calm she barely notices.

"It's out," he says, holding it up for her to see. Such a small device—the fishing lure—that caused so much pain.

Annie tells the doctor that the wife of one of the students in her program had an IUD in, but she got pregnant, and the baby came out during delivery holding the IUD in his tiny hand.

Dr. Smith chuckled. "It happens, though that is unusual. Are you ok? I understand you fainted the last time you were here."

"Yes, thanks, I feel ok."

"Glad to remove it. Stay well." The doctor left the room, and the nurse came in to see how she was doing. Annie had already jumped off the table and pulled her clothes on.

"Are you ok?"

"Yes, thanks. What happened to the other doctor, the older doctor?"

"He's not with us any longer," the nurse said with a meaningful look.

Annie left the clinic feeling free for the first time in a long time. No more pinching in her belly. No more fishing lures for lying men.

Annie asked the women in her therapy group if any of them went to the women's clinic. Did anyone know about the older doctor who used to work there? One woman said complaints had been stacking up against the doctor, about his cruelty to women. There was a lawsuit—the university center let him go after an investigation. Annie was not surprised.

She was free of Mitchell's lies, his wife, their Afghan hounds. She would never learn to speak French in Montreal, but maybe this was for the good. She had a dissertation to finish. She pledged to finish by thirty even if she had to go to therapy three days a week. She knew that doing original research and sustaining that research stopped many students. It was one thing to take courses for years—go on autopilot and let your professors lay out the requirements. But coming up with an original topic, figuring out how to collect and analyze the data, write it up, and defend it before a committee of faculty was a major step. But Annie was good at writing and glad to be done with coursework and finally on her own. She could do this. She learned in therapy sessions no one was going to stop her but herself.

The few women in her program banded together to figure out how to deal with male committees and sexist comments. Should they ignore them? Respond? At what jeopardy? There were no women faculty in her department.

Her friend, Liza, was asked to drop a paper that was due by their professor's house rather than his office. He said he wouldn't be in his office for a while.

"Will you go with me, Annie?"

"I can't—I have to work. It will be fine. Just drop the paper on his porch."

Liza drove to the professor's house the next day and rang the doorbell. He opened the door quickly. "Hey, thanks for dropping the paper by. Why don't you come in? I'd love it if you would take a bath with me." He said this so nonchalantly.

Liza didn't know what to say. Was this a joke? Her professor asked a second time, looking amiable and hopeful.

"Sorry, I need to get going—here's my paper." She called Annie when she got home. She was scared and talking fast. "Do you think he's going to fail me? Should I report him? Who would I report him to?"

"It's probably best to see what grade you get. Is there a thing between you? Do you like him?"

"Absolutely not. There's never been anything between us."

He was on another friend's dissertation committee and Annie's too. What would Annie do if he said something like that to her? Maybe the bath line worked with some students. Just weeks ago, Rachel defended her dissertation, but the committee did not pass her. One reason, they said she smiled too much. Rachel was one of those people who smiled a lot, it was true. The male committee didn't think she could take her place in the field of administration with that affect. She filed a lawsuit against the university that tied up her life in dispute for a long time. In the end, she lost the case.

Annie knew litigation was not so unusual. The first National Organization of Women lawsuits were filed against school districts for sexual harassment when Annie worked in Dallas. The superintendent called Annie into his office and asked her to write a first response.

"Sorry, sir, but I can't write that piece. I'm too conflicted about these issues, and I know of instances of sexual harassment in the building." She expected to be fired.

He nodded without asking her for any information and said, "Ok. I'll find someone else."

Annie and her friends fretted about Liza and Rachel's situation. Graduate school was hard enough. Remembering you're female, you don't fit in and would never fit in, was an ongoing threat.

Annie was preparing for preliminary exams. She received her questions from all the professors on her five-man committee except Dr. Collins.

"Come in, Miss Zechman. You're here for your questions today, right?"

"Yes." She smiled but not too much because she didn't want to look like Rachel.

"Sit down," he said, gesturing to the chair next to his desk. "Let's review how knowledgeable you are on one of the most important areas in administration—management. I noted in looking at your transcript that you have not taken any courses in management."

"That's right—no one advised me to take management courses." She knew that was a poor answer. She was supposed to know what was important in her field and should not be blaming her advisor for poor advising, even if that was true. So she added, "I'm not prepared to answer questions in management but would be happy to read in the field and answer questions in writing."

Dr. Collins looked impassively at her. He proceeded to methodically ask question after question about management.

She knew she could not make up answers, so she said, "I don't know," to each question. She must have said I don't know at least twenty times. She was sure she would be asked to leave the program next, academic career over, a fraud.

After more than half an hour of grilling, Professor Collins seemed satisfied he had driven her into the ground sufficiently. "You're not prepared to move to dissertation stage, Miss Zechman, without knowledge about management. I cannot approve you today. I will give you the option to write a paper about management. You have forty-eight hours to get me a report. I'll decide then whether I will approve you to continue your studies." With that, he stood up and waved her away.

Annie mumbled a fake thank you and walked out, legs weak. She headed immediately to the university bookstore to see what textbooks students cover in management courses in both the business and education departments. She bought two large textbooks and one workbook. Then she called Santos. "It was awful. I'm probably going to be dropped from the program. Collins hates me. He kept asking me questions over and over, knowing I didn't have answers. Why would he keep asking me questions when he knew I didn't have any answers?"

"He was raking you over the coals to see what you would do. You did the right thing. You didn't BS him. He's an ass."

"Does he do that to the men?"

"I don't know. Go home and study. I'll bring you dinner in a few hours—how about a turkey and cheese on rye, chips, and chocolate chip cookies?"

"That would be great, thank you."

"You've got this, Annie. Don't worry."

"I don't know. I just don't know."

He was worried about Annie. It wasn't that long ago she was talking about suicide. At least she wasn't carrying on all the time about Mitchell anymore.

At home Annie spread out the management books on the living room floor and compared the tables of content to see what topics they had in common. She would start with the main topics in the field—in both books, there was leadership, history of management, organizations, and ethics. She took notes and assembled key information to summarize in her report.

Santos dropped the welcome food by her house and told her not to worry.

She worked all night and most of the next day. She was running out of time but figured she did the best she could in the time she had to summarize the field. When she finished typing her report, she drove it to Professor Collins's office on the St. Paul campus. Thankfully, he wasn't there. She didn't want him to see how bad she looked. She left it on his chair.

She called Santos. "I turned it in. Can you meet me at Bridgeman's in a few minutes?"

"I'm on my way."

She got to the restaurant first and picked a booth at the back. When Santos arrived, she ordered a bacon, lettuce, and tomato sandwich on rye bread with a chocolate ice cream soda made with chocolate ice cream. She asked the waitress to put extra chocolate in the soda and two cherries. Santos ordered a grilled cheese sandwich with chips and a Coke.

"I'm sure you did great, Annie," he said, trying to raise her spirits.

"He has no respect for me. I think he wants me out of the program. I'm not well enough prepared, and he knows it." Annie was tired and disconsolate. "But this is the best chocolate soda I've ever had," she said, smiling ironically. "You know how guys on death row get to ask for their favorite meal right before they go to the electric chair? This is my last favorite meal."

"You're going to be fine, Annie. Collins is just running you through the hoops."

The tiredness was hitting her. He walked her to her car, and she headed home to get in bed, wondering what she would do if she were asked to leave the doctoral program. She slept deeply with the two cats stationed on each side of her like small lions protecting their library building.

Professor Collins called the next morning. "Miss Zechman, Collins here. Can you come by my office at noon tomorrow?" His voice sounded crisp and business-like.

"Yes—I'll be there. Thank you."

Annie arrived before noon and waited nervously in the hall until Dr. Collins called her to his office.

"Come in, Miss Zechman."

He was leaning back in his wooden desk chair, holding her report in his right hand. "If you can pull this off, Miss Zechman, in just forty-eight hours, think what you can do in your professional career. Had you not produced this level of work, I was prepared to advise against you moving forward. I am approving you to move forward based on the quality of this work. Good job." And with that, he signed the preliminary examination form she left with him a few days ago and handed her the form and her management report.

She thanked him and headed down the hall to her advisor's office. Dr. Browning was not in, so she left the approval paper on his chair. It contained the approving signatures of all the members of her committee. It was time to move to the dissertation stage—one huge hurdle to go.

———— ◆ ————

Annie's teaching assistant job didn't pay enough, and now that she was done with classes, it was time to go back to full-time work while she worked on her dissertation. She expected to stay in Minneapolis and find an administrative position. She asked some of her professors for ideas for a job search.

One of them was frank, "You're never going to get an administrative position as a female. It's best to go to a smaller venue."

Annie studied a map, figuring she could look for a job within a three-hundred-mile radius. This was the distance that would enable her to drive back in a day when she needed to get to the university for meetings related to her dissertation.

She asked the university career center for help in revising her resume. They looked through the list of nonprofessional jobs she worked at to pay her way through school for years and advised her to remove them. "You're focused on a professional course now. It's best to remove those other jobs."

So Annie revised her resume, focusing on her education and professional jobs. One of the colleges she applied to in Iowa wanted to interview her for a department head position. Annie drove to Iowa, excited for the full day of interviews with faculty and administrators. The meetings were going well, and Annie felt optimistic. The final interview was with the college president. He was a tall, big-presence personality with a frank, rough demeanor. He was sitting behind a large oak desk with nothing on it but Annie's resume when Annie was ushered in by the staff member who just interviewed her. The president stood up and loomed above Annie, thrusting out his hand to shake hers. His handshake was firm and his voice loud—he was used to dominating the rooms he entered, Annie surmised.

They sat down and talked amiably for a few minutes. He inquired about her PhD program and asked why she was interested in working at his college. Then he picked up Annie's resume and flung it high into the air. They both watched the several pages flutter to the desk, landing in a messy pile. "What makes you think you can relate to the type of students at our community college and the faculty who work here? We care about jobs and helping our students find their way." He leaned forward in his oak chair and looked directly at her with piercing blue eyes. He looked bemused as he confronted Annie about what he seemed to believe was her silver-spoon background.

Annie realized, 'He thinks I haven't done anything but sit in a school classroom my whole life.' The anger stirred in her, and her injustice voice took over. "I can relate to your students and faculty. I've worked part- and full-time paying my way through school for more than a decade. I've held nearly twenty nonprofessional jobs that are not included on my resume. I've worked since I was sixteen—as a lifeguard, camp counselor, secretary in a legal office, medical transcriptionist, waitress, secretary in a hospital cancer department, EKG technician, department store gift wrapper, freshman dorm counselor, in the registrar's office at college, in the art department at college, advisor to adults returning to school . . ." Her voice trailed off as she stopped to catch her breath.

His glasses slipped low on his ruddy nose.

She told herself, 'Don't say any more. It's his turn.'

There were a few moments of silence. Then he stood up and said, "If you want the job, you're hired." He smiled like he had achieved a victory round with a worthy foe.

Annie knew her injustice voice met his challenge. She had obtained her first administrative job, no thanks to the career office at the university.

Santos suggested renting the U-Haul. He would drive the truck with Annie's things, and she would drive her car with the cats. They would unload everything at the new apartment in Iowa. Santos would take a bus back to Minneapolis. They set the move for Christmas Day. There wouldn't be much traffic if the weather was bad, and she would have the new apartment set up in time to begin her new job in January.

In the weeks leading to the move, Annie boxed up her things. The afternoon before Christmas, they loaded the truck with everything Annie didn't need to leave out for that night. Early the next day, Santos came to Annie's house to help move the final items into the truck. "Merry Christmas," he said, handing her a bag of chocolate candies when she opened the back door. It was barely dawn and five below zero.

"Oh, thank you so much! I'm sorry, I didn't get you anything."

"It's ok. You can buy me dinner tonight in Iowa, if anything is open," he said with a smile.

They assessed what needed to be moved. Everything should go into the truck except for her purse, cat litter box, bowl with water, and bag with the cat food—those would go into the car. She was already wearing her parka. A couple of feet of snow blanketed the yard from last week's storm. The cats couldn't be out in a cold car for too long, so they would be last to move.

Santos and Annie made two trips to take the mattress and box spring to the truck, wrapping them in large sheets of plastic. Santos made the final trips to the truck with the remaining items while Annie loaded items in the car. They surveyed the house and agreed it was time to get the cats and lock up the house. The cats were sitting side by side in the center of the living room floor, wary in the empty house. Annie picked up Miss Kitty first and headed to the car with her. Santos was waiting with the car door open. Annie dropped the cat onto the passenger seat where she had folded a thick wool blanket, and Santos quickly closed the door.

Then it was back to the house to get Chester. Annie scooped him up, pressing him to her chest, but when she got halfway down the walkway to the garage, he wriggled out of her hold and landed in a snowbank. She yelled, "Chester, come here!" but he was hightailing it back to the house. She watched him disappear into an exhaust hole leading to the basement of the duplex. Annie had never been in the basement before—the landlord told her only he had access. Santos opened the door to the basement—she was surprised the door was unlocked.

Down six stairs was a large noisy furnace. Chester was squeezed into a narrow cubby above the furnace, peering at them. Annie looked around the basement to assess the area. "Oh my god," she let out a startled cry. Bird carcasses littered the concrete floor. There must have been twenty brown and grey-feathered birds—mostly sparrows. This is what the cats must have been doing when they were outside—stalking birds and dragging them through the crawl hole into the basement. Annie was mortified. She never noticed the crawl hole to the basement or imagined her cats would be able to get into the basement.

Santos reminded Annie they had to get the cat and get on the road. Annie tried soothing words to encourage the cat to come out. "Come on, Chester, let's go for a ride in the car." She held her arms out in front of the cubby. He retreated further into his space. She tried again to coax him out. Santos was getting nervous.

"Kitty is in the car, and it's freezing, Annie. We have to get on the road."

"I know, I know." Despite her feeling of panic, she tried more coaxing in a quieter voice: "Come on, Chester, come out." She held out her hands to the unmoved cat. "How about we clean up the birds before the landlord sees them," Annie suggested since they were getting nowhere with the cat.

"Ok—I'll get a plastic bag from the truck." He returned with a large black garbage bag. He and Annie hurriedly picked up the rigid carcasses one by one, using a paper towel to protect their hands. Chester edged forward to watch what was happening to his birds.

Annie counted them out loud while they bagged the bodies. "Oh my gosh, twenty-seven," she said as she dropped the last body into the bag. She wondered how many months the cats had been catching birds.

"I'll throw these in the trash," Santos said. "We have to leave without Chester if he doesn't come out, Annie."

"I'm not leaving without him."

Santos muttered they would never get out of Minnesota and headed to the garbage can by the garage with the bag of birds. Nearly an hour had passed since they were supposed to get on the road.

Interested in seeing what happened to the birds, Chester ventured out of his hiding place and jumped to the basement floor. He began to sniff around the floor close to the furnace where most of the carcasses had stacked up. Annie moved quickly to scoop him up, calling to Santos just returning to the basement, "I have him! I have him!" Annie emerged from the basement with Chester squirming and growling. Santos ran ahead to open the car door and ensure Miss Kitty did not jump out. The grey cat was nestled into the blanket Annie had prepared for the drive.

Annie climbed into the driver's seat and Santos closed her door. Once safely inside, she let Chester out of her arms to explore the car. She started the motor and rolled her window down just enough to talk to Santos. "Ok, we're ready. Can you go back and make sure the house is locked up? And you drive behind me, ok? I'll pull over if I see you stopping on the highway."

"Ok." He pulled his wool cap low over his ears and headed to the house for a last check. Annie had left her keys for the landlord on the counter. The lights were turned off. Santos closed the door and tested it to be sure it locked behind him. Then he ran to the U-Haul and climbed into the high driver's seat. The loud engine trembled to life in the cold. The heater in the Pinto was on high, blowing warm air gusts on the unhappy cats.

Annie gave Santos the thumbs-up, and the Pinto backed out of the driveway. The truck followed. Their motorcade drove for five hours south without stopping, the small white car leading the way. There were few other vehicles on the highway that Christmas Day and no new snow to slow them down.

It was late afternoon when Santos and Annie unloaded everything from the U-Haul and car into the two-bedroom apartment in Iowa. The cats hid in one of the closets. Santos was staying for a few days to help Annie. The first night, Annie slept on the top mattress of her bed in her new bedroom. Santos slept on the box springs in the second bedroom. They agreed months ago they were just friends though Santos told her while she was planning the move to Iowa one afternoon over chocolate sodas, "If you never find anyone to marry, Annie, I will marry you. I'll always love you."

"You're like my brother," she told him. They confided in one another about nearly everything. She talked his ears off throughout her affair with Mitchell. He knew she was still in love with Jonas. He knew about Oliver. He was dating a woman ten years younger—he said he liked younger women.

The day after Christmas, they returned the truck to the U-Haul dealer and celebrated by going out to breakfast. Then they headed to a furniture store to look for a sofa and a television. At twenty-nine years old, Annie had never owned a television or a sofa.

They looked at sofas first. Annie selected an L-shaped couch in a deep pumpkin-colored velveteen. She would pay for it monthly for a year. The store would deliver it the next day. They found a television and a stand for it next, which they carried to the car.

The two cats watched Santos and Annie assemble the stand. They set the tv on the top shelf and slid the stereo moved from Minnesota onto the second shelf. They sat on the floor against the wall where the new sofa would go, watching the screen come to life. The cats played inside the empty boxes. Annie could feel herself re-nesting. Tomorrow she would take Santos to the bus station.

"Are you going to be ok without me?" she asked him. She worried he would give up on school. He was getting restless as he neared dissertation stage.

"I'll be fine." She didn't believe him.

"I'm sorry I've been carrying on so about Mitchell. I'm always falling apart, and you're having to listen to me."

"It's ok. You're stronger than you think, Annie. And you're smart."

"I don't feel very smart sometimes." They had stuck together since the first day they met at orientation. "I think you should get a mattress for your apartment. I can lend you the money now," she said. Santos had been sleeping on the floor of his small apartment on piled-up blankets for more than a year. Annie couldn't understand how that could be comfortable.

"I'll be ok. Don't worry." He didn't like it when she nagged about his bed.

They went to dinner and talked about how often she should return to Minnesota to check in with Dr. Browning and the other professors on her committee. She thanked him again for driving the U-Haul and helping bag the bird carcasses.

The next morning they arrived at the bus station a few minutes early. When it was time to go, he said, "See you soon. Love you, Annie," and gave her the thumbs-up on his way to his bus.

She gave him the thumbs-up and a smile. The velveteen sofa arrived a few hours later.

Annie's new job took over most of her day life. She spent most evenings and weekends working on her dissertation, nestled into the new sofa with papers and books spread around the floor and the new tv on for company. The cats joined her on the sofa—Chester perched on one of the wide-padded arms, Miss Kitty stretched out on the ledge of the sofa back.

Annie didn't have time to obsess about what Mitchell must be doing in Montreal. Or what Jonas was doing in Wisconsin. Oliver was still calling sometimes—he wanted to come see her in Iowa. He asked if Annie wanted to think about marriage. She said she wasn't ready for marriage to anyone, and he should not wait for her. She and Meyer sent letters to each other. In his last postcard, he told her his divorce would be finalized soon and asked if she had mulberry jelly in her pantry.

She started to meet people at work to talk to. She rode her bike through rural roadways. She took a photography course at the college. Every eight weeks, she drove to Minnesota to meet with her advisor to check in with him about her dissertation research.

In the summer, Annie drove six hours to see Jonas in northern Wisconsin. She felt nervous driving, running questions through her mind like road signs. The first road sign blinking yellow— would he be glad to see her? The second sign, more ominous—would he think she was weak and cloying, still not able to accept they were broken up? Another sign— did he care what happened to her? And the green jealous sign—was he seeing someone else?

She pulled the car into the gravel apron next to the house on Fish Lake and turned off the motor, sitting for a moment to take a few deep breaths, as if her life depended on the next five minutes. He was walking down the path to greet her. She opened the car door and he reached to hug her. It was a short hug, a tentative hug. She quickly took in the house he had built on land his family owned, and the second smaller building on the other side of the driveway. They walked behind the house to the lake, the water calm and unmoving. It was like the water was waiting for a cue from them— should there be gentle waves lapping near them or deeply stirring waters?

In the path between the main house and the smaller cabin which he said he built first so he could live there while he was working on the larger house, she saw the sculpture made from large grey cinder blocks that were stacked to a man's height, his height. "What is that?" she asked.

"Ode to my life," he said wryly.

The blocks were turning dark from the weather she figured, wondering how long ago he built the block, unbending man.

He showed her the insides of the house and cabin. The furnishings were his mother's doing, he said. She spent the summers there and he stayed in the cabin or in a loft room he'd built in the main house.

He didn't want to stay inside, so they talked for an hour, kicking gravel in the driveway, mostly looking down or at the sky, not at each other. She complimented the small garden near the house—the pink and purple flowers. He said Mary visited and planted the garden. Annie wanted to sigh, but she held it in. He was withdrawn and quiet, not the good quiet she used to find calming. She decided it was best to leave, and he did not stop her. She backed out of the rocky driveway and drove the six hours home. Why didn't the lake waters kick up and protest? Why didn't the concrete man take a first step and stop her. If Jonas cared about her, why would he let her leave with such a long drive ahead?

Then hours of driving. Red blinking signs badgered her over and over —he was not happy to see her. Yellow caution signs—neither of them were in a good place and nothing could relieve the sadness between them, in them. And the green grating sign of jealousy—was Mary making her way to Fish Lake to plant flowers in his garden and try to bring his block man to life?

Annie's busyness with work and school did not lift her depression. It resided in her cells like heavy sacks weighing her down. She cried in her car driving home from work, from seeing friends, from the grocery, and when she drove by the concrete wall next to an overpass she had selected for the day she would end it all. She picked out the large structure in an isolated location outside of town. Large painted letters depicted the romance of M + S on the bridge. Three epitaphs written in different hands, in different colors, in different sizes, were on the bridge too, readable to everyone who drove beneath the overpass: *Whoever passes under this bridge dies. Class of 68. Motherfucker.*

One afternoon she parked her car just beyond the overpass, turned on the emergency blinkers, and walked under the bridge. In the weeds, she found a used Tampax and beer can. She tried to imagine what new pieces of trash would be left if she crashed there. The police and emergency crew would have to tow her wrecked car out of there. They would probably leave something. Cigarette butts. Pieces of paper from forms that had to be filed with copies in triplicate. Fragments of her car. Some of the Pinto's black-and-white checkered upholstery—maybe a big enough piece to resemble a chess board and everyone would know her king was checkmated—there was no possible escape.

Her car ashtray spilled over with crumpled Kleenex and the backseat was strewn with the tear-dried Kleenexes. It was time to find a new therapist—her sixth. She had almost as many therapists as lovers in less than a decade.

Annie called the university hospital to request a referral for a mental health practitioner with experience with sexual problems. They referred her to a man/woman team. At her first session, Annie tremored for the first thirty minutes as if she was in a snowstorm without a coat. This had never happened in a therapy session before. The twosome were sympathetic. The man was close to Annie's age. Tall, thin, brown hair, bland affect, glasses, clear skin. He led the conversation. The woman was also Annie's age. Dark-haired and listening well, the woman deferred to the man. They didn't get very far in the first session, perhaps because Annie was tremoring so. They didn't ask many questions about sex and didn't seem ready to get into a real conversation. Annie expected to get into a conversation whether she was tremoring or not.

At the second appointment, there was no tremoring. Annie told them she wanted help with having more effective sexual relationships. There was sexual abuse and incest in her past—she didn't know how to process this, let go of this. The man dominated the session. He asked a few questions, but there were no assignments, guidance, or insights. The woman seemed unable or unwilling to step forward.

Annie concluded the sex therapy couple didn't have much to offer. Maybe no therapy could help. She confided in her friend, Nelly, that the couples approach was not working for her. Nelly was going to the same couple for anxiety. She told Annie that the man in the team asked her to go on a date after their third session.

"What? Isn't that unethical?"

"I think so. I wasn't prepared for him hitting on me. My anxiety is worse, Annie."

Annie abandoned the couples' therapy. But she needed help—she was afraid she would give up one day and plow into the pillar at the overpass. She would find a seventh type of therapy.

***

"Have a seat. Dr. Elliott will be with you soon."

The receptionist gave Annie a card to fill out. Annie took a seat by the window and searched for a pen in her purse. She filled in her name, address, nearest relative, and questions about her health. She handed the card back to the receptionist and returned to her seat. She felt jittery. What should she say? I'm cracking up. Can therapy help me process traumas? She pulled out Flora's list. She could refer to the list if she couldn't think of anything to say. The list reassured her she had reasons to fall apart. But did she? Other people have lists worse than hers, and they weren't falling apart. Her mother was probably right—she was making a choice to wallow.

She speed-read the list like she was practicing for a test in school: *Parent dying. Incest. Date-rape. Stranger rapes—me and my friend the same month. Parent betrayal. Powerless to save a friend from sexual assault. Hit by a car. Jonas leaves me. Strip search in jail. Twice almost kidnapped from the street. Killing animals for science. Assassinations. Meyer throwing art project in the garbage dump. Jewish hate. Mitchell's lie. Abandoning cat in Bruchen. War. Racial injustice.* Maybe she had too many on the list. Maybe some of them weren't that bad.

"Annie, come this way." The receptionist directed her to the new therapist's office. Dr. Elliott explained she was a psychiatric social worker training as a therapist under a more practiced therapist. She began their session by making Annie a cup of tea served in an antique china cup. She looked like an earth mother, portly and substantial.

Annie told Dr. Elliott about her list.

The doctor asked if she would share what was on the list.

Annie started to read the bad things out loud, and the doctor clucked like a caring mother would. "Oh no, Annie. I'm so sorry. Oh dear. Have you shared the list with anyone, like your family?"

"No, I never shared the dream or the list." Annie was surprised the doctor was listening to her. She felt she could breathe. The doctor wasn't dismissing her. At least not yet.

Annie saw the new doctor weekly. They talked about why Annie dated emotionally unavailable men and married men, what her competitive feelings with other women might be about, and how to process traumas. Annie confided she was feeling suicidal and thinking of crashing her car into a concrete overpass she felt drawn to. Dr. Elliott made her promise she would not kill herself. Annie didn't like making pacts. She was a subversive personality—didn't her therapist know this?

TEN BEFORE THIRTY • 291

Annie struggled during several trips past the overpass not to turn the steering wheel too far toward the wall—just to show Dr. Elliott that she was not going to follow their pact. After weeks of fighting with herself, she asked Dr. Elliott to take back the pact. Dr. Elliott was aghast to learn the pact had only increased Annie's compunction for suicide. Annie figured Dr. Elliott was still too green at this business—she should talk more with her mentor before someone died here.

Annie was working on final edits in her dissertation. She was close to her goal to finish in August when she would turn thirty. That's when she would take a two-week vacation to drive to the West Coast to drop off resumes and explore job prospects. There was nothing to hold her in Iowa once she finished school. She told Dr. Elliot she would miss two sessions while she looked for another job. The doctor congratulated Annie for being so close to finishing her degree and suggested an assignment that might be helpful for her therapy.

"What would you think of writing a letter to Flora while you're on your trip? Tell her how the list of traumas has impacted you over the past twenty years. This could be a unique time to reflect on that as you begin this journey to find a new job."

"Maybe." One of Annie's roommates from the Mifflin Street apartment in Madison would be driving with her from Iowa to Vancouver, British Columbia—then head down the coast to Seattle, Portland, Eugene, and San Francisco. Annie and Sally would leave resumes at places to work in every city. Annie didn't think she would have time to write a letter going west, but maybe on the trip home when she would be alone because Sally was flying back to Madison.

Nelly stopped by Annie's apartment to say goodbye. She would feed the cats while Annie was gone.

The two weeks of travel passed quickly. Annie was leaving San Francisco to drive home on her birthday. She planned to find a motel to break up the drive when she got tired. A pile of papers rode shotgun on the passenger seat—remaining copies of her resume, application forms from potential employers, and the university's letter notifying her she completed all the requirements for the PhD. She had brought the notification letter to show employers who asked for verification. The tape recorder Duncan gave her when he left for Vietnam sat next to the paper pile—she might record a message to Flora, not write a note. She headed east on Interstate 80.

<hr>

Eight hours into the drive—near Salt Lake City—Annie pressed the ON button to the grey recorder. She'd been mulling over what to say to Flora since she left the gas station hours ago near Reno.

Hello, Flora. It's Annie. I hope you can hear me on the other side. I'm in the middle of a long drive home, hoping to get my many conflicted thoughts into the tape recorder Duncan gave me when he left for Vietnam.

I think of you often and have so many questions. Did you really visit me when I was ten? I think you did. Why did you make me choose when to have so many bad things happen? Why didn't you protect me—make the choice for me, or tell me to choose later in life when I had better coping skills and would be able to handle them better? I don't think a ten-year-old should have to make a decision like that, not even knowing what bad things are.

It sounds like I'm blaming you—that's not what I mean to do. Maybe you got instructions from God to visit me, and you had no choice. Or maybe you didn't visit me at all—maybe you were just a bad dream out of my own mind after we cleared out Dad's things from his office. But I think it was you, Flora, that night in my bedroom.

My doctor wants me to tell you what it's been like these twenty years. You probably didn't have mental health professionals in your day. And if you did, they probably were as unhelpful as they are now. I've tried seven types of therapy trying to figure things out. Mostly I have figured out I need to do this work on my own. No one seems very good at dealing with traumas. It's always 'eat a good diet, get more sleep, exercise more, do deep breathing, don't blame yourself, accept what comes and be flexible, and lower your expectations. Oh and this one, 'time will heal the wounds.' But Flora, time doesn't heal some of them. They stay with me—and just get older.

It's not so easy to bounce back after the really bad ones. I learned to give myself permission to take some healing time though Mother tells me I wallow too much. I don't agree. She thinks I'm headstrong and careless, that I brought bad things on by my own actions. But I haven't even shared most of my list with her, so how would she know? Actually, she doesn't even know about your list.

Annie stopped the tape recorder to focus on passing a long caravan of trucks travelling single file for what seemed like miles. Their motors were loud and ominous. They must have communicated on their CB radios to make a pact to blow their horns as she passed each one because that is what they did. Deep-bass toots. Long baritone brays. Tenor bursts like an unwelcome alarm clock. Whooshing alto air waves. She wondered if the Pinto would give out as she increased her speed past eighty. She wanted to get away from the men waving at her and leave the braying behind. Flora would have to wait. When it was quiet on the road ahead, she pressed the tape recorder ON button again.

Sorry, Flora, there was a disturbance on the road. Where was I? Oh yes, talking about the list. There are more than ten traumas on my list. I'm not saying that's unfair—how could you know, really know, what was coming? So, maybe the number doesn't matter. But it seems unfair that some people get more than others. I don't want to feel sorry for myself and come off like a victim. Maybe if you were here you would tell me that adage, 'you don't get more than you can handle.' I don't believe there's a master "trauma-assigner" God doling them out . . . more to stronger people, fewer to the weaker? It all seems so up to chance . . .

After twenty years of thinking about this, Flora, I have to ask if there is any value in counting traumas? Did you really want me to keep count? Here's why I'm asking. I think it's time to stop counting. It doesn't matter how many traumas happen from now on—I'll deal with them as best as I can. Sometimes I know I'm going to go numb and feel dead inside for a while. Or be angry. Or depressed. And for sure I'm going to try to be more careful, to protect myself better. But it's time to start focusing more on good things, Flora.

I hope I get to see you again in another dream someday and we meet up when I die, if that is what happens when people die. And I hope there is a life for your spirit wherever dead is.

She took several deep breaths while she tried to decide if there was more to say. The machine recorded her breaths for more than a minute.

Ok, signing off now. Like always I have reverted to too many questions and over-analyzing things.

Love you, your great-granddaughter, Annie, on my thirtieth birthday.

Annie pressed the recorder's OFF button, wondering if she should start over. She was not sure that was what she wanted to say. She was tired—it would be dark in a few hours—she'd been driving for nine hours, only a third of the way. She saw a large motel complex ahead and pulled into their driveway to find a single room. No vacancies. She stopped at three more motels over the next couple of hours, but every place was full. The last clerk said there were a lot of late summer travelers, and they had reservations. Annie was afraid to sleep in a motel parking lot or a remote pull-off along the highway, so she kept driving.

It was midnight somewhere in Wyoming when she noted she had been thirty for one full day. She had not planned to spend her birthday driving all night. She planned to stop at a motel with a pool and swim under the night time sky like she did most birthdays. Instead she was eating Three Musketeer bars, the lone car behind a few trucks on the dark highway. She decided to hang behind and follow one truck's rear lights ahead, grateful he was illuminating the pavement in front of them.

The dark night hours passed with the Pinto following the truck's square red lights until Annie could see the pinking of dawn. She knew about the first appearance of light before sunrise from a college science class. Red has the longest wavelength of any visible light, and the sun looks red on the horizon because its long path through the atmosphere blocks the other colors of the spectrum. The molecules in the atmosphere were scattering the violet and blue lights away from her line of sight, letting the other colors bathe her eyes—the yellows, oranges, and reds. In the warm and welcome hues of dawn in Nebraska, she was aware of deep tiredness. If she crashed, she promised Flora she would not blame her. This would be on Annie—she should have made a reservation and planned a better course. She wanted to stop by the side of the road to close her eyes for a while but held firm to the steering wheel and sped into the daylight. During her twenty-eight hours of driving, Annie had time to make a plan for life after thirty. She would become a vegetarian, lose the weight she piled on during her job and dissertation regimen, keep searching for love, find a new job, and stop counting traumas.

Two days after Annie returned to Iowa, she resumed therapy sessions with Dr. Elliott. She told the doctor she tape-recorded a message to Flora during the long drive home.

"How did that go?"

"You know, I kind of enjoyed talking to Flora. It gave me time to think about so many years of counting traumas. And afterward, I felt freer in a way I had not expected."

"What do you mean by freer?"

"I don't know . . . like I had learned so much . . . like she was listening to me."

Dr. Elliott smiled. "You might want to talk to her again sometimes if things build up inside your head around the list."

"Maybe." Annie had been thinking about making a second tape. "There's something else. Meyer and his wife are divorced and he's been writing to me. We're talking about seeing each other."

"Isn't this the man who threw away your sculpture piece in college? Isn't he on Flora's list?"

"Yes."

"Do you trust him?

"I don't know. We've always had a close connection—mentally. At least he won't be a married man," she quipped.

At next week's session, Annie told Dr. Elliott that a job application she submitted to a higher education think tank in Denver before she left on her trip called for an interview. The interview went really well and they made an offer—and she accepted it. She was moving in a month and would not be coming to therapy anymore. The doctor had already set the wind-up clock for their forty minutes and made their cups of tea.

"That's very good news about the job, isn't it?" the doctor asked, sipping the steamy chamomile tea.

"Yes—it's time to leave this job now that I finished school. I'm wondering about seeing Meyer—he lives in Denver."

"Maybe it's a good idea to see if there is something there now that he's single."

Annie nodded yes. After all her therapy, she still didn't understand why she was attracted to unavailable men. Probably she didn't think that any man, married or not, was going to stay with her. Maybe she didn't respect other relationships. Maybe she didn't want to stay with any man herself. They talked about the possibility that Annie might never find a long-term partner. Annie agreed. Maybe it was the times. Relationship musical chairs—she would be the lone woman out when the music stopped, no seat for her at the table of love. And there was Vietnam—trying to establish relationships with men traumatized by war—and the fear of taking on more risks in love.

Annie didn't want to raise any more questions in therapy sessions. She didn't want to answer any more questions. She wanted to be done with therapy.

Dr. Elliott told Annie how much she enjoyed getting to know her and hugged Annie goodbye, wishing her well in her journeys.

Santos was arriving late afternoon on the bus from Minneapolis. Annie was meeting him at the station. They were renting a U-Haul truck early tomorrow and Annie's friends were coming over to help load the truck. Santos and Annie planned to do the 800-mile drive over two days. Annie would drive her car with the two cats and Santos would drive the truck. Annie made reservations for them to stop at a hotel in Grand Junction, Nebraska, the halfway point.

It had been two weeks since Annie's final session with Dr. Elliott. Annie had concluded she needed to figure things out on her own. She had sampled so many types of therapy, surely she had acquired enough tools to figure things out even if she wasn't aware of them consciously. Maybe the tools were unconscious, and that's how therapy worked—coping tools are mysterious—they just get into your bloodstream but you aren't aware of them.

In her final visit with Dr. Elliott, Annie told her about the idea of a "non-trauma" list but she wasn't sure what to call it. She looked up antonyms of trauma in the dictionary, but none of them seemed quite right. She read the list of names she had written on a piece of paper to Dr. Elliott: *"healing, alleviation, help, relief, benefit, contentment, joy, order, remedy, cure, calm, comfort, health."* Annie had been wondering if she would have as many on the new list, whatever she called it, as the old list. She'd been thinking about the criteria—what makes a healing, joyful moment? Absence of pain and worry? A feeling that exceeds happiness, like euphoria? Forgetting yourself entirely? And how should she score them—like she scored the trauma list?

The doctor nodded approvingly at the idea of a non-trauma list through sips of hot tea. She had just refilled their cups with steamy water from the dented copper kettle on the hot plate next to their chairs. "I bet the new list will be longer than the trauma list when you start to focus on good moments, Annie."

"Maybe." How could Dr. Elliott be an optimist and work in mental health? Annie tried to sip her tea, but it was too hot. The steam rose like damp clouds up her nostrils. Annie had already started the new list but did not tell Dr. Elliott. No one could know what made Annie happy, truly happy.

The tree at the top of the Pennsylvania hill. Dad was alive. A few long branches were swaying in the wind like human arms. She grabbed one arm and started running down the hill, and the branch suddenly swept her up and flew her all the way down the steep hill. Oh, she was descending so fast and high in the cool air—she was a leaf on the tree, surfing wind waves. Over and over, she raced back up the hill, her dark braids giddy. She was never happier in her entire life.

Not even when she hid the small blue balloon under the toilet seat in the Pickney apartment with Jonas, and he lifted the seat and cried out with surprise, and they laughed so hard. Then she took a hot bath, and he soaped her back while they talked about the sailboat race he crewed for. And when they climbed into bed that late afternoon, he read her *Winnie the Pooh* while they had warm sex. She was sitting on top of him barely moving with him deep inside her, and he was showing her the pictures of the crying donkey who lost his tail. Then Pooh found the tail, and the usually depressed donkey waved his tail in joy and Annie had a surprise orgasm.

And not even when Jonas gave her the little poem she kept in a scrapbook next to the picture of the two of them by the lake:

If wishes
were fishes
the world
would be
water
and
Annie
Queen of
the Sea

Annie was carrying the new list in her wallet. She was done counting traumas. Good things would be coming. She would see Meyer soon. And maybe she would see Jonas. After she lived past thirty.

CPSIA information can be obtained
at www.ICGtesting.com
Printed in the USA
BVHW040303220423
662811BV00003B/563